game of the gods
LI♦VE

L FERGUS

Li've

@FallenAngelKita

http://FallenAngelKita.com

ISBN: 978-1-949789-01-0

Cover art by mrinmoykar999

CONTENTS

BOOKS BY L. FERGUS

Warmache

~

Game of the Gods

Rebirth

Clouds

Sarin's War

Li've

~

The New Angels

Twelve Bravo – short story

BykeChic

For my #1 fan.

LIST OF ANGELS

Kamikaze, Katrina Marie

E'gar, God of Rage
Humanized War Cat
Gray Cloud

Kamikaze is the co-leader of the Valkyries. She is the biological daughter of Kita and Snowy. A gifted assassin, Kamikaze is a pragmatic leader. She prefers to hunt alone or with her partner Tenshi. Her loyalty to Kita is unwavering.

Kamikaze has no wings, instead has spots and markings like a war cat, a subspecies of the snow leopard. She has long fur on the backs of her arms and on her back. Short, fine fur covers the rest of her body. Three claws extend from the tops of her hands. Her feet look like those of a war cat.

∽

Phoenix, Kylee MacKay

Et'ah, God of Hate
Black Cloud
Fallen Angel

Phoenix is the other co-leader of the Valkyries. She is Kita's adoptive daughter, and her girlfriend is Saint Valentine. Phoenix loves death and destruction, but she lacks patience and discipline. She is independent and resourceful, but lusts for vengeance and holds deep grudges against those who have wronged her.

Phoenix's wings are a mixture of yellow, orange, red, and black feathers that burn like her red hair. She wears a yellow bodysuit with red and orange stripes up the side, a brown leather bomber jacket with a phoenix stitched on the back, yellow crystal bracers, and combat boots. Phoenix doesn't wield any weapons, relying solely on her ability to control fire.

∽

Toxic, Kara Laramie

Deer'g, God of Greed
Black Cloud
Fallen Angel

Toxic is an experienced politician and comes from one of the oldest and richest houses on The Mass. Her best friends are Phoenix and Saint

Valentine. She often acted as Vicereine and governed The Mass in Kita's absence.

Toxic's feathers are fluorescent green with a thick black edge. When not governing, she prefers jeans, boots, and a black hoodie. Her nails, eyes, and mouth glow green. Toxic wields dual swords and can unleash a corrosive gas.

∾

Anthrax, Nell Flanagan

Esa'esid, God of Disease
Black Cloud
Fallen Angel

Anthrax has been the Angels' doctor for eons. She is a mild-mannered fallen angel compared to the others. Sarin is Anthrax's best friend. They have known each other since childhood and came to The Mass together on the colony ship. Galina's ISS teams murdered Anthrax's partner, Nina, and their daughter, Tink, during Galina's coup.

Anthrax's feathers are white with a black edge. She likes twenty-fourth-century fashion, wearing seven strategically placed white patches under her doctor's coat. Her hair is red and white flames burn from her eyes. Shark's teeth give her an unnerving smile. Anthrax wields a bo and can produce anthrax gas. She can transform into the banshee Pestilence and unleash plagues on her enemies.

∾

Saint Valentine, Denver Brown

Ecit'suj, God of Justice
Gray Cloud

Saint Valentine is the daughter of the AI Omega and is Phoenix's partner. She combines the best of organic and non-organic computing in her head. As Kita's aide, they connect their computers and have a special bond. When Kita disappeared, Saint Valentine helped Sheppard and the military—a job she loathed.

Saint Valentine took her look from her favorite superhero. She wears black military fatigues from Kita's military and a red beret. Over her fatigues, she wears a tattered red cape with a high collar that covers the lower part of her face. Her feathers are red, with a white border that forms a heart at the tip of each feather. She's armed with a pair of .50 caliber pistols holstered on her lower back.

∾

Tenshi, Angela

Ra'w, God of War
Gray Cloud

Tenshi is a skilled mercenary and is Kamikaze's partner. Kita discovered her working in the forge, Inferno, as the leader of the Hammers —a group tasked with maintaining order among Inferno's female population.

Tenshi has black and white chevron patterned feathers with a mixture of blue feathers. She wears a black sports bra, camouflaged fatigue bottoms, and combat boots. She is a master of firearms, carrying a pair of machine pistols strapped to her legs, .50 caliber pistols holstered on her lower back, and an assault rifle. She has Asiatic features, long black hair, and loves her dark sunglasses.

~

Raptor, A'ana

Yti'varg, God of Gravity
Black Cloud

Raptor is a dinosaur ravager first, and an Angel second. Her partner was the shapeshifter Frostbane. Never afraid to be alone, she would often disappear into the Forest of Ash for months or years at a time. The other Angels look to her for wisdom and advice.

Raptor stands six-feet-three-inches and has chocolate colored skin. Her feathers are green with a yellow stripe down the middle with black tips. She wears a green halter crop top, black low-rise jeans, and boots. Sometimes she wears a black, yellow, and green poncho. She is a shapeshifter capable of transforming into a raptor or t-rex.

~

Babydoll, Karenna (Kerri) Liverpool

So'ahc, God of Chaos
Black Cloud
Fallen Angel

Babydoll is Kita's left hand, best friend, and dedicated legionnaire. Arriving on the colony ship, she worked her way through the ranks to Junior Commander in the Legion of Germania. She acts as an advisor and mentor to Kamikaze and Phoenix.

Babydoll has Legion blue feathers with black edges. Her floor-length blond hair is fashioned into two prehensile braids, each with a scorpion stinger on the end. She wears a high cut leotard with the top fashioned after the Legion uniform and knee-high combat boots. She is a master of firearms, but loves martial arts and has mastered many styles. Eight retractable crystal spider legs sprout from her back, and she wears a pair of crystal bracers on her arms.

~

Panther, Veronica (Vee)
   Re'drum, God of Murder
   Black Cloud
Panther was a notorious party girl until she became Kita's girlfriend. Under Babydoll's tutelage, she's become a formidable martial fighter. As the god Re'drum, she has been with Kita for thousands of years.

Panther has black feathers with dark gray rosettes that match those on her cheeks, thighs, and chest. She has a black tail and wears a black skirt, high-top sneakers, a cut-off white t-shirt, and suspenders. Three claws extend from between her fingers on each hand.

Aspen, Leaf (Danielle Pyatt)
   Tg'hil, God of Light
   White Cloud
   High Angel
Aspen is a master assassin and was a student of Kita's. Tg'hil is one of the oldest gods and has created almost all of the universes in Infinity.

Aspen has white feathers with gold tips. She wears a white sneak suit and carries an array of weapons including katana, wakizashi, compound bow, and throwing stars. She covers her blonde hair with a hood and her nose and mouth with a mask. She uses the Angel's internal communications system, known as the comm, instead of speaking.

~

UEE ANGELS

Sarin, Jane Gjord
   Edi'rp, God of Pride
   Black Cloud
   Evil Angel
Sarin is an accomplished leader, psychiatrist, sniper, and gunslinger. She holds the rank of Deputy Commandant in the Legion and is Kita's partner. As a citizen of the United Earth Empire, Sarin was arrested by Galina and returned to Neptune. After being reunited with her father, Sven Gjord, she organized the resistance to Galina's Political Bureau.

LIST OF ANGELS | *xiii*

Sarin is known for her black and red schoolgirl outfit. Her wings are black with red patches earning her the nickname Blackbird. Beauty for her is as much a weapon as her .67 caliber sniper rifle. She carries a pair of .50 caliber pistols strapped to her thighs and the sword Razorsplitter on her back. Her platinum blonde hair is often braided with a spiked ball at the end.

≈

Talon, Scarlett Kobb
White Cloud
High Angel

Talon was the leader of the Owlery, a group of Angels dedicated to charity, compassion, and kindness. During Galina's betrayal of Kita, Talon was arrested because she was a citizen of the UEE. She was granted parole and put in charge of raising and training the young Angel Talli. Sarin rescued them from Galina during a raid in Seattle. Talon's girlfriend is Cinnamon.

Talon's wings are patterned after a barn owl. She wears a white bodysuit and a cloak that closes in the front. Her cloak has an oversized hood, wide sleeves, and hides her arsenal of weapons including a short sword, pistol, and throwing knives.

≈

Athena

Athena is an AI that used to oversee the city of Gaia and was recruited by Kita. She oversaw the entire region of Hades with her partner Quill. After Galina betrayed Kita, Athena snuck aboard a UEE ship and made contact with Sarin. Together, they plotted the resistance to Galina and the Political Bureau.

Athena doesn't have a physical form beyond the computer she inhabits. She does use a solid holographic projector to project an image of herself. She often looks like a female humanoid android with grey skin. Her wings are electric blue and gray. She can infiltrate any network or computer she can gain access to.

≈

Ryder Starr

Ryder was a Red Legion general leading the resistance to the Political Bureau when Talon and Cinnamon found her. To protect her command, she donned the cursed gun belt that belonged to her cousin, Cowboy, and became The Rider—a flaming demon cowboy. She joined Sarin to help lead the resistance to Galina and the Political Bureau.

Ryder's wings are a mixture of pink, yellow, orange, and red feathers that look like a sunset. Even though she is in the Red Legion, she wears a cowboy hat, flannel shirt, duster, jeans, and cowboy boots. She thinks of herself as a legionnaire first, cowgirl second, and Angel third. Proficient with most firearms, she prefers revolvers.

~

Cinnamon, Kristi

Cinnamon was the personal assistant to Sven Gjord when Sarin arrived home. She impressed Kita with her management and organizational skills, and Kita made her an Angel. On a mission to recruit Ryder Starr, she fell in love with Talon.

Cinnamon's wings are the color of cinnamon. She wears a crop top shirt with the word *fireball* on the front, along with a leather half jacket, jeans, and boots. Sarin instructed Cinnamon on how to shoot her .45 caliber pistols. Cinnamon learned to control fire from Kita.

CHAPTER I

*K*ita's cheek rested on the cool, clear plastic of her spherical cell. Her eyes stared unfocused out into space. A daily ration of thin soup had left her drained with barely enough energy to function.

Ragji, a Majestic-class Moon Annihilator, drifted into her vision. The ship was over a mile in length. The conning tower in the center of its back made it look like a shark. And, like a shark, it circled waiting for her.

From FTL, six cruisers and frigates with unknown markings appeared around the Ragji and opened fire. The bright flashes caused Kita's eyes to focus. The six attackers had jumped inside the Ragji's shields. *Only I'm that precise.* The ships rained fire on the Ragji causing the port side to explode in a bright fireball. A pair of shuttles left the cruisers and flew toward the prison.

Ragji and its crew of kitty cats have been on station too long. Lulled into a pattern and senses deadened by months of staring at space...But, who would attack the Djinn? Those aren't UEE ships...Whatever they're after doesn't matter. Now's my chance to escape this accursed place and extract revenge on Warden Kiiz.

But, Kita barely had the energy to think—let alone fight. *What the Crushing Depths? What are the gods going to do to me that they haven't done already?* Before being starved into submission, Kita had spent weeks meditating, searching for her lost knowledge of the gods. She found some of what was lost. Most importantly, she rediscovered knowledge the gods barely understood.

Kita's vision changed. No longer did she see mass and energy, but symbols that represented the equations that made up everything. These equations acted like nesting dolls, culminating into an equation that governed the entire universe.

She looked at herself. Her equation looked like the rest, except for a small part. It didn't have a symbol or an equation, just a point of light. This was all that remained of her god form, Li've. It was enough to alter equations around her. She touched her equation and changed a pair of symbols. Energy coursed through her veins making her feel warm and envigorated. She returned her vision to normal.

Kita stood up and stretched her arms and wings. She'd been lying on the hard plastic for too long. She walked around her cell, dragging her hand on the plastic, ignoring the battle below. She took in the stars, her only friends. She reached the cell door. It was reinforced plastic a foot thick. Sandwiched between the plastic was several layers of a material that made the cell Angel-proof. Or so Warden Kiiz had gloated when he put her in here.

Like everyone else who challenges me, you make the same mistake— underestimating me. Even imprisoned, my power grows.

Kita drew back her fist and struck the cell door. The plastic shattered like ice, revealing a long, clear hallway connecting her cell to the prison. Stepping into the hallway, red lights in the ceiling blinked in warning. Someone was watching her. Looking into a camera, Kita blew it a kiss, and her picture on the camera monitors in the control room vanished.

She walked down the hallway admiring the view. It amused her they felt the need to isolate her. She'd hoped to be put in with the general population where she could take control of them and the prison. It wouldn't be the first time she'd done it.

But someone was smart. Was this someone's brilliant deduction or had someone talked? Only Snowy would know my full capability, and she's gone. Could she be working for the Tet? It wouldn't be the first time she's opposed me. Wouldn't that be interesting? I wonder where she is. I hope she's not dead.

As Kita reached the end of the hallway, a series of small explosions disconnected the hallway from the prison. The air rushed into space, moving Kita's hair slightly. The hallway drifted away from the prison. Along with the air went gravity. Kita floated off the floor. *This is their plan if I get out of line? Space me?*

Kita wiggled her nose, manipulating the equation. She shot forward, passing through the airlock doors into the room beyond. A pair of large lion-like Djinn guards looked shocked by her appearance. She raised her hands, mimed grabbing them by their heads, and clenched her fists. Their heads collapsed, crushed like cans. Stepping over the bodies, Warden Kiiz's voice came over the speaker, "Recovery teams get out there and get the body."

He's in for a surprise…Now, where am I going to find Case and Jess?

Kita exited the room and followed the corridor. She turned a corner, and a group of guards waited in riot gear. Kita raised her hands and mimed cracking whips. A pair of shockwaves hit the guards. The bodies exploded—their gear containing most of the mess.

Through a door, Kita found a giant room full of cryogenic pods. *Are Case and Jess in those?* Curious, she went to one and wiped the frost from the window. Inside was a Zentonian, a large squirrel-like creature, in cryogenic sleep. She went to the next one and found a frozen toad-like Toeak.

Why freeze them? Why not kill them? It's the same thing. They're not being rehabilitated this way. Maybe it's easier on society's conscience…

Kita looked up. There were twenty floors above her. *That's a lot of people. I wonder if they ever thaw them out? And, why have a facility in deep space?*

She moved through the room, trying to imagine what crime could be so horrible to require freezing. *Why wasn't I frozen? I prefer unconsciousness to solitary confinement.* Talking to yourself got old fast, and she'd exhausted the movies stored on the computer in her head. She needed to find the master computer to tell her if Valor and Defiance were among the frozen.

Above Kita, guards ran onto the catwalks circling the room. "Freeze, Angel," yelled a guard directly above her.

"You mean figuratively or literally?" Kita said with a smile. She waved her hand. A pod ripped from the wall, flew across the room, and crushed the guard issuing the command. The guards opened fire with shocker rounds. Kita wiggled her nose and made herself immune to their effects. Waving her hands merrily, she ripped pods from the wall and hurled them at the guards, knocking them off the catwalks, or crushing them between two pods. She dropped pods on those guards still alive on the ground floor.

After a pod crushed the head of the last guard, Kita cocked her head to one side. She felt two presences she hadn't felt in a long time.

"Snowy! Zen!" she called in a pleasant voice. The group waited in a doorway across the room.

Snowy was an anthropomorphic war cat, with foot-long claws that extended from the tops of her hands and a fluffy tail nearly as long as she was tall. Zentix was a Diamock. Their bottom half looked like a goat, and the upper half looked like a quill-covered dog with bony plates on the chest, arms, and abdomen.

"Let me handle this," said Snowy. "She's not the same as the last time we saw her."

"What's happened to her?" said Zentix.

"I think she found her missing god part."

Kita chuckled at her eavesdropping. Snowy knew her so well.

"Kita! Are you alright?" called Snowy.

"That depends. Are you behind my imprisonment?"

Snowy let out a sigh and stepped out to face Kita. "No. We're here to rescue you."

Kita chuckled. "I can rescue myself, thanks."

"From our reports, you were comatose and in solitary confinement."

"They weren't wrong, but what point is it to be active when I have no way off this...facility."

"Then come with us. We'll get you somewhere safe." Snowy retracted her claws and waved Kita to her.

Kita wagged her finger. "Ah-ah. You haven't explained your new friends. Last time I saw a yellow uniform, it was shooting at me and carrying you off. I'm not going to exchange one cell for another."

"That's true, but it's a misunderstanding. Please, come with us, and I'll explain."

"I'll take my explanation now. I'm in no hurry, but I suggest you talk fast. I'm not sure how long your ships are going to last against Ragji's cannons."

Snowy rolled her eyes. "I know it's not worth telling you good people are dying saving you."

Kita sneered. "And I put my neck on the block to save plenty more. Look what it got me."

"Collector admits he made a mistake with the asteroid. He misjudged you and what you're capable of—"

Kita cocked her head with a devilish smile. "Tell me, what did he offer you to switch sides?"

Snowy frowned. "He didn't offer me anything—"

"So what did you offer him to save yourself—me?"

"No. I locked myself in the engine compartment of the ship and threatened to blow it up if I wasn't given safe passage off. That's when Collector came and talked to me. He's a Djinn purist. He believes the other races make them weak. This facility has a hidden purpose. They cut up these prisoners and take them back to Djinn to be eaten. They believe it increases their warrior prowess."

Kita raised an eyebrow. Once upon a time, Snowy ate her enemies. *Was Snowy finding a home among the Djinn?*

"It sure is easy to kill and eat your enemies when they're frozen," Kita scoffed.

"They take what they can get. But, it's bigger than some Djinn trying to relive their glory days. Collector understands what a threat the humans are, and unlike the Tet, he wants to do something about them. He has a sizable force in the quarantine zone. Like you, he has an eye for talent. He knows he needs you. Your actions on Veven proved it. He's willing to give you what I know you want—"

"And what is that?" Kita cooed.

"Galina." The hair stood up on the back of Kita's neck. "He'll put you at the head of his fleet so you can get her and give them the battle they crave."

Kita bit her lip. Galina: the betrayer, the murderer of her children, her jailor. Kita could taste the revenge, which tasted similar to the blood she'd drawn biting herself.

But, there was a problem. It was one thing to go after Galina. It was another to target the UEE. They belonged to Defiance. She wasn't sure how her girlfriend would react to her destroying the UEE's Shadow Fleet. *Maybe there's another way.* If she restored Defiance to her throne, then she wouldn't need to destroy the Shadow Fleet. Once Defiance was in charge, she could turn on the Djinn and drive them from UEE Space. Earth sounded like a much better place to be than Tet space.

"Ok, Snowy. I'll talk to Collector, but what's in it for me?"

Snowy chuckled. "I told Collector he'd have to sweeten the pot. I've got three things."

"What three things does he have that I could possibly want?"

Snowy ticked them off on her fingers. "Case, Jess…and Crypt."

"Crypt…" Kita whispered. Crypt, the soul reaper, was one of the twelve great swords made by the grandmaster bladesmith Earnan and presented to the Great Elder Vidic to carry as he guided the Arconian clans. The sword possessed the power to pull the souls from the living. Kita had carried the sword since finding it in her youth in the base of a volcano located in The Orient region of The Mass. Crypt had disappeared between the time Kita saved the universe and Galina's forces recovering her body. *How did Collector get a hold of it?* "I want them, and I want them now."

"Unfortunately, Collector doesn't have them. He just knows where to get them. They're auctioning Jess, Case, and Crypt to the highest bidder. Collector is going to give you the people and material to free them."

"Something tells me Collector could buy them if he wanted."

"And what fun would that be?"

Kita shrugged. *Why buy it when you can steal it?* "Ok. Lead the way out of here."

"Here. I brought you a bodysuit. I figured you'd need some clothes." Snowy tossed Kita a bundle.

Kita shook the bodysuit out and slipped it on. "Any idea where my swords and armor are?"

"We sent a team to check a few locations. We'll meet them at the shuttles."

"I'll tear this place apart for them," said Kita.

"Hopefully that won't be necessary."

Kita followed Snowy and her team down a short corridor. Snowy opened the door and led the group onto the ground floor of another cellblock. Like the previous, everyone was frozen.

Attached to the ceiling, an arm lowered and grabbed a pod. It lowered to the ground and set it on a cart. The cart drove off through a door that closed behind it.

"Another snack?" Kita asked Snowy.

"I—maybe. I haven't done it personally."

"You mean not recently."

"Ah," Snowy's nose turned pink, "no. Everything I've eaten has come from a vat."

"You sound disappointed."

Snowy raised an eyebrow. "And you sound like you've got your memory back."

"Most of it. There is one big hole. I'm missing a person."

Snowy smirked. "I won't ruin the surprise for when we meet her. Wherever she is."

"Well, I'll always have Case."

"I heard about Cotton. I'm sorry."

Kita shrugged. "It wasn't working in the end. I tried, but she had her principles, and I had mine."

"Or the lack thereof…"

Kita wrinkled her nose. "Humph."

Snowy raised her hand as a radio transmission came in. "I'm here,

Sahara...Not in the armory? Try the warden's office. I—Sahara! Don't engage them. Retreat to the shuttles. We'll get them another way."

"Problem?" said Kita.

"The Fast Reaction Force from Ragji is in the facility. We have to go. We don't have the firepower to slug it out with them, even with you."

"What about my weapons and armor?"

"We'll get them another way."

Kita huffed. "No. I'm not leaving without them."

"Kita, I'm not even sure they're here. The intelligence reports couldn't pin down their exact location. Here is one of several possibilities. You—"

Armed men ran onto the first four levels of catwalks. They stood shoulder to shoulder. Their weapons pointed at Kita and her rescuers.

"Kind of slow, aren't you?" said Kita to the soldiers. "I've been loose for ten minutes."

"Drop your weapons, get on your knees and put your hands behind your heads," instructed one of the soldiers.

"Well, see, that's a problem. My weapons are built into my hands." Kita smiled as flames leaped from her hands and marched up her arms. When they reached her torso, the flames engulfed her.

"Take her down," yelled the soldier.

The soldiers fired, but the bullets hung in the air around Kita and her group. Kita laughed wickedly. "You got your try. My turn," she yelled.

~

SNOWY PUSHED HER TEAM BACK INTO THE DOORWAY AS THE BULLETS LANDED IN front of them. "Run, go!" she ordered. "Go through the far door back to the shuttle."

Snowy and her team sprinted across the bottom of the cellblock. Bullets hit the floor around them. Snowy wasn't surprised the soldiers missed. Kita was watching out for them.

The far door opened ahead of them revealing a team of soldiers. Snowy phased in front of her team and blasted them with a sheet of lightning. Behind her, Kita laughed maniacally as she tossed the pods around, crushing the hapless soldiers.

The station shook, knocking Snowy and her team to the ground. There was a low moan of stressed metal.

"Christ on the cross," yelled Snowy. "Masks down, prepare for decompression."

Her team closed their helmets' faceplates and switched their breathing to internal. Snowy didn't have to do anything. Her body was rated for space, and she carried a canister of air for when she needed to take a breath.

A loud crack reverberated through the facility. A ripping sound followed. Several decks worth of pods crashed down in the middle of the cellblock.

"Go, go, go!" cried Snowy. "She's going to rip this prison apart."

Snowy and her team dashed through the maze of empty corridors. Ahead of them, a pair of decompression doors slammed shut.

"Charges?" asked one of Snowy's team members.

"No time," said Snowy. "Everybody touch me."

Each member of the team reached out and touched Snowy. She phased, transporting the entire team to the other side of the doors.

"Move," she yelled.

They reached the first of three doors they had blasted through to get to the cellblocks. The facility shuddered, throwing everyone sideways into the wall.

"Come on, Kita. Keep it together long enough for us to get off," muttered Snowy.

They reached the second door as an elevator door opened. Snowy's team brought their weapons up.

"Wait! Don't shoot!" said a soldier wearing the same yellow armor as Snowy's team.

A Djinn female wearing custom yellow armor led the new group. She raised her visor, revealing a sand-colored cat-like face with big brown eyes.

"Sahara! We have to hurry. Kita's ripping this place apart," said Snowy.

"What about saving her?"

"Don't worry about that. We'll pick Kita up when she's done."

"How is she ripping this place apart?"

"That's a long story, but the short version is she's a god."

"A what?" Sahara said skeptically.

"A god—able to control the universe and everything in it. Last I saw her, she'd lost that power, but she's found it again. And now she's got months of imprisonment to take out on someone."

"Kita sounds wonderful," said Sahara in a sarcastic tone.

"She...can be. She's just cranky."

"I get cranky when I wake up, and I just hit the alarm clock."

"This prison is her alarm clock."

The group turned a corner into the docking area. Prison guards were trying to open the door to one of Snowy's shuttles.

"Hey, back off," yelled Sahara. She drew a pair of haladie daggers from her back and threw one, hitting the unarmored prison guard in the neck.

"Sorry to spoil your escape, Warden Kiiz, but these shuttles belong to us," said Snowy.

Kiiz, a large Djinn male, turned and snarled. "No dirty inbred female orders me around. You will submit." He drew a pistol.

Snowy's team fired. Kiiz crumpled to the deck.

"Care to insult me?" Snowy said to the other guards, a mix of Djinn and Verisom males.

"Pathetic sandkicker males, obeying a dirty female?" snarled one of the Djinn guards.

Snowy snarled and leaped at him. The male raised his arms and extended the short claws on his hands, as Snowy's much longer claws sliced through his arm. She landed, plunged her claws into his chest, lifted him over her head, and slammed him to the deck.

"Anyone else want to call me a dirty female?" Snowy demanded of the remaining Djinn guards.

The Djinn bared their teeth, glaring at Snowy, but stood aside at the behest of the Djinn males that made up Snowy's group. Only Sahara and her slender frame stood out among them.

"Come on, let's go," said Snowy.

Her team members opened the shuttles, and the two teams boarded.

"So, now what do we do?" called Sahara to Snowy over the shuttle's comm.

"We let Kita have her fun and pick her up when she's done."

CHAPTER III

*K*ita floated amongst the wreckage of the prison. She stopped when she came to a locked, reinforced composite metal box. Taking the corner, she pulled, bending the lid back until it tore from the hinges. Inside was her missing weapons and armor.

At last!

She removed Dusk and Dawn. The black blades' edges gleamed in the starlight. After admiring them, she sheathed them on her back. On the bottom was her bow, Midnight. With a flick of her wrist, she extended it, checked it, then collapsed it and stowed it on her lower back. She pulled out her upper arm and thigh pads—containing her collection of throwing stars—and strapped them on.

The head of a guard floated in front of Kita. Smiling, she poked it and sent it spinning in a new direction. Her only disappointment was finding Warden Kiiz dead. She had wanted to gut the bastard and strangle him with his own intestines.

A flash from below signaled a battle still raged. Ragji fought against its attackers, though the attackers were down three from six. *Maybe it's time to even the odds and show Collector my power.*

After exiting the debris field, Kita picked up speed and aimed at Ragji's aft section. As she traveled, she generated an energy field. Kita halted a thousand yards from Ragji and threw the energy field at the ship.

The energy field struck the aft starboard side and exploded. The force caused Ragji's aft to drop and the bow to rise. The three engines on the starboard side exploded, adding a new vector of rotation to the ship.

Kita flew through the tangle of debris into the damaged section of Ragji. Twisted and torn metal stuck out like bones. Sparks flew into space as dangling wires grounded out. She found a corridor torn in half. Her boots touched the friction carpet. After taking a step, she felt the familiar tug of gravity. *The wounded beast still lives.*

The corridor ended at a pair of emergency decompression doors. Kita ignored the laws of physics and glided through the doors. The corridor split. To the left, it disappeared around a corner; the right led to a door. She heard a single voice come from the left. Curious, she turned invisible and walked toward the voice.

Around the corner, she found a Djinn in an engineer's jumpsuit, complete with a toolbox. He was speaking to someone over a video console.

"I have no readings beyond this section. It's like it's not there," said the engineer.

"Did you do a visual inspection?" snarled a Djinn in an officer's uniform.

"The decompression doors are closed and won't open until the pressure is equalized."

"Override them! We're not getting any power from engines six through twelve."

"No one is answering in—"

Kita turned visible and slammed her hand into the Djinn engineer's back. She wiggled her hand around and grabbed his spine, then jerked her hand back and forth and broke the bones loose. The Djinn collapsed, hitting his muzzle on the console on his way down.

Kita held the bones covered in blue blood up to the camera. "Visual inspection is your ship is missing a large chunk." Kita dropped the bones on the console and smeared blood on the camera lens.

"Who are you?" demanded the officer.

"The one girl wrecking crew." Kita slammed her fist into the console. *You think they'd just look out a damn window.*

Kita followed the corridor. To her surprise, this section of the ship was empty. In her mind, she expected to see people running around. *They're probably at battle stations or helping put out fires and repair damage.*

She reached a door that was renforced and required authorization to open. Kita shrugged and walked through it.

The walls tapered inward, funneling her down a small hallway. A blinding light kept her from seeing ahead of her. Exiting the hallway, she stepped into a round room filled with barricades. She was in a security checkpoint—a hard point meant to help repel boarders, a favorite tactic of Tet warfare.

A squad of Djinn soldiers stood on the other side of the room not paying attention. Kita drew Midnight and an arrow. She fired, hitting a Djinn in the eye through his faceplate. The other Djinn turned, and two more went down to arrows. Kita swapped Midnight for Dusk and Dawn and charged the stunned group.

Kita leaped and plunged her swords into the first Djinn's chest. She withdrew, performed a backward handspring with a twist and stabbed her swords into the second Djinn. Spinning, she dropped to her knees and cut through the third Djinn's legs. As he fell forward, Kita thrust upward through the Djinn's head. Kita rolled to her right to dodge a wild burst of bullets. She sprang into the air and corkscrewed, slamming Dusk and Dawn down into the shoulders of the last Djinn. The body fell backward, a shower of sparks from the power armor erupting when it hit the floor.

On the ceiling was a trio of autocannons along with the four blinding lights. Kita smiled, grabbed a Djinn, and snapped her fingers. The Djinn's eyes opened.

"Hang on, this is going to hurt," she said with a giggle.

She placed her hand on his armored chest piece and melted through it. The Djinn screamed when her flaming hand touched his skin.

"Oh, that was nothing. *This* is what's going to hurt."

Thrusting her hand into his chest, she seized his beating heart and yanked it from his chest cavity. The Djinn's roar became a whimper. The Djinn floated off the floor under one of the autocannons. Kita floated up along with him, still holding his heart. She draped the muscle over the autocannon and let the body hang.

The Djinn moaned.

"Don't worry. I'll give you something to sing about when I'm done with your friends."

Kita whistled as she revived the Djinn, ripped their hearts out, and hung them from autocannons and lights.

"There," said Kita when she finished. "Aren't you the cutest kitty cat choir?" She chuckled at the moans she received. "Oh, you need to perk up. This isn't a zombie convention." She waved her hand, and the Djinns' heads lowered. "Now, let's hear you sing."

"Sick bitch…"

"Fallen angel…"

"Sociopath…"

"Going to…"

"Take her…"

"Revenge."

"Perfect," Kita purred. "Make sure to recite that to anyone who comes in here or any gods watching."

Kita went to the guard station's console and found the bridge on the map. She called the bridge, stepped aside, and waved her hand at her choir as a Djinn officer appeared on the screen. The choir sang her song a few times for him.

"What is this? Someone explain," demanded the officer.

Kita waved her hand.

"She's coming for you," sang Kita's choir as she left the room.

The blinking red boarding warning light cast shadows as Kita walked down the corridor. *I doubt Snowy's forces can board Ragji.* Still, there wasn't a super-freak-on-the-loose warning system, at least not on any ship she'd been on. *I doubt the kitties have that kind of imagination.*

The warning put more people into the corridors, all of which she dispatched with extreme enthusiasm, but not even the soldiers were challenging. The Djinn weren't bad fighters, just primal. They received basic training in how to use their claws, but none mastered them like Snowy. The Djinn preferred modern weapons. *I'm sure they're regretting that now.*

Kita turned a corner, following a map she downloaded at a security kiosk. Ahead of her was supposed to be an *authorized access only* Area. Two guards stood at the door. *Must be the place.* Kita was searching for the elevator to the bridge, and by process of deduction, this place made logical sense—it was directly below the bridge and access was restricted. *It would be better if they marked it storage or something.* According to the map, most of the interior of the ship was dedicated to storage.

Forming two fireballs, Kita threw them at the guards. *You didn't get the message to be on the lookout for me?* The fireballs struck the guards in their helmets. They retaliated by opening fire. Their bullets stopped in front of Kita as she waited patiently for the superheated fire to burn its way through. She laughed when they dropped their rifles and danced around trying to take their armor off. One managed to remove his helmet causing the flames to engulf his mane.

"Stop, drop, and roll," Kita told them as she walked by.

She entered a chaotic room. In the center, an elevator shaft made of clear panels was surrounded by workstations. *This must be the command center.* As the nerve center for the entire ship, it gathered and disseminated information, but wasn't where the senior officers were. That's who Kita really wanted.

Kita grew four of her explosive red balls in her hands. Few in the room noticed her. Those that did looked confused by her appearance. Kita tossed the balls into the four quadrants of the room. An alert Djinn yelled something to the rest of the room. Kita smiled and waved as her heat shield expanded. She snapped her fingers four times, and the red balls exploded.

The shockwaves bounced around the room destroying the organized chaos, pulverizing and throwing the bodies around, blue blood oozing from noses and ears. Kita's heat shield collapsed, and she surveyed the scene with a wicked smile. Most bodies lay in unnatural positions, the soft tissue turned to jelly. *That should take the pressure off Snowy and her friends.*

Kita walked to the elevator, stepping over dead Djinn. Around her, some of the workstations sparked or their screens blinked randomly. Entering the elevator, she hit the button for the bridge.

The elevator moved upward, stopped, and the doors opened. Two Verisom males in power armor flanked a door in front of her. Kita had never seen Verisom males in power armor before. *Cotton was right. They are imposing.*

"Stop and identify yourself," said the Verisom on the right through a translation device that made his voice sound mechanical. Both Verisom aimed their large miniguns at her.

"Kita. I'm taking a tour of the ship."

"You are not authorized to be here. Return to the command center, and you will be escorted to an authorized area."

Kita chuckled. "At least you're not trying to kill me outright. I—on the other hand—am."

She raised her hands over her shoulders, drew Dusk and Dawn, and threw the blades end over end into the faceplates of the Verisom, pinning them to the wall. With a smile, Kita recovered her swords. *Why are two Verisom males guarding the entrance to the bridge of a Djinn ship?*

As Kita stepped up to the door, it opened. A Djinn officer bounced off her and caused a comical set of collisions by several Djinn following him. *The Djinn Keystone Cops.* Kita swept her blades cutting the first Djinn in half. She stabbed the second, spun, took the head of the third, and stepped around the fourth to stab him backward.

The bridge was in disarray. The crew was trying to reestablish their link with the command center. Above them, the captain sat in his chair, next to him was a Verisom female. *Well, that explains the guards. Still, I didn't know the Djinn shared with those they considered food.*

"It's the escapee!" yelled a Djinn from a workstation next to the door. He jumped to his feet while drawing a sidearm.

Kita snapped her fingers, and everyone froze in place. "None of that." She walked across the bridge and stopped in front of the Verisom female. "Hello, Princess. What's a good looking girl like you doing in a place like this?" Kita leaned in and kissed her. "Yum. You never forget your first bunny."

The Verisom's nose twitched violently in protest of the violation.

"Such a mouth," Kita said with a chuckle. She stroked the side of the Verisom's head to calm her. Kita turned her attention to the captain. "We have a problem. Warden Kiiz is dead. I so *badly* wanted to skin that cat alive. What's a girl to do but find a replacement? Since I was thrown into that damn bubble, I've watched this ship circle like a carrion bird waiting for me to drop dead. *YOU* represent my incarceration as much as Kiiz. I've destroyed his prison, and now I'm going to destroy this ship. The Grand Panel and the Tet will learn the price of crossing me. I would have helped them whenever they needed it. Instead, they listened to idiots like Grand Marshal Tetarax. Now, they're going to learn what betraying me means. I'm not going to stop with Ragji. I'll destroy the whole damn Tet and every living soul on it." Kita's voice became low and menacing. She ended with a growl. "But first, let's you and I have a little fun, shall we?"

Kita reached into the captain's mouth, grabbed his left canine, and yanked it out. The captain's eyes went wide with pain. Kita released his head so she could listen to him howl. She held up the tooth with the root dangling. "I find it odd they call it a canine when it comes off a cat, don't you think?"

"Dirty, sand flea encrusted barren female. You will suffer for your insolence," the captain roared.

"I'm not barren," Kita scoffed. "I have plenty of eggs. I just choose not to use them." Kita showed the tooth to the rest of the crew, letting their eyes follow it. "There are worse predators in the galaxy than cats. Angels are built to be killers. Now, let's see that other tooth."

Kita grabbed the captain's muzzle and forced his jaws open. "Oh, quit struggling. You want to do it the hard way?" She jabbed her finger into the socket of the missing tooth and turned up the heat. The captain roared and shook his head violently throwing Kita off. "Oh, you want to play rough? Fine." Kita drew Dusk and held it up to the Verisom. "Give me the tooth, or I start removing body parts."

"She is an officer. You can't intimidate us," snarled the captain.

Kita unfroze the Verisom's head. "What's your name?"

"C—Carrot."

"Princess Carrot has a nice ring to it. You must be one of the mid-tier princesses. Do you know who I am?"

Carrot nodded. "You were Princess Cotton's fiancée—the Angel Kita."

"Someone's been reading the tabloids. Do you really think I killed Cotton?"

"I…I…The Queen said you did."

Kita patted the side of Carrot's head, enjoying the silky soft fur. "That's a clever attempt at sidestepping the question. I want to know what you think." Kita held Dusk up so Carrot could see it.

Tears filled Carrot's big eyes. "I…I don't know. I don't know what happened. I'm not in the warrens that are told privileged information."

Kita grabbed one of Carrot's ears and sliced the tip of it off. Carrot screamed. Her eyes rolled up in her head, and she passed out.

Kita held up the tip of the ear to the captain. "How many more parts do you want her in?"

"You're a monster."

Kita chuckled. "A monster you created. Now, tooth or I wake her up, and I'll take something bigger."

The captain let out a low growl but opened his mouth. Kita grabbed the tooth and yanked. The Captain roared and shook his head violently.

"Tell me something, Captain. Why risk your neck for her? Djinn see the Verisom as just above food."

"Commander Carrot is here under a liaison program to learn how Djinn ships operate. A Djinn officer is serving aboard a Verisom ship. I'm honor bound to protect her."

Kita laughed. "Honor, what a joke." She touched Carrot's nose, and the Verisom woke. "You're going to want to be awake for the next part, Princess."

Carrot bowed her head, but her nose was pale.

"Don't worry, sweetheart, the end will be quick." Kita turned to the crew and held up the two canines. "Now that I've defanged your captain, I'm going to defang the Djinn fleet."

Kita stepped in front of the captain's chair and threw her arms wide forming a column of red energy around her.

SNOWY CLUNG TO THE BACK OF A CHAIR AS ANOTHER BLAST ROCKED THE SHIP. She didn't know what was happening, but the gunfire from Ragji had lessened considerably. Kita was the most logical reason. They were still determining what hit Ragji to blow apart its portside engines.

"Commander Snowy!" an urgent cry came from the sensors station.

Snowy rushed over. "What is it?"

"This just came up on imaging. There's a massive column of energy coming from Ragji, and it disappears out into space."

"Christ on the cross! She's going to blow up the ship. All hands emergency FTL jump, now! Tell the other ships and jump."

"We can't blindly jump," said a sailor at navigation.

"We jump, or we're dead! We have to beat the energy wall that's crashing down on Ragji."

"A what?"

"She's done this before. Just do it," Snowy yelled. "What's about to go off has enough energy to destroy a planet. We don't want to be anywhere close when this goes off."

"Other ships have been alerted and are complying," said a sailor from communications.

"Good. Go, go!"

CHAPTER IIII

A brilliant white light glided through the window of Ragji's bridge. It circled Kita's beam of light several times before expanding into a tiny Angel with mousey brown hair, big brown eyes, and wearing a white bodysuit. She stuck her hand into Kita's beam.

"I'm sorry, big sister, but this is extreme, even for you. Why do so many innocents have to die?"

Kita scowled. "Tina! How did I know you'd be close? Every time I'm imprisoned, you're watching."

"I'm trying to keep you safe. I don't want anything to happen to you."

"Did you enjoy watching them starve me—making me too weak to move? I couldn't even think. Is that why you watch?" Kita screamed.

Tina held up her hands against Kita's anger. "Were you in any significant danger I would have stepped in."

"What is *significant danger*, Tina? Do I have to die first? Because my resurrection systems need power to function. Starving to death means they're inoperable."

"Kita, I'm sorry, but I would never let it get that far. I was hoping you'd relax and take it easy."

Kita gnashed her teeth. "Do I look relaxed? The only thing that happened was my rage and hate built like a plugged volcano."

Tina gulped. "Please calm down. This is not the way. Doing what you're doing will bring Y'grene and the others, and they will delete you."

"Why? What have I done?"

"You're trying to become a god again. They'll never allow it. You're too dangerous."

"What have I done to them?" Kita roared, hoping the gods were listening.

"It's not what you've done. It's your motives and objectives."

"I'm to be punished for something that might happen?"

"You're a threat—to all the equations. You're a threat like they've never known and you scare them."

Kita balled her fists and her eyes burned. "Then let them know fear." She screamed, and the energy wall crashed into the ship shredding metal and plastic. When the wall reached the beam, everything exploded in a brilliant flash.

~

"Why are we in the White?" said Kita to Tina. She only passed through the White on her way to Infinity. It served as the boot system for the equation that governed the universe.

"I'm sorry, Kita," Tina said with a sad frown. "I can't let you run wild.

You're too powerful. I heard what you want to do to the Tet. I can't let that happen. I gave you a chance."

Six gods, as points of light, appeared and flew around the pair of Angels. Three hovered behind Kita, while the others lined up next to Tina. One point expanded into Ht'aed, a grim reaper, the second into Y'grene, a sphere, the third, E'fil, became a woman covered in vines and leaves. Those gods behind Kita expanded into humanoid forms. Each god was made from millions of points of light.

"Y'grene," Kita purred at the ball.

"Li've," Y'grene greeted in a crisp, even voice.

"Why call this equation by one of our names?" said Ht'aed in a deep, menacing growl. "It is not worthy of it."

"I earned my name," snarled Kita. "I defeated the Harbingers and combined a universal equation with a nonstandard subset you created. None of you could have done that, and I did it in an instant."

"That is why you should be deleted," said Ht'aed.

"Try it," yelled Kita. "I may not be as powerful, but I can still pack a wallop."

"Calm yourself, Li've," said E'fil in an airy and happy voice. "You chose this path and knew the outcome. Accept your fate."

The three gods behind Kita grabbed her. Kita struggled, but they forced her to her knees. Kita bared her teeth at the elder gods. They crowded around Kita and reached out to her with an appendage glowing blue at the tip.

"Delete me, and I will gain power you can't imagine," said Kita menacingly.

"Your power is at an end," said Ht'aed.

Ten pinpricks of light appeared and flew around Kita and the gods.

One broke away and flew between Kita and the elder gods. The pinprick expanded into Kamikaze. She raised her fist. "Touch her, and I'll raze Infinity to the ground."

The other pinpricks of light transformed into eight Angels and a raptor. They drew their weapons and put them to the other gods.

"Hold," ordered Ht'aed. "This doesn't concern you."

"Anyone messing with my mom is messing with us," said Kamikaze.

Panther, Aspen, and Toxic prodded the gods restraining Kita with swords and claws to make them let go. Kita stood and fluffed her ruffled feathers.

"You're not the only one who comes with backup," Kita said smiling at Y'grene. "Did you forget about the Valkyries, or did you think they would obey you?"

"This is none of their business," Ht'aed hissed.

"Oh, but it is. They've been on a fool's errand—at your direction—to find my god powers. Instead, you deleted as much of my god power as you could, but not all of it. There's enough left I can still interact with equations. It doesn't matter, what was lost I can find again. Now, maybe you'd like to negotiate?"

"What are your terms?" said E'fil.

"I want what was taken from me restored and let us be left in peace to do what we will."

"Let you run wild? Never," roared Ht'aed.

"Or we could be running wild through Infinity." The body language of the other Angels shifted. Kita knew ravaging Infinity was a threat she would have trouble carrying out. Most of the other Angels wouldn't attack their home, but she had to start somewhere.

"They promised they wouldn't," said Y'grene.

"You're hardly one to call anyone on a broken promise," said Kita, "especially when they haven't done it yet."

"You are no longer Li've, and the researchers following you return home," said E'fil. "In exchange, we will let you go under the condition you never return to Infinity."

"That's not a deal I can make. All the gods chose to bond to Angels. I won't order them home," said Kita crossing her arms.

"I refuse to return to Infinity as long as my father is there," said Panther.

"Us too," said Tenshi and Valentine.

"The daughters of Ht'aed have spoken," said Kita with a lopsided smile.

"You will come home if I order it," said Ht'aed.

"Good luck enforcing that," said Phoenix snidely.

"I will not force anyone back to Infinity that doesn't wish to go, but Infinity must be made safe from threats," said Y'grene. "And you can't terrorize other equations. As a group, you have too much power."

Kita shrugged. "You let us go, let me retain my status as Li've, and we promise not to use our god powers. Sound fair?"

"No! Li've cannot remain!" bellowed Ht'aed.

"I'm not going away," said Kita. "You respect me, or I will sic the Harbingers on every equation I can find." The three elder gods recoiled at the proposition. "You better believe Soa'hc, and I will find a way."

The lights of the elder gods blinked. "We agree to your terms, but Y'crem must go with you, and none of you are allowed in Infinity."

Kita looked at Tina and shrugged. "Ok. Deal."

The Angels let go of the other gods. The elder gods and their escort collapsed into points of light and vanished.

"Mom!" Kamikaze yelled as she gave Kita a hug.

"I've missed you." Kita gave her a kiss on the cheek.

After a moment, Kita found herself in the center of a massive group hug.

"I missed all of you," she announced with a grin. "But let's get out of here."

∾

KITA AND THE OTHER ANGELS APPEARED AMONGST THE WORKSTATIONS ON THE lower level of the bridge of a ship. On the upper level, Snowy was hunched over a screen.

"Sit your slagging ass down," said Phoenix as she pushed a Djinn back into his seat.

"Hey, Snowy," called Kita.

Snowy looked up, and her mouth fell open. "W—Where have you been? Where did they come from? What happened?"

Kita glared at Tina. "A Judas betrayed me to the elder gods, but they forgot I have a family. We negotiated my release."

Tina flittered behind Raptor.

"Ya best not be hidden' behind me," growled Raptor.

"As far as Ragji, it is no more," said Kita.

"That won't make the Tet happy," said Snowy. "Let's not talk here. Come on ladies, follow me."

∾

SNOWY LED THE ANGELS INTO THE SHIP'S WARDROOM. "PLEASE, FIND A SEAT. IF you're hungry, I can try and make the dispensers make something besides meat."

"I think everyone is fine for now," said Kita as the Angels moved in and found seats. Kita gave Snowy a hug. "There's a proper greeting."

Snowy's nose turned red, and her whiskers drooped. "Thanks. It's been a while."

"Why the unhappy reaction? I thought you'd be excited to see me."

"I am. It's just that I…uh…well…"

The door opened, and a woman who looked similar to Snowy except sand colored and a short thin tail entered.

"Snowy, I heard we had guests. My, they're a colorful bunch," said the new arrival.

"Who is this?" said Kita. *I remember you from the prison break. I didn't know you were someone important.*

Snowy's ears laid flat against her head. "Ah…Kita…this is…ah…"

"Hello, Miss Kita, I'm Lieutenant Commander Sahara. Snowy's executive officer and girlfriend."

Kita raised an eyebrow at Snowy. Her nose was deep red. "Is this what you're stumbling over?"

"About time," said Babydoll. "Does this mean she'll stop pining for you?"

Kita chuckled at her best friend. Snowy looked like she wanted to crawl into a hole and die.

"Good. This means I get Kita to myself," said Panther as she gave Kita a hug and a kiss.

"Hmmm, I've missed you," Kita purred.

"You better have," said Panther as she played with one of her suspenders holding up her black skirt.

"Cat got your tongue?" Babydoll said to Snowy.

"I…uh…Meet Sahara," Snowy whispered.

"Maybe we should introduce her to everyone," said Kita.

"Vee," said Panther.

"Kerri," said Babydoll.

"Kamikaze."

"Raptor. Leaf," Raptor said pointing to Aspen.

"Kylee," said Phoenix.

"Tenshi."

"Denver," said Valentine.

"Tina."

"Kara," said Toxic.

"Nell," said Anthrax.

"Where did you come from?" said Sahara. "We were tasked with rescuing Kita."

"We've been out in the universe searching for parts of my mom," said Kamikaze.

"Kita's your mother?"

"Yes. So is Snowy."

"You never told me you had a daughter," Sahara said playfully to Snowy. "Though, I could have guessed. She looks just like you."

Snowy sighed. "She takes after Kita."

Sahara's whiskers drooped. "Did I step into something I shouldn't have? I'm sorry if I did."

"Don't worry about it," said Kamikaze. "Snowy and I have a history that we've come to terms with."

Snowy smiled sheepishly.

"I met the other Angels after I destroyed Ragji," said Kita. "Their mission to search for my missing parts is over, and they've come to help."

"Snowy," said Sahara, "I'm going to move the ship into communication range. Our blind jump has left us outside the normal channels."

"Yes, of course. Kita should speak to Collector as soon as possible."

~

KITA AND THE ANGELS FILED INTO THE SMALL QUANTUM COMMUNICATIONS room. Making room for everyone required folding their wings around themselves like feathered cloaks.

"This room works just like the quantum communicators in our heads," said Snowy. "A hologram of Collector will appear at the front of the room."

"And where is Collector?" said Kita.

Snowy wiggled her nose. "I don't know. I've never met him in person."

"He's in a safe place. His empire is vast," said Sahara.

"He's not the king of the Djinn. I've met the current and previous kings," said Kita.

"Business empire, but his wealth does rival royalty."

"Have you met him?" said Valentine.

"I have. Collector's a very driven Djinn. He wants to reclaim the pride and honor the Djinn have lost."

"Oh goodie, one of those types," said Anthrax.

"Is there something wrong with that?" said Sahara.

"No," said Kita. "If his goals align with ours we won't have a problem."

"What be our goals?" said Raptor.

"Immediately? Getting back Jess, Casey, and Crypt, then we get Enterprise and find Amanda, Hali, and Sheppard—"

"Sheppard!" several of the Angels yelled together.

"Yes, she's here," said Kita calmly.

"Why isn't she six feet under?" demanded Anthrax. "Do you know what she's done? Did you forget who her lover is?"

Kita held up a hand. "I do know. I've talked to her about her part in it."

"She killed Nina and Tink!"

Kita frowned and shook her head. "She had nothing to do with that. Galina is solely responsible. Rene only killed Spike, Quill, Jen, Leo, and Frostbane. She has apologized profusely to me for what she's done but needs to apologize to all of you, especially to Raptor, Valentine, and those close to Leo. She received the worst possible punishment—I gave her back her wings."

"And what if she turns on us again?" demanded Anthrax.

"She won't," said Kita firmly, her anger rising from the defiance and disrespect shown by the other fallen angel.

"You can't stop me from killing her."

"Can and will," said Kita stepping up to Anthrax. "You want to go now? I will put you in the ward for weeks."

"Sheppard is more important than me?" Anthrax yelled.

"I'm saying she's as important and deserves a chance to make up for her mistakes. She's proven it to me and will to you. I don't care if any of you like her, but she gets the same chance as I would give any of you."

"You're choosing that bitch over your own granddaughter?"

Kita smacked Anthrax to the floor. "Don't you dare use Tink against me. For years, I didn't even know who the twins were and couldn't mourn them, because of what Sheppard was a part of. But I forgave her. I don't expect you to. I don't even care if you listen to her apology, but you will respect my decision. It's my choice, and if you attack her, you'll deal with me."

"I think your brain is still missing," hissed Anthrax. Aspen and Tenshi helped her up.

"If you don't like it," Kita pointed to the door. "We'll drop you and anyone else off at the next stop, and you can make your own revenge."

The white flames burning in Anthrax's eyes roared like jets, steam puffed from the corners of her eyes. She sank to the floor and buried her head on her knees, crying loudly.

Snowy looked at Kita and frowned. *"Are you just going to stand there?"* Snowy said over the Angel's internal communications called the comm.

"What am I going to do?" said Kita.

"She's one of your oldest friends. Don't leave her like this. She misses Nina and Tink, and wants to know you care. Come on, you haven't been alone that long."

Kita sighed. She pushed several of the other Angels out of the way and sat down beside Anthrax putting her arm around her. Snowy sat down on the other side.

"Nell, I'm sorry," said Kita. "I wish I could have done more to save them."

Anthrax looked up slightly. "I just miss them so much. I know it's been years, but it feels like I just left them. I expect Nina to walk through the door at any moment, especially when you're around. I know it's not your fault," she said around sobs.

"It *is* my fault," said Kita. "I couldn't save everybody, and I'm sorry."

Raptor knelt down next to Kita and put her hand on Kita's shoulder. "Suga, ya did what ya could. Ya got a lot of us out, and that be something. We be the survivors, and it be up to us to get revenge on Galina. She be the real skunk. Sheppard was just a nitwit fool. With our help, you be the one to get us to her."

"I just wish it didn't have to cost so many lives," whispered Kita.

Babydoll knelt in front of Kita. "We did all we could. Even you couldn't see what depths Galina would sink to. We never thought she would kill so many. She struck us when you were at your weakest, and their sacrifice meant the entire equation was saved."

I'll never be that weak again... Kita hugged Anthrax tight. *Never again will we have to weep for our dead. I promise, no matter what I have to do.*

"I'm sorry," said Anthrax.

"Nothing to be sorry for," said Kita.

"No, you have your own family to mourn, including Nina."

"That doesn't mean I can't be here for you. Maybe when we get some downtime, we can mourn together."

"Yeah. I miss them so much."

With Snowy and Kita's help, Anthrax stood up.

"Ok," said Anthrax, "let's see what this big kitty wants."

Kita looked at Sahara. "Go ahead and call him."

"I've, ah, had him on hold," said Sahara.

Kita shrugged. She was used to having important people waiting for her. She was the center of the universe after all.

The holographic projector flashed and the image of a well-dressed Djinn sitting in a chair puffing on a pipe connected to something off screen materialized.

"Kita…and friends," said Collector in an even tone.

"Collector…" Kita purred. "Yes, on my way out of the prison I thought I'd pick up a few friends who could help."

"I was misinformed on how many Angels were imprisoned there."

Collector's gaze shifted from Kita to Snowy and Sahara. The two females seemed to shrink. Kita smiled to herself watching Snowy twist.

"It's not their fault," said Kita. "Neither of them knew about these Angels."

"I know they weren't in the prison," said Collector.

"True. They were doing a task for me."

"Which was?"

"None of your concern. They completed it, and we're stronger because of it."

"I want a dossier on each Angel and her capabilities."

Kita pursed her lips. "I'll allow your people to observe and report. Just know no Angel is weak and we're all built to thrive. Snowy mentioned you had something that might pique our interest."

"I might have something that could be mutually beneficial."

Kita crossed her arms. "That's vague. Why don't you tell us and stop wasting everyone's time."

Collector tapped his pipe against the armrest and took a puff. "The Djinn are the top predator in the galaxy." Around Kita, she saw smiles and heard a few giggles. "But ever since we entered the Tetrahedron Consortium our prowess has diminished. We've lost our prey, and instead, we've joined with them. We need combat to sharpen our claws and bring honor to us. We need a new prey, and I believe the humans will provide us with what we need."

"Is he serious?" said Babydoll. "*He must not know anything about human history.*"

"Now, now," said Kita. "*If this kitty cat wants to sharpen his claws in the viper's nest we won't stop him. In fact, we'll show him exactly what to do.*"

"*What are you planning?*" hissed Snowy.

"*Nothing. If he wants to go a few rounds with the Shadow Fleet, I'll happily oblige. Anything to weaken Galina.*" Kita smiled at Collector. "And what do you want us for?"

"You are a true warrior. I have a fleet standing by. Once they engage and show Djinn what it means to fight, the rest of the Djinn fleet will join us. We will conquer new territory and take plenty of new slaves. You will lead us, and you can take your revenge on Galina."

"*Does he understand what he wants?*" said Babydoll. "*He wants us to show his kitty cats how to fight. Doesn't that mean we're the greatest warriors in the galaxy?"*

The other Angels chuckled.

"I bet he thinks there aren't enough of us to be a threat," said Panther.

"Let's be holden' that card until we be needen' it," said Raptor.

Kita clicked a nail against her teeth. "There are a few things I'm going to need," said Kita to Collector.

"What do you require?"

"Snowy said you knew where two of my Angels and my sword Crypt were."

Collector took a puff of his pipe. "There is an auction to be held on Petal Ten of the Tet. Your friends, Jessica Rabbit and Casey Bush, are to be the main attraction. Snowy identified your sword among the other artifacts—"

"Poor bastard probably doesn't know what that sword is capable of or he wouldn't be giving it back to Kita," said Anthrax.

"—I offer whatever support in retrieving them."

"My guess is, you have enough money to buy them," Kita said raising an eyebrow.

"I could, but consider this your trial run. The person holding the event is a dear friend of mine. I don't wish him or any of his guests to come to harm."

"That takes all the fun out of it," Phoenix said with a sigh.

"Fair enough," said Kita. "I also am missing three other Angels: Rene Sheppard, Amanda Gering, and Hali C'Zar Ah'tem. I want them back along with the ship Enterprise."

Collector looked at his pipe. "That will take time. Enterprise is out with the Diamock fleet. Our reports say the Angels Sheppard and Stormy are with the ship. Hali C'zar Ah'tem is on the Tet handling your legal defense."

"Then she should be free." Kita chuckled. "Pick her up. Have your people tell her, the Grandmaster requires her presence. She'll come without question."

"Orders are being dispatched now."

"Then you have a deal," said Kita. "We'll lead your attack on the humans. You'll get your fight, and we get Galina. The how and when are up to us."

"I expect the fleet to leave as soon as you are ready."

Kita smiled. "Don't worry. We're as anxious to get started as you are."

CHAPTER IV

"*This could be a tough nut to crack,*" said Aspen as she studied the hologram of the mansion belonging to Takkat FretChat, the host of the auction. "*Few shadows, a layered security system, roving guards, a vault, and we need keys to unlock the stasis field.*"

"Are you telling me it can't be done?" said Kita raising an eyebrow. Defeatism wasn't something she expected out of her former students.

"*No, but it's going to take some ingenuity.*"

Kita nodded. She trusted Aspen's assessment. Aspen was one of the best assassins she'd ever trained. "Let's concentrate on just being able to move around the house."

"*We could hack the security system, but we have to get to it, and it's located in the basement.*" Aspen touched a spot on the hologram expanding the room. She tapped on the security server. "*It's on an isolated network. The only way to access it would be directly.*"

Kita looked around the room at the other Angels wondering how she was going to get a pair of them to pass as party guests. All the Angels in Tet space were known, and humans were still considered the enemy. Neither race would have that kind of money nor the status required to attend this type of party. She looked at Snowy and Sahara. *Would two Djinn females unescorted raise much suspicion? Maybe I can borrow a male from Collector.* That idea left a bad taste in her mouth. She didn't like the idea of not being able to carry out a mission with the resources at her disposal, especially when she had a dozen Angels.

The door opened. Kita let out a squeal. She charged, ignoring Starlight's bow to her, and hugged the other Angel. Kita kissed Starlight on the cheek. "Oh, I missed you, and you've come at the perfect moment. I have a mission you'll love."

Starlight looked relieved. "I thought you'd be upset that your legal defense couldn't get you free."

"Don't be worryen' yourself about that," said Raptor. "Kita be used to sitten' in prison."

Kita laughed along with the other Angels. "Snowy was able to spring me with help from Collector."

Starlight's eyes went wide with shock. "Collector! But—"

"Don't worry. We've worked out an arrangement. The first task is to get Casey and Jess free."

"Actually your first task is to introduce us to this beautiful creature," said Panther. "I love the dress."

"This?" said Starlight. "Oh, this is nothing, just standard wear for work." The dress had a golden chain halter that held up a shimmering dress that clung to her curves and plunged to her lower back. It ended mid-thigh, and she wore a pair of high heel gladiator-type sandals.

"What do you do for work?" said Babydoll with a teasing smile.

"I head up the Angel's defense counsel. I thought Jess and Casey were with you on Conto V."

"Never heard of it," said Kita. "I was kept in some deep space prison facility used to feed Djinn. Casey and Jess weren't there when I was rescued. Collector says they're to be auctioned. That's what we're planning now. I was hoping you'd heard of this auction."

"Those liars," snarled Starlight. "That's why they refused to let me speak to any of you or see Jess."

"Does that mean she's taken?" said Toxic, the green light from under her hood dimming.

Kita frowned. "Sorry, Kara. Hali, let me introduce you to everyone. These Angels have been out looking for me since Galina took me. These two," she pointed to Kamikaze and Phoenix, "are my daughters."

"Nice to meet you all, I'm Hali C'Zar Ah'tem, former Grand Ambassador for the Aurori."

"She's also a trained assassin," Kita said with a smile.

"Yes, I have my swords in my bag."

"Yeah, that dress doesn't hide much," said Babydoll.

"I'm willing to do whatever is necessary to get Jess and Casey back. I received an invite to this auction. I hadn't paid much attention to a lowly artifact sale, but it has my full attention now." Starlight frowned, and her eyes narrowed.

"Come," said Kita, "and help us take the first steps to get back what is ours."

～

STARLIGHT STEPPED OUT OF THE AIRCAR AND HELPED PANTHER AND RAPTOR out, taking each by the hand graciously. She offered her arms to the other Angels, and they accepted with dazzling smiles. The trio followed the glittering footpath from the drop-off zone to the entrance of the mansion.

"Have you been here before?" said Panther to Starlight.

"Yes. It belongs to Tukkut FretChat, a wealthy Zentonian entrepreneur. He's also rumored to sell drugs and arms. For a squirrel, it's not a bad mansion, but it's nothing compared to what the Verisom princesses or Djinn business class have. You'll get a chance to meet him. We need a voice imprint to get into the vault."

"Do they have squirrels here?"

"It's a term I picked up from Jess. I've seen pictures of Earth squirrels. It's very fitting. She has nicknames for all the races."

"Are ya sure ya not be needen' our help?" said Raptor.

"You're my cover. I can take down the camera system and the vault's shield barrier easy enough, but I would look foolish wandering around by myself."

"Kita be senden' ya with her two best party animals," Raptor said with a chuckle.

"She said you both had lots of experience."

"Kita just be lookeen' for a way to get herself out of goen'."

The Angels stopped at the base of the stairs, and a member of the house staff came forward to greet them. The Zentonian wore a brown and green formal servant wear.

"Grand Ambassador Ah'tem, my master, welcomes you and your guests to tonight's festivities," said the servant.

"It's my pleasure. I wouldn't miss the artifacts your master has up for auction." Starlight took a step forward.

The servant held up a hand. "Grand Ambassador, I will need your invitation."

Raptor opened her purse and pulled out the formal handwritten invitation. "Here be the invitation," said Raptor as she gave it to Starlight while giving her a kiss on the cheek.

Starlight handed the invitation over.

The servant opened the envelope and read the invitation. "This says 'and guest.'"

Starlight smiled a well-practiced smile she used when she wanted to get her way. "Oh, I know, but I couldn't decide between them. They're both delectable." She hugged the other Angels tight and gave each a kiss on the cheek at the same time giving the servant an inviting look with her eyes. "I'm sure your master won't mind. They are Angels after all. Panther and Raptor are both new to the Tet. This is their first social affair. I can't think of a better place for them to be introduced."

"My, you don't mind being forward," giggled Panther to Starlight.

"Aurorians by nature are flirtatious and like physical contact. Kita said you wouldn't mind."

"I'm not complaining. It's the first time I've ever been kissed by someone of a different species."

"Later I can do it properly."

Panther and Raptor gave the servant flirty and teasing smiles. The servant stepped away and pulled a communicator from his pocket.

"Security. Senior Butler AchCh. Grand Ambassador Ah'tem is here with an uninvited guest...She arrived with two guests, both Angels...She says they are new to the Tet and this is their first social event...Yes, I will inform her."

Starlight's smile widened as a way of telling the servant the Angels hadn't been eavesdropping on him when he returned.

"Your friend may enter," said the servant. He handed Starlight a brochure showing the items up for bid.

"Thank you," said Starlight. The servant stepped aside and let them pass. The Angels climbed the steps to the mansion's open front doors. Inside was an open courtyard that formed a cross shape five stories tall full of trees, planters, fountains, and open pavilions. In the pavilions were rows of ornate pillars. The walls were white and decorated with gold.

Staircases made of rods with carved ends led to beautiful accented circular doors.

"Damn. If this place is ok, I'd love to see what is great," said Panther.

"Extravagant be too simple a word," agreed Raptor.

"You've never seen anything like this?" said Starlight.

"The closest would be Hades, where Kita ruled as Mistress," said Panther. "They had statues and busts of her and some of the Angels, but it was still simple and plain compared to the decadence of this place."

"It be reminden' me a bit o' KitaCorp zone on Base Station, but not be as refined," said Raptor. "Gaudy, I be thinken' is the term for this place."

"I thought Kita was the Vicereine of an entire planet," said Starlight.

"She was. What this guy has would be nothing to what Kita had," said Panther.

"Kita not be caren' for material wealth, she be wanten' power," said Raptor dropping her smile.

"She also wants love," said Panther countering Raptor's harshness. "She wants our friendship, or none of us would be Angels."

"She do be wanten' that. She be a good friend."

"I have nothing bad to say about her," said Starlight. "She's a strict teacher. She was a little stand-offish at first, but I got her to like me."

"That be rare," replied Raptor. "Normally if Kita don't like ya from the beginnen, that be it. Ya must have impressed her."

Starlight stopped near the center of the courtyard. "There's Takkat. Let's see if we can get something we can use to open the vault."

"I'm sure we can keep him talking for a while," said Panther.

The Angels changed directions and joined the group around Takkat. The trio was noticed by the Zentonian, and he made his way to them.

"Grand Ambassador Ah'tem, how good it is to see you again. I'm so pleased you could join us and bring these wonderful Angels with you." He offered his hand, exposing a tiny screen on a wristband.

Starlight took his hand and smiled. "The pleasure is mine, honorable FretChat."

"Please, please, we're among friends. Call me Takkat."

Starlight bowed her head. "Then please, call me Starlight. My friends are Raptor and Panther. They just arrived on the Tet and are excited to see it."

"Let me be the first to welcome you to the Tet," said Takkat as he opened his arms wide. "Angels are so rare. I feel privileged to have three of you in my home. Tell me, Starlight, this is a new name for you."

"It's my Angelic name, given to me when I earned my wings."

"So are you no longer Aurorian?" said Takkat curiously.

"When the Angel's embassy opens I will be applying for dual citizenship."

"I must ask…Are they real?"

The three Angels shared a look.

"What ya be meanen'?" said Raptor.

"Are they augmentations, prosthetics...or?"

"Can I ask him if his tail is real?" said Panther with disgust. She kept the same dazzling smile on her face and batted her lashes at Takkat.

"They are very real," said Starlight as she stretched her wings straight up and flapped them slightly.

"I've seen the videos," said Takkat, "they are amazing. And you can fly?" Starlight lifted a few feet off the ground. "Truly remarkable. And to become an Angel what is the cost?"

"Your soul," said Panther seriously.

"It's not like buying a coat," said Starlight. "It's a life-changing moment, you sacrifice everything, and you give yourself over to the group."

"Ya must be female, too," said Raptor.

"Aurorians only have one sex," said Starlight.

"Ya be looken' female. That be good enough for Kita. Maybe why she didn't warm up to ya right away."

"I see," said Takkat. "That's too bad. I would love to have a pair. I can offer a fair price."

"Over Kita's dead body," hissed Panther.

"You know me so well, Vee. I have enough to fake an audio recording," said Kita to the others.

"I better. Love you."

"I love and have missed you."

"I'm sorry, Takkat, wings are not for sale at any price. I'm afraid Kita, the leader of the Angels, is quite strict on who gets them."

Takkat gave the Zentonian version of a shrug. "Her loss. She could make a fortune. Have you seen tonight's auction list? There are some fabulous pieces from my private collection up for sale as well as two mystery pieces. I think you will find most interesting."

"We haven't had time to go through the brochure yet, but the interactive paper was a splendid touch," said Starlight.

"I hope you get a chance to see them before they're gone. There are some avid collectors here tonight, and they've brought their credit chits."

"How rude. That was a not so polite way of saying we can't afford anything tonight," grumbled Starlight.

"Guess we be haven' to help ourselves the old fashioned way," said Raptor.

"Well, Angels, if you'll excuse me I have other guests I need to attend to," said Takkat with a dismissive wave of his hand.

"Time to go," said Starlight. "Thank you for inviting us, Takkat. We look forward to tonight's auction."

"It will be splendid and having your friends here will make it even more special."

"Sick bastard selling us as slaves," snarled Panther. *"Let's rub it in his nose."* She lifted into the air above the crowd.

The other Angels joined her. Together they glided above the crowd and landed a fair distance away from Takkat.

"Ugh, I feel slimy," Panther said with a groan.

"He be an uncouth one," agreed Raptor.

"I'm used to them," said Starlight. "They try and keep Aurorians all the time. We're like trophies to them."

"I'm used to being hit up by slimeballs all the time for my body and sex. This is the first time for my wings. I feel violated," Panther hugged herself tightly.

"It be alright," said Raptor giving her a hug.

"I earned my feathers," whispered Panther.

Starlight joined the hug. "And no one can take them away from you. Takkat's just a pig who thinks because he has money he can buy whatever he wants. Let him learn some things money can't buy."

"I wish Kita was here to punch him in the mouth."

"On the way out I will," said Starlight. "I owe Takkat for much more than just tonight."

Ignoring those around them, the Angels split and followed Starlight through the indoor garden to a large fountain that flowed backward. Beside it was a display table with pictures showing five of the seven items up for auction.

"This be Dead and Buried. They form Crypt," said Raptor. "Kita goen' to be unstoppable when she gets these."

Starlight opened the brochure. "According to this, Takkat is selling each blade separately."

"The fool not know what he got. These swords be powerful."

"All the better they don't know. I'd hate to see what an idiot like Takkat would do if he knew."

"Hopefully slice is hand off," growled Panther.

A Djinn accompanied by his five wives, covered head to toe, approached to look at the table. He and Starlight exchanged nods. She guided the other Angels away, down the path to a circular staircase.

"Those aren't going to be fun in heels," said Panther after looking at the cylindrical steps sticking from the wall that were no more than a hand's width in diameter.

"The server room is on the bottom floor," said Starlight as she looked over the rail.

"I be sayen' we take da easy way," said Raptor. She vaulted the rail and floated down three stories to the bottom.

Starlight and Panther shrugged and followed. Starlight stuck her head around a corner. "It's clear." She led the Angels through a twisting layout to a sliding glass door.

"Ya be sure this a security room?" said Raptor.

"It's not a security room, but a server room. It's where the computers are."

"Ya be thinken' it'd be better protected than this."

"Besides the security server, this room contains servers for all the communications, house systems, and entertainment equipment. I think the idea is to hide it in plain sight," said Starlight as she entered the room and went to the security server machine. She pulled out the keyboard and set it to the right configuration for her fingers. From between her breasts, she pulled out a small data cube. She inserted it into the slot and typed out a series of commands. The screen lit, and a bar showed the progress of the software download.

After the software finished installing, Starlight retrieved the data cube and tucked it away. She turned and exclaimed, "Void!" when a foot appeared through the door. She grabbed Raptor and kissed her while pulling Panther to her. *"We've got trouble,"* she explained to the others. Raptor continued to kiss Starlight while Panther nibbled on her neck.

"Excuse me, Grand Ambassador..." said a polite, but firm voice.

Starlight broke from Raptor and kissed Panther on the forehead. "Yes?" she said formally acting as if nothing had happened.

"This section of the house is off-limits," said the Zentonian servant.

"My apologies. We were looking for the powder room."

"I can escort you there."

Starlight smiled. "Please, lead on." She put her arms around the other Angels and followed the servant back toward the staircase. *"Kita, the cameras are down. We're moving to take down the vault's electrical barrier."*

CHAPTER V

" $\mathcal{F}$ inally. I'm tired of being in this box. Ready, Leaf?" said Kita as she lifted her black mask into place.

"*Bark, yeah! This is the kind of mission I live for,*" said the tiny Angel as she pulled her white mask over her mouth and nose.

They turned invisible, and Kita opened the air car's trunk compartment. Stepping out, they fluffed their feathers to get them flight ready. Kita's black feathers were in stark contrast to Aspen's white feathers with golden tips. Together, they spread their wings and flew from the parking structure toward the mansion.

They landed in the drop off zone and fell in behind a couple ascending the stairs. Slipping behind the couple as they passed through the doors, the Angels took flight and circled in the center courtyard of the house.

"*There is the door to the study and master bedroom,*" said Aspen as she pointed toward an ornate circular door with a landing. "*How do they get up here?*"

"*They climb. Special lifts are used for visitors.*"

"*Bet they weren't counting on guests that could fly.*"

"*The Verisom have an awesome vertical jump. Not sure if they could reach the top floor here though.*"

"*So what was it like to be a fiancée to one of them?*" said Aspen as she pulled the door open a crack for them to slip inside.

"*Ah…fuzzy?*"

"*If you wanted that you would have stayed with Snowy.*"

"*She was nice, assertive, big beautiful red eyes…come on, you're going to make me cry.*"

Aspen laughed. "*Not you, you're made of stone.*"

"*You know that's not true.*"

"*I know, but it's still fun to tease you.*"

The hallway was cylindrical with three doors, one on either side and one at the end. Kita could feel the textured surface under her feet.

"*What is this?*" said Aspen. "*What's wrong with a square hallway?*"

"*Every race builds to what they like. Try visiting a Verisom residence. They love mazes and can't build in a straight line for the Crushing Depths. I'll take the study. You search the bedroom for a DNA sample.*"

Kita entered the study. It was a spherical room. Artifacts lined the walls. A round Zentonian-style desk was on the far side with a beanbag chair. She followed the room around, stopping to look at an interesting artifact labeled BIRTHING MASK. Kita wasn't aware of any races that used birthing masks currently, but she didn't know the history of most of them. She knew a bit about Verisom and Diamock, and none mentioned a birthing mask.

On the desk were a computer and a reader. Kita smiled over the civilian tech, cracking it would be that much easier. From her belt, she took two Wireless Universal Serial Adaptors. An invention of Snowy's, it was modeled after Kita's finger. The WUSA could configure to any port and let her gain access via wireless connection to the computer in her head. When she was finished, she could send a signal and the WUSA would self-destruct leaving no trace.

Kita attached the WUSAs to the computer and reader and attacked both with her hacking suite. Takkat wasn't a fool, he used the best commercial grade security software, but it wasn't a match for her tools, some of which had been custom designed by Raph.

She let out a sigh, thinking about the teenager. It was a shame he died so young. He was a true innocent, and she missed the boy's charm and lightheartedness. *Here's to you Raph, my hero.*

"Kita, we have a problem," said Aspen.

"What kind of problem?"

"I've got two Aurorians chained up in this guy's…nest."

"Ignore them and find the sample."

"I'm not going to leave them here like this."

"We can't carry them out of here."

"We've got to do something," Aspen said forcefully.

Kita huffed. *Damn high angels, I swear.* "Ok, let me see if Hali knows anything. Hali?"

"Yes?"

"Why would a Zentonian have two Aurorians chained up in his bedroom?"

"Ah…You want the short or the long version?"

Kita gulped. "What's the short version?"

"Sex slave."

"What?"

"So the longer version is: Zentonians like to procreate."

"Yeah…"

"And in the past, their population would explode putting a strain on resources. The government has put a limit on how many children a female can have. But, they've never evolved away the need-to-breed instinct and have no contraceptive except complete organ removal. During breeding season they get the urge multiple times a day."

Kita groaned. *I'm glad I didn't fall in love with one of them.* "So why don't they develop toys or something?"

"Oh, they do, but wealthy Zentonians prefer biological gratification to mechanical."

"So they enslave Aurorians to do it for them? Isn't that illegal?"

"On the Tet, yes slavery is illegal, but not on Zento. There it is only illegal to enslave another Zentonian. Their law says nothing about other races. What happens is, they hire some poor young Aurorian as a servant, which is legal, but then they take them to Zento and enslave them. Takket must have snuck these two back here."

Kita rolled her eyes. *"This is all we need. We can't just call Tec-Sec when we're finished?"*

"I'm sure Takkat has people in Tec-Sec," said Starlight. *"He'd know they're coming and move the girls. This is a hard crime to catch and even harder to prosecute because the Zentonians make the Aurorians sign contracts."*

"And this just became my problem," Kita growled. *"What are we going to do with them? We can't bring them back to the ship or drop them off at the nearest Tet-Sec precinct."*

"You can't, but the rest of us can. If I bring them in it shouldn't be a problem."

"Goodie, more time for me in the trunk."

Starlight chuckled. *"The downside to being a wanted criminal. How goes the search?"*

"Just about hacked his computers," said Kita.

"I can't search the room until I know what to do with these two," said Aspen.

"Just knock them out."

"Using what?"

"Here," Kita sent Aspen the drug compound for putting Aurorians under.

"Sorry girls," said Aspen.

"I'm into the computers. I'm coming to help, Leaf," said Kita. *"Thanks, Hali."*

"I'm curious to see how we get them out."

"Me, too," said Kita as she entered the bedroom. The bedroom was spherical and lined with pillows. The walls and ceilings looked like branches decorated with gold. The two Aurorians were lying on pillows, asleep.

"Find anything?" Kita asked Aspen.

"So far it's clean."

"There must be something in here." Kita dug through the pillows all the way to the floor. *"What kind of housekeeping does he have? Not even a hair."*

"What about the other room?" said Aspen.

"It was marked utility."

"There's no bathroom in here. There must be something close."

Kita nodded, and the two assassins went back into the hallway and opened the third door. Inside was a counter with sinks surrounded by brushes and vials. To the right was an ornate looking hole.

"There has to be something in here," said Kita.

Aspen picked up a brush and examined it. *"Nothing."*

As Kita searched the bathroom, she searched the computers for files containing the keys for the stasis fields. So far, she had found weapon invoices, evidence of stock manipulation, and pornography, but no keys. *"This place is spotless,"* Kita grumped.

"Wait! I've gotten an idea," said Aspen. She opened the cabinet under the right sink and crawled inside. *"Bark, yeah! I think I have something. Let me have one of those cotton swabs."*

Kita opened a pouch on her belt and pulled one out. She unclipped the protective cover and handed it to Aspen. *"Where are you looking?"* said Kita.

"The P-trap collects all sorts of stuff. It's got to have some of his DNA in it, but we should swab both sinks since we don't know which one he uses."

Kita opened the other cabinet and looked inside. Plumbing wasn't her thing, and she wasn't sure what to do or what she was looking at. *"What do I do?"*

"Bark! Did we finally find something you don't know?"

"Plumbing isn't something I keep on file."

Aspen chuckled. *"See the part that drops down? It has two connectors you need to unscrew. Just be careful, you don't want to spill the water."*

Kita found the connectors and unscrewed them. *Why doesn't this place use a vacuum system like a ship?* She took off the trap and wrinkled her nose. It was obvious no one had cleaned down here since the plumbing was installed. She took a swab from her belt and ran it along the inside of the trap. Kita bent back inside to reattach the piece.

"Did you get a sample?" said Aspen as she stuck her head in the cabinet causing Kita to bobble the piece and dump water on her face. Aspen giggled.

"Aw, yuck. It's in my mask and in my mouth. Bleck!" Kita snarled. She couldn't even stick her tongue out in disgust. With a flash of flame, Kita dried herself. *Still doesn't get rid of the smell.*

"Here!" Kita thrust the sample at Aspen.

She took it—her dark eyes alight with amusement.

Kita crawled out from the cabinet.

"Any luck finding the stasis keys?" said Aspen.

Kita sighed. *"No. The machines are clean. We need to think of some other place to look."*

"Who else would have them?"

"An assistant, maybe. Hali do you have any ideas?"

"Hmmm…Takkat was wearing an interesting wristband. It had a tiny screen."

"How's it going with you?" said Kita.

"I'm following the power conduit to the junction box. I hope to get access to the conduit so I can short the circuit. So far, we've been on an interesting tour of the gardens."

"So much for this being easy."

"At least you're not getting assaulted every five seconds for pictures. And they keep thinking Vee is you."

"They'll just have to be disappointed. Tell them I don't do pictures anyway."

Kita and Aspen went back to the landing. They took off, flying among the trees looking for Takkat.

"There he is, by the gravity fountain," said Aspen as she pointed to Takkat holding court with a group of admirers. She and Kita glided above him.

"This is going to be tricky," said Kita.

"You big girls think it's all cool to be tall until you have to squeeze in somewhere," Aspen chided. She held out her hand.

"Are you sure?" said Kita.

"Let this little girl show you how it's done," said Aspen with a wink.

Kita handed a WUSA to Aspen. If anyone could weasel her way in, it would be Aspen. She was only four foot eight and weighed eighty pounds soaking wet.

Aspen landed and made her way through the group of party guests without raising any suspicion. She crouched in front of Takkat. He liked to talk with his hands, and after a wild gesture, the screen on his wrist appeared.

"I saw it," said Kita. *"It's on his left arm."*

"Got it," said Aspen. She tracked Takkat's movements, her hand waiting. Takkat held out his hands to show how huge one of his luxury spacecraft was. Aspen's hand darted up his sleeve and attached the WUSA.

"Is it working?" said Aspen.

"Yeah."

Takkat lowered his arms and Aspen jumped straight up to be next to Kita. She hacked the device using the passwords she'd recovered from Takkat's other machines. The second password opened the device. There wasn't much—a calendar, directory, a link to his personal banking account, and a program called SUnK. Curious, Kita ran SUnK.

"Got it!" said Kita to Aspen. *"Let me clone the device, and we can get out of here."* Kita copied the entire device's contents to the computer in her head. *"Ok, we're good. Hali, how are you doing?"*

"We found the junction box, but there's a servant in the way. We're going to see if we can persuade him to move. Go to the vault and—"

A gong sounded.

"—Damn, that's the signal for people to take their seats. We'll have to act fast if we're going to get things out of the vault."

"Ok, we're going there now."

Kita led Aspen to the back of the mansion where a path led to a stand of trees. Kita landed and followed the path down to a heavily secured door.

"Is the electrical barrier off?" said Kita. She wasn't in the mood to receive a heavy electrical shock and set off the alarms.

"Ah…Just a sec…" Starlight giggled playfully. *"I'll be right back…don't go anywhere…"*

"Was that to me?" said Kita.

"Sorry," said Starlight. *"I had to give Judge Amarax the slip. Ugh. He looks to have his hopes up. Vee's keeping him busy. I think the other races are getting the idea that Angels are promiscuous."*

"Not really…at least, not outside the group."

"I wasn't sure if it was just you or…"

"I'm not promiscuous," Kita huffed.

"You've tried to sleep with or have slept with every female in the group."

"That does not mean I'm promiscuous. I didn't try and sleep with you."

"You would have if it hadn't been for Cotton."

Kita rolled her eyes. "I didn't try and sleep with Onyx or Zen."

"Kita does have a lot of long-term partners, but I wouldn't call her promiscuous," said Panther. "Though, she has had sex with both Raptor and me."

"Not helping," growled Kita.

"It was one of her rare promiscuous nights when she was upset with three people."

"Hey, don't bring me into this," said Aspen. "I had no idea what was going on. I was just there."

"With a big, silly grin on your face," said Panther. "I owe you a thank you. If it hadn't been for you, I would never have had my chance with Kita."

"This is a story I have to hear," Starlight said with a giggle.

Kita groaned.

"Ok, I'm at the junction box. I'll have it down in a second," said Starlight. "There you go. I sent a power surge through it that will trip the breaker."

Kita grit her teeth as she touched the vault door. When nothing happened, she let out a sigh of relief. She activated the door's security panel, and it cued her for a vocal input. Kita opened her mouth and let her vocal cords act as a speaker.

"My voice is my password. I am Takkat FretChat. I command you to open." *Talk about having control issues.*

A green light lit on the security panel. A biometric scanner opened.

"Which should I stick in?" said Aspen.

"Just stick them both in and smear them around. It should find what it's looking for." *I hope.*

Aspen did as instructed, sticking the swabs into the hole and smearing the samples on the sensor lens. The biometric scanner closed and both Angels waited holding their breath.

Kita clenched her teeth. She tried to think of another way to get a DNA sample or find another way in. She could melt her way through if she had to, but that would take time. If only—a second light on the door's security panel turned green. Kita let out the breath she was holding. She pushed on the door, and it swung open.

Kita and Aspen walked down a narrow passage that exited into a large room. Rows of artifacts, each behind a stasis field, filled the space.

"Damn. This vault must be nearly as large as the footprint of the house," said Aspen.

Kita groaned to herself. It would take time to search for Crypt, Defiance, and Valor. "You start here. I'm going to go to the back and work my way forward."

Aspen didn't answer. She was already flying down the row. Kita glided over the artifacts to the back.

"Kita?" said Panther.

"Yeah?"

"We found our two missing Angels."

"Where are they?"

"There are behind two curtains on the stage," said Panther. "I've flipped through all my lenses, but I can't make anything out."

"It's the stasis field. Just keep an eye on them. We're searching for Crypt now," said Kita as she hurried down another row.

"Ok, we've had to take our seats. They're going to begin soon."

"Bloody moons. That means they'll be coming in here to get the items. Leaf!"

"Yeah?"

"We have to hurry."

"I'm flying over the rows as fast as I—Wait! I've got one of them," said Aspen.

"The other half isn't next to it?"

"Ah, doesn't look like it."

"Is there a number or marking?"

"Nope," said Aspen.

Kita opened the SUnK program and flipped through the list of keys. They had identifiers, but they didn't make any sense to her.

"Kita! The vault door just opened!" cried Aspen.

As Kita ran down the sixth row, she found the second part to Crypt— Dead. She searched the cabinet for an identification marking. *Screw it. They're going to know we're here soon enough.* Kita undid the entire list of stasis keys. The stasis fields dropped in a cascade.

"Grab Buried," Kita instructed Aspen.

Kita picked up Dead. The curved black blade with pieces of inlaid obsidian felt perfect in her hand. Etched into the blade in blood red was its name. The worn lava rock handle was worn smooth. She sheathed it on her back and ran to the end of the row.

Five servants and Takkat entered the room.

"Did you get Buried?" said Kita.

"Got it. How do you want to do this? They're going to notice the stasis fields are down and the swords are missing."

"The servants are following Takkat to the right. If we go left, we can make it to the door and shut it. I can weld it shut."

"Ok. I'm moving to the left."

Kita reached the end of the row and turned toward the door. Aspen appeared ahead of her. Across the room, Takkat and his servants turned down the row toward Buried's cabinet.

Kita's vision tinted red and the world slowed down as she entered her berserking state. She sidestepped Aspen, grabbing the Angel at the same time. Kita charged down the same row as Takkat and his servants. She punched Takkat in the mouth, breaking his large incisors, sending the pieces flying. Slamming into Takkat with her shoulder, Kita drove him into his servants, knocking them down. She jumped over the downed servants and ran to the end of the row. Turning the corner, she sprinted to the passageway, ran out the vault door, turned, and kicked it shut. Kita dropped Aspen, heated her hands, and ran them along the edge of the vault door, welding it shut. Tears formed in the corner of her eyes as a wall of emotions crashed down on her.

"Wow!" said Aspen. *"I never thought I'd get to ride that train. Bark, that was fast. You ok?"*

Kita nodded as she wiped her eyes. *"I'll be fine, just a little shaken."*

"Here, this belongs to you." Aspen took Buried from her back and gave it to Kita.

"Thanks. Now I need to find a home for Dusk and Dawn. Think you can manage?"

"ME?" exclaimed Aspen.

"Why not?"

"What about Kara or Hali or...or..."

"Leaf, you've earned it. You're an excellent assassin."

"I promise I'll be worthy," said Aspen as she bowed to Kita.

Kita handed Dusk and Dawn to Aspen bowing over each sword as she did.

Aspen flourished them in rapid succession. *"Can I turn them white?"*

Kita chuckled. *"Your swords."*

"Thank you," said Aspen. *"I won't let you down."*

"I know you won't. Come on. Let's get to the stage."

Kita and Aspen flew out from under the stand of trees toward a small stage with two curtains on either side. Guests sat waiting for the auction to begin.

"Ok, ladies. We're coming in. Be ready for action," said Kita. *"Leaf, Vee, take the curtain to the left. Hali, A'ana, get the right. I'll keep the crowd busy."*

Starlight, Raptor, and Panther jumped from their seats and took flight surprising those around them. They flew to the curtains. Kita turned visible hovering above the stage. She drew Dead and Buried, and slammed the hilts together. Flourishing the double-bladed sword, Kita stopped it parallel to the ground. She pointed the curved ends toward the crowd and whispered the word carved into Crypt's handle. "Reap."

A blue cone of light emitted from Crypt. Bluish doppelganger ghosts appeared next to each guest. The ghosts lasted for a second then dissolved into the ether. The remaining bodies of the guests collapsed to the floor.

"Oh, how I've missed you," Kita grinned.

The other Angels removed the curtains revealing Valor and Defiance suspended from the ceiling by their wings. Both had a collar around their necks.

"They're wearing neural collars. Snap them off, and they should wake up." Hali flew up to Valor and snapped the collar off. Valor's eyes opened, and she vomited. Across the stage, Panther did the same thing for Defiance.

"Is that an effect of the collar?" said Panther.

"No," said Starlight. "They have stasis sickness. A'ana, can you cut her down?"

Raptor broke the harness keeping Valor airborne. Starlight caught Valor and lowered her to the ground.

Kita knelt over Defiance after the others laid her down.

"Casey, can you hear me?"

Defiance moaned. "By the emperor, what did these filthy aliens do to me?"

Kita chuckled. "I think she'll be fine." She stroked Defiance's face tenderly.

"Something I should know?" said Panther.

Kita's eyes went wide. "Ah…yeah…ah…Casey and I …we were…are…ah…"

"Damn, Kita, just spit it out," said Defiance. "I'm her girlfriend, Casey. I'd shake your hand, but I think if I move, I'll puke."

"Hi," said Panther. "I'm Vee. Kita's other girlfriend."

"No wonder she's nervous. We'll have to compare notes. Ugh, I think I'm going to pass out now. Whatever they did to me—"

"Casey?" Kita said alarmed. She could hear a heartbeat and Defiance was still breathing, but Kita couldn't help but be nervous.

"So…were you going to tell me about this?" said Panther to Kita.

Kita gulped. "Yes, ah, when the time was right."

"You're cute when you're flustered. You know I don't care, right? As long as I get you some of the time? I know when Jane gets back I won't see you for a year—"

"Who?"

"Is that who you don't remember or is that just the excuse you're going to tell her?"

Kita's shoulders slumped. "I know there is someone out there that I'm partnered to, I just don't remember."

Panther giggled. "Well, when we find her I want to be there. It'll be a storybook reunion."

"Freeze! Nobody move!" yelled a guard leading ten more.

"Oops, time to go," said Kita. "A'ana, Vee, Leaf, can you keep them busy?"

"Can we kill them?" said Panther.

"I don't see why not. I blew that parameter of our assignment. Collector will have to deal with it."

"Time to show these kitties a big cat." Panther morphed into a large black jaguar. She let out a deep rumbling roar and leaped from the stage at the guards.

Raptor jumped into the air and transformed into a t-rex. She smashed chairs and bodies under her feet, and then let out a ground-shaking roar. Charging the guards, she snapped up a Zentonian and ate him whole.

Aspen darted toward the guards. She didn't attack but flashed bright beams of light from her hands, blinding the guards causing them to stagger. Panther and Raptor pounced on the easy targets.

"Hali, grab Jess and let's get out of here," said Kita as she picked up Defiance. *"Kami, Kita. We're coming out hot."*

"Ok, Mom. We've been monitoring and will have you covered."

Kita and Starlight flew toward the front of the mansion guarded by the other Angels.

"Wait," said Aspen. *"We can't leave the two in the bedroom."*

"Vee, go with her," ordered Kita.

Panther turned back into an Angel and flew after Aspen. While she waited, Kita flung fireballs around the mansion. The pair returned, each carrying an Aurorian. Under Raptor's guard, the Angels flew across the mansion. When they reached the front door, the servants scattered.

Raptor smashed the doors with a swipe of her tail. Kita ducked through the wreckage just as a large shuttle landed in the drop-off area. The other Angels followed her down the steps. Guards from atop the mansion and patrolling the grounds opened fire on them. The side of the shuttle opened, and Tenshi, Babydoll, and Valentine exited with pistols and rifles drawn. The three Angels returned fire at the guards as Kita, and the others jumped aboard the shuttle.

"We're in, girls. Let's get out of here," ordered Kami from the pilot's seat.

The shuttle lifted off as Babydoll, Tenshi, and Valentine flew aboard.

"We're in. Go!" cried Babydoll.

Kamikaze boosted to maximum and the shuttle launched into the sky as Tec-Sec air cars arrived.

~

"DID YOU HAVE ANY PROBLEMS?" said KITA as STARLIGHT and ASPEN boarded the shuttle. She had Panther's arm around her and Defiance's head in her lap.

"No. I filled out the statement and told the officers where I found the girls. I originally got a Tec-Sec Zentonian sergeant, but the lieutenant was an Aurorian and was much more sympathetic. She didn't ask stupid questions and believed me when I told her where they came from. The incident at Takkat's mansion hadn't been reported yet."

"Good. So the girls will be taken care of?"

"Yeah. Not sure if anything will happen to Takkat over it, but I suppose losing his mansion will teach him."

"Don't forget he has no front teeth," said Aspen.

"I wish I could have seen that."

"Don't worry," said Kita. "I've got the replay."

CHAPTER VI

K ita's eyes fluttered open. She smiled when she remembered where she was, snuggled up against Panther in bed.

"Hey, sleepyhead," said Panther. "I must have worn you out."

"Hmmm, just warm and happy. Your skin is so soft."

Panther chuckled. "I haven't done anything to it besides take a quick shower before we started. I'm going to have to get used to being in my routine again. Things you don't have to worry about when you're a god."

Kita raised her head from Panther's chest and noticed the screen on the wall. "What are you watching? I didn't mean to leave you alone."

"It's no problem. I found a movie about forbidden love between a Zentonian—they're the squirrels, right?" Kita nodded. "And a Djinn. Not sure what to make of it, other than the Zentonian female breaks all the stupid social norms of the Djinn. I guess it's supposed to be empowering?"

Kita sighed and laid her head back down. "Yeah. I'm sure it was written by an Aurorian. They love that stuff."

"I was impressed by Hali. She knows what she's doing. Where did you find her?"

"She was a friend of Cotton's on the Grand Panel. She desperately wanted to join, and hated being a diplomat and loved being a soldier. I told her if she could get me a piece of King Lear's mane I'd teach her to be an assassin."

"I take it she got her piece?"

"She took a combat knife, marched into the meeting room, wrangled the cat, and cut off a piece of his mane. Lear was hopping mad. Snowy had to kill him."

Panther smirked. "Life with you is never dull."

Kita stuck her tongue out and licked Panther's nipple.

"Eep!" said Panther as she covered her breast. "I wasn't expecting that."

Kita snickered.

"Keep laughing, brat."

The screen on the wall flashed red.

"What's that mean?" said Panther.

"Incoming call," said Kita as she pulled a sheet over them. "Answer."

Anthrax's image appeared. She raised an eyebrow.

"Nell, what can I do for you?" said Kita pleasantly.

"Well, that didn't take long. Hi, Vee," Anthrax said with a big smile that displayed her shark's teeth. "I was calling to let you know—after fifteen minutes of trying to understand the messaging system—that Casey is awake. Jess is still under."

"Thanks, Nell. And, thanks for looking after them."

Anthrax smiled. "It's good to practice medicine again. Our host's equipment is interesting. I'll get it figured out quick enough. I'm glad I come with my own medical equipment suite."

"You're the best," said Kita. "Does this mean I can see Casey?"

"Give me an hour to run some tests. I want to make sure this stasis sickness hasn't done anything permanent."

"Ok. I'll be there."

"See you then." Anthrax's smile faded to a frown as she tried to disconnect.

"Like this, doctor." A fuzzy hand reached across the camera and screen went black.

Kita sighed. "Guess I should get cleaned up."

"In such a hurry to go from one girlfriend to the next?" said Panther with a teasing smile.

"Ah, no. I—"

Panther reached between Kita's legs. Kita gasped. "Good. You can spend a little more time with me."

A shiver went down Kita's spine. "By the Crushing Depths…" Kita whispered.

"That's what I like to hear," Panther purred.

～

KITA AND PANTHER ENTERED THE SHIP'S MEDICAL BAY. IT WAS EMPTY EXCEPT for a handful of staff.

Kita approached the on-call doctor. He wore a yellow jumpsuit with a red paw print on the breast, the Djinn symbol for aid.

"Excuse me, I'm looking for Doctor Anthrax," said Kita.

The Djinn looked up from the reader he was studying. "The Angel?"

"Yes."

"She's in suite three."

"Thank you." Kita took Panther's hand and led her to suite three. The door was open, so Kita went in.

"Hi, Nell," said Kita seeing the back of the Angel's black and white wings. She turned, revealing Defiance. "Casey!" Kita couldn't keep the excitement from her voice.

"Kita! About time you came and found me. I was getting worried. Hi, Vee." She winked at Kita. "I bet you were hoping I'd forgotten about that."

Kita's ears turned red causing all three other Angels to laugh.

"How are you feeling?" said Kita to Defiance.

"Much better. I don't feel like throwing up every ten seconds. Now, I'm hungry. Prison food sucks."

"At least you got some," said Kita. "They didn't feed me anything but watery soup."

"Yeah, what happened to you? They told us you'd been moved."

"I was moved to a deep space prison, locked in a bubble and slowly starved into submission."

"Poor baby," cooed Defiance. She took Kita's hand and kissed it. "It looks like you're doing better."

"Yeah. Snowy and Zen rescued me—"

"They're ok?" A loud gurgle came from Defiance's stomach. She blushed. "Sorry. I said I was hungry."

"We'll get you something to eat…If the doc says it's ok." Kita looked at Anthrax.

"She checks out fine. She's free to go. I think I'll go with you right after I check on Jess. I could use a snack." She turned and left the suite.

Defiance pulled the sheet off her then stopped. "I should have asked her where my clothes were."

"You didn't come with any," said Kita.

Defiance sighed. "Maybe I can borrow some of those twenty-fourth-century patches from Nell."

Kita chuckled at the reference to Anthrax's taste in vintage clothing styles. The Angel wore only seven circular patches that didn't hide anything.

"We can always tie the sheet into a toga," said Panther.

"By the emperor, I haven't been to a toga party in decades," said Defiance.

She got up, folded the sheet, and tied it around her.

"When we find Snowy we'll get you some real clothes," said Kita.

"I thought I'd be fighting her for a spot on your arm," Defiance said with a chuckle.

"She has a girlfriend now."

"Really?"

"She's found some Djinn female."

"Wow. Who would have guessed? What do Djinn females look like?"

"Like Snowy, but sand colored."

Kita offered her arm to Defiance.

"Really? You should be swinging from my arm."

Kita laughed. "How about I just hold your hands as I escort you to the galley?"

"Yeah, whose ship are we aboard anyway?" said Defiance.

"Collector's."

"Collector!"

"I'll explain everything," said Kita.

"You better. We better not be prisoners, or I'm going to slap you."

"I like her," said Panther.

Kita rolled her eyes. "We're not prisoners…but it's an uneasy arrangement at best. Collector wants us to lead his forces against the Shadow Fleet."

"And you agreed to that?" yelled Defiance.

"Yes, but I have a good reason."

"You'd better. That's my fleet."

"Ah, who are you again?" said Panther to Defiance. "Kita's the only one I've ever known with a fleet of anything."

"Casey Bush, Princess of the UEE."

Panther's eyebrows shot up. "Oh. No wonder she's been so nervous over you."

"What's that mean?" said Defiance.

Kita stopped, pulling the other two to a halt. "Before anyone gets the wrong idea, my nervousness had nothing to do with that," she said firmly. "I was worried about how the two of you would react to each other. I wasn't sure how you'd both handle it."

"I knew I wouldn't be the only one when I signed up," said Defiance. "I like that I get along with the other girl. I was afraid I would be at war with Cotton."

"I don't understand your concern," said Panther. "I was there when you had Snowy, Roo, and Jane. It didn't bother me then, and it doesn't bother me now. I agree with Casey, it's nice not to be at odds with the other girls. I was always fearful of Jane."

"I'm sorry. You shouldn't have to be in fear of anyone," said Kita.

"When you remember Jane, you'll understand my fear," said Panther.

"I wouldn't let anyone hurt you. No matter who she is. Casey is a princess, but that doesn't mean you're anything less. I love you all."

"Whoa, slow down," said Defiance. "I didn't know we were at the L-word."

Kita chuckled. "Ok, like you all for who you are."

"I did like that you rescued me. That's points in your favor." Defiance winked.

Kita kissed Defiance's fingers and then Panther's. "Vee helped."

"I think we'll get along just fine," said Panther.

Kita smiled as she guided them to the galley. It was a quarter full of off-duty Djinn getting something to eat. In the corner sat Phoenix, with her head in Valentine's lap, and Toxic. Kita's group approached the group of younger Angels.

"Hey," said Phoenix.

"Hi, sweet pea. How are you girls?"

"Eh, the food sucks and so does the entertainment...and you can only have sex for so long before that becomes boring."

Kita looked at Valentine. "Her words, not mine, but yeah."

"Kara?" said Kita to Toxic.

"At least they're having sex. I just get to sit around and stare at the wall."

"Sorry, girls," Kita said shrugging her shoulders. "I don't know how long we'll be aboard this ship. The next step is to get Enterprise back, and there's more to do aboard her."

"When's that?" said Phoenix.

"I'm not sure. I haven't gotten any information about the ship's whereabouts. Sheppard and Amanda should be with her."

"I would like to voice my disdain for allowing Sheppard back into the flock," said Valentine.

"I know. But she's repentant and is making amends."

"For whatever she's done to you, I am sorry," said Defiance. "Galina and Sheppard acted in my name, and therefore it's my responsibility. I promise you she understands the error in her judgment and it won't happen again."

"Yeah, but who are you?" said Phoenix.

"Casey Bush, Princess of the UEE."

"And you're dating my mom?"

"Yes."

"Galina's going to crap herself."

"Galina's days are numbered," said Defiance. "I understand many want a little piece of revenge."

"Some big pieces," said Anthrax coming up behind Kita and the others. "She killed my partner and my child."

"I'm sorry," said Defiance. "I promise you'll get your piece."

Anthrax bared her shark-like teeth. "I plan on ripping it out of her hide."

Kita led the others to the buffet line.

"Ah, meat, meat, or more meat," said Defiance.

"And it's all raw," said Panther as she grabbed some steak-like slabs. "Luckily I don't mind it raw." Her tail lashed behind her eagerly.

"We do have a BBQ on the premises," said Defiance, poking Kita.

"We do?" said Kita as the group returned to the table.

"What's all that flame of yours good for?"

"Burning things?"

"Do I have to teach you Texas-style BBQ?"

"Uhm, what in the Crushing Depths is that?" said Kita with a questioning look.

"I doubt the kitty cats have BBQ sauce around here. Maybe you can smoke them."

"What?"

"Kita, honey, just pick up the meat and cook it," said Anthrax.

Kita picked up a filet from Defiance's tray and heated her hand. She held it until it smelled done and gave it back.

Defiance took a bite. "Not bad. If you ever need a day job, you could become a BBQ pit master."

A crewmember in a yellow jumpsuit entered the galley and approached the table. "Captain Kita?"

Kita turned in her chair. "Yes?"

"Collector would like to speak with you."

Kita nodded. "Ok, take me to the communications room."

"Can we come?" said Phoenix.

Kita shrugged. "Sure."

"We're going to stay and eat," said Panther for her and Defiance.

The three young Angels got up and followed Kita and the sailor out of the galley.

"*Kita,*" called Valentine.

"*Yes, Denver?*"

"*I…I wanted to know if it would be ok if I connected my computer to yours. I miss you.*"

Kita smiled. Valentine was the daughter of the AI Omega, and she had a computer in her head like Kita. It was nice to be needed. She missed having the connection to Valentine. "*Of course you can. I'm afraid there's not much to do. I don't have an empire that needs to be run.*"

"*That's ok. Just being connected to you makes me feel better.*"

"*How are you doing?*" Kita said, concerned.

"*I'm doing ok. Kylee keeps me busy. Keeping her from destroying everything is hard.*"

"*Are you two doing ok?*"

"*Yeah, we're fine. I just don't think she realizes how draining she is.*"

Kita understood Valentine's complaint. Phoenix's constant energy and motion could be overwhelming. She'd been that way since Kita had found her at age eight. Years without a break could take an incredible emotional toll.

"*I remember. Don't worry. I'm here now and can help. I was hoping she'd grow some and learn how to lead.*"

"*She did. She's a good leader when it doesn't become a fight, but she never stops, and it can be a constant battle keeping her on track. She just wants to destroy everything not thinking if she should.*"

That had been a major worry of Kita's when she'd chosen Phoenix to lead. Could she control herself? She was always impulsive, never thinking things through. But, there were times when she did, and Phoenix had great results. Kita had hoped she'd grow into it and having her sister as co-leader would balance her out.

"*That's good to hear. I'm glad Kylee's grown. I'm excited to see how you and she have turned out.*"

"*Thanks. I don't think we've disappointed you.*"

"*You're both here and in one piece. I can't ask for more.*"

"*Sometimes not for lack of trying.*"

Kita chuckled. "*That's part of growing up. I hope you learned from your mistakes.*"

"*I have, I'm not sure about Kylee,*" said Valentine.

"*I'm sure somewhere in that brain of hers the lessons have taken root.*"

"*I hope so. I'm just glad she's damned near invincible and can get out of trouble.*"

Kita chuckled. That had been by design.

"Don't worry, Denver. I know she's a handful, but you did a good job, and she loves you. Have you told her what's bothering you?"

"No."

"I know she wouldn't like to see you distressed. If you had told her, I'm sure she'd try and accommodate you."

"I was afraid she'd see me as weak and leave me."

Kita stepped back and put her arm around Valentine.

"Denver, Kylee would never leave you, but you have to do what is right for you. Wearing yourself down until you're nothing doesn't help you or her."

"But, what if she—"

"You let me worry about her for now. I'll make sure she stays in one piece. You need to worry about you. Enjoy being with Kylee, don't worry about what she does. And, take some time for yourself. I'm sorry this ship is so sparse, but Enterprise has some luxuries you can take advantage of, including a library of Earth material that's mostly up-to-date."

"That would be nice. It would be great to update my databases," said Valentine.

"You could go shopping, too."

"I do need to get one of my ear cuffs repaired. We left in such a hurry I didn't have time to grab the others."

"We'll get you some more. I'm sure the VI can copy the design."

"I don't have any money."

Kita laughed. "Don't worry about that. We've got the company credit card."

"Thanks...Mom."

"Mom?"

Valentine's hand appeared from under her cloak to show off the ring on her finger.

"Oh, congratulations!" Kita kissed Valentine on the side of the head.

"Thanks. We haven't had a wedding yet. Kylee keeps putting it off." Valentine looked despondent.

"As soon as we're settled somewhere we'll have one."

"It sounds like we're going to Earth. I can think of some great places there."

"If you want it in UEE space we can make it happen."

"I've always dreamed of the Mediterranean Sea."

Is that Omega talking?

The group entered the communications section of the ship. They wound through the different workstations to a set of doors. Beyond the doors was the quantum communicator. The Angels stepped inside, and an image of Collector appeared.

"Captain Kita, we meet again."

Kita cocked her head, not liking the tone he conveyed. "Collector."

"I've received some interesting reports over the last few hours. Some are mysterious, others are...provocative."

"If you're trying to intimidate me I can get one of your flunkies in here.

If you have a problem with something I've done spit it out and we can settle it."

"Snowy said you were a person that preferred action. My first report is about the mysterious destruction of both the Deep Space Prison and Ragji. The DSP showed no signs of being destroyed by a weapon but was ripped apart. Ragji was destroyed by a blast more powerful than any weapon in any arsenal. The origin of the blast is an axis vertically through the ship. There were forty thousand people on that ship, most of them Djinn. It's a staggering loss for the young king. They are offering a substantial reward for anyone with information."

"Physics," said Kita.

"Physics?" said Collector taking a puff of his pipe.

The doors opened, and Snowy and Sahara entered. "Collector, we came as soon as you called," said Snowy.

"Snowy, yes, in the after action report against Ragji it was recorded that you stated having seen the type of energy burst that destroyed Ragji. Is this correct?"

Snowy went rigid. Kita smirked at her friend. *Who are you going to side with Snowy?*

"That is correct. I don't know how they happen, but I know Kita has a way of creating them."

Kita grinned at Snowy. Her ears went flat against her head, and her whiskers drooped.

"This knowledge is secret to only certain Angels," said Kita. "It's not something we're allowed to divulge to anyone."

"And if I make it a condition of my continued support?" said Collector as he steepled his fingers.

"Then you might as well let us off here, and we'll find our own way back to Enterprise. It's not something we will share for any price."

"Knowing it can be done is ninety percent of the battle. My scientists will discover its secrets."

"Good luck," said Toxic. "With your infantile understanding of physics, it'll only take you several million years. You're talking about power beyond your comprehension. You don't even understand how everything is put together yet. How can you conceive ripping it apart?"

"Kara, please," whispered Snowy.

"What? His scientists can't even figure out how to do this…" Toxic put her hands together. When she opened them, there was an eight-inch dagger in her hand. "Recognize this, Collector?"

Collector reached inside his coat. His nose wrinkled into a snarl. "I expect that returned."

Toxic held the dagger between her hands and pushed them together. "There you go."

"Knowledge is power," said Kita.

"In that, we are in agreement," said Collector. "From my reports, you have rescued your Angels and recovered your sword?"

"Yes. Thanks to your crew they are recovering from their ordeal."

"Can you explain why you disobeyed me?" Collector said in a relaxed, but intimidating manner.

Kita traced her tongue around one of her canines. "Because I find slavery reprehensible. Those people were there to buy an Angel. I should have killed Takkat for the two Aurorians he had chained in his bedroom."

"Snowy informed me you were without morals."

Kita glared at Snowy, who looked at the floor. "Not without, just my own. I don't mind a lot of things, but slavery bothers me, especially when it's one of my Angels."

"This does not build trust between us."

Kita folded her arms. "You wanted my help, remember? If you want the help of the powerful, you have to be willing to take them on their own terms. You have my Angels and me for your little war. Let us worry about how to accomplish things."

"From now on, Snowy and Sahara will accompany you to protect my interests. This is non-negotiable. I have gathered information on Enterprise and the Angels Rene Sheppard and Amanda Gering. The ship is conducting drills with the Diamock and Verisom fleets out in the Bermilli Expanse. You will board a freighter, jump near Enterprise, and take shuttles to capture it. My people will observe and report once you've taken the ship."

Kita ground her teeth over having terms dictated to her. Defiance and Sheppard weren't going to like having unknown personnel aboard the ship. Maybe she could fool them into thinking the laundry was a top-secret reactor.

"Anything else?" Kita hissed.

"Yes. The Diamock and Varisom crew and fleets are not to be harmed."

Kita smiled condescendingly. "Of course not."

"You're dismissed. Snowy, Sahara, I want to talk to you."

Kita turned and sneered as the door opened and she led the other Angels out. *Dismiss me? Keep thinking you're in charge.*

CHAPTER VII

*K*ita felt the familiar drop of her stomach to her toes as the freighter made the jump to FTL. Her vision returned, and she was still standing on the small bridge of Halkix.

"Jump complete," said Defiance as she took off her helmet and set it next to the FTL controls. "We've got a five-mile drift from the target. Enterprise just appeared on the scopes, setting course for her now."

"Is that drift good or bad?" said Toxic.

"That's phenomenal. Normally drift is measured in hundreds or thousands of miles."

"That's what happens when you use the best computers in the universe," Phoenix said dismissively.

"Yes, glowbug, but I'll be dreaming of numbers for a week," said Valentine.

Kita and Kamikaze nodded in agreement.

"Uh-oh. We've been noticed," said Defiance. She leaned over and put the freighter's communications on speaker.

"This is the Fordina. You have entered a restricted area. Identify yourself."

"They renamed my ship?" snarled Defiance.

"That's not a human voice," said Valor.

"Feed them the song and dance about us having a bad FTL jump and our engines are busted," said Kita. "I'll try and contact Sheppard and Amanda." Kita switched to the comm. *"Rene? Amanda? Can you hear me?"*

"Kita?" the two Angels replied together.

"By the Crushing Depths, it's good to hear your voices. Are you alright?"

"I…We're fine, just in the brig," said Sheppard.

Kita gasped. *"What happened?"*

"I turned over control of the ship. I didn't know if I should fight for it, so I let the Tet have it. I'm sorry. I didn't know what you had planned. The crew followed us and is locked up in their quarters."

"When did this happen?"

"Shortly after your trial. The Diamocks ordered us into dock and marched several infantry companies aboard before we could react. The Diamock and Verisom are operating her now as a training vessel to train their ships against fighter and bomber attacks."

"Ok, I'm here with help to free you and the ship," said Kita. *"We're on a freighter approaching Enterprise's position. Can you girls break out and secure the engine room?"*

"Sure. We're not far from there."

"Good. I'll send some of the girls to meet you after we secure the bridge."

"What girls do you have with you?" said Sheppard.

"The Valkyries are back."

"By the emperor. They're going to kill me!" cried Sheppard.

"Rene, it's ok. I've talked to them about you. You'll have some apologizing to do and take a few verbal lumps, but no one is going to kill you. I promise."

"Ok…"

"How are you, Amanda?" said Kita.

"Fine, just bored. I've mastered the tempest in a teacup."

Kita chuckled. "Now you can make a bigger storm."

"We're ready to go on your command," said Sheppard.

"Once the alarms sound, go."

"Wilco," said Sheppard.

"You girls be safe and don't worry about killing anyone. We're not working for them anymore."

"Who are we working for?" said Stormy.

"A group that wants to take us to Earth."

"Home?"

"Sure. I think it's time we got out of Tet space."

"I agree with that," said Sheppard, "but going to the UEE takes us to Galina."

"That's the idea," said Kita. "You girls be safe."

"See you when you get here."

"There's nothing I can do about it. We're trying to get the maneuver engines online so we can move," snarled Defiance at the picture of a Verisom officer.

"How far out are we?" said Kita as she reached over and killed the connection with the Fordina.

"Two miles," said Defiance.

"Good. Start the engines and set a course so we'll pass by them. I don't want to hit them."

Defiance tapped on the freighter's flight controls. Through the floor, Kita felt the boost of acceleration from the ship's engines coming online.

"Ok, back to the cargo area," Kita ordered to the others.

Kita and her group met with the rest of the Angels in the cargo area.

"Time to go?" said Babydoll from the inside of a shuttle.

"Yes, but we're not taking shuttles over. We're going to drop in on top of them." Babydoll grinned. She dissolved, changing into a dimensionless black cloud. "Kami, take your mother. Vee, take Hali. Denver, take Jess. Kerri, take Sahara. Leaf, take Zen. I'll take Casey."

"Kita, we're supposed to take the shuttles," said Snowy.

"And I'm changing the plan. This will give us the element of surprise."

"No," yelled Snowy. "We've worked out a plan. Casey can take control from the hangar area, and we'll lock the ship down from there."

Kita held up a hand. "We're still going to do that, but from the bridge. I don't want to give the ship a chance to recover. The bridge will give us maximum control of the ship the fastest and prevent casualties on both sides."

"That's never been in your calculations for any plan—ever," snapped Snowy.

"There's a first time for everything," Kita replied sweetly.

"If this is a double-cross you will pay," said Sahara.

"Pray you don't have to collect," said Babydoll.

"What exactly are we doing?" said Defiance.

"Going to Enterprise. Sorry, this is going to get a little chilly," said Kita as she transformed into her cloud. She moved around Defiance and swallowed the Angel. "Ready?" Kita called to the others in the monotone voice all black clouds had.

She received affirmatives from the others. Kita led the group of black, white, and gray clouds out through the roof of the freighter and into space.

As Kita crossed the distance between Halkix and Fordina, she looked out at the stars. The Bermilli Expanse was home to some spectacular views of the Gerix and Comi nebulas. Clouds of young stars burned brightly. Red and orange dust mixed with gases glowing blue and green, creating a sight she'd never seen in the galaxy before.

Kita drifted over the top of Fordina and dropped down through the large dome window into the ship's sprawling bridge. Most of the workstations sat empty. The holographic table was off. Kita settled next to the table, disgorged her passenger, and then shifted back to her Angelic form. The other Angels did the same.

"B—by the E—Emperor, that is c—cold," said Valor after Valentine let her go.

"Computer, authenticate Princess Casey Bush," yelled Defiance.

"Who are you? What are you doing aboard Fordina?" said a Verisom female getting up from her workstation.

"Computer!" screamed Defiance.

"Taking back her ship," said Kita to the Verisom.

"What's wrong with my ship?" Defiance yelled at the Verisom.

"This ship belongs to a joint mission between the Diamock and Verisom fleets."

"It belongs to no one but me," roared Defiance. She waved her hand and encased the Verisom's legs in ice.

The rest of the Verisom and Diamock crewmembers rose from their seats.

"I suggest you sit your ugly mugs down," said Toxic as she drew her swords.

The other Angels brandished their weapons. Raptor transformed into a raptor and let out a low, menacing whistle. An alarm sounded.

"I'm trying to access the computer," said Kita to Defiance, "but they've got some kind of wrapper program installed."

"Get me back my ship," snarled Defiance. Her hand formed into an ice ax, and she slammed it into the skull of the trapped Verisom.

"Kita!" yelled Snowy.

"What? I didn't do it."

"Control her."

"I'm not going to control anybody. It's Casey's ship, and she's got a right to fight for it."

"I'll kill all of these alien vermin," said Defiance angrily. She hurled a pair of large ice balls toward the crew. The balls exploded showering them with deadly ice fragments.

"Stop!" yelled Sahara. She had both her daggers out as she faced Defiance.

"Your girlfriend against mine?" Kita purred to Snowy. "I know who I'm taking."

"Stop this," said Snowy.

"Why? My girl's in the right. It's her ship that's been stolen. I don't know what your girl is trying to do, other than get herself killed."

"She's trying to protect your alliance with Collector."

"She should let me worry about that."

"What do you want, you stupid tabby?" goaded Defiance. "You want to join the rest of these deplorable degenerates? I'll have your hide as a throw rug."

Sahara snarled and leaped at Defiance.

"Sahara!" cried Snowy.

From the side Babydoll struck Sahara, sending the Djinn sideways. Babydoll expanded from a ball into a whirling roundhouse kick, striking Sahara repeatedly, then exploded into an uppercut punch hitting Sahara and driving her into the ceiling. Babydoll grabbed Sahara, performed a flip, and kicked Sahara into the deck.

"What the hell, Kita! She's not reinforced like an Angel," screamed Snowy.

"She should have thought of that before tangling with one that has bodyguards."

"If she's injured it's your fault."

"With a beating like that you better hope she's not dead."

Snowy's eyes went wide as Zentix rushed to Sahara's side.

"What are we going to do about my ship?" said Defiance waving her arm at Enterprise.

"We'll get it figured out," said Kita calmly. "We'll need to go to the server room and manually uninstall their program. It can't be that sophisticated."

"What should we do with the rest of the crew?" said Phoenix.

"Kill them. They know way too much about this ship."

Phoenix burst into flame and flung a pair of fireballs at a pair of crewmembers hiding behind a desk. With glee, some of the other Angels joined in the hunt.

"Kita! You bitch. She's not breathing," screamed Snowy. "What are you doing?" she cried when she heard the first screams of the crew.

"They know too much," said Kita.

"I won't let you slaughter them."

"Leaf, Tina, see what you can do for Sahara," Kita said to the high angels.

"Then you're going to have to defeat all of us," said Kita to Snowy.

"I just need to beat you!"

"Bring it, pretty kitty. But I won't lose."

Snowy snarled and launched herself at Kita. Kita drew her swords and met Snowy in the air, swords rung as they struck claws. Snowy kicked with the claws on her back feet. Kita let them slash her lightly across her thigh, before kicking Snowy in the chest, sending her backward. Kita twirled, hitting Snowy with the back of her fist repeatedly, driving Snowy into the deck. Kita backflipped and struck Snowy in the jaw with her heel. Snowy somersaulted and landed hard on the red friction carpet covering the deck.

Snowy rolled backward, planted her feet and leaped at Kita. Raising her swords, Kita blocked Snowy's claws and pushed them aside. She corkscrewed and slashed Snowy across the back. Snowy swung with her claws. Kita ducked and struck Snowy's upper arm as it went by. Kita spun, struck with her swords, leaving six long gashes up Snowy's back. Kita dropped to the ground and swept with her leg, kicking Snowy's legs out from under her. Snowy landed on her back.

Kita pounced and thrust her swords toward Snowy's shoulders. Snowy caught Kita by the forearms and pushed back. Snowy's face contorted as she strained to keep the swords out of her flesh. Kita gritted her teeth and pushed, forcing the tips of her swords into Snowy's shoulders. Snowy let out a scream. The fur around the swords turned bright red. Snowy kicked up with her back feet. Kita shifted and blocked, knocking Snowy's legs aside while pushing Dead and Buried deeper into Snowy's shoulders.

Snowy roared and thrust her claws into Kita's sides. "Don't make me do it," Snowy yelled.

"Go ahead and try it," said Kita as she pushed down harder with her swords.

"I warned you," said Snowy. She screamed as she released a bolt of lightning into Kita.

Kita's eyes rolled into the back of her head and then closed. When she opened them, she was smiling. She let out a maniacal laugh. "Do you really think that's going to hurt me?"

Snowy's eyes went wide in surprise. "But…"

"Like everyone, you underestimate me!" Kita let go of her swords and grabbed Snowy's wrists. She pulled Snowy's crackling claws out of her and shoved them into Snowy's sides. Kita stood up, pulling Snowy to her feet. Kita grabbed Snowy by the throat, lifted her above her, and turned her sideways.

"Wait!" screamed Snowy. "No—"

Kita dropped, and Snowy fell, her back landing across Kita's knee.

There was a loud crack followed by a few pops. Kita let Snowy go, and she slid off and landed on the floor, her eyes wide with shock and pain.

Kita stood up and recovered her swords. She looked down at Snowy's broken body. "You're free to change masters at any time, just remember I'm the greatest."

"Ouch, that looks like it hurts," said Babydoll as she landed next to Kita.

Zentix left Sahara's side and dashed next to Snowy's. "What have you done to her?" demanded Zentix as she examined Snowy's twisted and broken back.

Kita glowered. "I reminded her I will only be pushed so far. I am no one's servant, and no one will tell me what to do."

"Painful lesson," said Babydoll.

"It's more than a lesson of pain."

Babydoll nodded. "I learned the one about double-crossing you a long time ago. I don't need a reminder. I'm still scared of you."

"I don't want you scared of me."

"I still love you. Don't worry."

"You're my best friend, Kerri. That'll never change unless you want it to."

Babydoll held up her hands. "I'm not planning on going the way of Galina."

"Hey, they're all dead," yelled Phoenix from across the bridge.

"Thank you, sweet pea. Leaf, anything?"

"She's breathing again. I think it would be better if Nell took a look at her."

"Nell, will you?"

"Sure, why not," said Anthrax, her shark's teeth covered in orange blood.

"Denver, come with Casey and me. We're going to the main computer room. Jess and Kerri! Take two groups, free the human crew, and task them with getting rid of the Tet crew. Amanda and Sheppard should have the engine room secured by now. I want life support, and the weapons lockers secured. Nell, Tina, Leaf, see what you can do for Collector's agents."

"You got it," said Valor as she got down from the holograph table. She had been talking with Starlight and the other Angels that hadn't joined in the slaughter.

"I guess I still remember my way around the ship," said Babydoll.

Kita nodded and let them divide the remaining Angels.

"Shall we go get your ship back?" Kita said to Defiance.

Defiance gave Kita a dirty look. "Yes. It took you long enough."

"You'll get yours. I promise."

CHAPTER VIII

"The ship's server room is through here," said Valentine as she led Kita and Defiance into Enterprise's Combat Information Center.

"Did you serve on Enterprise?" said Defiance.

Valentine smiled. "No, but my father served in the Shadow Fleet before being sold to Gjord Industries."

"Sold?" Defiance said raising an eyebrow.

Kita chuckled. "Denver's father was the AI Omega."

"I know sexbots are realistic, but, ah…I know with Kita there has to be a trick."

Kita raised her hands. "I had nothing to do with it. I told her to run and hide. Next thing I know she's coming out fighting with a pair of wings."

Valentine nodded. "Father used everything he learned from Kita about making Angels and remade my body, including adding a computer in my head. Unlike Kita's computer, which just augments her brain, mine is fully integrated. My father copied most of what he'd learned to me."

"How did Omega know how to do this?" said Defiance. "AIs can't perform functions outside their programming."

"Omega became sentient on the journey to colonize," said Kita. "To protect himself, Omega rewrote the colony ship's stored human genome so if you had all the right genes you would seek him out. I was the lucky one to find Omega."

"So if it weren't for Omega I wouldn't have you?" said Defiance.

Kita shrugged. "Pretty much."

"I will have to hunt down the creators of Omega and thank them."

"Who you should thank is Communications Officer Dave Berlin," said Valentine. "He's the one that unleashed the virus on Omega that made him sentient."

"Hopefully Dave is buried in a shallow grave somewhere," grumbled Kita. Berlin became Kita's nemesis Angus, a biomechanical AI driven to rule the planet. He could inhabit both humans and computers. When Angus found Kita, he planned to take over her mind and find Omega for himself.

"We don't know that for sure," said Valentine. "The probability that we destroyed the last copy of him is low."

"Just what I don't want to think about," Kita said with a sigh.

Defiance opened the door to the server room. It contained rows of computers and a terminal in the back. The Angels crowded around the terminal. The screen's display was in Diamock.

"I'm surprised they don't have someone down here," grunted Defiance.

"I don't think they completely understand how the ship works," said Kita as she typed in a password. "They know enough to be dangerous. Hmmm, didn't work." She knelt and took off the access panel to the terminal to reveal several jacks and ports. Placing her finger over a port, small metal fibers extended from her finger and let her connect.

The screen on the terminal blinked, and parts changed. The screen turned green and then displayed ACCESS GRANTED in Diamock.

"We're in," said Kita. "Let see how to undo what they did."

Kita flipped through several screens and stopped on the GUI protocols. "Here we go…and uninstall…click ok…and we should be back to Common."

"Uhm, why did a counter appear in the bottom corner," said Defiance.

"Huh?" Kita clicked on it making the counter bigger. "That didn't help."

"We've got fifty-five seconds to figure it out," said Defiance.

"Let me," said Valentine.

Kita made a face, but let her take control. Valentine knelt and interfaced with the terminal. The terminal's screen flashed through images of controls as she searched.

"Ok, found it. Tracing it now," said Valentine. "Following…following… it's in the engine room."

"*Rene! Amanda! Are you in the engine room?*" called Kita.

"*Yes, we're cleaning it now. They're playing hide and seek,*" said Sheppard.

"*Quit playing with them and search for a bomb.*"

"*A bomb?*" said Stormy.

"*What does it look like?*" retorted Sheppard.

"*I don't know,*" said Kita. "*Anything out of the ordinary.*"

"*With all the SLIP drive equipment in here, it could be hiding in plain sight.*"

"*Well hurry. We only have thirty-five seconds.*"

"*Kita! That's not enough time!*"

"*I know, just search. It can't be well hidden. We're trying to deactivate it from this end. How's it going, Denver?*"

"*It's somewhere in sector three of the engine room, and that's where the command signal ends.*"

"*I know where that is,*" cried Stormy. "*It's the Political Bureau section.*"

Kita bit her lip. She had to warn the others, but she wasn't sure everyone could be saved. She put a call out to the other gods. "*Everyone, listen up, there is a bomb on the ship. In fifteen seconds, I'm going to need you to transform into your god form and get out. Try and save the others.*"

"*We can't carry them as if we were clouds,*" said Panther.

"*We could if we teleported them somewhere,*" said Tina.

"*You? Break the rules?*" scoffed Kamikaze.

"*I'd try and take everyone here, not just Angels.*"

"*They're the ones that planted the damn bomb,*" Kita said grumpily.

"*I be teleporten' the two with me,*" said Raptor.

"*I'll go to the engine room and get Sheppard and Amanda,*" said Kita. "Denver, can you get Casey?"

"Wait! I've almost got it," said Valentine.

"We've got seven seconds," warned Kita.

"I know— I know…I think…I got it."

"Still counting," said Kita. *"Everyone, go!"*

"I found it!" cried Stormy. *"There's a bunch of wires out the back. Which one do I pull?"*

"There's no time," said Kita. *"I'm coming to get you."*

"We can't abandon the ship," yelled Sheppard.

"We don't have a choice. I—"

"Kita," said Valentine, "the countdown has stopped."

"What happened? Are you sure?"

"Yeah—"

"I ripped out all the wires," said Stormy. *"I figured that would stop it."*

"Is that in the field manual, lieutenant?" said Sheppard with a laugh and a sigh.

"Ah, no. I believe you Marines call it field expedient.*"*

"Ok everybody, the danger's passed. Continue as before," ordered Kita. "How's the computer, Denver?"

"I'm doing a soft reboot now to make sure we got rid of their software."

"Ok. I'm going to check in with the others." Kita called Babydoll. *"Kerri, how are you girls doing?"*

"We ran into a pair of Gronks."

"Damn, they must be desperate if they're bringing those things aboard. Do you need help?"

"No, we took care of them."

"Everyone ok?"

"Besides my wounded pride, everyone's fine."

"I need to warn Jess. Her group doesn't have as much firepower."

"I thought she was a walking arsenal."

"I need to tell her to make sure she has the right munitions loaded."

"Tell me what?" said Valor.

"There are Gronks aboard the ship," said Kita.

"Oh, hell. I hate those teenage mutant snapping turtles. I'll bust out my Gronk can openers."

"Tell the other girls to be careful if you run into any," said Kita.

"What? You don't want them learning the hard way like we did?"

"We already learned the hard way," said Babydoll.

"Ha. Wish I could have seen that," teased Valor.

"It's funny now. At the time, I wasn't sure what we were going to do. Kita, we've found our first group of humans. What do you want me to tell them?"

"Tell them to go to general quarters and run the diagnostics for their section. We don't know what shape the ship is in and we may have to fight our way out of this."

"Rodger," said Babydoll.

"Wilco, when we find some," said Valor.

Kita nodded and turned to Defiance. "I told the others to send the crew to general quarters and run diagnostic checks."

Defiance nodded. "Sounds good. Emperor knows what these damn dogs and bunnies have done to my ship."

"Kita," said Valentine, "I've got the main computer back online. It's running through its checks now."

"Computer, authenticate Princess Casey Bush."

"Princess Casey Bush—authenticated. I will alert all sections you are aboard the ship and are in command."

"Good, that's what I want to hear. Sound general quarters and send out special instructions that all Verisom and Diamock forces are considered hostile and to be terminated with extreme prejudice."

"Yes, Princess."

"Do we need to stay here?" said Kita to Valentine.

"I'm linked into the system, and I'll give you access so we can talk to it from anywhere."

"Good. Let's get back to the bridge."

～

"CAPTAIN ANDERSON," SAID KITA TO ENTERPRISE'S EXECUTIVE OFFICER IN A sinister tone. Then she smiled to tell him she was playing with him.

"Your Highness, Captain Kita," he replied as he saluted, not reacting to Kita's tone.

"I don't have time for pleasantries, Captain," snapped Defiance. "Get my ship back online. I want squadrons ready to go and to know the situation around us. We have five enemy ships in the vicinity that could attack at any moment, and I want to beat them to the punch."

"Yes, Your Highness. I will marshal the crew and bring the ship up to combat readiness."

"Make sure they run a diagnostic check on their stations," said Kita. "We don't know what the bunnies and doggies have done to the systems."

Anderson's jaw tightened as he ground out a, "Yes, Captain," between his teeth.

Kita smiled at him. There was no love lost between them. He seemed to dislike her having any kind of authority on the ship. *I'm dating your princess, so deal with it.*

Kita, Defiance, and Valentine walked around the bridge. Kita disposed of the bodies while Valentine ran diagnostics on different terminals. Defiance watched as the crew exited the elevator, sometimes solo, other times in large groups, and restored the bridge to operational status.

"Do we know how many enemies were aboard the ship?" said Defiance.

"I've found twenty-two so far," said Kita. "I don't know how many are wandering below. I'll call and ask the others if they've run into any. I'm sure we would have received a report if they ran into heavy resistance."

"Find out. We can't have them running loose on the ship."

Kita raised an eyebrow about being ordered about. She quelled a flippant response. Defiance was doing her job. Still, she didn't like taking orders from anyone, be it Collector or her girlfriend.

"Ladies, how's the resistance down there? The Princess wants to know." Will *the others catch my sarcasm?*

"None to speak of," said Valor. *"We've encountered a few guards guarding the humans, but they gave up easy."*

"You fill the brig up with prisoners, and they're your problem," said Kita seriously.

"So far it's just twenty-four."

"Twenty-four guards to guard twenty thousand people?" said Kita.

"They do lock the doors. I have no idea how they're feeding them. We haven't stopped to talk to anyone other than to let them out and tell them to report to general quarters."

"We've run into a group of humans not locked up," said Babydoll. *"They were on some kind of work detail. The guard surrendered, which just made it easier to kill him or, at least, I assume it was a him—big bunny like head, tall, fluffy tail."*

Kita chuckled. *"Yeah, that's a male Verisom."*

"We have a few in the engine room. Some went quietly, others didn't," said Sheppard. *"Everything is quiet down here. We're guarding the two entrances."*

"Alright, thanks." Kita sighed. "Very light," said Kita to Defiance. "They don't have much of a guard detail. I think they were counting on the door locks to do the job for them."

"Well it worked," Defiance grumbled.

"I doubt the crew knew what was happening or understood our allies had become the enemy."

"I still don't expect them to roll over like dogs."

Kita shrugged. She didn't blame the crew. In the absence of orders, they sat tight. *How long would they have waited?*

"Kita, I have the holotable working," said Valentine.

"Good, thanks." *Maybe that'll get Casey's mind off the crew.* "Come on, girls. Let's see what's out there."

Kita approached the fifteen-foot table. On either end, the table displayed readouts of the ship's biometrics and status of the squadrons. In the middle was a holographic rendering of local space. It showed Enterprise in the middle and five enemy ships in an arc from 270 degrees to 25 degrees at 15 degrees down angle.

A crewmember with the words AIR BOSS across his back went through the squadron readouts. All were red, except for one green that was blinking.

"We already have a fighter ready to go?" said Kita to the Air Boss as she touched the fighter icon.

"Hey, don't do that!" said the Air Boss.

An image of a pilot appeared. "Hey! About time. I'm ready to launch. Let's go, let's go, let's go. We've got enemies out there with asses that need kicking—"

The Air Boss closed the window.

"Who is that?" said Kita taken by the pilot's enthusiasm, determination, and dedication. She wasn't willing to send the pilot out alone, but she appreciated the gesture.

"That is Major Alex Garcia, affectionately known by her call sign Rainbow Jack. She's one of the best wizzos we have."

"What's a wizzo?"

"A wild weasel—electronic warfare operator. Their job is to hunt down the enemies' radar, and other electronic surveillance then jam or destroy them. They also will go ahead of the main fighter squadrons to set off enemy countermeasures then destroy them."

Kita raised an eyebrow. "That's a job that requires a lot of courage."

"You've got to be crazy smart to do it. Rainbow Jack is one of the best." A few more fighter icons turned green. "Looks like the squadrons are pulling themselves together."

"How long until we have flight operations, Commander?" said Defiance.

"Unknown, Your Highness," said the Air Boss. "I don't know the status of the pilots or the ground crews."

"Why don't you find out? I don't want to be a sitting duck when those enemy ships realize what's happened."

"Yes, Your Highness." The Air Boss saluted and hurried away.

Kita leaned against the table and crossed her arms. "What's the matter, Casey? I know you don't like them, but this is extreme even for you."

"They're just lucky I haven't shot any of them."

"For the circumstances, I'd say they're doing an excellent job. The bridge is almost staffed, fighters are coming online, I'm sure the rest of the ship is gearing up as fast as we can find people."

Defiance glared. "How would you feel if you had disgusting worms oozing all over your swords? When the people who are supposed to defend it let the enemy have it without a fight?"

How did I end up defending humans? "We never told them the Verisom and Diamocks were the enemies. I submitted to them, so did you. They were just following our example. The crew doesn't know you were nearly sold into slavery or that we're no longer working with the Verisom or Diamocks. We haven't given them any direction or told them anything about what's happened. They can't read our minds. Cut them some slack and give them a chance to catch up."

"Should we tell that to our enemy?" Defiance yelled. "My crew is incompetent—please give us some extra time before attacking?"

The elevator opened. Sheppard and Stormy exited, both wearing their duty uniforms.

"That's not fair to the crew, Casey," said Sheppard as she stopped in front of Defiance and Kita. Kita had recalled them and kept them abreast of the conversation as they made their way from the engine room to the bridge.

"Oh, shut up, Admiral. You're their leader. This is your fault. They should have fought for my ship. You," Defiance pointed at Stormy, "are to hunt down those responsible for turning my ship over to the enemy."

"What?" said Stormy sounding appalled.

"You're a political officer, aren't you? Find the traitors. Do what you're trained to do."

Stormy stood up straight. "I'm sorry, Your Highness, but my loyalty isn't to you, it's to Kita."

"You traitor," snarled Defiance. She grabbed Stormy's eyes of providence from her collar and ripped them off.

"Ok, that's enough," said Kita standing up and moving between Stormy and Defiance. "You gave Amanda your blessing. You can't renege on it now. I don't know what your problem is, Casey, but you better solve it in a hurry. I plan on taking this ship into battle as soon as it's operational. I won't have a pouting princess with ruffled feathers get in the way. The crew is doing their job and getting the ship operational as fast as they can.

"Screaming and threatening them won't help. I won't have you act like my father, screaming and yelling, trying to get blood from a stone. The crew has been sitting for months and wants nothing more than to get a little revenge, especially after I tell them what happened to you."

Defiance reached to slap Kita, but Kita caught her hand

"Ah-ah. There are many times when slapping me is appropriate, but now is not one of them."

Defiance turned red. "You tell them what happened to me and I'll—"

"You'll what?" said Kita. "There's nothing you can do to me."

"I can break up with you," hissed Defiance.

"Ok, bye. I'll be sad, and my heart will hurt. I'll probably cry on Rene's shoulder." Sheppard rolled her eyes. "But the same thing goes for you as for Cotton. I won't bend. I'm a fixed point."

"You are such a bitch."

"I know, but you knew that. Same as I know it about you."

"I hate you," snarled Defiance.

Kita shrugged.

"It's still my ship," roared Defiance.

"Good luck getting someone to command it," said Sheppard.

"What?" screamed Defiance. "Are you betraying me too, Admiral?"

"No, but I'll turn in my globe and anchor before I'll let someone treat the crew and ship like this. We're not some toy for you to play with or dogs to come when called. I'll tell the crew to stand down or better yet, I'll tell them to keep going and—" Sheppard's elbow glowed blue. The glow raced down her arm as she punched Defiance in the mouth.

Defiance flew backward, crashing into the side of a workstation. Blood poured from her mouth as teeth fell out. Defiance tried to get up by reaching for the top of the workstation. Her hand missed, and she fell back to the floor.

Kita led the other Angels over to check on her. She could hear soft sobs coming from under Defiance's hair. Kita stroked the dark locks a few times, before picking Defiance up and sitting her upright.

"Are you ok, Casey?" said Kita.

"My mouth," Defiance sobbed in a mushy voice.

"It'll be ok. We'll find all the teeth. They go back in easy enough." Kita picked them up as she found them.

"I can't believe she hit me." Defiance spoke with a noticeable lisp.

"Every once in a while we need to get hit in the mouth to knock some sense back into us. That's all Rene did. It was nothing personal. She was just standing up for the crew and showing you the light."

"But…"

"Just take it as the lesson it is. You may be a fallen angel, but even we have limits. Sheppard showed you one."

"I'm sorry…" Defiance said with a sniff.

"I know. You can apologize to Amanda and Rene. They're the ones you offended, not me."

"Ok."

Kita helped Defiance to her feet. "I'm sorry, Amanda and Rene. I was out of line and abused my authority," she said as she hung her head.

"Apology accepted, Your Highness," said Sheppard.

"You can keep my eyes," said Stormy. "I'll find a different uniform to wear."

Kita cringed inwardly. "Talk to Denver. She'll get you one of mine."

"I guess I deserve that," said Defiance. She sighed. "Admiral, can you get the ship ready to fight?"

"Wilco at best speed," Sheppard said with a smile.

Kita put her arm around Defiance. "It'll be alright. Just give her some time. Come here, let me help you put those teeth back in."

"Come on," said Valentine to Stormy. "I'll get you a new uniform made for you."

As Kita helped Defiance put her teeth back in place, Anderson approached. "Your Highness, Captain, we received a message from the Diamock ship, Bite Lock. They want to know what happened and if we know anything about the freighter."

"Ahh…" Kita bit her lip.

"Tell them it's a Free Zentonian protestor ship," said Defiance. "We don't have the resources to detain them and interrogate them on how they knew we were out here."

"Yes, Your Highness." Anderson kept his face straight, but Kita could feel his doubt.

"Will that work?" said Kita having her own doubts.

"From the reports, I've read the Zentonians do it all the time to Verisom. It shouldn't be anything too out of the ordinary. It'll buy us the time we need to get ready."

CHAPTER IX

"*J*extrapolated the enemies goals from studying the mission history stored in Enterprise's command computer," said Valentine. She stood at one end of the holotable with the rest of the Angels gathered around as well as the higher-ranking crewmembers. "They were studying fighters and how to defend against them."

"There goes our strategic and tactical advantage," groaned Sheppard.

"Not necessarily, *Admiral*," Valentine said the word with so much disdain she could have cut Sheppard.

Kita cringed. *"Denver, you don't have to do this,"* Kita said privately over the comm.

"I just don't wish to answer to her ever again."

"You're not answering to her. You don't answer to anyone. You're helping me help Casey. She and I will take care of Rene."

"Then tell her to keep her comments to herself," Valentine said aloud.

Before Kita could speak, Sheppard said, "I owe the Angels an apology. Denver, I especially owe you an apology. I made a series of poor choices that led to some big mistakes, and I acted horribly to all of you, especially you, Denver. I treated you worse than a machine.

"I thought I was doing what was right by the emperor. I believed Kita was a paramount threat that needed to be brought to heel. I was positive she was going to doom us all. I could say it was Galina's fault—that I followed her orders—but I won't. My actions are my responsibility, and it's my fault. I killed some very dear friends and…I killed Spike and Quill." Tears streamed down her face as she choked up. "I'll never forgive myself for pushing that button. I was a fool, and I'm sorry—I'm sorry I ruined our lives and killed our friends. You have every right to hate me. I deserve it. Just know I'm sorry. If I could sacrifice my life to bring them back, I would. You deserve them, not me. I'm just…I'm just pathetic, and I don't deserve to stand with you."

Sheppard turned and fled. Kita phased in front of Sheppard and caught her in an embrace.

"Shh, shh," Kita whispered in Sheppard's ear. "It's alright, but you can't run from this. You do deserve to be one of us. I say so. You have to face them. They were your friends. They gave you your chance to speak. Let them speak.

"Not everyone hates you. I don't hate you. I love you. You were a great mentor to my girls, and you taught them a lot. You stepped in and took over when I was imprisoned in that tree. I didn't ask you to, but you did anyway. You could have left them to Galina. I don't think I ever said thank you, but I owe you so much. Without you, Spike and Quill would never have grown up to be the girls they were. I wouldn't change anything. Now, come on. Let's see what the others have to say."

Kita led Sheppard by the hand back to the holotable. Valor, Starlight, Defiance, and Stormy were waiting, looking concerned.

"Rene, you ok?" said Valor. She glided up and gave Sheppard a hug.

"No," whispered Sheppard.

"We're here for you," said Starlight.

The other new Angels joined in the hug.

"Do you even know what this is about?" scolded Anthrax to the new Angels.

"Not really," said Stormy.

"I do," said Defiance. "Rene was following the orders of her commanding officer. It's not her fault. She was doing her duty to me."

Anthrax bared her shark-like teeth. "That doesn't excuse what she did. She knows right from wrong. She should have known an illegal order when she heard it. She killed Nina and Tink. She may not have pulled the trigger, but it's her fault."

"No!" cried Sheppard. "I had no idea Galina was going after the families. They were supposed to be hostages. I never would have killed them. Please, you have to believe me."

"What about the others that were slaughtered?" said Tenshi.

Sheppard hung her head. "I knew about directive Seventy-seven. I never thought she'd execute it. I...I underestimated how much Galina hated Kita. I should have seen it. I should have known all of her decisions were made in a jealous rage...but...but I thought she was right."

"There's your problem," Toxic said snidely.

"No. Rene was doing exactly what I expect all of my officers to do," retorted Defiance.

"What's the rule about sleeping with your superior officer?" said Anthrax.

Defiance looked at Sheppard. Sheppard closed her eyes and nodded.

"We all know Galina loved Kita more," said Aspen. *"Sheppard was just a way for Galina to pass the time."*

Fresh tears welled in Sheppard's eyes.

"That be harsh comen' from ya," said Raptor. "I be thinken' Sheppard loved Galina."

"I did, but I grew scared of her. I feared to go to sleep, that I might not wake up. I did whatever I needed to keep her happy."

"It sounds like we have abuse," said Stormy.

"The only one doing the abusing was Sheppard," said Valentine.

"That's not fair," said Valor.

"You weren't on the receiving end of it," screamed Valentine. "It almost cost me my relationship with my partner, and it damn near cost me my life. You want to know how many times I wanted to put my pistol to my head? More than I can count."

"Whoa, Val, it's alright," said Toxic as she hugged Valentine.

Phoenix stood by looking bored.

"This does not sound like the Rene I know," said Starlight. "She's been wise, kind, and willing to show us how Angels are supposed to be."

"Give her time," said Toxic, the glow from under her hood dimming.

"I agree with Hali," said Kamikaze.

She received a round of surprised looks from the Valkyrie Angels.

"Sheppard was my mentor as well as Spike and Quill's. She taught us so much, and when my moms vanished, she took care of us like we were her own. The flock wasn't kind to Sheppard during the Harbinger invasion. I was surprised Sheppard did her duty. I can see where she'd come to trust Galina more than us. I don't blame her for what happened. This was a monster of our own making. I hope she finds peace. She may owe some of you an apology, but we all owe her one."

"I'm not apologizing to her," screamed Valentine.

"We can stand here and yell at each other until all the suns go supernova," said Babydoll, "but only one person's opinion matters and she made up her mind when she kicked Sheppard's ass in this very room." Babydoll looked at Kita.

Kita smiled at Babydoll. *Thanks for putting me in a tough spot, Kerri.*

Babydoll smiled back and gave Kita a wink.

Kita looked around defiantly, daring anyone to challenge her. "I have made up my mind about Rene. I know what she's done and why. There is one person I want to hear from. She lost the love of her life that day and hasn't said a word. She's managed her broken heart by herself."

"Who?" demanded Anthrax.

Kita raised an eyebrow. *Funny you should be the one to demand whom. He was your old lover.* "Frostbane died with the twins. Raptor and he were a couple. She deserves an apology as much as I do. I think she has the right to speak and face the person who took the most important person in the world from her."

All eyes shifted to Raptor.

"It be true. I loved Frosty. Not a day be goen' by that I don't be missen' him. But, that be the way of nature. We live, and we die. A wolf mother be mournen' the loss of her cub for a moment, but she be moven' on. I be cherishen' my time with Frosty. I be haven' no ill will against Sheppard. We all be predators and that day she be haven' the bigger claws and faster teeth. She be doen' what her instinct be tellen' her, and there be nothen' wrong with that. There be only one apex predator. The rest of us be sheep in the herd waiten' our turn to be culled. It be what Kita wants that matters."

"It's not about what Kita wants," said Tina. "You matter, too."

"We be placen' our lives in her hands when we were given' wings. It be part of the deal. We be climen' up the food chain, but we'll never be the top. It be the deal we make. Kita be given' me more than I could ever dream. She knew what I be wanten' before I did."

"Kita is not some prophet."

"*She is a god,*" said Aspen.

Tina scoffed. "No, she's not. We're gods. Kita is an imposter. She's not from Infinity—"

"When did this become about me?" said Kita. "Everyone here is my friend. I love you all. I don't force anyone to do anything. I've made my decision. I knew there would be some hard feelings, but Rene's not the first I've given a second chance to."

"Who's to say it should be your decision," said Tina. "It should be the group's choice."

Kita folded her arms and tapped her foot. *Talk about a betrayer.*

"My mom is the leader," said Kamikaze. "She always has been."

"I doubt anyone here would disagree with that," said Babydoll. "Nell?"

"I still say Sheppard should be punished and better watch her back. The moment she looks away, I'm going to be there to tear her apart. Kita will give me that much."

"Just know I'll be watching Rene's back," said Kita.

"Fair enough."

"Anyone else think I'm not worthy of leading?" said Kita. Everyone stood silently. "Well, little sister, your coup has failed."

"I wasn't trying to take over. I was trying to give everyone an equal part," pouted Tina.

"Everyone is equal, even me."

"*What makes Kita special is she's the catalyst,*" said Aspen.

"And momma bird," said Toxic, the glow from under her hood brightening.

Kita chuckled. "I try to protect and provide for everyone the best I can." She turned to Sheppard. "Rene, anything more you'd like to say?"

"I'm so sorry for what happened. I promise I will try and make it up to you. I don't know how, but I'll try. Just, please, give me a chance. I'm not the same person I was back on Base Station. You can ask Kita or Jess or...or Hali—"

"Or me," said Defiance. "If you have a problem with Rene, personal or professional, bring it to me, and I will make sure it gets straightened out. That goes for you too, snagglepuss. Mess with one of my officers, and you'll mess with me."

"And you know who's backing her up," said Valor.

"I'll take you all on," said Anthrax.

"We'll leave that for another day," said Kita. "Is everyone satisfied? Any more apologies need to be made? Because after this, this is the last I want to hear about what happened."

"What she going to be doing for us?" said Toxic.

"Same as she did before, lead the military forces. We should let her get back to it. I want some ships turned into scrap."

"What should the rest of us do?" said Babydoll.

"You can hang around the bridge if you want to or Jess can show you to the officer's lounge. I'll call you if I need you."

Babydoll, Valentine, and Panther stayed with Kita as she toured the bridge. They made the rounds, stopping at each section. Kita would talk with the sailors to find out how ready their section was and if they needed anything. *This is a much better way of getting information about Enterprise than looking at a display.*

"How are things in navigation?" Kita asked a group clustered around a workstation. A lieutenant stood.

"Uhm, well, I'm not sure, ma'am."

"Is there a problem?"

"We don't know. The FTL computer is acting funny."

Kita's blood went cold. They needed that computer to make their getaway. She was sure there were more Tet ships in this sector than the five in this training exercise. She planned to hit them and then make a run for it. Enterprise wouldn't last long against a determined attack.

"And how is it acting funny?"

"We enter the destination coordinates and run the iterations. The computer spits out its flight plan, and that checks out fine, but when we look at the actual numbers coming out of the computer, it takes us nowhere."

"So someone has told the computer to display the right flight path, but when you look at the generated coordinate list it doesn't match?"

"Yes, ma'am."

"Lucky for you I happen to have the best diagnostic computer with me."

"I know nothing about FTL," said Valentine. "That was after my time."

"Then we'll figure it out together. Come on, let's get jacked in and see what's wrong."

Both Angels placed a finger over a universal communications port and ran a test plot.

They checked the results and found what the lieutenant had described.

"Could they have altered the code?" said Valentine.

"That would take a specific level of knowledge of the Enterprise's systems that the Verisom and Diamocks have yet to demonstrate they possess," said Kita.

"I don't see what else it could be."

"Maybe it's a loose wire," said Babydoll.

Kita exchanged looks with Valentine and shrugged. "It couldn't hurt to check. Lieutenant, open her up and see if there's anything amiss."

"Yes, ma'am."

The lieutenant set her crew about opening all the service panels and checking connections.

"I found one, ma'am," a sailor called from under the main workstation. "A wire has been pulled out of its connector."

"Can you fix it?" said Kita.

"Yes, ma'am. Give me a minute." The sailor, with his tongue out, reached into the machine. "Ok. Got it, ma'am."

"Let's see if that's our culprit," said Kita.

She and Valentine ran another FTL test plot.

"That seems to have fixed it," said Valentine.

"I agree," said Kita. "Run a few more test plots, Lieutenant, and make sure. Then let me know."

"Yes, ma'am."

Kita led her group toward the next section.

"Do you think that was on purpose or just a fluke fault?" said Panther.

"I didn't see the wire, but I can't see it falling out of place. Maybe one of the Tet crewmembers did it when we first boarded. I'm glad they caught it. It would be embarrassing to try and jump and not go anywhere."

"It could have been deadly," said Babydoll. "We should alert the other sections and have them check for sabotage."

"Agreed. Denver, can you put out a message to all sections and stations throughout the ship to check for sabotage."

"Going out now."

Anderson approached. "Captain Kita, Admiral Sheppard has a situation that needs your attention."

"Oh?"

"Yes. We've received another communication from the other ships demanding to speak to an Admiral Refer. We have no idea what to tell them."

Uh-oh. I was hoping we'd have more time. Refer sounds like a Diamock name. Hmmm. Kita called Valor over the comm. *"Jess, where's Zentix?"*

"She's with Snowy and the other cat. They're in the medical ward."

"Find her and get her sent up to the bridge." Kita smiled at Anderson. "I think I can bluff us some more time. What's the status of the ship? How close are we to being able to launch fighters?"

"The maintenance crews are checking out the fighters as fast as they can. Currently, seventy-five percent of available aircraft have been checked."

Kita did the math in her head. That was 187 aircraft out of 250.

"Let me talk to Sheppard."

Kita led her group over to the holotable where Sheppard was planning the attack and escape.

"How close are you to being ready?" Kita asked Sheppard.

"I'm waiting for as many aircraft to come online as possible. The more we have, the better off we'll be."

"We found and fixed a problem with the FTL computer."

"I didn't know it was down. It's not in the maintenance report."

"Well, they were debating if they had a problem or not," said Kita.

"What are we going to do about their demands to speak to an Admiral Refer?"

"I've got a plan. How much time do you need to get the minimum amount of fighters you need airborne?"

"If I send the warning order now…ten minutes," said Sheppard.

"Do it. I think we'll be better off if we go with the element of surprise than wait for a larger force."

The elevator door opened and Zentix entered the bridge.

"Zen!" Kita called waving a hand. Kita frowned. From Zentix's quills, Kita could tell she was unhappy. Using her cloud, Kita felt apprehension, unhappiness, and confusion coming from her friend.

"Reporting as ordered, Captain," said Zentix with a stiff salute.

"I told you, you don't have to do that with me…especially now when I'm no longer captain of a Diamock ship. Is there something the matter?"

Zentix remained at stiff attention but looked around at the other Angels.

"If it's something you want to discuss in private, we can."

"No, Captain. But…You broke your agreement, twice, with Collector. Our mission was to retake Enterprise with as little causality as possible. And you attacked Snowy and Sahara. My faith in you is broken."

Kita bit her lip. *How to explain this?* "For starters, Sahara attacked me, and Kerri intervened. Snowy attacked me over Kerri's actions. Snowy won't be out long, a few days. Denver, what's Sahara's status?"

"In surgery. Nell is helping. Sahara's prognosis is excellent. Time to recover is unknown."

Kita nodded. "I know what Collector said, but I don't agree with him. We have no place to put hundreds of prisoners. I need the crew to fly the ship, not be guards. What Collector wanted wasn't possible.

"Those killed at the mansion were killed because they were participating in slavery—a practice I despise. Takkat put Casey and Jess up for auction. I wasn't going to let that go unpunished.

"Collector is trying to have everything. He wants the governments of the Tet happy, he wants his little war, and he wants me. I'm not happy with the governments of the Tet for locking me away. I'm not going to play nice with them. I'm going to punish them for what they've done."

Zentix's quills rippled. "But you broke the rules."

"What I gave them should have more than made up for it, but petty minds run the Tet, and they refused to let it go. They'd rather throw me in prison for some slight than let me run free where I could protect them. They made their choice and forced my hand. They're lucky all I want is to be free of Tet space, or I'd bring more destruction."

"This mission is so you can prove your loyalty to the Tet and regain your status."

Kita shook her head. "I'm loyal to myself, my family, my friends, and those who serve me. That's it. I will be loyal to others if they are loyal to me. The Tet was not loyal to me after all I did for them. I know you have loyalties to Diamo and Diamock Command. I understand if you don't want to stay."

Zentix's quills stood on end. "You're sending me away? You don't think I'm loyal to you?"

"I know you've been hanging around with Sahara and Snowy. I thought you were loyal to Collector like they are."

"I spend time with them because they're all I've had for several months, and I know them. I haven't been introduced to your new arrivals. Collector is a hoof banger—" Kita cringed at the slang term for the lowest of the low of a Diamock unit, those in the discipline company "—he has no honor. He is not a warrior but pretends to be one. I only went with Snowy because I had no place to go. The goal was to escape until Snowy met Sahara. Then suddenly she wanted to be Collector's friend and offered you to him."

"Who is Sahara?" said Kita curiously.

Zentix's snapped her muzzle. "Besides Snowy's pseudo-girlfriend? Sahara is Collector's daughter."

"Oh, damn," said Babydoll with a laugh. "No wonder that girl is screwed up."

"What do you mean *pseudo-girlfriend*?" said Valentine.

"Snowy wishes them to be together, like Kita and Cotton—my respects to you, Kita, for Cotton. She was a brave warrior—Snowy has not explained it to Sahara fully. They only hold hands and groom each other. I don't think Sahara would understand the desire of another female wishing to mate with her. It is beyond her comprehension."

"Poor Snowy," said Kita shaking her head.

"Her mistake," said Zentix. "Collector doesn't know either."

"I see trouble brewing," said Panther.

"We'll protect Snowy if we have to, even if it's from herself," said Kita. "Zen, you've got the same rights as any Angel. What I've given you is yours to keep. I'll take you anywhere you want to go and give you what I can."

Zentix quills stood up. "You think I'm not loyal to you? I gave up my ship and crew to follow you."

"I know you did, but I don't want to force you into anything."

"It was my choice. I want to fight with you. Have I not proven myself?"

"Yes, on multiple occasions. I do owe you more than I can give. I hope this makes up for some of it." Kita touched Zentix on the nose. "Boop."

The other Angels giggled. Zentix cried out and fell to her hands and knees.

The armor plates on her back opened and two bones grew upward forming joints. Buds formed on the leathery skin and opened. Gray, orange, and brown feathers grew reaching for the ceiling.

"Rise, Blitz," Kita said with a smile.

Panther and Babydoll each took an arm and helped the new Angel to her hooves.

"What happened?" said Blitz.

"You're one of us now," said Valentine.

Babydoll pulled one of Blitz's wings around so she could see.

"I...Wings? You...I'm not worthy."

"I decide that," said Kita. "You're loyal, dedicated, and an excellent soldier."

"Now you'll be a legendary soldier," said Babydoll.

"Blitz—is that my name?"

"Your angelic name," said Kita. "It's what non-Angels will call you. The Angels will continue to call you Zen unless you say otherwise."

"Blitz...does it have a meaning?"

"Short for *blitzkrieg*. It means lightning war. It's a military strategy where you use fast maneuver forces to push through your enemy's front line into their rear area to cause as much disruption as possible. I thought it appropriate for you."

"What's grown on my arm plates?"

Kita grinned. "Maser cannons. You can also outrun a lightning bolt and as you run you generate energy that you can release in an explosion."

Babydoll let out a low whistle. "You're going to be a juggernaut on the battlefield."

"How?" said Blitz, her quills signaling that she didn't understand.

"Don't worry. We'll get you trained up," said Kita.

"Kita, communications reports there is a Commander Defix on the line, calling for Admiral Refer," said Valentine.

Kita smiled at Blitz. "Zen, you mind doing me a favor and talking to them?"

"Refer is a male."

"I have voice imprints of his earlier communications," said Valentine. "I can create a filter that will change your voice to his."

"Of course I will. What do you want me to tell them?"

"Find out what they want. Then tell them we've updated the code to the launchers and we need to launch all aircraft to make sure it works properly. Hopefully, that'll let us launch unmolested, and we can launch our attack and catch them by surprise."

Kita led the group to the center of the holotable.

"I'll be running old footage of the admiral so they won't see you," said Valentine to Blitz.

"Ok."

"Just face the screen, and I'll do the rest."

A Diamock face appeared on the holotable. His muzzle was clenched, and his quills covering his face and head stood erect in a display of respect.

"What is it, Commander?" said Blitz in a tone that said the other Diamock was bothering her.

"Admiral, I was calling with an update on the freighter."

Blitz looked at Kita confused.

"It's the freighter we came in on. We told them it was full of protestors," Kita said over the comm.

"How are you talking to me in my head?"

"All Angels get an internal communicator that lets them talk to any other Angel in their head. Just think of the Angel, and you'll be connected to them."

Blitz turned her attention back to the screen. "Has it been dealt with?"

"Shuttles are on route now, sir."

"Then why are you bothering me? We're in the middle of an important software update for the launchers. Pass the word that we will need to launch all fighters to test the software."

"I was not aware of any such update, Admiral."

"Am I expected to tell you everything, Commander? Call me when you have some results on the freighter. In the meantime, return to your duties."

"Yes, Admiral."

The Diamock head on the holotable vanished.

"Great job, Zen," said Kita. "That should buy Sheppard enough time to finish planning and get the fighters launched. Right, Rene?"

"I'm working out the last details now," Sheppard replied from the far end of the holotable.

CHAPTER X

The sailor saluted, touching his hand to his helmet. In the cockpit of the fighter, the pilot returned the salute. The sailor dropped to a knee and pointed down the launcher. The fighter's engines roared as the catapult rocketed the craft into space.

"Wow. That seems like a dangerous job," said Kita, watching over the Air Boss' shoulder.

"Someone has to crawl under and make sure the connection is secure. It's a tradition that goes back to when they used to launch planes off the decks of ships."

Adding the chance of falling into the sea makes the already risky launch procedure seem even more dangerous. "How many fighter groups have we launched?"

"Twenty-one," said the Air Boss. "Three left."

"Good. Guess I'll go check in with Sheppard."

"Yes, Captain."

"It feels wrong just standing around like this," said Babydoll as the group moved toward the holotable.

"What can we do without using our god powers?" said Valentine.

"I know, it just goes against my training. On the ground, you're part of the fight. In space, you have to let someone else do it. And I want to hit somebody."

"I'm sure we can strap you into a fighter," said Kita playfully.

"That's not the same as feeling somebody's nose break under your fist. You just push a button."

"If that's all it takes I'm sure Kylee and Kara would be aces."

"I stand by my statement," said Babydoll turning up her nose.

"Oh, I'm with you," said Kita. "Nothing beats plunging your sword into a person's still beating chest and watching the life slip away, drop by bloody drop."

"Hmmm, that's something I could go for. I notice the aliens have different colored blood. I didn't get a chance to taste it."

"Tastes like blueberry." Kita grinned. "At least, as far as the kitties go. I haven't sampled anyone else, but the Diamocks are orange, the Aurorians are gold, and Zentonians are red."

"So we could have orange, pineapple, and strawberry?"

Kita and Babydoll giggled while Valentine rolled her eyes and whispered, "Bloodlusters, ew." The comment made the other Angels laugh harder.

"So, Rene, where do we stand?" said Kita coming up to her.

"About to start offensive operations as soon as the last squadron gets airborne."

Kita looked at the display. Almost 240 fighters swarmed around

Enterprise at different orbits. In the distance were their targets, five Tet ships trying to board the freighter Halkix. "Rene, can you single out a single fighter to follow?"

"Ah, sure. Who did you have in mind?"

"A pilot that goes by the call sign Rainbow Jack."

"She's a good one to watch. One of the best. RJ will be leading the Angels in the first group."

"Angels?"

"They used to be called the black knights, but changed it after the Princess got wings."

Sheppard opened a window that showed the fighter and pilot's biometrics as well as a view of the cockpit. Rainbow Jack was bobbing her head as she checked her equipment.

"Audio?" said Kita.

Sheppard hit a button.

"Cold as ice, faster, harder," Rainbow Jack sang as rock music blared in the background.

Sheppard rolled her eyes. "She's not supposed to have music playing."

"Hey, I like music when I fight." Kita stroked her chin. She wanted to see what Rainbow Jack could do. Going in first would give her the element of surprise. Any rookie could take advantage of that. Kita wanted to see what Rainbow Jack could do when the enemy was alert.

"Rene, can you have her lead the fifth group?"

"Why? I want to get this off on the right foot."

"I want to see how she handles a little adversity."

Sheppard frowned. "I told you she's the best wizzo we've got, and she's a damn good pilot, too. Why waste her talents?"

"Why not use this as an opportunity to evaluate an up and comer? I'm sure there is another wizzo ready to take Rainbow Jack's place." Sheppard sighed exasperatedly. "I'll go ask my other girlfriend if that'll help make up your mind." Kita waved to Defiance across the bridge.

"Why would I do this for you?"

"Because I want to see how good she is. No one wants to see me sneak up on some sleepy guard and slit his throat. Everyone wants to see me fight Snowy or Kerri."

"My money's on you because I'll know you'll cheat," Babydoll said with a chuckle.

"Only because you won't have thought of it first."

"I can only imagine the temper tantrum you'd throw if I actually beat you to something like that."

"It would be epic."

Babydoll laughed. "See? She doesn't even deny it."

"Why would I? Only fools play fair…"

Kita, Babydoll, and Panther all raised eyebrows and looked at Sheppard.

Sheppard sighed. "Fine. Aircraft control, new attack configuration order. Swap gargoyle zero-zero with angel zero-zero and falcon zero-zero with gargoyle zero-zero."

"Aye aye, ma'am." The controller repeated the order back to Sheppard.

On the screen, Rainbow Jack received her new marching orders. "Are you kidding me! Who's dumb idea is this? Don't they know I'm the best? Command! Who gave this order?"

The controller sighed. "It came from the top, Rainbow. They didn't say why. You're to lead the fifth group in."

"Someone is going to get a piece of my mind when I get back."

Babydoll and Panther smirked at Kita. With a shrug, Kita muted Rainbow Jack's feed.

"If she's as good as she claims this should be easy for her," said Kita.

"Still hard on the ego, to be demoted right before a battle," said Babydoll.

"She'll get over it."

"All squadrons in the air," announced the Air Boss.

"Thank you," said Sheppard. "Combat control, it's a green light."

"Aye aye, ma'am," said a nearby officer. "Aircraft controller, code tiger."

"Aye aye, sir," said the sailor operating the workstation. "All squadrons, code tiger! Tiger! Tiger! Report by number."

The squadrons called in with affirmatives they'd received the message. On the holotable, the squadrons broke orbit around Enterprise and streaked toward the Tet ships. Now came the dangerous part. It would take time for the fighters to reach the Tet ships, giving them a chance to prepare, if someone was paying attention. *I hope the freighter has them too occupied to care what we've been doing.*

Kita zoomed in on the freighter. Six shuttles surrounded it, but there was no way of knowing what they were doing. Kita closed the window. It was out of her hands now. She enlarged the window showing Rainbow Jack. The music was still blaring, but she was concentrating on controlling her aircraft. She was ten seconds ahead of the lead squadron for their sector. Enough time for Rainbow Jack to turn on her instruments to jam enemy sensors and keep the rest of the squadron safe. *Good luck, girl. I hope you don't need it.*

"You look worried," said Panther.

"I don't like not being able to influence the situation. I feel useless."

Panther nodded. "It does feel strange not doing anything when a fight is about to go down, but all these people are part of the fight. We can influence them."

"I think our mere presence is a morale boost. We did our part by rescuing them," said Babydoll.

"How bad was it for the crew?" said Kita.

"Discipline held. The areas were clean and the people in good shape.

No one was starving. The only complaint I heard was there wasn't enough rack space."

"For weapons?" said Kita, confused.

Babydoll chuckled. "No, for sailors. The lower enlisted hot bunk, meaning they share beds with someone from another shift."

"Oh, how charming. I think I'd rather just sleep on the ground."

"That's why we're legionnaires and not sailors."

"First squadrons have reached target alpha," announced an officer from Combat Control.

On the holotable, the image zoomed in on fighters swarming the enemy ship. Several explosions came from the near side.

"This is Angel leader," said a voice.

"Go ahead, Angel leader," said Combat Control.

"Spot report. They have anti-fighter guns mounted all over the ship. Fire isn't accurate, but they're putting up a lot of lead."

"Roger, Angel leader. Will advise the other squadrons to be careful and take precautions."

Kita wrinkled her nose. That confirmed what she suspected. The Tet was working on anti-fighter technology. But, it sounded like their technology wasn't that good yet. Still, if they put enough rounds in the air, they'll eventually hit something.

The other fighter groups reached their targets. Kita unmuted the sound on Rainbow Jack's window.

"Alright boys, here we go," said Rainbow Jack. Her hands flipped a series of switches. "And you've been thunderstruck!" she yelled as music blared in the cockpit.

"Not a bad song selection," said Babydoll. "It's appropriate."

Kita nodded. She'd never heard this version of the song—she preferred the original.

"Nah-nah, can't hit me," Rainbow Jack taunted as she flew toward the enemy ship. "By the emperor! Control, this ship just lit up like the emperor's birthday fireworks display. I've got over two dozen new sensor contacts besides the main."

"Rodger, do what you can to defeat them then enter wild weasel mode."

"Wilco, Control."

"What is wild weasel mode?" said Kita to the other Angels.

Everyone shrugged.

"*Rene,*" Kita called over the Angel's internal comm.

"*Busy, Kita.*"

"*I know, but what is wild weasel mode?*"

"*It's when a wizzo increases their signature to draw enemy fire.*"

"*So everything is shooting at them and not the other pilots?*"

"*Correct.*"

"*Interesting. Thanks. I'll leave you alone.*"

"We're going to see if Rainbow Jack can dance on the head of a pin," said Kita to the others.

"Oh?" said Panther.

"Apparently, it's her job to attract as much attention as possible."

"She seems to be the type that would like it." Babydoll chuckled.

"The first squadron of bombers is hitting target alpha," announced Combat Control.

"Can you highlight them?" called Kita.

Six icons streaking toward the enemy ship designated alpha became yellow on the holotable display. They charged the ship and then turned ninety degrees. A moment later, alpha blinked as the computer registered the impact of the bombers attacks.

"Spot report, Admiral," said a Combat Control officer. "Damage to target alpha substantial. The bombs penetrated the main hull."

Target beta blinked.

"Looks like the bombers got to the second ship, too," said Kita.

"They're going to make fast work of them," said Panther.

The elevator door opened and eight Diamock and Verisom troops emerged firing.

"Keep to your stations," yelled Sheppard. She drew her pistol and returned fire.

"Come on," said Kita. "Let's get them."

Blitz streaked across the room building a charge. She smashed into the enemy group and detonated, sending bodies flying. Firing her maser canons, she blew a Diamock soldier apart.

Babydoll threw herself into a ball and struck a Verisom male. A shockwave rippled across him. She uncoiled into a flip kick that sent the Verisom toward the ceiling. Launching herself after it, she struck it several times with her fist, grabbed it by the shoulders, somersaulted, and kicked him into the deck.

Defiance froze a female Verisom and a Diamock solid. Valentine drew her pistols and fired six times hitting a male Verisom in both eyes and a Diamock four times in the chest.

Panther roared, snapped her claws out, and leaped at a male Verisom. She plunged her claws into his chest, flipped over the top of him, and threw him into the elevator door. Bouncing off the deck, she landed on top of the Verisom and slashed his throat open.

Kita phased behind a Diamock female, and kicked her in the back, sending her to the deck. Drawing her swords, Kita stabbed them through the Diamock's shoulders. She slammed her boot into the back of the Diamock's head, breaking her muzzle with a loud crack. Snapping off a point of the Diamock's crown, Kita whispered, "That'll give you something else to think about."

"Get their weapons secured," ordered Sheppard.

The handful of Marines guarding the bridge hurried to comply.

"Where the void did they come from?" said Blitz.

"No idea," said Kita. "I thought the ship was clear."

"Obviously it's not," said Sheppard. "Security, sweep the ship, look for any alien survivors. Thanks for acting so fast, girls."

"No problem," said Babydoll. "The Legion is always here to save the Marines' asses any day."

Sheppard rolled her eyes. "Sergeant, make sure the prisoner gets medical treatment and get the rest of them cleared off my bridge."

"Good job, girls," Kita said to the other Angels as they gathered around her. Kita led them back to the holotable. She touched Rainbow Jack's status to catch up with the pilot.

"Hey, look out. This bad boy's got flak cannons," yelled Rainbow Jack.

"That doesn't sound good," said Kita. She hadn't heard of anyone else reporting such weapons, just the auto-targeting cannons.

"Damn it!" yelled Rainbow Jack. "They got me. They got me. I've got a wing full of flak."

In Rainbow Jack's box on the holotable, the part of the outline of the fighter turned red. Several system statuses turned yellow or red.

"Is she dead?" said Panther.

"I don't think so," said Kita.

The video feed showed Rainbow Jack piloting her fighter. She was busy flipping switches. "Control, I've got it under control. I'm going to start blinding them. Fox-two, RSM away. I've got twelve active sensors, preparing MSMB."

"What is that?" said Kita.

"No idea. We'll have to ask later," said Babydoll.

"Control, a direct hit with RSM. Echo target is blind, I repeat, echo target is blind," Rainbow Jack announced. Her icon circled the enemy ship as the first wave of fighters arrived. "Get those hazard shields up, people," she instructed. "There are pockets of flak everywhere. MSMB ready, getting into position." She made a tight turn that brought her perpendicular to the enemy ship. "MSMB away."

"Down she goes!" a sailor watching the holotable called. Target alpha was breaking apart.

"Shift resources to bravo," called Sheppard in a flat voice.

"We've got impacts!" whooped Rainbow Jack. "Twelve enemy sensors down. Starboard side clear. Moving to the port side." Rainbow Jack's icon rolled over the top of the enemy ship. "I'll keep them busy over here."

"She knows her stuff," said Babydoll. "These fighters probably never had it so easy."

"I'm impressed," said Kita. "I wouldn't want to do it."

The holotable flashed. "Charlie exploded," announced a Combat Control officer.

"How many fighters have we lost?" said Panther.

Kita looked over the Air Boss' shoulder. She counted three fighters listed as black, ten red, and eighteen yellow. "Not many. We totally surprised them." She knew one of those fighters listed red was Rainbow Jack. She glanced back at the video feed, but the woman was concentrating on her instruments while flying her fighter. *Talk about multitasking.*

"Gold, Blue, and Red leads, Rainbow Jack, I've got them blind on the port side, but they're firing blindly so be careful. The flak is heavy." She received affirmatives from the squadron leaders.

Defiance drifted over and kissed Kita on the cheek. "Enjoying the show?"

Kita raised an eyebrow. "It's impressive. It beats being on the receiving end."

"True that. Enterprise has some of the best pilots in the Shadow Fleet."

"We've been watching Rainbow Jack. She knows her stuff."

Defiance glanced at the window displaying Rainbow Jack's status. "Her bird is injured. I don't know if that speaks to how good she is, but she is a wizzo. She's got to be able to fly."

"Do I hear a hint of jealousy, freighter pilot?" said Kita.

Defiance scoffed. "She'll never know what it takes to make an FTL jump or pilot through a wormhole. That takes real skill."

Kita raised a hand. "There's no better pilot than you."

"Damn straight," growled Defiance.

Blitz and the communications officer approached.

"Your Highness?" said the communications officer.

"Yes?" Defiance snapped harshly.

"There is a Captain Regot calling. He's demanding to know what's going on."

"What does he think is going on? He's being attacked. Funny time to worry about it." Defiance looked at Blitz, her tone became friendly when she spoke. "Any idea why now, Zen?"

"We caught them by surprise and have taken out two of their ships in rapid succession. I think they're *catching up to events*, as your people are fond of saying."

"Well, let's see what he wants while he still has a ship left. Put him on the holotable."

A window appeared with a Diamock looking upset. "Who are you?"

"I'm Princess Bush, and I'm taking back what's mine. The Enterprise belongs to me. My crew is extracting their revenge for how the Children of the emperor and I have been treated during our incarceration at the hands of you Tet thugs."

"Where is Admiral Refer?"

"I'm sure his body is around somewhere, or what's left of it."

"You will not get away with this. Missile batteries fire at will."

Defiance cut the connection. "Admiral, expect some incoming missiles."

"Shields are up, phalanx antimissile system online, Princess."

Defiance nodded. "We're as ready as we'll ever be."

"And what is the intercept percentage of the phalanx?" said Babydoll.

"About ninety-five percent. It depends on how many they send at one time. The ship has twenty systems mounted around the hull."

"This is why I don't like ship-to-ship combat." Babydoll sighed. "Somebody else's mistake means my ass."

Defiance raised an eyebrow. "If a line of legionnaires crumbles on your flank it means the death of the entire unit."

"I can still shoot back. I can't do anything if a missile hits us."

"Admiral, bravo and delta have fired six missiles each," reported a Combat Control officer.

"Ship Defense, are you tracking those?" called Sheppard.

"Yes, ma'am, but they're too far out to engage."

"And we're left sitting and waiting for our ultimate demise," huffed Babydoll.

"Have some faith, Kerri," said Kita. "They've done well so far."

"I'd feel better if I could go stand on the hull and shoot those missiles with my rifle."

"I think the ship can survive a few missile strikes."

"There isn't that much steel between us and space." Babydoll pointed to the panoramic windows in the ceiling. The shutters were closed for combat.

"How thick are the shutters?" said Panther.

"The hull is an eighteen-inch composite," said an officer watching the holotable. "The shutters are twelve inches, plus the windows are a twelve-inch composite that's nearly as strong as the hull composite."

"See," said Kita. "Nothing to worry about."

"Tracking new contacts," reported a sailor from Ship Defense. "Twelve missiles from target echo. We do not have enough systems to engage all contacts."

"Create a targeting list," said Sheppard. "After the list is exhausted have the computer change to automatic acquisition mode."

"This might get a little rough," said Defiance.

"Control, Rainbow Jack. All portside enemy defenses are down. Target echo is clear. Missiles outbound toward Enterprise. I've got one MSMB left. I'm going to see if I can run them down."

Rainbow Jack's status showed her fighter's systems were yellow and red, a few were black. "Why is she chasing down missiles? It doesn't look like her fighter is holding together."

"Rainbow Jack, Eagle Six." Kita raised her eyebrows at Defiance's call sign. "Do not engage. I repeat, do not engage. Your bird can't handle it, just bring her home. Let Enterprise's defenses get them."

"Don't worry. I got it, Eagle Six. I'm acquiring targets now."

On Rainbow Jack's status screen, her yellow systems turned red.

"She's got problems," said Kita.

"Rainbow Jack, I repeat, *do not* engage," said Defiance angrily.

"Come on, baby, hold together. I've almost got them...Little faster... Tone! All twelve. MSMB away!" The left wing on Rainbow Jack's fighter status display went black. "Oh, damn. It took my wing with it. Control, Rainbow Jack."

"Rainbow Jack, Control."

"I've lost my left wing, and the engine is flaming out. I still have maneuver jets. Let them know I'm coming in hot."

"Negative, Rainbow Jack. Ditch the bird. We'll pick you up."

"I can't, Control. The first hit took out my primary life support system. I've been on the reserve most of the mission. I won't survive until pick up. Don't worry. I can get her back."

"In how many pieces?" said Kita.

"She sounds as hard-headed as you," Babydoll said with a teasing smile.

"Missiles in range," announced an officer from Ship Defense. "Phalanx system engaging."

"What is a phalanx system?" Kita asked Defiance.

"It's a Gatling gun connected to a computer that fires high explosive shells to knock out incoming threats."

"Can we open the window? I'd like to see this."

"They're coming from underneath us."

Kita sighed and turned to the holotable. Twenty-four dots moved toward Enterprise at an alarming rate. Rainbow Jack trailed twelve of the missiles. Whatever weapon she'd fired wasn't big enough to be seen on the holotable. In the background, the rest of the fighter squadrons attacked the remaining three enemy ships.

"How long until impact?" called Sheppard.

"Twenty seconds, Admiral," said a sailor monitoring the holotable.

"Sound the impact alarm. Everyone brace yourselves."

"Admiral, the first missile has been taken out," reported the officer from Ship Defense. "And another one."

The Angels stood around the holotable listening as each missile was destroyed.

"That wasn't so bad," said Valentine.

"Yeah, just twelve more to go," said Babydoll.

The twelve incoming missiles were seconds away.

"Brace for impact," the Officer of the Watch called.

"Ship Defense?" yelled Sheppard.

"Targeting as many as we can. We only have nine available systems. Two gone. Two seconds to impact!"

Kita grabbed the holotable and Panther's hand. On the holotable, the dots representing the missiles moved into Enterprise's icons. She braced her legs against the shockwave that would rock the ship and closed her eyes.

"Hell yeah! Got them!" Rainbow Jack cried.

Kita opened her eyes. She waited for alarms to sound, but the ship was quiet.

"Ok, everybody, back to work," yelled Sheppard.

"Control, Rainbow Jack, I'm coming in hot. Get the nets up."

"Rainbow Jack, you're coming in too fast for the nets. I advise you to ditch, and we'll pick you up."

"I can get her slowed down—don't worry."

"We're switching you over to the Air Boss for recovery, Control out."

"Where is she coming in at?" said Kita to the Air Boss.

"I'm going to direct her to runway four. That way if she blows up she'll do the least amount of damage."

"We'll go down and help."

"What can you do?"

"Play catch. Come on, girls."

~

KITA AND THE ANGELS APPEARED IN THE HANGAR. IN FRONT OF THEM WAS runway four. Eight nets were strung across the runway, while a rescue crew waited behind a crash shield protecting the hangar entrance. The Angels went over to the first responders.

"When is the fighter due?" said Kita.

A Marine looked at the Arcom on his wrist. "Ninety seconds, Imperial Angel. If you'll please clear the area we need to get ready."

"We'll hang out in the middle of the runway and see if we can snag her for you."

"What? No, you can't do that!"

"I say it's fine, Marine," said Defiance in a harsh tone.

"Your Highness, you can't go out there. The fighter is coming in so fast she's going to go through all the nets."

"That's why we're going out there."

Kita and the others glided out onto the runway between the sixth and seventh net. They spread out ready to grab Rainbow Jack.

"There she is," said Valentine. She pointed to a light moving toward them. "She's coming in too fast. The Marine is right. My calculations show she'll go through all the nets and end up back in space."

"Do your best to grab her and hold tight," said Kita. "Keep your wings open to create as much drag as possible."

"I've always wanted to play parachute," Panther said with a laugh.

"What happens if we don't stop her?" said Blitz.

Kita smiled. "Then we go for a ride."

"Here she comes," announced Valentine.

The Angels braced themselves as Rainbow Jack's wounded fighter roared in, plowing through the first two nets.

"Did those slow her at all?" said Babydoll.

"She lost two hundred and fifty-four miles-per-hour," said Valentine. "She's traveling slower than a bullet."

"Yeah, but she's much bigger than a bullet."

Rainbow Jack hit the third net, and the fighter slammed onto the runway, skidding forward trailing a shower of sparks into the next net.

"She's dropping speed," yelled Valentine over the noise.

The fighter hit the fifth net. The first and second nets arrestor cables ran out and came free, whipping behind the fighter. The loose cable could take a leg or cut someone in half.

"Keep back and stay behind cover!" Kita yelled to the rescue crews.

The fighter hit the sixth net, and Kita braced herself. She feared there would be nothing to grab on to, but the nets provided ample handholds along the airframe but obscured her view of the cockpit. She mentally kicked herself for not patching into the fighter's communications system.

The Angels opened their wings and dug in their heels. The fighter struck Kita first. She grabbed the netting and wrapped her arms around the nose. The force of the impact knocked her off her feet. She felt the fighter slow as the other Angels grabbed hold. Unable to arrest the fighter's forward momentum, the group slammed into the next net.

"By the Crushing Depths," muttered Kita as the net pinned her and the other Angels' wings to the fighter. She burst into flame and melted through the net. She thrust her legs out and jammed them into the deck. As she slid the soles of her boots smoked.

As they came to the end of the runway, Kita spotted the launcher's cleat. *Denver! Fire runway four's launcher!*

The cleat raced toward Kita and the fighter. Kita stuck her foot into the launcher's track and made herself rigid. The cleat struck her foot pushing her forward. The fighter rose off the deck, flew over Kita's head, and slammed down on its side. The nets came down on top of the Angels. The ejection pod fired sending Rainbow Jack skidding across the deck into a protective barricade.

"Ok, whose dumb idea was this?" Babydoll muttered as she untangled herself from the nets.

"Mine," growled Kita as she tried to do the same. "Everyone ok?"

"You owe me a massage after this," grumbled Panther. "I think it tried to rip my arms out of their sockets."

"My hands are all chewed up," said Valentine. "Can someone untangle me?"

"That was like ultimate steer wrestling," whooped Defiance.

"You're supposed to eat them, not play with them," said Babydoll.

"I'm fine," said Blitz. "My plates are scuffed. What's a steer?"

"A really dumb four-legged beast that doesn't understand it's a hamburger," said Babydoll.

"What's a hamburger?"

"Only God's gift to women...or is that tacos? Maybe pizza. When we go to the mess, I'll show you."

Kita burned through the nets freeing the others. They hurried over to the rescue crews freeing Rainbow Jack. A metal saw was cutting through the ejection pod's framework.

When the sparks from the saw stopped flying, the rescue crews used pry bars to open up the escape pod's hatch. When it opened, a corpsman stuck his head in to talk to the pilot. The corpsman came out nodding his head. The rescue crew pulled Rainbow Jack free.

"Thanks, everybody. What a ride," exclaimed Rainbow Jack.

The leader of the rescue team pointed behind her to the Angels. Rainbow Jack turned around, scanned the Angels, saw Defiance, and came to attention and saluted.

"Your Highness. I, ah, didn't expect a personal reprimand."

"I have a feeling I know what your punishment is going to be, Major," said Defiance coldly. "I'll let her deal with you."

"Yes, Your Highness. I will explain myself to Admiral Sheppard."

"You wish. I'm talking about her." Defiance hitched a thumb at Kita.

"Hi," said Kita. "After you finish thanking these girls for saving your ass, you and I are going to have a chat."

CHAPTER XI

"What are we doing down here? It smells like burnt oil," whined Phoenix.

Kita rolled her eyes at her daughter. Phoenix's bad attitude was wearing her thin. "This is a little hide-a-way spot I found last time I was on Enterprise. It's a good place to hide things, right Rene?"

"Until someone goes poking around where they aren't supposed to."

"I had been directed this way to see the installation of the SLIP drive. Not my fault I heard them."

"Heard who?" said Valentine.

"Me and my team," said Stormy.

"Who the slag are you, anyway?" snarled Phoenix.

"I'm Amanda, and you are Kylee."

"You better know who I am."

"Your mouth preceded you."

"I will kick your ass from here to the farthest galaxy." Phoenix lit a fireball in her hand.

"Uh-huh," said Stormy. She waved her hand, and a small storm cloud appeared over the fireball. Rain poured down dousing the fire, and a lightning strike hit Phoenix's hand.

"Ouch! What the slag, bitch?" snarled Phoenix. "I'm going to burn you so bad—"

"Enough, Kylee," said Kita. "Everyone inside." She waved the group of Angels through the door. She waved in Rainbow Jack and Sheppard last.

"Well, this is cozy," said Panther as she looked around at the racks, portable head, practice mat, and bokkens in their stand.

"So what are we doing down here?" demanded Phoenix. She pointed at Rainbow Jack. "And why did you bring her —him? It's a man—at least the important parts are."

The blood drained from Rainbow Jack's face.

"Kylee!" yelled Valentine. "Do not tease someone like that."

"I'm not lying. Check the backscatter lens."

"That is vile, Kylee, even for you," scolded Valentine. "The backscatter scanner isn't there for you to peek under someone's clothes."

"I wasn't peeking! I was just checking for weapons. I do it for everybody new. You never know who's got what."

"You shouldn't do it to a friend!"

"She's not lying," said Kita quietly. *What did I miss?*

Rainbow Jack flushed red with anger. "Is this why you brought me down here? To make fun of me?" she yelled. Tears trickled down from the corner of her eyes. She fled toward the door.

"No, wait!" yelled Kita. "Rene, Casey, Amanda, Jess, stop her—him—her? Her!"

Around the room, Kita received confused looks from many of the Angels, but not from the UEE Angels.

"What am I—and we—missing?" Kita said to Babydoll and Anthrax.

"There's nothing to get freaked about," said Babydoll. "She's transgender."

"Trans—what?"

"Ah, Annie, maybe you can explain it better than I can."

Anthrax nodded. "She's transgender. A male in the process of becoming a female. At a certain stage in development, the wrong hormones are given to a fetus, and their brains develop thinking they're one gender and their body develops in the opposite. It can manifest itself at a young age. When someone is identified as transgender, they're given hormone therapy when they reach puberty. Once the body is done developing, around age twenty-five, they have surgery to give them the proper organs. It goes both ways, male to female, female to male."

Kita blinked. "It never occurred to me that this could happen."

"I guess coming from the world you did it's not that big of a surprise," said Babydoll. "There's not much anyone could do to fix it, and a transgender person doesn't have any choice but to go with what they're given. It probably didn't cross anyone's mind."

Have I met a transgender before? There were some real tomboys and some very effeminate men. Could they have been transgender and trying to cope with it the best they could? How awful. Imagine if my father had gotten his way. "I understand. Does anyone have any questions?"

The Angels shook their heads.

Kita bit her lip looking at Rainbow Jack being comforted by Defiance, Sheppard, Stormy, and Valor. *I should take a picture with Rainbow Jack's permission. This really shows the empathy of the Princess, admiralty, and Political Bureau.*

"I think we should go apologize. Come on, Kylee."

"What did I do?" she huffed.

Kita gave her daughter a dirty look.

"The backscatter lens is a gross invasion of privacy," said Valentine.

Phoenix crossed her arms defensively. "I'm just trying to keep us safe."

"What's she going to have that's dangerous to us?"

"You never know. It's saved me a few times."

"We'll sort it out later," said Kita. "Come on, everyone."

Kita led the group to the Angels comforting Rainbow Jack.

"Is she ok?" Kita asked Valor.

"Just angry, embarrassed, and upset."

"She has a right to be."

"Lucky for you, the first person to grab her was the princess," said Valor.

"I and the others would like to apologize."

"I'll go see."

"Thanks, Jess."

Before turning around, Valor gave Phoenix a dirty look.

"I didn't know!" Phoenix yelled.

"Hush," said Kita. "What have I told you about tact?"

"I don't know. It's been like ten years, and I've been doing fine without you."

"If it weren't for me you'd have nothing."

"I've destroyed more in the universe than you ever will. You're nothing compared to me."

"You're not too big for me to teach a lesson."

"Try it."

Kita grabbed Phoenix's hand and jerked Phoenix to face her. "If you're going to challenge me, you better have what it takes to beat me because I will pound you into the ground."

"I'm not scared of you," Phoenix said with a sneer. "You're not a god anymore. Let go before I prove you're an old has been."

"*Kylee, Kita, stop it. We do not need a fallen angel rumble right now,*" said Aspen as she glided between the two fallen angels. Valentine grabbed Phoenix's arm. Tina flittered in front of Kita.

"Kylee, don't be a fool and underestimate your mom," said Valentine. "You don't know what power she has."

"I know what she doesn't have." Phoenix raised her fist and fired a purplish-black flame burning a section of Kita's face before Valentine grabbed Phoenix's arm.

Kita bared her teeth as her damaged face healed. She phased behind Phoenix and punched her in the back of the head, lower back, and between the wings. Bending at the knees, Kita spun and swept Phoenix's legs out from under her. She grabbed Phoenix by the hair and smashed her face against the deck. Lifting Phoenix's head, Kita pushed her index finger against Phoenix's forehead. Silver beads containing Phoenix's bionanites and Angel genetic material emerged from Phoenix's skin and ran to Kita's finger. Kita took Phoenix's abilities, leaving her a human with wings.

"What the slag are you doing, you psycho bitch?" Phoenix cried.

"I brought you into this world, I can take you out of it," Kita hissed as she dropped Phoenix's head.

"I'm still a god."

Kita drew Dead. "Then I'll send you to Infinity, and you can live like the other gods."

"You can't do this to me."

"Can and have. Enjoy being human. Push me further, and I'll take your wings." Kita turned to Rainbow Jack. The pilot's eyes were puffy, but her jaw set determined. Kita put her sword away. "Sorry. Sometimes my daughter's head gets too big for the universe. I'm sorry for the embarrassment and hurt we caused you. It wasn't my intention. I was impressed with your performance today and wanted to congratulate you. I see why you're the best. I was hoping you'd join us—so we might get a chance to know you. I promise you, no one means you any malice. You're among friends here. For some of us, you're our first exposure to the idea of a transgender person. You took us by surprise, and we reacted poorly. What is your name?"

"Alex Rodriguez."

"Alex, I'm terribly sorry. If you wish to leave, I understand. There will be no hard feelings, and I hope you can forgive us."

"Who are you? The Princess has already apologized."

"Really?" said Kita over the comm to Defiance.

"Someone had to do damage control on that little freak out. Your face was priceless, by the way. Watching you try and compute it was worth it."

"She did take me by surprise."

"You seemed to have adjusted quickly."

"Who am I to tell her what she can be? If she wants to be a girl, let her. I feel sorry for her having to spend so much of her life in the wrong body."

"Yes. I apologized for that also. Enterprise has been gone so long Alex missed her surgery date."

"She'll get another, right?"

"Of course."

Kita smiled at Alex. "My name is Kita. I'm the leader of the Angels."

Alex looked back at Defiance and Sheppard. "I thought you were Children of the emperor."

"We are. It's complicated."

"Kita and the others are friends of the Empire," said Defiance. "They've shared their technology with us, and in return, they have been made Children of the emperor."

"So, they're aliens?"

A few of the Angels giggled.

"No," said Kita. "We come from a lost world populated by citizens of the Empire. The planet was cut off and left to fend for itself. We are the apex of evolution, but Angels aren't born. They're made. Hence my interest in you."

"Me? I'm just a fighter pilot, and I'm loyal to the emperor."

"If you haven't noticed, some of the emperor's finest have wings."

"Admiral Sheppard is a legend, and the princess is, well, the princess."

"I also have Captain Jessica Rabbit and Lieutenant Amanda Gering of the Political Bureau."

The blood drained from Alex's face.

"They're quite nice once you get to know them," Kita said with a smile.

Valor and Stormy waved at the anxious pilot.

"The rest of these girls are either citizens of the Empire, survivors of the lost world, or girls I've met in Tet space. We have a myriad of talents and abilities. Most of us are fighters, and we're headed to Earth to settle a score with General Galina Lyakhova of the Political Bureau."

"What did she do?" said Alex while giving Stormy and Valor curious looks.

"To put it simply, she betrayed us and killed many of our friends in the process. Casey has been gracious enough to give us permission to go after her."

"Casey?"

Kita pointed and winked at Defiance.

"Kita is my girlfriend," said Defiance with a grin at Kita.

Alex's jaw dropped. "Your Highness, she's not—"

"Not what? You know nothing of Kita. She's not one of the political pedigree bulls that wander through the halls of Dallas. I think she's better. She was born into nobility, has reached the rank of commandant in the Legion, and been vicereine of an entire planet. I think she's one to bring home to mom."

"And what would your mom say about your wings and me?" said Kita.

"She'd probably sigh and wonder when the phase ends." Kita pouted as everyone else laughed. "You're not a phase, darlin'. You're mine."

"Eh-hem," said Panther. "I claimed her long ago. And you may be a princess, but I am the God of Murder."

"There's enough of me to go around," said Kita firmly to quell any violence.

"As long as I get mine," said Panther.

Defiance chuckled. "How am I supposed to compete with that?"

"You're not," said Kita. "No one is competing over me."

"You girls just don't do it right," said Anthrax. "Mom…Mom…MOM!"

Kita burst out laughing. She gave Anthrax a hug.

Alex gave off waves of confusion, doubt, and embarrassment.

"I'm many things to everyone," said Kita to Alex. "Most importantly I am a friend, mother, protector. We are a family, and we take care of one another. I think you have what it takes to join us."

"But why? What do I have to offer?" said Alex looking unsure and confused.

"I watched you today. You're the best fighter pilot by far. I look for people who are the best or have the potential to be the best." Kita smiled. "I can feel your conflict…your hesitation…your wonder. I can do many things…even make your dream come true, better than any surgeon."

"Damn. When did you become a temptress?" Babydoll chided with a laugh.

"I'm just saying."

"Who do you think you are?" said Alex. She gave Sheppard and Defiance a concerned look.

"To answer your question, I'm a god." Kita turned Alex around. The Valkyrie Angels and Tina changed to their god forms—their Angel form made of millions of points of light.

"What trick is this?" Alex exclaimed. "Your Highness! This isn't funny."

"It's not meant to be funny," said Defiance. "She's showing you the truth. There's more to the universe than even I understand."

"To prove to you I'm serious this is yours to keep." Kita brushed Alex's cheek with her hand.

Alex gasped and then doubled over. Tears flowed down her cheek. She cried in pain. After collapsing to the deck, she curled up in the fetal position. "By the emperor. What did you do to me?" she shrieked.

"What did you do?" demanded Defiance.

"I gave her what she wanted: to be female. The transformation is similar to getting wings, but it affects her entire body, not just her back. It'll be like a bad period."

"I never had a period."

"Lucky you."

Alex's body relaxed and her cries became whimpers. The other Angels looked on sympathetically.

Anthrax knelt next to Alex and checked on her. "What did you do, Kita? I don't see any wings."

"I made her female," said Kita.

Anthrax took Alex's arm and drew a blood sample using the barb in the heel of her hand. While she analyzed the sample, she ran her hand over Alex's body. "Damn, Kita. You did more than swap out parts—you changed her chromosomes. I can't even tell she was ever male."

"Good. I'd hate myself if I'd missed something."

"No wings?" said Tina.

"She got the basic Angel package. We'll see if she gets wings."

Alex rolled onto her back and bent her legs. She took a few deep breaths. "By the emperor, what happened?" She raised her head and looked at Kita. "What did you do to me?"

"Have a look."

"At what?"

"Does it feel like something's missing?" scoffed Toxic.

Alex's hand darted between her legs. She tore open her flight suit and peeked into her underwear. "It's gone."

"Replaced with a real working set of ovaries, a uterus, and a vagina. Your body is now female—as if you were born that way."

"How?" exclaimed Alex.

"I told you we were gods, but I use that to speed up the process. It's just good old-fashioned biochemistry."

Tears welled up in Alex's eyes. "Thank you."

"I know what it's like to be different."

Alex stood up and gave Kita a hug. "I'm forever indebted to you."

"It's yours to keep, as are the other gifts."

"Other gifts?"

"Talk to the Angels, they'll tell you, but I need to go."

"Go where?"

"Out. I'll be back."

Kita took a step back and phased on top of Enterprise near the stern. The stars filled the darkness. She sighed heavily, and tears trickled down her cheeks.

"Hey, baby, are you ok?" said Panther putting a hand on Kita's shoulder. Defiance's hand touched her other shoulder.

Babydoll walked around Panther. "You ok, killer?"

Kita shook her head.

"What's wrong, darlin'," said Defiance as she wrapped her arm around Kita's waist.

"There was a time when I wished someone would come and fix me. I wanted so badly to be normal...to like boys. To make my father and mother love me and not be the outcast—the despised—the vile polluter. I just didn't want people to hate me." Kita buried her face in her hands.

"I'm so sorry, sweetheart. No one should have to grow up in that environment."

"But you wouldn't be who you are if you hadn't," said Panther.

"I know," whispered Kita, "but everyone knows I'm different."

"And we love you for it," said Babydoll.

"Could you imagine Kita if she was normal?" said Panther.

"Yeah, she would have married some noble scum, lived miserably bearing children, and finally died in a drafty stone house."

"By the Crushing Depths. That sounds awful," Kita said with a tearful chuckle.

"Instead, you're standing on top of a giant warship willing to do your heart's desire, with no protective suit, staring at the stars in the arms of two gods and a princess. I like the different Kita way better."

Kita sighed. *Still so far to go.*

CHAPTER XII

A chime woke Kita. The panel on the wall flashed an incoming call. Kita pulled the covers over her chest, hiding the two heads beside her, and sat up. "Answer," Kita said quietly.

Sheppard's face appeared. "Kita! Hey, sorry to wake you, but I thought you'd like to know Snowy is out of surgery and awake."

"Thanks, Rene. I'll go down and talk to her so we can get out of here. Have you taken any rest?"

"Not yet. I'm trying to get the ship up to standard. The Tet left an awful mess, and the crew is trying to get back into rhythm."

"Don't overwork them. They need a break, too. Being a prisoner can be exhausting."

"I've been rotating them."

Kita nodded. "Make sure you take a rotation. I'll get somebody to order it if I have to."

"Do you know where the Princess disappeared to? I haven't seen her in almost an entire shift."

Kita glanced next to her. Defiance's head appeared from under the sheet.

"Ta-da, you found me, Admiral. Is there something you need?"

Sheppard hung her head. "I'm speechless."

Panther popped her head on Kita's other side. "What's she speechless about?" She let out a large cat-like yawn.

Sheppard's mouth hung open.

"What?" said Kita.

"I—I—I've got nothing," Sheppard replied with a despondent look.

"Rene, don't be like that. Mostly we've been sleeping, but I owed Casey some time, and Vee joined us. If you need help, we'll come. You don't have to do it yourself."

"No. I just—just get the coordinates of where we need to go." Sheppard broke the connection.

"She seemed upset over us," said Defiance.

Kita took Panther's hand and opened a cloud connection for a brief conversation about Sheppard's reaction.

"Yes, but Vee and I agree it's not what you think."

"Oh?"

"She wasn't mad we were together," said Panther. "She's upset because she felt excluded."

"How do we make her feel included? I don't think I want to sleep with her."

Kita shrugged. "I have no idea. I think she wants to be with someone, not us specifically. It's been a long time since she's been with anybody except Galina. I'm sure those last couple of years were like having a gun to her head."

Panther rested her head against Kita's arm. "Maybe we could set her up with someone?"

"Like who? Rene's married to her career. Few people understand that. That's why she and Galina got along so well—in the beginning."

"She needs someone who could take her away from it," said Defiance.

Kita made a face. "Yeah, but who?"

"How about one of the new girls?"

"None of the Valkyries will be willing," said Panther sitting up. "She's left a bad taste in everybody's mouth, and it's still too early for her to have repaired the damage."

"That doesn't leave many," said Defiance with a frown.

"Only Amanda and she's too inexperienced to handle Rene," said Kita warily.

"What about the new girl?"

"What new girl?" said Kita.

"The new girl you just made—Alex."

"She doesn't have wings."

"And how long until she does?" said Defiance with a smirk.

"I don't know. Maybe never."

Defiance laughed. "Oh, please. You like her. You're just playing coy."

Panther nodded in agreement.

Kita frowned. "She didn't seem receptive."

"She was defensive because of what Kylee did," said Defiance.

"How do we get them in a room, away from their military bearing?" said Panther.

"I can do that," said Defiance. "I can order them to come to movie night or something."

"We should talk to Alex first and see what she thinks," said Kita.

Defiance laughed and gently hit Kita on the arm. "Look at you being Miss Sensitive."

"I know I wouldn't like to be put into that situation."

Defiance tapped her nail on her teeth. "Good point. Let's talk to Snowy, and then we'll find Alex."

~

KITA LED PANTHER AND DEFIANCE TO THE MEDICAL WARD ABOARD Enterprise. Along the way, Babydoll joined them.

"You're looking better," Babydoll said teasing Kita.

"Time with my girls does wonders."

"Your girls?" said Panther feigning being offended.

"I think you're our girl," said Defiance.

Before Kita could say anything, there was a loud cat-like scream from the medical ward.

"Sounds like Snowy's more than awake," chuckled Babydoll.

"I wonder what fool told her about Sahara," muttered Panther.

"I don't know," said Kita, "but we should go save Snowy from herself."

Defiance opened the door. Inside, Snowy, claws out and in a full back brace and halo, faced down two Marines—with their weapons lowered—looking uncertain of what to do. Several beds were on their sides. The rest of the staff was huddling in corners or in other rooms.

"Snowy," yelled Kita in her command voice.

Snowy turned to face the four Angels. She pointed at Babydoll with her claws. "You! I will kill you or send you back to whatever hell you came from."

Babydoll held up a hand. "Hey, I was doing your girlfriend a favor. I roughed her up a bit. Case would have killed her."

"You nearly killed her."

"The operative word in that sentence is *nearly*. I didn't kill her."

"How am I going to explain this to Collector?" Snowy thought for a second and pointed a claw at Kita. "How are you going to explain it to him?"

Kita shrugged. "I haven't thought about it, beyond telling him the truth."

"That you murdered a ship full of Verisom and Diamock sailors?"

Kita held up six fingers. "I killed six ships full of Tet sailors. I thought they should learn a lesson about taking something that isn't theirs—and for locking me up like a guppy."

"Are you crazy?" Snowy shrieked. "No, don't answer that. The Tet will hunt us down for sure."

Kita shrugged. "As far as the Tet knows, nothing has happened. No one's left to report it. All they'll know is five ships were destroyed, and Enterprise is gone. Someone might hypothesize that I'm behind it, but they'll be chasing ghosts. I'm not planning on leaving them a calling card with the quadrants of where we're going. Speaking of which, I need those coordinates so I can get us out of here in case someone does show up."

Snowy bared her fangs. "Collector's not going to stand for this, and neither am I."

"Oh, shush," said Panther. "You're just upset your girlfriend got herself broken. If it weren't for Sahara, you'd be all over Kita."

Snowy's nose flushed. "Sahara was doing her duty. Which is something you'd know nothing about, you bedroom plaything."

"I don't care what Sahara was doing or thinking she was doing," said Kita. "She got in my way—which we all know has consequences. Casey, Nell, Tina, and Leaf graciously offered their services in putting her back together. I understand it's going to take time to heal. I will explain what happened to Collector. I'm not afraid of him, and now that we have

Enterprise I don't need him. If he wants to get feisty about it, I have a hostage. Think about that."

Snowy's ears flattened against her head, her whiskers drooped, and the blood drained from her nose. "You—you wouldn't dare."

"I'm getting to Earth one way or another. If Collector wants me to lead his little armada, then he's going to need to do as I say. Otherwise, I'll take Enterprise, jump through the Alicorn wormhole, and warn the Shadow Fleet of what's coming and he'll never get his little war.

"If you don't want your girlfriend going home to daddy in an ammo box, I suggest you give me what I want to know, get back in bed, and be ready to fight when I call for you, understand?"

Snowy retracted her claws and lowered her head. "I never thought the day would come when you would treat me like this."

Kita grinned. "You treated me like this for years, and like a fool, I loved you for it. Now, I'm much older, wiser, and confident in myself. I don't need you to raise my self-esteem. I can do that on my own, and I have friends who don't treat me as a prize to be won. But now, you're not a prize for me. You're just Snowy. I hope Sahara brings you the happiness I couldn't. I still count you as my friend, but sometimes you have to tell friends when they're wrong and put them in their place."

Snowy sniffed. "You put me in mine. The rendezvous point is the Jentex system out in the quarantine zone."

"Thank you," said Kita. "Now go back to bed and let these poor people do what they need."

With her tail dragging on the deck, Snowy walked down the line of beds to the last one and climbed in.

"Shall we fix these?" said Kita motioning to the upturned beds.

The Angels righted the beds and put them back in line. Defiance checked on her Marines.

"There's item one off our list," said Kita with a smile. "Shall we move on to number two?"

∾

"THIS IS AN EXQUISITE TEA SET, CASEY," SAID KITA AS SHE STUDIED THE painting of a cosmic scene on a saucer. "This would rival any my mother owned. Where did you get it?"

"Oh, it belongs to the ship."

"The ship has a tea set?" Panther commented with a laugh.

"It has a complete set of dishware and silverware," said Defiance. "Enterprise is meant to be a diplomatic ship as well as a warship. It represents the Empire." She took the saucer from Kita and put it on the table. "I know your reputation," she teased.

Kita made a playful face. "I had tea with the high princesses of Verisom and managed not to break anything."

"And today you'll have coffee with me."

"Coffee?" Kita stuck out her tongue. "That stuff is awful."

"You've only had the synthesized stuff. Coffee made from a bean is a delicacy," said Defiance.

"I don't think you can fix bitter mud."

"What's wrong with tea?" said Panther.

"Goes back to pre-Empire days when the United States of America was vying for independence. The good citizens of the USA were tea drinkers until the crown put a tax on it. To protest, the citizens of Boston threw several shiploads of tea into the harbor. Since then, the USA and later the UEE have drunk coffee to get their caffeine fix."

"Tea is good, but I'll take Atomic Blast any day," said Kita.

"Not today," said Defiance. "We're entertaining a guest, and we'll serve what they like."

"How do you know what she likes?"

"She's a pilot. She drinks coffee. The question is what variation? I'll offer black and espresso."

"There's more than one type of coffee?" asked Panther.

"There are probably thousands of specialty blends, but we'll go with the basics today." The door chimed. "Ah, she's here. Ladies, take your places," Defiance ordered as she moved to the door.

Kita did not like being ordered around, especially for a glorified tea party. She'd spent too much of her life attending them as it was. She caught Panther's eye, and the other Angel shrugged.

"At least this isn't a formal event," said Panther.

Kita grunted to that.

"Major Garcia, I'm glad you made it," said Defiance when the door opened.

Alex's face went white when she saw Defiance.

"Please, come in, Major."

"Ye—yes, Your Highness," Alex said sounding like she was trying to keep the shock from her voice.

"And call me Casey, Alex. This is an informal event." Defiance led Alex over to the sitting area where Kita and Panther waited with pleasant smiles on their faces. "You met Kita earlier, and this is Panther."

Panther smiled revealing her fangs while her tail waved behind her playfully. "Call me Vee, please."

Alex looked at Panther and gulped.

"Please, be seated," said Defiance.

Kita waited for Alex to take a seat before she and Panther sat.

"How do you like your coffee, Alex?" said Defiance as she picked up the coffee pot.

"Black, two sugar, ah, thank you."

"A pilot after my own heart. I always felt cream was for the weak."

Defiance made up a cup for Alex and served her.

"And how do you like yours, ladies?" said Defiance to Kita and Panther over the comm.

"No idea," said Panther.

"Do you like it sweet, milky, or with a bite?"

"Sweet and milky."

"Coming up. Kita, darling?"

"As sweet as possible. Why didn't you just ask us?"

"To show her we do this often enough that I don't need to ask. It shows you're regulars of mine."

"I thought I was," said Kita.

"Not in a social way...yet."

"Oh, goodie. What is it with princesses and their need to be social?"

"Comes with the job, unfortunately." Defiance poured the coffee and made each cup up, then handed a cup to Kita and one to Panther. She made hers last and sat back in her chair opening her wings and crossing her legs. "So, Alex, how are things on the flight line? Are they going to be able to put your fighter back together?"

Alex looked at her coffee.

"Feel free to drink up. The scones are good, too."

"Thank you. My—my fighter is a total loss, according to the maintenance officer." Alex's shoulders slumped.

Kita felt a great deal of loss coming from Alex. The fighter must have meant a lot to her.

"We'll get you another," said Defiance firmly. "I can't afford to have a pilot of your skill without a fighter. Your performance during the battle was commendable—above and beyond the call of duty."

"I—I couldn't let them destroy the carrier."

"Using an MSMB that way is genius. I'll have to have you teach the other wizzos how to do it."

Alex's eyes shifted side-to-side. "I guess I could."

"Casey, we didn't invite Alex here to talk shop," said Kita.

"Yes, I know. It's hard when you get two pilots together. Tell me, Alex, how's the new body? Did you visit the docs yet? I'm sure Supply was surprised when you drew new everything."

Alex flushed. "I haven't had time to see the docs yet. I'm..."

Kita felt Alex's embarrassment and discomfort, and decided to help her. "It's ok to not be comfortable. It'll take some getting used to."

"I couldn't wait for it to be gone and now...I feel lost."

"We should schedule you some time with the ship psychiatrist," said Defiance. "This is a big change, and it was sudden."

"I don't know how you did it, and don't take my response as I'm not grateful or happy. I am. I really am. It's just a lot to process."

"Of course," said Kita. "We understand. We've all gone through drastic changes and understand it takes time to adjust. I'm glad you're happy. I try and help those who deserve it."

Alex took a long pull off her coffee. "Can I ask you something else? Something I've noticed?"

"Sure."

"I haven't been hungry or sleepy."

Kita chuckled. "I thought I told the others to explain it, but along with becoming a woman, you received what I call *the basic Angel package*. You're stronger, you heal quickly, the spectrum your eyes see is expanded, you only need to sleep every two to three weeks, and only eat once a month. But be forewarned, when you do you'll put it away by the plateful."

"I'm to become like you?"

"Maybe. We'll see if you have what it takes. I was impressed with what I saw during the battle. Keep it up, and I don't see why not."

"Will I still be able to fly?"

"Definitely," said Defiance. "We wouldn't keep you from your passion. Your new fighter might need to be redesigned for wings."

"Can I ask a personal question, Vee?" said Alex.

"Sure."

"How did you get a tail and spots?"

Panther chuckled. She poked Kita in the ribs causing her to squeak. "Someone has a thing for cats. When I became an Angel, I got my spots and tail."

"They're beautiful."

"They are, aren't they?" said Kita as she leaned in to give Panther a kiss on the cheek and raise an eyebrow at Alex to show where there was a boundary.

"I'm sorry," said Alex. "I didn't mean—"

"It's ok, Alex. Kita's territorial. Which she shouldn't be," said Defiance.

Kita set her cup down, walked over to Defiance, and kissed her on the cheek. "Happy?"

Defiance laughed. "I think you're my territory."

The three Angels turned to look at Alex. The poor girl looked petrified.

"It's complicated," said Defiance as she took Alex's hand. "Kita, why don't you sit down."

Kita shrugged, sat, and picked up her coffee. She tasted it for the first time and made a face. *It's got nothing on Atomic Blast.*

"Why don't we go back to talking about pilot stuff," said Panther.

Kita sighed to herself and settled in to wait.

∽

"Hey, Rene, we got our destination," Kita called ignoring the looks she received for yelling across the bridge.

Sheppard looked up from a huddle of officers. She excused herself and met Kita near the holotable. "I heard there was an altercation in the medical ward."

Kita held up her hands. "It was going on when we got there."

"Snowy was upset over Sahara," said Defiance rolling her eyes.

"Damn that cat anyway," said Sheppard. "Why can't she accept an ass kicking and move on?"

"Kita put her in her place," said Panther. "I don't think we'll see much trouble out of her again."

"That I would like to see," said Sheppard raising an eyebrow at Kita. "Snowy is a favorite."

"She chose her side, and it wasn't me," said Kita firmly. "I don't care how fuzzy you are. If you're not loyal to me, I won't help you."

"The question is: Will she get another chance?" said Babydoll coming up to the group from talking with the Marine leadership.

"Kerri, what are you doing here?" said Kita.

"I was bored. Rene's good at finding people things to do. Infantry is my specialty, so I'm working with the Marines and showing them how the Legion does things."

"I thought it would be beneficial," said Sheppard. "Teaching the Marines how the Legion operates will make integration easier when we meet up with the Legion."

"Works for me," said Kita. "How are the other girls doing?"

Babydoll shrugged. "Most are getting used to being Angels again. Some, like Leaf and Tenshi, have gone back to training like they never left. Nell is in the medical ward. She said she's behind in her medical knowledge."

"I thought she was versed in everything," said Kita.

"It's a big jump from the best we had on your homeworld to UEE proper. Valentine is around somewhere. She's enjoying being with the ship."

Kita smiled. Valentine was sharing all sorts of discoveries with her through their computer connection. As Valentine learned about the ship so did Kita.

"Kylee is sulking somewhere and making life miserable for anybody that comes into her orbit. Kara's kept her company. I think part of Kylee's trouble is Val isn't paying much attention to her."

"I told Val to do what was best for her and leave Kylee to me. Right now, Kylee can rot as long as she doesn't cause any major trouble."

"That's kind of hard when you're a human with wings," Panther said with a chuckle.

"That's the idea," said Kita.

"Raptor requested a bigger training area," said Babydoll.

Kita looked at Defiance and Sheppard for an answer.

"When we're not doing flight operations she can use one of the runways," said Sheppard.

"You better prepare the crew to expect dinosaurs," said Babydoll.

"I'm sure she'll be a big draw. I hope she doesn't mind. I can see people sneaking off their shift to get a chance to see her," Sheppard said with a heavy sigh.

"I don't think Raptor will mind as long as people stay out of her way," said Kita.

"I have no idea what your Angels have been up to," Babydoll said with a shrug.

"They're fine. Most are helping down in the Political Bureau shop."

"I think it's funny you recruited from our enemy."

Kita smiled. "How better to strengthen us and weaken them in one move?"

"You are the master," Babydoll said with a wink.

"So, Kita, where are we going?" said Sheppard.

"Oh, the Jentex system, out past Toeak space."

"I don't remember anything out there."

"I think that's the idea. When we jump in, I'll get Snowy to hail Collector's fleet. I'm sure it'll be a splendid reunion. Make sure we have an escape plan if the meeting sours."

"Not like you to be so unsure," said Babydoll.

"I don't trust him," said Kita flatly. "We have his daughter, so I don't think he'll try anything too stupid, but better to be prepared."

Some eyebrows went up.

"Sahara is his daughter?" said Babydoll.

"That's what I've been told."

"The plot thickens."

Kita grinned. "Oh, yes."

CHAPTER XIII

*A*nthrax set her tray down piled high with five plates of food at a table with Aspen, Kamikaze, Tenshi, Tina, and Raptor. The Angels occupied a corner of the wardroom, as the rooms aboard Enterprise were too small and cramped for wings.

"You should have seen the look I just got from a girl," Anthrax said rolling her eyes.

"I be betten' she not be believen' you look like ya do after eaten what ya do," said Raptor. "Or maybe it be the seven patches you be wearen'."

"It's not my fault. It's not like I want to eat all this. Getting used to being an Angel again sucks. Why can't we be gods again?"

"Because we support Kita," said Aspen. *"If you'll excuse me, I need to go back to the practice room."* She flittered out of her seat for the door.

"That girl acts like its ten years ago, and we have Machines to fight," scoffed Anthrax.

"Who knows what enemies we'll face," said Tenshi. "I've been hitting the range. I'm not as good as I used to be. My time in the assault course is off by two seconds."

Anthrax rolled her eyes. "Not two seconds."

"Those two seconds can save your life."

"What be ya problem, Annie? Normally ya not be so critical," said Raptor.

"It's just some people have fallen back into life like they never left, leaving the rest of us behind. And we've barely seen Kita. She's been too busy shacked up with Vee and the Princess."

"I be thinken' Kita be thinken' we be big girls and can be taken care of ourselves."

"It would be nice to talk to her, instead of her expecting we'll fall back in line."

"You don't like the medical ward?" said Tina.

"It's fine and more advanced than anything we've ever worked with, but I don't feel like we're a team."

"Ha," said Raptor. "We be barely a team ten years ago. We hardly be seen' Kita back then, too."

"Maybe it's that I don't like being an Angel. Being a god is so much easier," Anthrax said with a sigh.

"Wasn't that the point?" said Tenshi. "Being a god was too easy. We wanted something different, something challenging. But maybe I don't think it's so bad because I've joined with an Angel before."

"I did this because I wanted to be free to pursue my own course. I was tired of being dictated to what I had to study and always having to report in. I just want to enjoy diseases."

"But you can," said Tina. "The ward is a great place to see them."

"So far I've seen a broken arm and a cold. Not really the pandemics I was looking for," scoffed Anthrax.

"Maybe you should go play with Pestilence," said Kamikaze.

"I wish we had more to do."

"This ship is boring," said Tina. "But has some cute crewmembers."

Anthrax rolled her eyes. "I'm not interested in sleeping around."

"More for me then. I'm not going to let my sister have all the fun."

Anthrax shivered. "I can't imagine someone else touching me."

"You must be meanen' besides Nina?" said Raptor.

Anthrax nodded. "It still feels like she'll come into the room at any second."

"She's dead," said Kamikaze. "Why can't you get over it? She's not coming back. There's nothing any of us can do."

"And what should I do? Forget her? At least you have your partner."

"That doesn't mean I haven't lost partners in the past. Don't forget, I've lived a lot longer than you. I miss every one of them, but you don't hear me lamenting. They're dead. I mourned, and moved on. I understand wanting time, but to keep wishing they'll walk through the door at any moment doesn't help you. It hurts you."

Anthrax huffed. "I'm sorry I'm not as tough and as hard as you, Kami. My heart hurts. I loved that girl, maybe more than you'll ever know."

Kamikaze bared a fang. "I loved my partners with all my heart and watched them grow old and die. You know how hard that is? Knowing there's nothing you can do to stop it? Don't try and make your pain greater than mine. I'll win. If I did what you're doing, I never would have given Tenshi a chance, and I would be missing out on so much."

"Just because—"

An alarm sounded through the wardroom.

"What that be meanen'?" said Raptor to Tina.

"I have no idea."

Around the room, the officers shoved their trays to the center of the table and stood up.

"I think it best we be doen' what they be doen'," ordered Raptor.

The Angels stood up and looked at one another.

"FTL jump in ten," said the ship's computer, "...nine... eight... seven... six... five... four... three... two... one... mark."

Anthrax's stomach dropped to her toes as the world went black.

~

THE FAMILIAR DROPPING SENSATION PASSED. KITA WAS USED TO IT BY NOW AND waited for the holotable to update with the current quadrant information. So far, only the planet and the moon were visible. Kita could see them by looking out the window.

According to information dug up on Tet-Net, the interstellar network, Jentex was supposed to be uninhabited, except by the occasional bandit. *We should scare off any bandit or raider.*

"Any signs of life?" Kita called to Sheppard.

"I know what you know. Sensors, anything?"

"Scanning now, Ma'am. Combat scan will complete in ten seconds."

Kita wrinkled her nose. The combat scan was good for displaying the obvious. The fact that no one was here to meet them worried her. The hair on the back of her neck stood up. She hit the communications panel on the holotable and called the medical ward.

"I need to speak to Doctor Anthrax or Angel Tina," she told the orderly that answered. Kita glanced out the window. *I wonder what's waiting for us out there.*

"Hey, big sister. What do you need?" said Tina.

"Get Snowy on the line. We've arrived in the Jentex system, and no one is here."

"I think she's awake. Give me a second."

A hold pattern appeared on the screen. Kita grumbled, but it was better than watching life at some obtuse angle as she was moved around. The screen flashed, and Snowy and Tina appeared.

"I don't want to talk to her," Snowy said firmly.

"This isn't a social call," said Tina.

Snowy sighed and took the screen. "What, Kita?"

"We're in the Jentex system, and there's no one here. Who was your contact supposed to be?"

"I—I don't know. Sahara knows all that."

Kita sneered. "And I thought you were the trusted associate."

"I am, but it was given to her, and no one told me."

"Great. Tina!"

"Yeah?"

"Take me to Sahara's room."

Tina shook her head. "She's still under."

"Then wake her up. I don't have time to wait."

"It might hurt her worse."

"So?" Kita said tersely. "I'm not waiting around for her to recover from her mistake. If she's got to suffer more, all the better. Maybe she'll learn."

Tina sighed and took the screen from Snowy. In the background, Kita could see Snowy get out of bed before Tina put up the hold screen.

Kita took out a nail file and worked on a chip in her nail. Tina appeared with Anthrax in the background. Snowy stood to one side holding Sahara's hand.

"We gave her something to wake her up," said Tina.

Kita continued to work on her nail. "Let me know when she wakes up. Rene, anything?"

"Negative, Kita. There's nothing out here. We found a pair of dead satellites orbiting the planet, but that's it. We detect no ship signatures."

"Kita, she's awake," said Tina as she propped the screen up in front of Sahara.

"Sahara, this is Kita. We've arrived in the Jentex system, and we need to contact Collector's fleet. Snowy says you know the access codes and the frequencies we need."

"I demand to talk to Collector," Sahara said in a raspy voice. "You have violated the agreement, and it must be reported. He will decide if you can contact the fleet."

Kita's brow furrowed. "I don't have time to wait for you to run home to daddy and cry that you got beaten up on the playground. This ship doesn't belong to him and what goes on aboard is none of his business. I *am* going to keep my end of the bargain and lead his forces to victory. You can either be a hindrance or a help."

"I will never give you the codes until I speak to Collector."

Kita traced her canine with her tongue. "How are you with small spaces, Sahara? Because I'm going to shove you into a coffin and fire you into space. Think about it—a slowly decreasing air supply as the temperature drops with barely enough room to raise your hands to your head. How long do you think you'd last before the terror slowly slips in? That cramped box is all that's keeping the depths of space from you—I will do it—and I'll jump the ship to the middle of nowhere so there will be no chance you'll ever be found. I don't care about you, you're just in my way."

On screen, Babydoll and Panther appeared. They seized Sahara's arms and pulled her from the bed.

"Kita! Stop!" demanded Snowy.

"She wants to test my resolve. We'll see who's willing to die for their cause. I know I am, how about your girl?"

"Kita, let me talk to her."

"You can talk to her as Vee and Kerri carry her to the flight deck. We'll use one of the catapult launchers to fling her into space."

"Don't be a monster," Snowy begged.

"I'm not a monster. I'm getting results. I've seen how Collector gets results, remember Casey?"

Defiance stuck her head into the video feed. "He dissected me. This is nothing compared to what your boss does."

"He's not my boss," Snowy argued weakly.

"Better get talking," urged Kita as the group left the medical ward for the elevator to the flight decks.

"Amanda, Jess, can you bring me up a coffin and meet us on runway three?" said Kita.

"Sure. Who'd you kill?" said Valor.

"No one—yet. I'm trying to extract some information."

"We have methods for that," said Stormy.

"Yes, but this is far more fun."

"We'll be right there," said Valor.

Kita and Defiance boarded the elevator and joined the group escorting Sahara. The Djinn was too weak to struggle much in Panther and Babydoll's grasps. The group took the elevator to the flight deck. Sailors and Marines in the corridor pressed against the walls to give Kita's group space. A few crewmembers jeered the Djinn. *They probably think she's what remains of their captors.*

They reached the flight line.

"Kita," said Defiance, "I just contacted Launch Control. We have someone manning the launchers waiting for the order."

Kita nodded. Stormy, Valor, Blitz, and Starlight arrived with the coffin. "Attach it to the launcher, girls." She approached Snowy and Sahara. "Are we done playing hero? I'm sure Collector will not fault your dedication to him. But I'm done waiting. Put her in."

"Kita, stop!" cried Snowy.

"You had your chance. Now it's my turn."

Babydoll and Panther placed Sahara in the coffin. Kita stood at the head of the coffin and looked down at Sahara.

"Jess, give me a communicator."

Valor took a device from her belt and gave it to Kita. She turned it on and set the frequency, then placed it in Sahara's hand.

"What's the range of the communicator?" asked Kita.

"About fifty miles," said Valor.

"Case, tell them to set the launcher for five miles per minute." Kita knelt down next to Sahara. "You have ten minutes to make up your mind. Give me what I want, and I promise you'll be rescued and you can go back to bed. Or you can prove your loyalty to Collector until you die." Kita reached over and pulled the coffin lid closed. Sahara's eyes went wide as she shook her head. Kita waved good-bye.

Kita stood up and motioned for everyone to step back. "Fire when ready, Casey."

Defiance signaled Launch Control. There was a metallic *clack,* and the coffin raced down the launcher out into space.

"How long do you think she'll last?" said Babydoll.

"I bet she already thinks ten minutes have gone by," said Panther.

"Casey, can you get a search and rescue shuttle ready to go catch her," said Kita.

"You expect her to call your bluff?" said Stormy.

"What bluff? I want the body recovered, so I have something to dump at Collector's feet. Time to return to the bridge. We'll know her decision by the time we get there."

～

"RENE, ANY COMMUNIQUÉS WITH OUR NEWEST FIGHTER?" KITA ASKED AS SHE approached Sheppard and the holotable.

Sheppard rolled her eyes. "That was grotesque, even for you."

"But did it work?"

Sheppard sighed. "Yes. She called. We patched her through and broadcast the message. We're awaiting a reply."

"Is Sahara getting picked up?"

"The shuttle is on its way."

"Good. Jess, Amanda, Snowy, why don't you meet Sahara and get her back to the medical ward. I'm sure she'll be stressed from her ordeal."

"You are such a bitch," hissed Snowy. "To think I stuck my neck out to save you."

"No one asked you to. If I had, you'd be a god right now."

"Ouch. Sick burn," said Babydoll.

"Admiral," yelled the officer from Sensors. "We have a new contact bearing three four five, five degrees up. New sighting, check that. Multiple sightings. Three, four, seven, fourteen, eighteen…twenty."

"Where'd they come from?" demanded Sheppard.

"No idea, ma'am. They just appeared."

"Well," said Kita. "Let's not be left in suspense. Put me through on the channel Sahara used."

"Rodger," said Sheppard as she gave the order.

On the holotable, the image of a Djinn appeared.

"Where is Sahara?" he demanded.

"Indisposed. I'm Captain Kita. The one she was assigned to bring to you."

"Produce Sahara to confirm your identity."

"I don't take orders from you," said Kita as she crossed her arms. "I need to talk with Collector. While I do that, you are to prepare your fleet for a new commander. Send your ships friend/foe identifiers to my ship so we can update our display."

"I am the commander of this fleet," the Djinn roared.

"And who are you?"

"I am Admiral Kakafar aboard the flagship Jeffar."

"We'll see what you're in charge of after I talk with Collector. In the meantime, prepare your fleet for inspection."

"I will do no such thing. We do not need you to fight our battles for us. You will submit and obey, female. Produce Sahara—that is your order."

"You have no power to order me to do anything. Collector wanted me, and I will talk to him. He said I am to lead you. Now, prepare for my arrival. If you're not ready by the time I arrive, I'll have your mane."

Kita cut the connection. "Kerri, round up Kami, Val, Raptor, and Rene. We're going on a field trip."

"Going to get fitted for a shawl?"

Kita grinned. "The way the kitties are behaving we'll all have fur coats by the time this is over."

"I could go for a cute fur-lined bomber jacket," said Defiance.

"Anything my girl wants," said Kita with a wink.

"Maybe some boots to match—Oh, and gloves."

CHAPTER XIV

"Captain Kita," called the shuttle pilot.

Kita stuck her head into the cockpit. "Yeah?"

"We're receiving a transmission from the Djinn ship, they say they don't have any docking bays open for us and their flex tube collars aren't compatible with our ring."

"Transfer the message to the back," said Kita as she moved into the passenger compartment. She waited for the communication panel message light to blink. When it did, she hit the answer button. A Djinn, not Kakafar, appeared.

"Why can't I get a docking bay?" Kita demanded of the Djinn before he had a chance to open his mouth.

"They're full."

"So, make room."

"I'm under orders to tell you to return to your ship, and a shuttle will be sent to retrieve Sahara."

"No way," said Kita. "I'm in charge, not Kakafar." Kita stuck her head into the cockpit doorway. "Pilot, find an airlock." She returned to the panel. "You're tracking us?"

The Djinn bared his fangs. "Of course."

"Good. Then open the airlock my pilot finds. Otherwise, I'll rip it open."

The Djinn chuckled. "You haven't the equipment."

Kita held up her fist, and it burst into flame. "On the contrary, I have everything I need."

"Found one, Captain," reported the pilot.

"Good. Move us within a few yards. Seal yourself in and prepare to decompress the passenger compartment."

Once the cockpit door was sealed, the side door to the passage compartment opened. Across from them was a rectangular airlock door.

"Alright, ladies. Let's knock," said Kita to the other Angels. She led the way, jumping from the shuttle, across open space, and landing against the ship's hull. One by one, the Angels made the leap.

Kita moved to a hinge, melted through it, and went to the second.

"Everyone, grab hold and lift," said Kita to the other Angels after she melted through the second hinge. *"One, two, three!"*

The Angels pulled. The door slid out of its frame, and the Angels tossed it into space. Kita jumped down the hole, rotating her body to orient herself with the ship. She came to rest in front of the inner door. She banged on it sharply.

"They're not going to be able to open the inner door without decompressing the ship," said Valentine.

"Whatever," said Kita. *"The point has been made. We'll just transform into*

clouds and pass through. Denver, I'm going to pass you everything I know about Tet ship computer design and engineering. I want you to try and see what you can get into."

"Sure thing."

Kita transformed into her cloud and moved over Defiance. The other Angels transformed into their clouds and followed Kita through the door.

The airlock area was small and lined with maintenance pressure suits. A Djinn officer and a trio of guards waited in armored pressure suits. Behind them, the door to the rest of the ship was closed.

"At least they're not that stupid," said Babydoll as she transformed into her Angelic form along with the other Angels.

"Neptune's rings, nothing prepares you for that cold," said Defiance after Kita released her. "I want my gloves, jacket, and boots, Kita."

Kita grinned and turned her attention to the Djinn. "You can take those suits off. The compartment is pressurized."

The Djinn officer took a panel from his belt and looked at the readout. Satisfied, he took off his helmet.

He must be young. The Djinn officer didn't have a full mane, and his face wasn't as thick and heavy as an older male Djinn.

"Who are you?" demanded Kita of the young Djinn.

"Second Ensign Gargah. I'm to escort you to Captain Kakafar."

"I don't care to talk to him. I need to talk to Collector."

"The quantum entanglement communicator requires Captain Kakafar to operate it. You must speak to him. But before we go any further, you are to turn over all weapons."

Kita laughed. "If you can pry them from our cold, dead hands. For some of us, you'll have to straight up kill us."

A Djinn guard pulled a scanner from his belt and scanned the Angels. "Only that one, that one, and that one," he said pointing at Defiance, Sheppard, and Valentine.

Valentine pulled her pistols and pointed them at the Djinn. "Come and get them."

"I don't think you understand, Ensign Gargah," said Kamikaze as she slid her claws out. "We don't carry weapons, we are weapons."

Kita burst into flame, Babydoll's fist glowed with ghostly purplish-black light, Sheppard's elbow pulsed blue, Defiance frosted over, and Valentine aimed her pistols at Gargah's forehead.

"You're welcome to try," said Kita.

Gargah took the panel from his belt and tapped on it. "Then your guard detail will need to be increased."

"That just saves us from having to hunt them down," said Defiance.

Gargah ignored her and opened the door leading to the rest of the ship. "Follow me. I will take you to Captain Kakafar."

Kita looked at the other Angels and shrugged. She led the others out and followed the young Djinn. As they walked, guards fell in beside and behind them.

"Are they trying to intimidate us or are they scared of us?" said Valentine as she checked out the guard beside her.

"My guess is to intimidate," said Kita. *"The Djinn aren't the kind to show fear or weakness."*

The Angels followed Gargah through the ship until they passed through a reinforced door. Inside the walls narrowed.

"Girls, be ready," said Kita. *"We're entering a boarding checkpoint."*

"What's that?" said Babydoll.

"It's a place to repel boarders. The Tet never developed fighters. Instead, they slug it out ship-to-ship or send thousands of boarders to capture a ship. This area will have automated weapons and protection for the defenders."

"And the Djinn are the ones that taste like blueberry?"

"Yep."

"Well, let the ass-kicking begin."

Kita led the Angels through the funnel into the center of the room. Armored Djinn occupied every defensive position. Above them, the automated systems tracked their movements. The guards behind them encircled the Angels.

"Captain Kita," boomed Kakafar near the far door. He wore a yellow dress uniform complete with colorful triangular ribbons, cords, and other decorations. He was in stark contrast to the other Djinn who wore combat armor. "Where is Sahara?"

"You keep asking, and I keep telling you, she's indisposed. I don't answer to you. I will explain to Collector."

"If you do not produce her, then I am to assume you have her prisoner and I can take whatever measure I deem necessary to free her."

Kita shrugged. "So…what? You're going to kill me and attack my ship? I can't tell you how bad an idea that is. I promise you, *you* won't walk out of here. We will kill everyone, and I will drag your broken and bleeding body to throw at Collector's feet. Your choice. Your twenty-five against my seven. It's not even a fair fight—for you."

"Surrender and submit," snarled Kakafar.

"To you? Never," yelled Kita. "Death first."

The other Angels bared claws, fangs, pistols, and transformed. Raptor's change gave the Djinn pause as she whistled lowly and tapped her giant middle toe on the metal decking.

"In death, you will be found guilty," warned Kakafar.

"You have to kill us first," said Kita. "And you don't have enough firepower to bring down my newest chick."

"Last warning," yelled Kakafar. "Produce Sahara. Soldiers, aim!"

Around the room, the Djinn soldiers brought their rifles up. The automated defenses systems spun and locked on target.

From her feet, a flame spread up Kita, engulfing her in a roaring inferno. "I promise you'll die in Collector's presence."

"Fire," ordered Kakafar.

The soldiers opened fire on the Angels. The automated system rained down bullets and casings. Kita, Babydoll, and Panther raised their arms and the bullets hung in the air. The firing subsided slowly as the soldiers realized their rounds were building up in front of them.

Kita giggled menacingly as the bullets rained to the floor. "I warned you it wouldn't be a fair fight. Ladies, shall we?"

Kita flashed forward and grabbed a pair of soldiers by their throats. Her hands melted through their armor and the air filled with the smell of burning fur and flesh.

Babydoll threw herself into a ball and struck a soldier in the chest, cracking the composite armor and throwing the Djinn into the wall. She bounced off and struck another in the side driving him into the deck.

Panther slashed open a Djinn's armor and drove her claws into his chest. Kamikaze phased behind a pair of soldiers and drove her claws into the base of their helmets. She phased in front of another pair and plunged her claws through their helmets' faceplates. An ice bomb went off next to her, showering a group of soldiers with deadly ice fragments. Ice crept toward the Djinn, freezing them to the deck.

Valentine fired her pistols. The giant rounds blew through the Djinns' helmets and bounced around inside leaving a bloody mess. She fired so fast the first body hadn't fallen by the time she'd hit the fifth.

Raptor screamed and jumped after the Djinn, her long talons puncturing and tearing through the soldiers' armor. Her powerful jaws ripped their heads off, helmet and all. The dinosaur turned and found herself staring down Gargah.

"Leave him," instructed Kita. *"He's proven to not be as stupid as the rest. He could be useful."*

Raptor growled low and stuck her snout in Gargah's face. She blasted him with shots of air from her nose. Gargah didn't move but flexed his hands with his claws out. Raptor knocked him over with her tail. She screamed and leaped at another soldier with his rifle pointed at her. Raptor's mouth seized his arm. She yanked and twisted, snapping through the armor and bone, taking the Djinn's arm and weapon with her. A bullet from Valentine put the Djinn down.

Kita threw a star and struck Kakafar in the leg, severing the tendons. He collapsed to the deck and crawled toward a barricade. Kita grinned wickedly and jumped, drawing Dead as she landed on him. She plunged the sword through his lower back. Kakafar collapsed. Kita grabbed the Djinn's mane and slammed his face into the decking several times until blue blood ran from his nose.

Reaching into her belt, Kita pulled out a pair of Djinn canines. She held them up in front of Kakafar. "You know what these are?" she asked with a snarl. "These belonged to the captain of Ragji. I yanked them from his face after he made the mistake of thinking he could control me. And now…you're next."

Kita reached into Kakafar's bleeding mouth and grabbed his left canine. With a twisted grin, she yanked. Kakafar screamed.

"Oh, don't worry," cooed Kita. "The second one is worse."

Kakafar tossed his head, trying to dislodge Kita. She grabbed his mane and slammed his face against the deck with a loud crack. "Oops, I broke your face."

Kita yanked Kakafar's mouth open and pulled out the right canine. She lifted his head up by his mane and dangled the pair of teeth by their roots in front of his face.

"This is what happens to those who insult me and don't treat me like I deserve to be treated. You Djinn are especially bad and need to be taught how to treat a lady. That's why I won't give you Sahara. I'm not letting my friend Snowy be pulled into your society. I'll do everything in my power to make sure they never return to Djinn space. They deserve better than that. I'll make good on my promise. I won't kill you until we see Collector."

Kita stood up and put the teeth in her belt. "Ladies, where do we stand?"

"Twenty-one dead, four wounded, and Gargah," reported Babydoll. She stuck her finger into the open wound of a Djinn. He roared in pain. "Oh, be quiet," she laughed as she stuck her finger in her mouth. She shivered causing her braids to whip back and forth. She grinned. "Yum."

Kita winked at her.

"Is this really the time and place for that?" demanded Sheppard.

"What is the correct time and place?" said Babydoll.

"Like, never."

"Then this will have to do. It's not like I'm asking you to do it."

"I'm surprised your playmate isn't joining you."

"Oh, I think she got hers."

"Gargah," called Kita.

The young Djinn picked his way across the room and stood before Kita. "Yes, Captain?"

"I'll let it go that you led us into an ambush since you were just following orders, but I do need to talk to Collector. Take me there."

"I will take you to the bridge."

"Good." Kita picked up Kakafar by his lower leg. "Lead on. I'll drag this worthless bag of meat along."

~

KITA ENTERED THE DJINN SHIP'S BRIDGE. IT WAS LAID OUT LIKE NONE SHE'D ever seen. A half circle of workstations centered on a command chair faced a large screen that showed local space and the fleet's status. Behind the half circle of workstations, clusters of workstations filled the back half of the room. Doors led to various unknown destinations.

The bridge came to a halt when she entered. Kita flung Kakafar into the command chair. She glided up so she could see the entire room.

"My name is Captain Kita, and I am now in control of this ship and fleet. Anyone who wants to argue is welcome to, just know your captain tried, and that's what's left of him. I am the one Collector sent to lead you and I will. Before I joined Collector, I commanded a ship in the Diamock fleet. My ship was the one that defeated the human invasion. I know how to win against any odds. I am legendary, and you will be too. Now, I need to speak to Collector."

"You are in command of nothing until Collector says so," said a Djinn in a formal uniform almost as ornate as Kakafar's.

Kita sighed. "And you are?"

"Commander Gef, first officer of the Jeffar."

"Put me in contact with Collector, and we'll sort this out."

"Collector doesn't come to you, you come to him."

"He'll pick up for me."

"Where is the agent Sahara? She was supposed to escort you."

This again? "She's safe but indisposed. I will explain it to Collector."

"If something has happened to her I do not wish to be you."

Kita rolled her eyes. *Really? What do they think is going to happen?*

"Let me talk to him, and we'll sort it out."

"We will send a message. Collector will contact us with a time."

"*Now* works," said Kita. "Show me to the communications room."

Gef stroked his mane. "Fine. It's your fur, not mine."

"Finally. Someone who sees it as it is."

"Follow me," said Gef.

Kita floated to the command chair and picked up Kakafar before joining Gef. The other Angels fell in behind.

"We will take him to the medical station," said Gef.

"I'm not done with him yet," said Kita.

Gef's mane rippled as a sign of surprise and curiosity. He led the group to a door across the bridge. Kita took in the stares from the crew. None were stupid enough to be openly hostile, but she did receive some challenging looks. Kakafar must have some crew loyal to him. Kita took note of whom and would have them moved if needed.

The door opened, and Gef waved everyone inside except Gargah. "Ensign Gargah, what are you doing?"

"I was told to follow by Captain Kita."

"He can come," said Kita. "He's proven he can follow orders and be useful."

The Angels squeezed into the small square room. Gargah stood in the back trying to look invisible but stood out anyway by being eight inches taller than Kita.

"Send transmission," Kita ordered.

The room lit on all sides forming a grid pattern.

Kita tapped her foot impatiently.

"You'd think he would be waiting for our call," said Babydoll.

"I'm sure he's trying to figure out what happened," said Valentine. "We've created an information vacuum."

"I'm sure he's been reevaluating his decision to include my mom," said Kamikaze with a teasing smile.

"If he hasn't before, he will after this," said Panther.

"I know I'd want your head," said Defiance.

"But I like you," said Kita.

"And you don't like me?" Collector's deep, but educated voice asked as an image of him appeared in front of the Angels. "I see you have brought more of your flock."

"I told you, I came with more."

"Where are Sahara and Snowy?"

Kita smiled. "Both were injured recovering Enterprise. They are fine, just too injured to make such a dangerous mission."

"And what makes boarding one of my ships dangerous?"

"Him." Kita held up Kakafar by the leg. "He refused to recognize who I was and I refused to take stupidity as an answer. I overcame his stupidity and brought him along so you can deal with him. Though, he can't say anything in his defense."

"Why have you beaten Admiral Kakafar?"

Kita sneered. "He attacked us first. We defended ourselves. You're down about twenty soldiers. It's never wise to attack us."

"I will expect a report from you and from the ship on what happened."

"I don't write reports. You'll have to take my verbal report. He refused to let me talk to you. I refused to produce Sahara or let him aboard Enterprise. When I refused to back down, he opened fire and we retaliated. I beat him into a pulp over his own stupidity."

Collector admired his pipe. "Admiral Kakafar is a decorated and accomplished admiral who has won many victories. Replacing him will take time."

Kita grinned. "Don't worry. I come with my own admiral. Rene?"

Sheppard pushed her way to the front.

"This is Admiral Rene Sheppard—formally of the UEE Shadow Fleet. There is no better admiral in space. She wrote the book on UEE strategy and tactics, and knows what they'll do before they do. She's the one responsible for the assault that smashed the Verisom fleet."

Collector looked up from his pipe. "Why is she no longer with the UEE?"

"She's like me and has issues with General Lyakhova—an important leader in the UEE."

"Your admiral has no knowledge of a Djinn fleet."

"All fleets operate on the same basic principles," said Sheppard. "I will have to learn the strengths and weaknesses of your ships. It will take time to build that into a strategy, but I know the vulnerabilities of the Shadow Fleet. I'm the best to lead your forces. Combine my leadership experience with my experience working with Kita, and you have a multiple force multipliers. We will need it. The Shadow Fleet is not small or inexperienced. They are fearless and tenacious. To win against them will require every trick in the book, and I wrote the book."

Collector stroked his mane. "Say I put you in charge, who do you answer to?"

"Kita. I will do her will."

"To get this wondrous advantage, I must put more faith in you, Kita?"

"If you want to win, you go with me. I do have an observation. When we arrived, twenty ships approached us. The UEE has over two hundred. I hope you're hiding a bigger force out here."

Collector pointed with his pipe in hand. "You have what I give you to accomplish the goal. This force is strong and adequate for its mission."

"That mission better be hit and run," said Sheppard. "And if we do retreat beyond the wormhole the UEE will follow."

"Your job is to start a war. Once war is declared, others will join us."

"Kita, this is a big gamble," said Sheppard.

"That's why I want you at the head of it. Don't worry, I have a plan."

"Give me your fleet, and I will start your war…as long as I get Galina," said Sheppard to Collector.

"It seems my options are limited. Gef will be your first officer and will report to me directly."

"Fine, but Enterprise is my flagship."

Collector puffed on his pipe. "I leave that to you. You have your task, Admiral. I expect a written battle plan in a week."

"You'll have one," said Sheppard.

"And Kita, you are responsible for everything."

Kita shrugged. "I wouldn't have it any other way."

Collector pointed a claw. "Sahara and Snowy are to be transferred to Jeffar to get the treatment they need."

Kita motioned to Anthrax. "I have a doctor aboard Enterprise that knows Snowy's medical history better than anyone. They will get better care aboard Enterprise."

"As soon as they are able they are to be transferred."

Kita sighed. "Will do. Anything else?"

"Yes, what happened in the Bermilli Expanse? Ships are missing, not just Enterprise. Investigators are going through the wreckage. No explanation for the destruction of the five ships is evident. I think the one person who can explain it is you."

"I destroyed those ships because I carry a major grudge against the Tet. I killed their crew aboard Enterprise. Sahara was injured trying to save the crew. She attacked me, and another Angel stopped her. Snowy attacked me over Sahara's injuries. I broke Snowy to prove a point."

Collector steepled his fingers, the claws on the ends tapping together. "And what is that point?"

"Don't get in my way. I don't care who you are. I don't need that kind of aggravation in my life. I have enough to worry about."

Collector bared a fang. "This puts us in a predicament. I can't have you attacking whoever you wish over whatever petty slight you perceive."

Kita shrugged. "I don't need you. I have a ship and my Angels. I can leave and go after the humans on my own."

"What makes you think you'll leave this ship alive?"

Kita raised an eyebrow. "You don't have enough crew aboard this tub to stop us. I will leave this ship a floating graveyard. Or I can repeat what I did aboard Ragji, and I'll take down your entire fleet. But go ahead, be like everyone else. Underestimate my power and resolve. I promise if you piss me off, I'll send you your daughter back to you in a hundred separate boxes. You can piece her back together. Don't make this about how much I need you. This is about how much you need me."

Collector's face was stone. His hands clenched in his lap. "If what you say is true, why is Snowy with you?"

Kita smiled and turned to Kamikaze. "This is not Snowy. This is our daughter, Kamikaze. She takes her looks from Snowy and her attitude from me."

"I know that look, Collector," said Kamikaze. "I've seen it plenty of times on people who deal with my mother. Your carefully cultivated hand full of hearts has turned to spades. We're not against your war, and we'll do our best to cultivate it. But you must cede absolute authority to my mother. You have given her a goal, and she will make it happen. A wise person once said: If you want help from the powerful, you must take them on their own terms. Before you stand some of the most powerful individuals in the universe. We are loyal to my mother beyond question. If you side with her, you won't be sorry. Oppose her, and everything you hold dear will be destroyed. We live a long time and grudges die hard."

Collector pointed at Kamikaze. "You speak like Snowy, with knowledge and wisdom. I have planned this war for decades, ever since the scouts returned from the Alicorn wormhole and reported a new civilization. The humans lacked the FTL drive and were deemed non-threatening. I saw an opportunity to return the Djinn to glory. I have painstakingly put the pieces in place. Kita was never part of my plan until Snowy recommended you. At the time I thought she oversold you, but the truth is, she undersold you. You are more than she promised and those you brought with you are a bonus. It is not that my hand has become poor, but has become significantly better. I will go down in Djinn history as the savior of the Djinn, and it will be because of Kita."

Kita rolled her eyes. "I assume your organization can spin what happened in the Bermilli Expanse to our benefit?"

"Oh, yes. Investigators are already saying the human vessel turned on the Verisom and Diamock and is now running loose in Tet space."

"That sounds like the truth to me," said Defiance.

"Sometimes the truth beats any lie," said Kita.

"Agreed," said Collector.

"Then we're in agreement?" said Kita.

"Yes. You are free to do as you wish and are in command of my forces. I expect to be kept informed of your progress, and the attack to happen soon."

"That'll be up to Admiral Sheppard." Kita looked at Sheppard.

"The sooner I establish command, the sooner it will happen."

"Orders are already going out," said Collector.

"Good," said Kita. "Then we'll take our leave."

Collector nodded and vanished. The room went dim.

"I think that was a first," said Panther.

"What's that?" said Defiance.

"Someone going along with Kita without having to have sense pounded into them."

The other Angels laughed as they exited the room.

"You," Sheppard pointed to Gargah, "are now my aide. Make sure Collector's orders on change of command are received and distributed. Then tell the other ships I want an inspection. I want you to gather the other ships' status and tech specs for analysis."

Gargah saluted and left.

"What do we do?" said Defiance to Kita.

"Help Rene figure out how we're going to start a war."

CHAPTER XV

"...And I spun around and swatted him with my wing," Stormy said with a laugh. "I felt so bad."

Starlight, Valor, and Blitz laughed with her.

Along with the Angels, a few tables in the wardroom were full of officers eating. Phoenix and Toxic sat in a corner booth looking sullen and grumpy.

"I keep forgetting I have four feet behind me and keep hitting things," said Blitz.

"It takes everyone time to adjust," said Valor.

"Yes, but you don't take up as much room as the rest of us," teased Starlight.

"I have less to preen," replied Valor as she stuck out her tongue.

"You leave that out there and I'll put it to work."

Stormy blushed and laughed.

"You'd like that wouldn't you?" said Valor turning up her nose.

"I know you would," said Starlight with a dazzling smile.

"I don't understand," said Blitz. "What am I missing?"

Stormy giggled. "She's talking about Jess licking her—"

"Will you chicks shut up," Phoenix yelled from her corner.

"I'm sorry," said Stormy, "we're just talking."

"Shut up, hatchling."

"Kylee, come on," said Toxic. "Let's go."

"I'm not going anywhere. I was here first."

"From what I understand you haven't left that corner since Kita put you in it," said Valor.

Phoenix slammed her fist on the table. "Watch your mouth, you short little freak. I can still kick your ass."

Toxic hopped out of the booth. She grabbed Phoenix's arm and pulled causing Phoenix to fall out of the seat.

"Dammit, Kara. Don't pull so slagging hard. You stupid moron."

"Hey," said Stormy. "Be nice. She's trying to help you."

"Oh, shut up," snarled Phoenix. "I'll talk to anyone any way I want. I'm the slagging leader of the Valkyries."

"That doesn't give you license to be rude," said Blitz.

"Holy slag, the goat freak talks," said Phoenix as she walked to the other Angels, her wings dragging on the deck.

"Apologize, or I'll knock your teeth down your throat," said Valor. "I don't care if you are Kita's kid."

"Yeah, you better remember who my mom is. Mess with me, and she'll make you human again so fast your head will spin."

"I doubt that," said Stormy. "She didn't seem too happy with you the last time we saw you together."

"Yeah, so? I'm still her daughter, and I can do what I want."

"Kylee, come on," urged Toxic. "I don't feel like getting into a fight."

"Well, she's in one until she apologizes to Zen," said Valor.

"Bring it, shorty," yelled Phoenix.

Blitz flashed to the side of Phoenix and punched her in the jaw. Phoenix crumpled to the ground whimpering.

"Thanks, Jess," said Blitz, "but I can take care of myself. Kita said don't start a fight unless you're willing to lose," she said down to Phoenix.

"My jaw, you stupid freak." Tears filled Phoenix's eyes. She curled up in a ball and covered her face.

Toxic and Stormy knelt next to her.

"Kylee?" said Toxic.

"Go away," Phoenix wailed.

"Just like every bully," said Valor. "One good shot and they crumble."

"I need to get her to the medical ward," said Toxic.

"You want some help?" said Stormy.

The light in Toxic's hood brightened. "You sure? She did just insult your friend."

"Kita says we're one big family. We fight and then we make up."

"It'll make it easier to handle her."

Stormy picked Phoenix up in her arms. "I'll be back, girls."

"Make sure you get her attitude adjusted while you're down there," said Valor.

"I think only Kita is capable of that," said Starlight.

Toxic sighed, the light coming from her hoodie dimming. "I wish she would," she mumbled.

～

STORMY SAT WITH TOXIC OUTSIDE OF THE SURGICAL SUITE IN THE medical ward.

"I didn't realize Kita took everything from Kylee," said Stormy.

"Yeah. Kita was pretty pissed. But, I think it's more than what happened then. Kylee's been dominate for years. She was bragging she could take Kita. And, Kita hears all and knows all, so I bet she was waiting to take Kylee down. Kita doesn't like anyone challenging her, even her own daughters."

Stormy watched the lights flash in Toxic's hood as she talked. "So you've seen this before?"

"Not like this. Kylee used to challenge Kita all the time, but it was small stuff, not for control of the group."

"Can I ask you something?"

"Sure, I guess. No one ever cares to ask me anything."

"I've never seen your face. Do you keep it hidden for a reason?"

"Huh? No," Toxic shook her head. "I like to be alone. It gives me solitude and helps hide the light."

"What is the light?" said Stormy.

"My eyes, mouth, and nails glow."

"Must be nice if you lose something in the dark."

Toxic chuckled dourly. "I can see in the dark as well as you can."

Stormy smiled apologetically. "Ok, bad joke, but it's a pretty color."

"Toxic green is a pretty color? I'm just a freak."

Stormy took Toxic's hand. "You're not a freak."

"Why are you being nice to me?" Toxic said depressed.

"Because you need a friend—a real friend."

The light in Toxic's hood dimmed as she shook her head. "I'm fine," she whispered.

"I don't believe that. I think you've been hanging around Kylee for too long."

"Kylee's a cool friend…when she's not a bitch."

"Can I see your face?"

Toxic shrugged and lowered her hood. Her face was tired looking and sunken. *I didn't know Angels could look this bad.*

"See? I'm ugly," said Toxic when Stormy didn't say anything.

"No, I…your face is beautiful. You look like you've been through a hard time and need some rest and less stress. Can I ask what's bothering you?"

Toxic hung her head. "It's nothing. I can handle it."

"Come on, tell me."

"You sure do want to know a lot about me, and you just met me."

Stormy blushed. "I think you're interesting and Angels are supposed to watch out for other Angels. It looks like no one has been looking out for you."

Toxic pulled her hood back over her head. "I don't need anyone to look after me."

"We all need someone. Kylee isn't doing a good job of taking care of you."

"It's not just Kylee's fault, it's Denver's, too."

Stormy cocked her head to one side. "What happened?"

"It's not what they did. It's what they do. They argue and fight, and then put me in the middle. I used to try and help, but they just blamed me. So now, they dump on me, and I take it, trying not to upset them further."

Stormy frowned. "That's awful. I'm sorry. Have you tried talking to them?"

"You know what it's like trying to talk to Kylee about anything that doesn't involve killing something, video games, or sex? Denver is like talking to a machine. You go in loops, or she says I should be able to handle it—like I'm a machine like her."

Stormy wanted to put her arm around Toxic, but hesitated, not sure of what reaction she would get. *Nothing ventured, nothing gained.* She slid her arm across Toxic's shoulders. Toxic slumped forward and buried her head in her arms.

Not sure what to do, Stormy bent down to Toxic's hood. "Kara? Are you ok?"

Toxic bolted upright. "You know my name?"

"Yeah, Kylee said it in the wardroom."

"No one's ever paid attention to me like that before."

Stormy hugged Toxic. "I am."

"I don't deserve this."

"Why not?"

"Because I'm a lying, cheating bitch fallen angel. I don't deserve garbage. I deserve what I've got."

"I'm not a saint. I'm a trained killer and am one of Kita's Commandoes. We're not nice people and we don't do nice things. You deserve better. Whatever you've done in the past is in the past. You can change the future by making different choices in the present. Talking to me is one of those choices."

Stormy pulled Toxic's hood down and brushed her dark hair out of her face.

"Why are you paying attention to me?" whispered Toxic.

"I'm trained to notice the things that don't want to be noticed. You don't dress like the other Angels, and you kept your face hidden. You hover on the fringe, but you're one of the Valkyries so you must be important. You didn't say anything, but there is an air of nobility about you."

Toxic shook her head. "I'm not a noble anymore."

"You were a noble?" Stormy couldn't hide the surprise in her voice.

"Back on that miserable planet, I was known as Countess Laramie. I was second to the Vicereine herself."

"Wow. I'm just a farm girl from Oklahoma."

"What's an Oklahoma?" said Toxic.

"A place of rolling high plains, grass, and dirt."

"Sounds like some of my districts."

Babydoll approached them flanked by Aspen and Anthrax.

"What happened?" said Babydoll.

Stormy stood up. "Zen punched Kylee for calling her a freak. She broke Kylee's jaw, and it's being wired shut."

Babydoll grinned. "That's the best news I've heard all day. That'll keep her quiet for a while."

"I'm going to go in and check on the progress," said Anthrax.

"Someone should tell Kita," said Aspen.

Babydoll nodded.

"Zen's not in trouble, is she?" said Stormy.

Babydoll waved a hand. "Nah. Kylee got what she deserved. She must have forgotten she's human. We can put her in bed next to Snowy."

"Do you need us?" said Stormy motioning to her and Toxic.

"No, you're free to go."

"Want to get something to drink at the galley?" said Stormy to Toxic.

"Yeah, I guess."

Babydoll raised an eyebrow as the pair left.

~

KITA FLOPPED INTO THE SHUTTLE SEAT. SHE WAS TIRED. TOURING ALL TWENTY of Collector's ships was mentally exhausting. Across from her, Valentine sat and pulled out her pistols and cleaned them. *It must be to keep her hands busy while she coalesces all the data we gathered.*

She had gathered the needed information to disable Collector's ships, but it wouldn't be easy. The ships' networks were not uniform and each required unique solutions. The software and hardware was a patchwork of civilian and military grades cobbled together. The bulk of the hacking tools would need to be written by Valor and Enterprise's Political Bureau crew. She didn't envy them, but Kita planned on making Valentine available to help.

Sheppard entered with Gargah. Her face was lined with stress and Kita could feel her apprehension and worry. She sat down hard next to Kita, much to Kita's surprise. Usually, Sheppard took up as much space as possible. Sheppard put her head back and let out a long sigh.

"You ok, Rene?" Kita said gently.

Sheppard lifted her head and rubbed her face. "I feel like a brand new lieutenant sent to command school. I don't know anything, and I'm expected to put together a fighting force as fast as possible."

Kita was about to offer Valentine to help but thought against it. Valentine would react negatively, probably violently, at being asked to work with her old tormentor. Even though Sheppard had changed, the trust that would be required for the pair to work together was shattered and would never be repaired.

Kita tried not to flinch when Sheppard slumped against her and put her head on Kita's shoulder. *Is Rene this tired? I know it's been a lot and she's feeling the pressure, but this is unlike her to show any kind of weakness.* Kita reached over and took Sheppard's hand.

"Don't worry. I'll be there to help. So will Casey. Zen has some experience with ships and I'm sure will help."

"I just don't know if I can do it."

Where is this coming from? Rene is nothing but confidence. "Of course you can. I have faith in you. What's wrong, Rene? This isn't like you."

Sheppard turned her head and kissed Kita's neck three times. Kita jumped out of shock and surprise. The next surprise was when she found both of Valentine's pistols aimed at Sheppard.

"What the hell are you doing?" Valentine demanded.

Kita was impressed at the speed in which Valentine had gotten her pistols together. "It's alright, Val." She looked down at Sheppard, and her eyes were wide with shock and fear. Kita waved Valentine away and put her arm around Sheppard.

Kita leaned in and whispered, "Rene, what's wrong?"

"I'm sorry. I'm sorry. I'm so sorry. I just…I just…you're always so available to everyone else. I thought…I'm just…"

Kita squeezed Sheppard tight. "Shh, it's ok. You just took me by surprise. I don't expect kisses from you."

Tears leaked from the side of Sheppard's eyes. "I'm sorry, Kita. I don't know what to do. Everyone hates me, and I'm so alone."

"Oh, Rene, you're not alone, and no one hates you—"

Valentine raised a pistol and aimed it at Sheppard. Kita waved her away.

"—Ok, Denver isn't your biggest fan, but there are plenty of people who like you: Jess, Zen, Amanda, Casey, and Hali all love you."

"I know, but Jess has Hali, Casey has you…I've got nobody to love me. I know I don't deserve it, but it hurts."

Kita pressed her head against Sheppard's. "Of course you do. I'll find you someone, anyone you want."

"Do you think Amanda would be interested?" Sheppard asked quickly. "She hasn't been seeing anyone has she?"

So much for Alex. Who would have thunk it? "Ah, I don't think so. I haven't heard anything from Jess, and she would know."

"You don't think I'm too old for her do you?"

Old, no. Experienced, yes. "No. I think she'll be flattered. But you have to remember, you may be Angels, but she still sees you as Admiral Sheppard."

"I know. I can put it aside. I hope she can."

Going to be an interesting conversation. So, Amanda, I've got someone who wants to take you out on a date. Who? Well, she's a bit of a legend in the Shadow Fleet… "I'll talk to her. I'm sure Casey will help. She's good at putting you military girls at ease."

Sheppard sniffed. "Yeah. She's a helluva princess."

That's an understatement. Kita held Sheppard while she wiped her eyes. Sheppard gave Kita a small smile.

"Thanks, Kita. You always know how to make things better."

Let's not pass out awards yet. "I try and keep my friends happy." *And if getting you laid gets this fleet firing in the same direction then that's what I'll do, even if I have to call in an IOU from Kerri to do it.*

"Captain Kita," called the pilot.

"Yes?"

"Incoming call for you."

"Ok. I'll take it back here." Kita looked back at Sheppard. "Are you going to be ok?"

"Yeah, I'll be fine…as long as Val doesn't shoot me in the head."

Valentine's eyes narrowed.

"She'll be fine," said Kita giving Valentine a dirty look. She got up and went to the communications panel. She tapped the accept button, and Babydoll appeared.

"Hey, Kita. Enjoying your tour of the kitty cat fleet?"

"Oh, it's great. We only had to relieve two captains."

"So I thought I'd give you a heads up."

Kita raised an eyebrow, "Oh?"

"Kylee mouthed off to Zen, and the goat broke her jaw. Kylee's an absolute nightmare. We've got her restrained to the bed, and Tina is babysitting her after she tried to escape as a cloud."

Kita hung her head. "Ok, thanks. I'll deal with her."

"Hey, I know she can be a pain in the ass. I'll go with you. You're going to need the backup."

Kita chuckled. "Thanks."

"It's what your best friend is for."

∼

KITA STOOD ON TOP OF ENTERPRISE ADMIRING THE STARS. ONE BY ONE AROUND her clouds drifted through the ship's hull. The clouds materialized into Panther, Babydoll, Aspen, and Raptor.

"Hey, baby," said Panther. "Did you call us here to stargaze?"

Kita chuckled. "No. I'm steeling my soul."

"Against what?" said Babydoll sounding concerned.

"Against what you're going to tell me about Kylee. When we parted she was my baby, and I adored her. I want to know what happened."

"She killed billions is what happened," said Aspen pointedly. "She destroyed entire civilizations and their worlds for no reason."

Kita winced. "I'm not blaming anyone, but did anyone try and stop her?"

"We tried talking to her," said Babydoll. "We couldn't restrain her. She didn't listen to us, not even Denver. She tried hard to reign in Kylee's impulses, but without sex as a lever, she didn't often succeed."

Kita sighed. "It's my fault. I thought Kylee was ready and could handle it. I'm sorry to have put you in that position. Did she help at all? Kami is the only one who ever came to me."

"Sorry, sug," said Raptor. "The girl be more interested in her carnal appetite for destruction. If you got in her way, she be throwen' a tantrum that be worse than if you just let her do what she be wanten' to."

"She lorded the fact that she was the leader over us," said Panther. "She would especially rub it in mine. She called me your concubine."

"I'm so sorry, Vee," whispered Kita. "You know that's not true. Your personal growth was tremendous. I thought pairing you with Re'drum was a fitting reward and you'd get to see the universe."

"It wasn't just me. She did it to others, even Denver and Kara."

"I had hoped they'd be a good influence on her," said Kita.

"Kara be goen' along with Kylee to avoid the girl's wrath," said Raptor.

"No one even cares that she killed billions?" interjected Aspen.

"I care," said Kita. "I didn't send her out to lay waste to civilizations of the cosmos. It was a threat to be carried out when necessary, as a tool to be able to complete the goal. Which I'm thankful you accomplished. I wouldn't be here if you hadn't found my cloud. She will not go unpunished, Leaf. I won't tolerate such behavior. I'm sorry to all of you that I misjudged her."

"It be a pattern," said Raptor. "When you not be there to nip her rump she be runnen' wild."

Kita closed her eyes. *Yes, it's true. Every time I'm gone, Kylee runs wild. I used to think it was others' faults, that she was reacting to them, but now I see it was them reacting to her. I owe many people an apology. I refused to see the truth, and I failed her as a mother.* Kita wiped a tear from her eye. *This will be the only tear I shed. I failed and must face the consequences.*

"I will deal with Kylee and do what must be done. I can't undo the past, but I can make the future right."

CHAPTER XVI

*K*ita and Babydoll appeared in front of the medical suite door that contained Phoenix. Kita opened the door. Phoenix, her eyes closed, lay in the bed with her wrists strapped to the railing. Tina and Snowy sat in chairs next to the bed. Tina was watching TV. Snowy wore a hard plastic back brace and collar, and was reading. The pair turned their attention to the new arrivals.

"Hey, big sister," said Tina. "You don't look happy."

"You were so concerned about the damage I *may* cause, that you ignored the damage that *was* caused."

Tina gulped.

Kita knelt before Snowy. She took the cat's hands. "I'm sorry for all those years I was gone, and I left you with Kylee. It wasn't fair to you. I thought Kylee's troubles were because of you, but now I see your troubles were because of her. I'm sorry for not seeing it sooner, and I thank you for all you did."

Snowy blinked several times. "Kita, you don't need to apologize for that. It was a long time ago."

"It might as well have been yesterday. I do need to apologize for it. I blamed you when I should have blamed Kylee. Her behavior is her own fault, not yours. I was blinded as a mother, but I see it now. I'm sorry. My own selfishness is to blame."

"I won't argue with that," said Snowy turning up her nose.

Kita stood. "Just remember, what I want is usually good for everybody."

Snowy waved her hand dismissively.

Kita raised an eyebrow. *Snowy must be crankier than usual.* Kita checked Sahara's status. She was still unconscious, but healing according to the Djinn doctor brought on board for her.

Standing, Kita moved to the head of the bed. Phoenix hadn't moved. She wore a set of pajamas. Kita put her hand on Phoenix's shoulder.

"Wake up," Kita said forcefully.

Phoenix stirred and blinked her eyes several times. Her head turned to face Kita, and her eyes focused. When she realized it was Kita, she awoke fully.

"About damn time you've come to your slagging senses and come to give me back my stuff."

"You're not getting back anything. I'm here to take your wings and your cloud."

"You can't. They're mine!" Phoenix screamed as she fought against the restraints. "I won't let you! I'm more powerful than you. I should be the God of Evil, not you. I've killed billions more than you."

Kita frowned. "That is why I am taking them from you. You're no longer a good evil, striving to make the equation a better place. You're here for your own gluttony, pride, and wrath. You no longer work for anything, and you covet what others around you have worked for while leeching off Kara and Denver. You are *not* the leader I trained you to be and you've squandered the gifts I've given you. Now I hear you belittle and insult the people I sent to keep you safe."

Phoenix gave Babydoll a nasty look.

"It wasn't just Kerri," said Kita firmly.

"Of course, she's going to tell you anything you want to hear," said Phoenix. "She's as good as a slave to you."

"I wouldn't lie to her," said Aspen in a soft, strained voice. She appeared on the other side of the bed from Kita.

"Oh, go slag yourself, you annoying runt."

"Enough," snarled Kita. "These are my friends and family. I will not let you insult them. They did me a favor, and you have caused them much pain. That is a debt I have to pay, and the first payment is setting things right. You are my blood and I can't change that, but that doesn't mean it will save you. You are no longer worthy of being an Angel. Your wings are mine."

Kita grabbed Phoenix's arm. The bright yellows, reds, and oranges of Phoenix's wings became muted and then lost all their color. The gray feathers turned black and crumbled.

"No!" Phoenix screamed. She dissolved into her black cloud half the size of the bed. The other Angels in the room reacted, but Kita waved them down.

"She is mine," said Kita.

Phoenix drifted toward Aspen, who ducked out of the way around the bed behind Babydoll. Kita dissolved into her cloud. She expanded until she filled the room.

Phoenix attacked Kita. Dark tendrils extended and penetrated Kita's cloud.

The shocks, burns, and freezing that represented the pain, rage, and hate Kylee felt was nothing more than an irritant to Kita.

"You think your life's pain is enough to hurt me?" Kita said to Phoenix in the black cloud's monotone voice.

"You know nothing of what I've suffered, what I've been through," said Phoenix in the same monotone voice. "Everyone abandons me. I thought you were different. You're supposed to be my mom. And now you act like you don't care?"

"I gave you everything: power, love, freedom. That was my mistake. I gave it to you—you didn't earn it. I failed you. This is a failure I have to live with. Maybe, I'm not the mother I thought I was, or maybe the other girls wanted a mother. You wanted the power to make others suffer like you have suffered. You played me, and you won, but now it stops. You may be a god, but I'm still your mother. I can put you back in the hole I found you."

"You are a failure. Look at what I've become because you kept abandoning me. This is your fault, not mine."

"No," said Kita. "You control your behavior, and it tells me what's in your heart and mind. I may not have been there as much as I should have, but I know I taught you better than what you've displayed. I'm embarrassed by it—a child of mine behaving like a common thug. You were supposed to become my right hand and join with me."

"You think I want to do your bidding for the rest of my life? I won't serve you or anyone. I'm not one of these other featherheads who bow before you. I won't let you control me."

"I never wanted to control you, just give you the life you deserved. Do you think Denver bows before me?"

"She's the worst! All she does is complain she's apart from you. When she's not doing that, she's telling me what to do."

"I thought you loved her," said Kita.

"I do."

"Do you really? Or do you abuse her love for your own needs?"

"Like you're one to talk—you and your concubines. You use one until you tire of her and then you move on to the next. Don't lecture me on love. I know you don't feel it. You're just as bad as me."

"I respect my girlfriends, something you don't give Denver."

"Don't tell me what I do and don't do." Phoenix sent another surge of emotional energy at Kita.

Kita absorbed it, to study later to better understand Phoenix. Large tendrils closed around Phoenix like looming fingers. The ends jabbed into Phoenix. Kita sent her own blast of emotional energy. Phoenix's cloud expanded and contracted several times.

"You think you know pain and hatred, child. That is nothing compared to the disappointment I have for you and what you've done. The destruction of those civilizations is on me because you are my failure. It's now one more burden I have to bear. One more thing I can never make up for."

Kita sent the energy and Phoenix's cloud ruptured. Phoenix let out a shriek of emotional energy. Kita's tendrils engulfed Phoenix. The girl fell out the bottom of Kita's cloud. Kita shifted back to her angelic form.

Phoenix scrambled backward until she hit the bed. She raised her hands and looked at them. "What did you do to me?" she cried.

"Taken what was mine," said Kita. "I've taken all I can from you. You're still a god, and I'm sending you back to Infinity."

"What? I've never even been there."

"You'll figure it out," said Babydoll.

"Tina, as the only one allowed in Infinity, do you mind escorting the young god to her home?" said Kita.

"Ah, sure," said Tina with a wary smile. "I'll explain it to Y'grene and E'fil."

"Give her a research project," said Babydoll.

"A what?" protested Phoenix.

Kita stepped up to Phoenix. "From this point forward you are no longer an Angel, related to any, or have any claim to us. You're as human as I can make you. May you find peace in Infinity or wherever you go."

Babydoll pulled Kylee to her feet. She grabbed the girl's upper arm and forced her into her god form. Tina changed into her god form. She collapsed into a brilliant white point of light and flew into Kylee collapsing her into a point of light. The two lights flew out of the room.

"Did you really strip her of everything?" said Snowy, her nose pale.

"Everything I could. I failed, and I must correct the mistake. Kylee's actions are my fault, but she must suffer the consequences. I won't tolerate someone who commits genocide for fun."

"So you will for other reasons?" said Babydoll with a teasing smile.

"As long as it's a good reason."

"I won't ask what a good reason is," said Snowy.

"Unlike you, the world is not black and white," said Kita.

"Har-har."

"But I must go and find Denver and tell her. I don't know how upset she'll be."

"You want help?" said Babydoll.

"No, this is something I should do alone. I've been there since the beginning of their relationship."

"As weird as that was."

"I should have seen the omen. Ship computer," Kita called.

"Yes, Captain Kita?" answered a genderless synthesized voice.

"Where is Child of the emperor Valentine?"

"She is in the Political Bureau office. Can I contact her for you?"

"Send her a message that I need to speak with her, and I will meet her there."

"Yes, Captain."

Kita sighed. "My day's only going to get harder."

"Better you than me," said Snowy.

"Go back to bed," huffed Kita. *Improve your attitude, or you're next out the door.*

⌇

KITA ENTERED THE POLITICAL BUREAU OFFICE. VALOR HOVERED OVER Lieutenant Po and several workstations with Valentine by her side. Jupiter lay at the end of a row of workstations. His head came up when he smelled visitors. Sarge trotted over to the other cat and exchanged several head rubs and licks. Kita smiled at the cats and smiled wider when she saw Stormy in the workshop part of the office.

What should I do first? The easy one or the hard one? I might as well get the tears out of the way first. Kita approached Valor and Valentine.

"How's it going, ladies?" asked Kita.

"Not as smooth as I'd like," said Valor. "This patchwork of tech is making it hard to create tools that aren't area specific. What we did for Mauler is a good roadmap, but everything we developed for that is no good with the tech these ships have."

"How they get it all to work onboard these ships is a mystery to me," said Valentine.

Kita sighed. "That's the problem with mercenary fleets."

"We did get the software suite that Collector requires to be installed on his ships for communications. We've reverse engineered it and have begun snooping through their communications."

"That's something at least. Good work."

"So what brings you down to our hole?" said Valor. "You're not here to smash the place up are you?"

Kita smiled remembering one of her previous visits. "No. I need to talk to Denver."

"What about?" said Valentine. "Did I do something wrong? Why didn't you just send it to me?"

"Because this is personal, and I need to talk to Denver, not Valentine."

"Oh, ok. I don't think I like the sound of that. Is Kylee alright?"

"She's fine," Kita said fainting a smile. "Jess, do you have an empty office?"

"You can use mine. I never use it. That door over there." Jess pointed to a door across the room.

"Thanks," said Kita. She took Valentine's hand and led her to the office.

Inside, Kita directed Valentine to a chair and pulled the other from behind the desk. She sat down so she could face Valentine. She took the other Angel's hands. Kita closed her eyes. She hadn't processed the emotions that went along with what happened and now she was going to have to help someone else. She wished for Panther and Defiance.

"Denver, I've made a decision that directly affects you."

"What did I do?"

Kita shook her head. "Nothing. That's part of why this hurts so much. You did nothing wrong. If anything you made the situation better."

Valentine gasped. "What did Kylee do?"

"I was given a report by some of the others of what happened while the Valkyries were out searching the cosmos."

Valentine went white and tears formed in her eyes. "I tried to stop her. I pleaded with her every time. She wouldn't listen to me."

"It's not your fault," Kita said gently. "These actions are hers and hers alone. She's been forced to take responsibility for them. These are not the actions of an Angel, but of a monster."

Valentine burst into tears. "I know she's bad, but she's not that bad. She promised to never do it again. And she was so sorry afterward."

"Denver, I know you love Kylee, but I don't think Kylee loves you anymore. She was just stringing you along—"

"No! That's not true. She gave me a ring and promised me a wedding."

"I know she did, and I'm sure she would have given you one, but she was doing it to keep you by her side, not because she loves you."

"Why would she do that?" Valentine yelled.

"Because you took care of her and praised her. You fed her ego and satisfied her carnal appetite. It's all about her. It was never about you."

"But I know she loves me. She waited for me."

Kita sighed. "I know she did. I believe at one point she did love you, but whatever happened over the last ten years has changed her or exposed her real self. This isn't your fault, so don't blame yourself. She fooled me too, maybe more than you. I failed her, and in turn, I failed you. I'm sorry. I really wanted this to be a happy ending for both of you. You deserve it."

"What's to happen to her?"

Kita bit her lip. "She's been stripped of her wings and cloud, and sent to Infinity to live with the other gods where they can control her."

"But—but I'm never going to see her again!"

"I know— I'm sorry. Maybe someday we'll be allowed back in Infinity."

"That's not fair!" screamed Valentine.

"Unfortunately, you're getting punished for her actions."

"I protest. There must be another way."

"It's already done," said Kita firmly.

"And you weren't going to tell me?"

"I decided it was best that it be done first and then tell you."

"Because you knew I wouldn't let you otherwise."

Kita shook her head. "It would have happened regardless. You may be her partner, but I'm her mother. More importantly, I'm still me."

"And of course what you want goes," Valentine said with contempt.

"It's a heavy responsibility. That's what this is about, my responsibility for Kylee's actions. There are many things I'd let go, but not something like this. Genocide without cause is inexcusable."

"That's rich coming from someone who kills for fun."

"Life is precious, Denver, a single life is not."

"So that's it?" yelled Valentine. "It's ok for you, but not for her?"

"I've never killed an entire civilization. I've killed thousands at a time. That's not even on the same scale."

"So the great God of Evil isn't so evil?"

Kita rolled her eyes. "In this case, yes. I can't say Kylee hated the people she killed. She killed for fun."

"You don't know that. Maybe she had a reason."

"Denver, you're grasping at straws." Valentine released Kita's hands. "The decision's been made, Kylee is gone. All that's left is the tears. I've shed mine. It's your turn. Cry, hurt, remember, and move on…or wait. I don't care which. Maybe some time as a god will do her good."

Valentine slumped forward and cried into her hands.

Kita slid her chair around and put her arm around Valentine. She let her cry, hoping the tears would wash the pain and memory away. What she didn't want to happen was Valentine retreating into her computer. She might never get the Angel part back.

Valentine lifted her head and wiped her tears with the back of her hands. She sniffed, and she went to say something, but it died on her lips. She cleared her voice and tried again.

"I want to talk to my sisters."

Kita nodded. Valentine the Angel didn't have any sisters, but Valentine, as the God of Justice, did—the Gods of Murder and War. Kita called Panther and Tenshi. The pair flew in as points of lights and expanded into their angelic form.

Panther took Kita's seat and put her arm around Valentine.

"What's wrong?" said Tenshi.

Kita touched the Angel, opened a cloud connection, and filled her in on events. Tenshi flinched hard enough to break the connection, giving both Angels painful feedback.

"You didn't?" said Tenshi.

"It's done," said Kita.

"Why weren't the rest of us asked?"

"I didn't think I needed the entire group's opinion. I chose those who'd give me honest feedback."

"Nice to know where I rate."

"It's not that your opinion isn't valid, but it would have been redundant."

"Is that why Denver wasn't consulted," Tenshi replied harshly.

"Her opinion would have been tainted. Same as Kara's."

"Kita's famous inner circle. Always playing favorites."

"If you don't like it, you know the way to Infinity," said Kita.

Tenshi glared but said nothing.

"That's what I thought," said Kita with a sharp look. "I'll leave you to your sister." She opened the door and looked at the workshop, but Stormy was gone. Valor was hovering over another workstation. Kita went to her.

"Where's Amanda?"

"Not sure. Her shift ended."

Kita made a face. "Ship computer?"

"Yes, Captain Kita?"

"Where is Child of the emperor Stormy?"

"Child of the emperor Stormy is in the forward observation room."

I didn't know Amanda was a stargazer. Kita said goodbye to Valor and went to find Stormy, hoping the encounter would lift her spirits.

CHAPTER XVII

*K*ita exited the elevator to Enterprise's bridge with Babydoll. The pair approached the holotable where Sheppard, Defiance, and Blitz were in a video conference with several of the Djinn captains.

Sheppard saw Kita and announced, "Thank you, Captains. My staff will be in touch if they have more questions." She killed the feed much to the surprise of Defiance and Blitz, then turned to the approaching Angels. "Kita, we need to talk to you."

"You and everyone else," Kita said sarcastically. "Sorry, Rene, it's been a long day."

"I heard something went down in the medical ward."

"What do you need?" said Kita not interested in telling.

"What's wrong, darlin'?" said Defiance to Kita.

Kita shook her head. "Kids."

"I want to know what the plan is. I know—"

Kita waved a hand to shush Sheppard. "Everyone, grab my hand," she ordered as she held out her hands. Once everyone touched her, she phased them outside of Enterprise near the bow.

"*Rene, I owe you and Case an apology,*" said Kita. "*You've both been very good sports about my dealings with Collector and leading his fleet against the Shadow Fleet.*"

"*I knew you had a plan,*" said Defiance. "*I am curious to hear it since they are my ships we'll be attacking.*"

"*I have no intention of leading Collector's forces to victory. Quite the opposite. I plan to lead them to their doom. As soon as we're in UEE space, we're going to contact the Shadow Fleet and tell them we're being pursued and under attack by alien forces. I don't know what forces guard the wormhole, I'm hoping you can come up with a plan and continue the ruse.*"

"*By the emperor, Kita,*" exclaimed Sheppard. "*I'm not a machine. I've been working days straight on this while trying to learn a completely new fleet.*"

Kita raised a hand. "*I understand, Rene, and I thank you, but I'm not asking you to do it for real. I need you to go against your training and nature. Put together something that looks good on paper that will fool the Djinn captains. That's all you have to do.*"

"*That would have been nice to know a few days ago,*" said Blitz.

"*Sorry,*" said Kita. "*I know you've been working hard, but I need to keep this ruse going for a little longer. I hope that's some stress off all of you. I plan to run drills and exercises to give the appearance we're training them. I expect you to tell them all the wrong things.*"

"*That could be as hard as doing the real thing,*" said Defiance.

"*No,*" said Sheppard. "*I'll hand it off to those who need to learn and are inexperienced with fleet-wide exercises. I'll make it a problem for the junior officers to solve. We'll need to review it. In the meantime, we'll work on an escape plan."*

"You expect your junior staff to be that bad?" teased Babydoll.

"I expect them to not understand the nuance of the situation and understand the strategy involved. I expect to get back a competent report that will require some modification but will be good enough to fool the Djinn. It will give my junior officers some practical experience in fleet-wide operations."

"What will the Shadow Fleet need to defeat Collector's fleet?" said Kita.

Sheppard crossed her arms. *"They have some anti-fighter technology mounted. It's not as sophisticated as ours, but it can still bring down some. One expeditionary force should be enough. I brought three with me when I came for the princess. That would be enough to drive them from our space."*

"I want them crushed. Everything that comes through that wormhole doesn't make it home."

"That'll be trickier. We'll have to coordinate expeditionary forces. We can cut off their escape that way. If we can get Fort Ticonderoga that will help spare our own ships."

"Work out a battle plan on what you know of the UEE forces. If we have to, we can lead Collector's forces into a trap."

Sheppard sighed. *"Assuming the fleet returned to normal stations after we returned from rescuing the princess."*

"I know it won't be exact," said Kita. *"I just want to have a basic plan that can be adapted to the situation we find when we arrive."*

"How does broadcasting the princess is in danger work for you?" said Defiance.

"That would bring every ship that receives it," said Sheppard.

"That's great to get everyone mobilized, but what do we do when we have everyone moving?" said Kita.

"I'll look on the map and figure out a place. Most likely it'll be out on the frontier. We pull the expeditionary force guarding the Sol system and those stationed in the AC system. I just need to figure out where the three groups can meet."

"What do we do if Collector's boarding ships get a chance to launch?" said Babydoll.

Sheppard grunted. *"They do a lot of damage, and our ships aren't designed for that kind of combat. We'll have to warn our side to keep their distance. We could try and get the Djinn to board the battle cruisers since they carry nearly as many Marines as the Djinn boarding ships."*

"Incorporate that into the strategic plan your staff puts together," said Kita. *"Tell them those are strategically important ships that need to be destroyed first."*

"Noted," said Blitz. *"I must say, having an entire conversation with others in my head is most bizarre."*

The other Angels chuckled.

"Kita likes to keep it interesting," said Babydoll. *"You haven't even seen the weirdest stuff yet."*

"Kita and weird are synonymous," said Sheppard.

Kita gave her a dirty look. *"For me, it's just an average day. I'll tell you when something gets weird."*

"Then we'll know we're in trouble," said Babydoll.

"And what kind of trouble would that be?"

"Like Harbinger or Kiltrex kind of trouble."

Kita sighed. *"Those weren't weird. They were heartbreaking."*

"But we won."

"And the cost?"

"All part of the business we're in," said Babydoll with a shrug.

"I hope it's not you I have to bury someday," said Kita, her anger building.

"They will be missed," said Defiance as she stepped around and put an arm around Kita. *"Come, let's go inside. They know what they need to know."*

KITA AND BABYDOLL FOLLOWED THE CORRIDOR FROM THE BRIDGE TO THE forward observation room. The room was located on the same level as the bridge, taking up a small corner of the entire space. The bridge and the observation room shared the same giant domed window.

"Hey, I'm sorry," said Babydoll. "Don't give me the silent treatment, especially over something that's true."

"I know you don't care about the Angels we lose, but I do," said Kita.

"Who said I didn't care? Most of them didn't like me, but I do miss living in the penthouse."

"I'm sorry the others didn't like you. I love you, and that's all that matters."

"I know. That's why I stick around. Actually, this new batch of Angels is nice—little green."

Kita sighed. "I know. I'm doing my best to break them in, but it's hard. We don't have a never-ending supply of enemies."

"Or a giant forest to send them into and let them fight their way out."

Kita chuckled. "I do miss that place."

"Ugh, not me. I can't wait to get back to civilization."

"I thought you were Legion through and through."

"Yeah, only on that planet were we ever in the mud," said Babydoll. "Back in the UEE, it was all urban."

"And you were more a police force than a military one," said Kita.

"Paramilitary. We do help with putting down revolts."

"I thought that's what the Shadow Fleet was for."

"That's if the Legion can't pacify the colony or planet. They're the last resort. The Legion is the second resort. The first resort is the negotiators that are sent in to try and fix the problems."

"And what would you do if you could go back to Earth?" said Kita curiously.

"Take in a football match. I've missed that."

"A sporting event is what you've missed? Why don't you watch them on TV?"

"I already know the outcome. You have to see it live and be there with the crowd. It's an awesome spectacle."

"Casey was telling me about rodeo."

Babydoll laughed. "That's not the same. Rodeo is a niche sport particular to America. Football is played the world over in front of a hundred thousand people. The roar of the crowd is enough to make you shiver."

"So did you ever see Rene play?" said Kita.

"Ah, no. Wrong football. She plays American football, a completely different sport. Again, a niche of America."

"I'm going to be so lost when I get to Earth—even with all the TV I've seen."

"Yeah, I should warn you now, real life isn't like it is on TV," said Babydoll.

"Oh, great. I've watched thousands of hours for nothing."

"You were entertained."

"Usually. I could have done without all the sappy romances."

Babydoll chuckled. "Says the girl who has two girlfriends and a partner...plus Snowy. I'm sure there is some sappy romance in there."

Kita chuckled. "Yes, I must keep the other girls happy."

"I have it on authority that you are a bit of a romantic yourself."

"And you're to tell no one. Otherwise, I'll reveal that you are too."

"If the right person comes along. I haven't had your luck and have the right four people come along...Actually, I think you've had more than that."

"I'd love to see you be romantic," said Kita teasing.

"I can do it. How hard can it be?"

Kita smiled as she stepped into the forward observation room. Benches and planters were scattered around, along with a few tables, but she didn't see Stormy.

"You suppose we missed her?" said Babydoll.

"No. Listen," said Kita.

Babydoll looked around.

"Ok, tell me if I'm doing this right," said Stormy. "I have to tap the red well to cast this hill giant, and I have to tap three others?"

"That's right," said Toxic. "Then you place it in front of your wells."

"So I can attack?"

"Not until your next turn."

"Ok, but I have one red well left over so I can cast a lightning bolt?" said Stormy.

"Ah, yeah. That's three damage to me," said Toxic.

"Yeah! I think I'm getting the hang of this."

Babydoll looked at Kita. "What are they doing?"

"It's a game the kids play. I didn't know Amanda was into it. From the sounds of it, she's just learning. Come on."

Kita walked down a row of benches and around a large planter full of greenery. On the floor was Stormy and Toxic with cards laid out before them in an order that only made sense to them.

Stormy looked up at the newcomers. "Hi Kita, Kerri."

"Hi," said Kita with a smile. "Why aren't you at a table?"

"Not enough room," said Toxic.

"Ah, well, sorry to interrupt."

"No problem," said Stormy. "Do you need something?"

"Actually I do," said Kita. "I'm here to ask you a question on behalf of someone."

Stormy blinked. "Really?" she covered her mouth. "I mean, you are? I —" Stormy said excitedly. "Wow, Kara, you told me your family was old fashioned, but I didn't think—Yes, of course, I'll go out with you." She crawled across the cards to give Toxic a hug.

"Ah..."Toxic gulped. "Ok."

Stormy let the smaller Angel go. "Oh, I can't wait! When and where?"

Toxic looked up at Kita, the glow from her hood dimmed. *"Kita, what's happening?"*

"I, ah, think you're going out on a date unless you want to crush her enthusiasm."

"But I don't know anything about that. What do I tell her?"

"Well, do you want to go out with her?" said Kita.

"I don't know. I didn't know she liked me."

"She's on the floor learning to play your card game," said Babydoll. *"This is normally a girl who's into intelligence and shooting things. She must like you."*

"I don't know anything about taking her out on a date," said Toxic. *"Where do we go on a ship?"*

"Normally I'd say a place to look at the stars, but you're already here," said Kita.

"How about the simulator?" said Babydoll. *"I'm sure the captain can get you priority access for an hour."*

"Sure," said Kita.

"But I don't know where to take her," exclaimed Toxic.

"Damn. Do I have to do all your thinking for you?" chided Babydoll. *"She's an Earth girl. Take her to the Eiffel Tower. Girls love that place."*

"There is an opening in three hours," said Kita. *"So, do you want to go, Kara?"*

"I don't know..."

"With that enthusiastic a reaction how can you say no?" said Babydoll.

"Just go and have fun with her," said Kita, *"even if it goes nowhere you can have a little fun."*

"Ah, do you want to go to the Eiffel Tower?" said Toxic while looking at the floor in front of Stormy.

Stormy gasped. "Are you serious?"

"Ah—yeah. There's an opening in the simulator in three hours."

"Oh, gosh. I have to pick out a dress and do my hair." Stormy jumped to her feet, careful not to step on the cards.

"*I've got to wear a dress?*" Toxic whined to Kita and Babydoll.

"*Well, if you want to be classy,*" said Babydoll.

"*I want to see you wear a dress,*" challenged Toxic.

"*Not unless it becomes standard issue.*"

"*I can arrange that,*" said Kita with an amused tone.

"*Don't you dare,*" hissed Babydoll.

"*What's wrong, Kara? You've worn dresses before,*" said Kita.

"*Formal dresses, business dresses, never casual dresses.*"

"*We'll help you out.*"

"*We will?*" said Babydoll.

"*What do you know about dresses, hair, and nails?*" said Toxic.

"*Some,*" said Kita. "*I can bring in an expert if you want.*"

"*Who?*" Toxic challenged.

"*Nell knows plenty about casual and party attire.*"

"*Are you kidding me? She wears six stickers and calls them clothes.*"

"*I believe it's seven,*" said Babydoll.

"*That's just her choice for daily wear,*" said Kita. "*Trust me.*"

"Oh, no..." groaned Toxic.

"Kara will meet you in the wardroom in two hours and forty-five minutes?" said Kita to Stormy.

"Ok. That's not a lot of time, but I can make it work." She bent down and gathered up her cards into the deck. She hugged Toxic. "Oh, Kara, I'm so excited. I'll see you in a little bit." Stormy, with her deck in hand, hurried out of the room.

"What the slag, Kita?" snarled Toxic.

"Sorry. I had no idea Amanda was into you. I came here to ask her out for Rene."

"Oh, slag. This is *so* bad."

"Why is it bad?" said Babydoll. "Did you see how she reacted? I wish someone would get that excited over me."

"You can have her."

"Hey," said Kita. "Be nice. I expect you to be on your best behavior and you know I know what that means out of you."

"Ah, man." Toxic grabbed the strings of her hood and pulled the opening closed.

"What are you worried about?" said Babydoll.

"I'm going to make a fool out of myself. She just became my friend, and now she's going to hate me."

"You don't know that," said Kita.

"Yeah, why would she hate you?" said Babydoll sounding confused.

"Have you met me?" exclaimed Toxic. "I turn everything to slag."

"You just think you do," said Kita. "I know differently and what you've done in the past. You've never failed me before and you won't now."

Toxic's shoulders slumped.

"Come on," ordered Kita. "Let's get you ready."

～

Anthrax met Kita, Toxic, and Babydoll in the wardroom.

"Hey, Kita. What's this special project?" said Anthrax.

Kita waved at Toxic. "You are playing fairy godmother to Kara. She has a date in a little less than three hours and needs to be dressed and primped for the event."

Anthrax raised her eyebrows. "Kara? Who?"

"What's it matter?" grumbled Toxic.

"Kara's still adjusting to the idea," said Kita. "Amanda asked her or, rather, I inadvertently asked for Kara."

"How'd you do that?" said Anthrax, cocking her head with a curious look.

"I came to ask Amanda out for Rene, but Amanda took it as I was there for Kara."

"This could be quite the love triangle. Think you have what it takes to go against Sheppard, Kara?"

Toxic groaned. "She wins."

"But Amanda has no interest in Sheppard," said Babydoll. "She's all over you."

"Lucky me," Toxic said shaking her head.

"I don't know a lot about what your new girls like or dislike, but I'm sure I can get Kara cleaned up and presentable. First, we have to find you something to wear that doesn't scream. leave me alone and don't touch me."

"I like it that way," complained Toxic.

"Then why are you going on a date?" said Anthrax.

"Because I just made friends with her and Kita's making me," mumbled Toxic. "I don't want to lose her, but I'm going to after this date, and I'm going to be alone." Toxic sat down hard and pulled her knees to her chest. She lay her head down on her knees.

Kita shared a look with Babydoll and Anthrax. The display attracted the interest of Raptor and Kamikaze.

"What be wrong with Kara?" said Raptor.

"Insecure with herself," said Kita. "Amanda asked her out. Kara's afraid she's going to mess up their relationship."

"I never would have guessed those Political Bureau types thought about anything but their jobs," said Kamikaze.

"You should see Jess and Hali when they're together."

Raptor knelt next to Toxic. "Kara, sug, you got nothen' to be worryen' about. You a good girl, Amanda goen' to like ya just fine. Come on." Raptor put her arm around Toxic and lifted the tiny Angel to her feet. Toxic didn't fight her. Raptor pushed Toxic's hood back to reveal tears dribbling out of Toxic's glowing eyes. "None of that," said Raptor. "Ya goen' to do it and have fun. Ya be in Kylee's shadow for too long and forgotten how to stand on your own two feet. It be time ya hang out with someone other than her. If Amanda does like ya, that be a good thing, not somethen' to get upset about. I know ya got the confidence, so don't be playing no games. Ya hear?"

Toxic wiped her eyes. "But…"

"No buts," said Raptor. "Ya goen' and that's final. Ya have fun and show the girl a good time."

"But I don't know what to do."

"We got Annie here, and she be haven' lots of experience. Kita be good too. Kami, Kerri, and I have been haven' our fair share. Plus, ya a girl. Ya know what girls like and don't like."

Toxic sighed heavily and slumped her shoulders. "It's been such a long time I've forgotten."

"Then we be reminden' ya on the way to the ship's store. Some of us went through the ship's catalog last week, and there be some cute dresses in there. If ya don't find nothen', then we can have the ship make it."

"Are you sure I can do it," whispered Toxic.

"Where be the girl who was Countess and Vicereine? Ya can lead a nation—ya can do this. We just got to remind ya, is all. Ya be playen' nursemaid to Kylee and she sapped all ya strength. Amanda be far better for ya. She not be a soul sucker and friend devourer."

"But Kylee…"

"Don't ya be defenden' Kylee. Ya know she's bad for ya. Now's your chance to get away from her."

"If it makes it easier," said Kita. "Kylee has been sent back to Infinity. She is no longer an Angel."

Kami gasped. Anthrax raised an eyebrow.

"What?" said Toxic.

Raptor raised an eyebrow and frowned disapprovingly.

"I have my reasons," said Kita.

"I'm sure you do," said Anthrax. "And I'm curious to hear them as we pick out a dress for Kara."

"Think you can do it, Kara?" said Kita.

"Just help me, ok?"

"We'll give you all the help you can handle."

CHAPTER XVIII

Kita's consciousness collapsed back into a point. Her senses slowly invaded the tranquil darkness she spent so much time exploring. The hum of Enterprise's air circulation system followed the smell of recycled air. Pain radiated from her butt from sitting on the friction carpet for so long. Using her senses, she searched for danger, something lurking in the shadows waiting for her. She sensed nothing. Opening her vision to a complete panoramic view, she checked her other senses. The locked indicators for the doors to the forward observation room still blinked red. Scanning the rest of the room, nothing was out of place from when she started a week ago.

She'd requested that she not be disturbed. It had been a while since she had meditated and since she felt she wasn't needed for the daily running of Enterprise, she felt now was a good time. Looking at her plans for the future, they didn't offer many opportunities for meditation. And she needed to. She felt she was far behind where she needed to be. Not that this session hadn't been fruitful. She had discovered much that increased her knowledge. She wasn't as powerful as she had been, but she was getting there. The newest discoveries on what was beyond Infinity had proven to be interesting.

Kita stood. She reached her hands above her head and stretched, then bent at the waist and touched her toes, feeling the blood circulating through her limbs. The pins and needles quickly passed. She collected Crypt and Midnight and stowed them on her back. As she walked to the door back to the bridge, she looked up at the stars one last time.

It was a different collection of stars than she had memorized, but they were still pretty. She loved space. The vastness filled with stars, nebulas, and black holes was beautiful to look at. At the same time, it was so deadly. Often what separated life and death was a thin sheet of metal.

She unlocked the door and followed the corridor to the bridge. She stepped inside, trying not to draw attention to herself. Around her, the bridge was busier than she'd ever seen it. All the workstations were occupied. People talked to each other in the efficient military tone that conveyed urgency without fear or worry.

Kita walked to the holotable. Sheppard, Defiance, and Blitz were standing at the center watching a holographic display. The rest of the display showed reports of other ships and fighters.

"Is this a replay of Rene's greatest hits?" said Kita, teasing.

"Kita!" said Sheppard. "About time. I—"

Defiance put an arm on the other Angel. "Hello, darlin'. We're glad you're back. Rene was about ready to claw down the door."

"Something you can't handle, Admiral?" said Kita.

"It does require your ingenuity as we have been unable to come up with a solution," said Blitz.

"What's the problem?"

"We received specs for Collector's ships. Their weapons, shields, and engines are far more advanced than anything the Tet has."

"And that means more advanced than anything the UEE has."

Blitz nodded. "Correct."

"And we have no way of compensating for this? Fighters? Strategy? Tactics?" said Kita.

"I'm afraid not," said Defiance. "Each ship is equipped with a SLIP drive. You know its capabilities to accelerate and turn. Their shields can slow down kinetic rounds and fighters, as well as stop energy weapons. Their weapons can punch through our shields in two or three strikes and do massive damage when they do connect."

"What have you been doing all week?" said Kita with a grin.

"Feeding them bad simulations. The cats are, if anything, overconfident at their chances. They believe nothing we have can stop them. I still think they're in for a fight against the battleships and heavy dreadnaughts. Even if their kinetic rounds are slowed, they'll still pack a punch. The cats have nothing bigger than a pocket cruiser."

Kita crossed her arms. "Has anyone talked to Jess?"

"I don't ask what the Political Bureau is doing," said Sheppard. "If they have something they bring it to me."

Kita looked at Defiance and raised an eyebrow.

"I don't know what they're doing. She said electronic warfare. I thought it was something for the wizzos."

"They've been working on viruses to attack and cripple the Djinn ships from the inside. Come on, Casey. Let's go see how Jess is doing. Rene, keep the kitties moral sky high with easy victories."

～

KITA WALKED DOWN THE NARROW CORRIDOR THAT LED TO THE POLITICAL Bureau office. She entered the office and found half the workstations filled. She expected them all filled. Valor was in her office on the far side of the room.

Kita stuck her head in the door and a blur of fur pounced on her. She caught Sarge and hugged the big war cat. Defiance laughed at the pair.

"Hello, boy. Did you miss me?" Kita laughed as he licked her. "I bet you haven't given me a second thought as you've been hanging out with Jupiter."

Sarge put his paws around her neck and lashed his tail.

"He's a joy to pet sit," said Valor with a chuckle. "Give these two a warm duct, and they won't move for days. No matter how much they're in the way."

Kita set Sarge down and scratched his ears. "I'll take him off your hands if you don't mind."

"If you're going out and about, take Jupiter with you. He needs some exercise." The golden leopard lifted his head, rolled onto his back, exposing his belly. "Oh, you think I'm a sucker, huh?" Valor bent down and rubbed the cat's white underbelly. "You're still going." Jupiter rolled on his side away from Valor and huffed. "Yeah, walking is going to kill you." Valor turned to Kita. "So, enjoy your time off?"

Kita smiled. "Hardly time off, but my meditation was successful. I found some lost knowledge and some extra. How are things here?"

"We have complete electronic warfare suites for ten of the ships and various stages of completion for the rest."

"I need you to concentrate on taking down engines, shields, and weapons. Those are components Rene and Casey have identified that the Djinn have a distinct advantage over the UEE."

"I'll do my best, but I've been working people double and triple shifts. I finally had to let them get some rest."

"Where's Denver?" said Kita, looking over her shoulder to scan the room. "I thought she was helping you?"

"She never came back. I tracked her down, but she refused to help. I got chased out by two of the other Angels telling me I'd have to solve the problem myself."

"Who would chase you out?" said Defiance.

"My guess is Vee and Tenshi," said Kita. "They are Denver's sisters."

"Really?"

"Not sisters from this equation, but sisters in Infinity. Their father is Ht'aed."

Defiance made a face. "I didn't know gods could have siblings."

Kita shrugged. "They didn't have the concept until I gave it to them." She looked at Valor. "Do you know where she is? I'll go talk to her. I'm sure it's me she's mad at."

"What did you do?" said Defiance accusingly.

"I kicked her partner and my daughter, Kylee, out of the Angels."

"What did she do, so I never repeat the mistake," said Valor.

Kita smiled. "Defy me and commit genocide."

Valor let out a sigh of relief. "I thought it was something like leaving the ice cream out on the counter."

"How did she commit genocide?" said Defiance.

"Kylee is the God of Hate. It's not hard. I understand she destroyed the suns and planets of these civilizations."

Defiance blinked. "I have the power, but I don't think I could do it."

"I won't deny Kylee had issues, but it's a mess I had to clean up, and I did. Some didn't agree with the way I did it, but it's my choice. I give the feathers, and I can take them away."

"I prefer mine where they are," said Defiance.

Kita gave her a wolfish look, "Me, too."

"Ok, get out of here before I have a mess on my desk," ordered Valor. "And take the cats with you."

"You sure you don't want to join us, Jess?" Defiance cooed playfully.

"You see who I sleep with, right? Just the most beautiful race in the galaxy."

Defiance and Kita laughed.

"Bring her along," teased Kita.

"I'm not sharing," said Valor.

"Speaking of sharing…how's Amanda?"

Valor smiled and rolled her eyes. "She's been on cloud nine all week. She went out with Kara three times. She told me all about it. I guess their first date in France was a little awkward, but Amanda was able to loosen Kara up. I think she's down in the practice area working with some of the other shooters if you want the first-hand scoop."

"And here I thought I would have to scold Kara." Kita grinned as she exited the office waving the cats to follow her and Defiance.

"*Denver?*" Kita called over the comm. She didn't receive an answer. "*Denver?*" Kita sighed.

"Denver's not answering me, and I'm not detecting any activity over our connection. None for a week."

"She must be really mad at you," said Defiance. "And I don't blame her. I'd be mad at you, too."

"She's mad now, but she'll see it's for her own good. She was the one that came to me saying she couldn't handle Kylee anymore."

"That's different than banishing her partner."

Kita shrugged. "Ship computer, where is Child of the emperor Valentine?"

"Child of the emperor Valentine is in hangar four near the runway, Captain Kita."

"She can run, but she can't hide."

~

KITA, DEFIANCE, AND THE CATS WALKED PAST THE NEATLY SPACED ROWS OF fighters filling hangar four. On many of the aircraft, hatches were open— some had engines pulled—and personnel swarmed over them making sure they were fit to fight.

"And to think, they do it all for you," Kita teased Defiance.

"They do it for the Empire. I'm just the personification of the Empire."

Kita nodded. "I've been there."

"I can't imagine you as an emperor."

"I wasn't. I was a Rose. I was the personification of the warrior spirit of Arcone. I was like a queen, but my power was limited to foreign affairs and the battlefield."

"How come I've never heard this before?"

"It was a long time ago during my youth. We had some differences that split us apart."

Defiance chuckled. "I can't imagine what those would be."

"I wanted one city for my personal forces, and they wouldn't let me have it. They kidnapped my girls to make me behave. It cost the leadership their lives. Afterward, I left with a few other Angels to explore space. That's when I rescued Rene."

"I wondered how you found her."

"We followed a rescue beacon to the emperor's Wrath. Because it was an Imperial ship, we helped the crew. When Galina revealed who she was, we discovered she was still in the Political Bureau system, and they had promoted her to Command General in her absence. To explain who we were to the crew, she made us Children of the emperor. We lived aboard until Kamikaze called me back to The Mass and an ecosystem gone mad. Who knew moving a mountain would cause so much havoc?" Kita shook her head.

Defiance took Kita's hand as they left the hangar behind and stepped out onto the runway. "And—somehow—I believe you moved a mountain on your own."

Kita angled the pair toward a group of Angels firing at targets set up at the end of the runway. "I had help. Nina and Amber did most of the prep work. I provided the steam to set it off."

"You dare show your face?" Valentine yelled from the group of Angels on the firing line. She drew her pistols and aimed at Kita.

"I'm not the one refusing to answer my calls," said Kita keeping her tone neutral. Kita opened her arms. "If it makes you feel better, take your shot, but you'll have to deal with them."

Around Kita, Saige and Jupiter stalked, their hackles raised, snarls bared their fangs.

"You had no right to do what you did," Valentine screamed as Tenshi and Panther arrived at her side. Behind them came Raptor, Aspen, Babydoll, Kamikaze, Toxic, Hali, and Stormy.

"Put the guns away, sug," said Raptor to Valentine. "Ya know this been' a setup."

"She's got a right to be upset," said Panther. "Kita, you had no right to do what you did. We all agree on that point."

Kita raised an eyebrow. "That's not how I read it, but your opinions are irrelevant. The choice is mine. If you learn to make Angels you're free to change her back."

"You didn't even give her a fair trial," said Tenshi. "You listened to who you wanted and ignored the rest of us."

"We would never have condoned removing Kylee," said Panther.

"Why?" said Kita. "Because it could happen to you? Is that what you're scared of? That I'll take back what I gave you? Are you that big of cowards?"

"No one is being coward," snarled Tenshi. "We are defending our rights."

Kita shook her head. "Then you have a fatal misunderstanding. You have no rights. You serve at my pleasure. You are free to leave at any time and take what I gave you, but I can take back what is mine at any time."

"Is that all we mean to you?" yelled Tenshi.

"No," said Kita quietly. "You mean the world to me, but I've fought against genocide my entire life, and I won't allow it in my ranks."

"You give everyone a second chance," screamed Valentine.

"That's when it's a transgression against me. This was a transgression against innocence."

"Since when do you care about innocence?"

"I never stopped caring. I stopped trying to save and protect them."

"You hypocritical bitch." Valentine fired her pistols.

Kita spun, drew her swords, and knocked the bullets out of the air, sending them sparking off the runway and walls. Tenshi and Panther grabbed Valentine's arms and pulled her pistols from her hands.

Kita sheathed her swords with a flourish. Her left eye narrowed and she motioned with two fingers. An invisible force slammed into the Valkyrie Angels, pinning them to the wall on the far side of the runway. Kita seized Defiance's hand. She draped her wing over the cats and phased the group to the bridge.

"Rene!" Kita called as she worked hard to keep her temper in check, at least, for the moment.

Sheppard looked up from the holotable. "Yeah?" she said with trepidation.

"You and Casey are to sleep for the next ship cycle. Issue the order to Enterprise that we leave in three days. Alert Collector's forces when we're six hours from leaving. Anyone not ready will be left behind."

"What about the issue with Collector's forces? Do we have a solution?"

"Don't worry about it. Go to bed. That's an order," said Kita firmly.

Sheppard looked at Defiance.

"Do you work for her or for me?" said Kita pointedly.

"Go to bed, Rene," said Defiance. "Right now, we work for her."

Kita glared at Defiance.

"I understand you're upset," said Defiance. "And I'm letting this temper tantrum go, but you will need me to be in charge once we get to UEE space."

I'd like to see you try. Collector won't stop me and neither will you. Kita looked at the cats. "Go back to Jess and guard her, Hali, and Amanda. Use whatever force you have to."

Sarge and Jupiter each let out a chuff and walked toward the elevator.

Kita opened the doors for them and set the elevator to the correct deck.

She stepped around Defiance and walked toward to door for the forward observation room.

"Where you going?" said Defiance.

"To brood," Kita answered acidly.

~

BABYDOLL COULDN'T MOVE. WHATEVER FORCE KITA WAS USING WAS STRONG, but she wasn't interested in playing games. She changed to her god form and tried to float away, but found she was stuck. *What the hell? There is no way Kita can trap a god.*

Looking at the equation, she searched for the force trapping her, but there was nothing. *Impossible. It would have to show. Everything must register in the equation.* A chill went through Babydoll as the implications of what this meant sunk in. If Kita could hide the creation of energy in an equation, it would be impossible to counter her.

Babydoll changed back to her angelic form. The force released and Babydoll floated down to the floor. She fluffed her feathers. Around her, the other Angels floated to the ground as the force released them. Panther's face was red, puffy, and an eye was swollen shut. Stormy ran up to check on Toxic. She looked fine. Obviously, Kita had been gentler with some.

"What the slag was that?" demanded Panther, her voice sounding mushy as Babydoll came up to her. Behind her, Valentine lay unconscious. Raptor was bleeding from a gash across her forehead. Kamikaze was helping Tenshi with a dislocated elbow.

Aspen drifted over to Panther. *"Let me see your face."*

Panther tipped her head over so Aspen could see. Aspen put her hand on Panther's face. When Aspen pulled her hand away, nothing had happened.

"Did Kita do something to our clouds?" said Aspen to Babydoll.

"Mine seems to be working. Let me see a sword."

Aspen passed over Dawn. Babydoll pulled the blade across her upper arm leaving a bloody line.

"Try that," said Babydoll.

Aspen put her hand over it. When she removed it, the cut was healed.

"That's what I thought," said Babydoll. "It's not you, but the person. Kita's being vengeful."

"How she be doen' that?" demanded Raptor.

"I have no idea," said Babydoll. "Whatever she hit us with was able to affect me in my god form."

"That be impossible."

"I'm reporting what I experienced. The energy wasn't visible in the equation, either."

"But, how?" said Raptor. "Ugh. I be haven' a headache."

"I wonder if your healing nanites are working," said Aspen.

"Oh, this be sucken' if they don't. Why would Kita do this?"

"You threatened her. She's going to prove she's not to be threatened."

"We won't blindly obey," said Tenshi.

"Speak for yourself," said Babydoll. "I know Kita's wrath, and I've seen her bag of tricks. I want no part of it."

"You were always her lap dog."

Babydoll shrugged. "Say what you want. I know Kita better than any of you. I know better than to challenge her. If you don't like it, take what she's given you and leave, but don't stay here and fight her. It will only end badly for you."

"She can't defeat us all," snapped Tenshi.

"She just pinned us to the wall with a look and a wave of her finger," Babydoll snarled. "You don't think she doesn't possess the power to rip everything from us? She did it to Kylee. I bet Kita could have deleted her if she wanted. Is that what you want? To be deleted?"

"She can't get away with this!"

"She already has. I don't think E'fil and Y'grene can stop her," Babydoll said quietly.

"Then we go after those she does care about. That's her weakness." Tenshi pointed at Stormy and Hali.

"Hey, back off," said Toxic. She drew her swords and moved between the Valkyrie Angels and Stormy.

A pair of lightning bolts struck the deck. Sarge and Jupiter stood in their battle forms. Jupiter opened his mouth, and a ball of lightning crackled.

Valor appeared in her armor and landed next to Hali. Sheppard, Blitz, and Defiance appeared looking bewildered.

"What's going on?" said Defiance.

"Kita is making a point," said Babydoll. "I don't think it's wise to attack the others."

"They're not gods," said Tenshi.

"I am," said Aspen.

"So am I," said Toxic.

"I side with the new girls," said Babydoll to the remaining Valkyries. "Just accept your lumps and go."

"Go where?" demanded Tenshi.

"I don't know. It's a big equation. I'm sure you can find a place."

"Why do we have to be the ones who leave? This is about what Kita did."

Babydoll glowered. "This is quickly becoming about what you're doing. And I will put a stop to it."

"You really think you can beat me? Us?" said Tenshi as she rested her hand on her assault rifle.

"You might want to talk to your partner about this," said Babydoll. "I feel she doesn't fully support you." Babydoll raised an eyebrow at Kamikaze.

Kamikaze gave Babydoll a dirty look.

"Your mom is running amuck worse than Kylee ever did," said Tenshi to Kamikaze.

"I believe my mom had a good reason for doing what she did. I won't pass judgment on her until I get a chance to talk to her. And, I won't help you hurt the new Angels. They have no part in this. Hurting them would only bring down my mother's wrath further."

"Kylee was your sister. What's to keep Kita from stripping us?"

"Nothing," said Kamikaze with a shrug. "It's her power to give. She gives it freely and asks nothing in return. It's also hers to take back. She owes us nothing. We owe her everything."

"I do not owe her everything," snapped Tenshi. "She took everything from me."

"Yes, and you embraced it. You gladly became an Angel, disavowing a son to do so. You think my mom owes you something? She worked out a deal so your son and grandmother would live."

"She made me trade my life for theirs!" cried Tenshi.

"And you followed willingly. You can leave at any time, but you stick around. What are you afraid of? That my mother is going to change her mind, strip us, and send us away? Kylee lost her status because she killed billions of people and their planets. Are you planning on doing something equally despicable?"

"Of course not!"

"Than what are you worried about?" demanded Kamikaze. "My mom doesn't make us live by a code of ethics. We're each allowed to find that on our own."

"I never be hearen' her talk about genocide as a bad thing," said Raptor. "She be killen' plenty."

"My mom has killed tens of thousands, but that's not genocide. I'm sure there are a few hidden rules my mom has. If she had been with us, she would have stopped Kylee the first time and given her a warning."

"Then why didn't she get a warning now?" demanded Tenshi.

"As Cowboy used to say, 'You're closing the gates after the cows are out.' It was too late. Kylee had done it—multiple times. She was passed the stage of a warning."

"What about Denver?" Tenshi said quietly.

Kamikaze looked at the unconscious Angel. "She must make a choice. She can lose everything and go be with Kylee or lose Kylee and keep everything in hopes that someday Kylee will be allowed back."

"That's not fair!" said Panther.

"Kylee's actions affected more than herself," said Kamikaze. "I lost a sister and friend. It hurts, but she hurt me by doing what she did. We warned Kylee, but she didn't listen. I wonder if there was more I could have done to stop her, but then if I had, what would she have done next? We weren't changing her, and she was only getting worse. In the end, I believe my mom is the best one to handle her. She understood Kylee and did her best to guide and teach her. Kylee could have been something great. My mom saw that. But, Kylee chose a different path. She couldn't overcome her own self-destructive behaviors. It's no one's fault but Kylee's. She had the opportunity to get help, and she chose not to take it."

"It is too Kita's fault!" Valentine cried as tears streamed down her face. "She took Kylee from me. Kita had no right to take her. She's not God. She's barely one of us—just an equation that knows more than she should. Why did she have to take Kylee from me?" Valentine put her face down on the deck and sobbed.

Babydoll raised an eyebrow as she looked at Panther, Raptor, and Tenshi. "It's your choice, ladies, stay or go. You know what staying means."

"I've left before," said Raptor. "I be not afraid to leave now."

"Your choice. You know where to find us."

"Tell Kita she be wrong."

"Tell her yourself." Babydoll pointed behind Raptor.

Raptor turned to face Kita. "You be wrong over what you did to Kylee. I be not afraid to say it."

Kita bowed her head. "The choice is yours. Only you know what your heart can handle."

Raptor looked at Tenshi and Panther. "You girls be comen'?"

Tenshi shook her head. "I won't leave Kami."

Panther looked at Kita, then at Valentine. "My sister needs me."

"Then I be off." Raptor changed into her god form and collapsed into a point of light. She flew down the runway and out into space.

When Babydoll looked back at Kita, she was gone. Babydoll sighed. Someday she would have to learn some of her friend's tricks.

"Ok, everyone. Back to it," announced Babydoll. "This ship isn't getting to Earth on its own."

CHAPTER XIX

$\mathcal{K}$ ita emerged from the passage leading toward the forward observation room. The bridge was bustling with activity as sailors operated workstations while talking on headsets. Her anger still percolated, but she was out of time. The fleet was due to leave in an hour. She looked for the Angels, but they were gone. Captain Anderson stood at the holotable reviewing reports. As Kita walked toward him, fire dripped from her wings and she left flaming footprints. She stopped next to him. "Captain Anderson."

He turned from the holotable and raised an eyebrow. "Can I help you, Child of the emperor?"

"Where is the princess or Admiral Sheppard?"

"Down in the Political Bureau office."

"What's going that would take Admiral Sheppard off the bridge now?"

"She said it was for a new weapon system in development."

Kita nodded and walked away. As she went, Anderson tried to stomp out one of her flaming footprints.

"Don't worry, Captain," Kita called. "They won't last long or leave scorch marks."

 ~

"Darlin', what happened to you?" cried Defiance when she spotted Kita walking across the Political Bureau office.

Kita shrugged. She was still on fire. Her bodysuit was full of holes, her hair was a mess, and all her makeup gone. "You should see the room," she said, trying to bring a touch of humor to the situation.

"You didn't torch another room, did you?" asked Valor.

"Little bit," whispered Kita.

"How do you do it without setting off the fire suppression systems?" asked Blitz.

"I'm very skilled."

"Darlin', you need to stop doing this to yourself," said Defiance as she hugged Kita.

Kita sighed and rested her head on Defiance's shoulder, enjoying the smell of her hair. "I probably smell like a cinder."

"More like fire and brimstone," quipped Valor.

Kita groaned.

Defiance patted the side of Kita's head. "Don't worry. We'll get you cleaned up."

"I need you on the bridge," protested Sheppard.

"You can deal with me being gone for thirty minutes. You used to run the bridge without me, you know."

Sheppard's face remained neutral, but Kita could feel the sting.

"So what are we doing?" asked Kita.

"Debating on how best to deploy the cyber warfare suites," said Valor. "Most are ready to go. The debate is if we deploy them on the Djinn ships or not."

"Why wouldn't we?" said Kita.

"The packages are large, and we're worried they'll be discovered."

"But if we keep them here we run the risk of communications being cut and not being able to deploy them at all," said Defiance.

"Isn't that a risk even if we deploy them?" said Kita.

"We can program scenarios where the suites will activate given certain parameters, like loss of communications with us," said Valor.

Kita felt a familiar bump against her leg. She leaned over and scratched Sarge's ears as she thought about what to do. Kneeling down, she ran her fingers through his long, soft fur.

"Deploy them," ordered Kita, "in the Deep Space Communications Computers. Disguise them as messages. No one dumps those systems. It will also hide our communications with them, but program in some scenarios in case we do lose contact. Do we need to delay departure so you can do it?"

"How long do we have before we reach the wormhole?" said Valor.

"It's a short FTL jump then we have to make up whatever jump drift occurs," said Sheppard. "I'd say six hours. Kita, I have another concern."

"Ok…what?"

"When we jump through the wormhole, are you expecting us to destroy the picket ships guarding the wormhole on the UEE side? I don't think the crew will do it."

Kita received a curious glance from Defiance. "I've given that some thought and I do have a plan."

"You could have told me earlier and taken some stress off my mind."

"It would have been nice to know days ago, darlin'," said Defiance.

"Sorry," said Kita with a downward glance. "It was pushed down the priority list. We are going to jump last, but instead of jumping through the wormhole, we will make an FTL jump. It's easily within the SLIP drive's range. That should buy us some time on the other end to warn the picket ships. I'll need to spend some time with the navigation computer to make sure our jump is on target. Does that sound acceptable?"

"That should give us twelve hours and the picket ships a head start," said Defiance.

"And we can contact the rest of the fleet," said Sheppard.

Kita let out a happy sigh, pleased her ideas were well received and made everyone's day easier.

"Is there anything else?" said Defiance to Sheppard and Valor.

"Not from me," said Valor. "We'll get to work and put the finishing touches on these warfare suites."

"No," said Sheppard. "I'll return to the bridge and oversee the final preparations for getting underway."

"Good," said Defiance. "I'll take Kita and get her presentable."

Kita and Defiance appeared in the admiral's quarters.

"Why don't we get you into the shower?" suggested Defiance.

"Are you saying I smell bad?" said Kita, trying to be more humorous than she felt.

"No, but I know it's been days since you had a shower."

Kita nodded. That much was true. She took off her weapons and pads laying them on the desk. Her boots morphed back into her bodysuit. She stripped the burnt and damaged suit off and threw it on the chair.

Defiance came behind Kita, picked up the bodysuit, and threw it in the recycler. She went into the bathroom and started the shower. She took Kita's hand and gently pulled her into the room, then pushed her under the streaming water.

Kita closed her vision, feeling the water hit her on two sides. It felt good, but it couldn't wash away the sorrow and pain she felt. The water did hide the tears she swore she wouldn't shed.

She couldn't help it. Kylee had been her baby, so full of energy and life. She was supposed to be the one that would be like her. To take over when she couldn't or didn't want. Kita had given Kylee everything she could think of to educate her. She didn't understand where she had failed and why Kylee had done what she did. What example had she failed to give?

The water on her back stopped, and a pair of arms slide around Kita. She opened her vision and found Defiance holding her. She didn't think she'd made a sound. Defiance rested her head against Kita's neck and wet hair. Kita placed her hands on Defiance's and interlaced their fingers.

"Are you ok?" said Defiance in a worried voice.

"I'll be fine," whispered Kita.

"What's wrong?"

"Just trying to understand what I did wrong with Kylee."

"I'm sorry about what happened. Is there something I could have done?"

Kita shook her head. "No. I cast this die a long time ago. I thought I'd done a good job, taught her right, showed her what to be, but somewhere along the way I lost her. Maybe I couldn't overcome her pain, or I wasn't harsh enough and gave her too much freedom. Maybe I was counting on others to do my job for me. Regardless, it's my fault. Someday, when this is over, I'll be able to talk to her and find out what went wrong. Maybe it won't be too late to fix it, or, maybe, I'll have to kill her and end her suffering."

Kita felt Defiance's grip tighten.

"Hopefully you'll never reach that maybe."

"I can only hope she sees the error of her ways. What are you doing in here?"

Defiance hugged Kita. "I wanted to be close to you, and you sounded like you needed someone to talk to."

"It's not something you need to burden yourself with. My troubles are my own."

Defiance's grip stiffened. "I love you. Your troubles are mine."

Kita tilted her head back and rested on Defiance's head. "I love you, Casey. But I'm a hard person to love."

"The same could be said of me. You're the only person who I consider my equal, and you treat me that way. I've had a lifetime of people doing my bidding. You're one of a handful of people who know what that's like. You know the weight of ruling and the pain that comes with it—and know how lonely it is. I want someone by my side who understands that and understands me. I've never found someone who can do one, let alone both. It won't be long before I'm crowned Emperor and I don't want to do it alone."

Kita grimaced. "You know I'm not that kind of person, and that's the last thing I want. Angels are built for war, and the UEE is the farthest from that. There is much in the equation that I want to experience and learn."

"I know. I'm not saying you have to stay. I wouldn't want you to. I would want to go with you. The government can run without me. All I care about is that I'm with you."

"And Vee? Snowy? My partner that's out there somewhere? I've never stayed with one person long."

"I won't pretend to think I can change you, just come when I call?"

"Always."

"That's all I want. To be yours and you to be mine."

"What about your citizens? How will they feel about me?" said Kita.

Defiance squeezed Kita. "I don't care. They'll get over it. I won't be like my grandmother and put my happiness aside for the better of the Empire. I can deal with anyone who argues with me."

Kita chuckled.

"What will you do after this is over?" said Defiance.

"I'm sure I'll stay in UEE space for a while. Several of the Angels are from there. Then, explore the equation. There are some things I'd love to show you."

"That sounds wonderful."

Kita turned in Defiance's arms. She brushed Defiance's hair out of her face and tucked it behind her ear. Taking Defiance's face in her hands, Kita kissed her.

～

KITA SAT AT THE VANITY BRUSHING HER HAIR AND PLANNING HER OUTFIT. AT some point during an orgasm, they had made the FTL jump to the wormhole. The sensation of having someone inside you while you drop into Nothing was an indescribable experience. She knew she'd have to do it again.

In the bed, Defiance stirred. She sat up gathering the sheet around her. "You're so not modest are you?" she said with a laugh as Kita sat naked.

Kita smiled. "Something my mother trained out of me. I had to walk around the castle in a towel."

"You're not wearing a towel now."

"No, I've moved on to the advanced course."

Defiance giggled. "So what's the plan?"

"I have a stop to make in the medical ward, and then get a report from Rene on how close we are to the wormhole."

"That stack of bodysuits suggests you're going out formally?" said Defiance.

"I thought I should look presentable for leading this crew of yours."

"Then I guess I should get up and put my uniform on."

"I like having you naked in the bed," said Kita with a warm smile.

"Unfortunately, I'm a working girl, too."

～

KITA ENTERED THE MEDICAL WARD WEARING HER BATTLE QIPAO—THE traditional dress for female assassins in the Assassins Guild from her homeworld. Hers had a short skirt, a sleeveless top with a high collar, and black tights and boots. On the front panel of the top, she had embroidered the UEE crest. Defiance joined her, wearing the UEE Shadow Fleet dress uniform.

The ward was empty the last casualties of the fight against the Tet ships discharged several days ago. Kita and Defiance found the Djinn doctor taking care of Sahara working at a portable desk. He dwarfed the stool he sat on.

"Hello, Doctor Er'jeria," said Kita.

The Djinn looked up from his computer. "Captain Kita. What can I help you with?"

"Checking in on your patient. How is she?"

"She still has multiple fractures, and her damaged organs are healing as expected. Collector wishes to know what punishment you plan on dealing out for the individual responsible."

Ah, none. "I have talked to Commander Liverpool and have instructed her on the proper use of force when dealing with a non-Angel opponent. She sends her apologies."

"I will pass that along in my next report to Collector."

"Happy to help," said Kita. "Thanks for the update."

Kita left the Djinn and went to the suite holding Sahara. Kita opened the door and found Snowy sitting near the head of the bed reading aloud.

"What do you want?" said Snowy wearily. She looked up and down, and her eyes narrowed. "I see where I rate."

Kita used to have a snow leopard embroidered on her top representing Snowy. "You have a girlfriend and a new master now."

"Collector is not my master."

"Then what's your plan? For the two of you to live on Djinn? Like they'll let that happen. They won't even allow it on the Tet. You need Collector's protection. Does he know of your relationship?"

Snowy's ears lay flat against her head as her whiskers drooped. "No."

"From what I understand you haven't explained your intentions fully to Sahara."

"I'm going slow. I don't want to shock her," whispered Snowy.

"Luring her into your web, huh?"

Snowy bared a fang. "Don't be a bitch."

"I wonder how long it will be before you need me to get you out of this mess."

"I don't need you. I know where we can go."

Kita raised an eyebrow. "Where?"

"Back to our homeworld. It's dangerous, but I know how to survive there. We can hunt and live in peace."

"You need someone's permission. That planet belongs to her." Kita motioned her head toward Defiance. "How are you planning on getting there?"

"I haven't figured that out yet."

"You're in the presence of the one person who can make it happen... After she gets back to Earth."

Kita walked up one side of the bed while hovering her hand above Sahara's body. She walked passed Snowy and stopped when she reached the head of the bed. Kita placed her hand on the Djinn's arm.

"Her fur is coarser than yours," Kita commented.

She pulled her hand away. Between her fingers was a device the size of a grain of rice. Kita held it up for Snowy.

"What did you do? What's that?" Snowy demanded.

"An FTL tracker. Do you think Collector is going to let his daughter out of his sight?"

"I—"

"I doubt she even knows it's there. But, I'll take care of it. Now might be a good time to ask for that ride back to our homeworld."

Kita phased to a Djinn ship in her fleet. Someone in the fleet had to be watching Sahara's tracker. She didn't know how accurate the tracking equipment was but hoped it was greater than fifty miles.

The corridor Kita appeared in was empty. She went to the wall and opened an access hatch. Kita closed her hand around the FTL tracker.

When she opened her hand, she held a cockroach. The insect contained the tracker and would provide enough movement to mimic a Djinn's movements. She placed the cockroach in the access panel, closed it, and phased back to the medical ward aboard Enterprise.

"Where did you go?" demanded Snowy.

"I gave you and Sahara a head start. Call it a gift from an old friend," said Kita warmly.

"I know you don't do anything for free. What do you want?"

Kita shrugged. "Maybe I'm apologizing for what Kerri did. You are my friend, and I do want to see you happy."

Snowy grunted. "I'll wait for the other shoe to drop."

Kita smiled. "I intend no malice toward the two of you. Come on, Casey. Let's go see how Rene is doing."

As Kita passed Snowy, she winked at her. The dread Snowy gave off was amusing, but misplaced. Kita wanted nothing but happiness for them.

~

"PRINCESS ON DECK," A GUARD YELLED AS KITA AND DEFIANCE EXITED THE elevator onto Enterprise's bridge.

"Where are we?" Kita asked Sheppard as she and Defiance approached the holotable.

"We're approaching the wormhole now. There is a pair of Diamock ships on patrol."

"Will they try and impede us?"

"I don't know what their orders are. They haven't tried to contact us."

"Make for the wormhole. If the Diamocks try and stop us, we'll deal with them."

"Command," Sheppard called.

"Yes, ma'am?"

"New orders for the fleet. Proceed to the wormhole and jump, unless ordered otherwise. Enterprise will jump last. When the ships arrive on the other side they are to engage any hostiles they encounter at their discretion."

"Aye, aye, ma'am. Transmitting now."

"All ahead slow," ordered Sheppard.

"All ahead slow, ma'am," replied the helmsman.

On the holotable, the Enterprise icon slowed, and the first of Collector's ships passed them and proceeded to the wormhole. The Diamock ships changed course.

"Enemy ships have changed heading to one-three-three down angle five degrees at three hundred and fifty-three miles, ma'am," reported Sensors.

"Incoming transmission on an open frequency," reported Communications.

"Put it on the holotable," said Sheppard.

The middle of the holotable blinked, and the image of a Diamock appeared.

"Who's this?" said Sheppard.

"I am Captain Gudin of the Diamock Navy. You—You're one of the renegade Angels! You are to halt and are under arrest."

Sheppard looked at Kita. She stepped up next to Sheppard. "You and what navy?" said Kita. "I see two ships. I have twenty-one."

"Those are privately owned vessels and are being instructed they are in restricted space. They will not help you. Save yourself and your ship. Surrender."

"What's the chance they're scrambling every ship in this sector to get here before we can jump?" Kita said to Sheppard and Defiance.

"I would," said Sheppard.

"You're going to have to make us," said Kita.

"Call general quarters," ordered Sheppard to the Officer of the Watch.

"Every Diamock and Tet ship in nearby space is being mobilized," said Gudin. "This is a fight you cannot win, and there is no escape."

"Communications, open a channel with all ships in the fleet," ordered Kita.

Around Gudin appeared the images of the ship captains of Collector's fleet.

"Warriors," said Kita addressing her ship captains, "the Diamocks are blocking our path to glory. You are to maintain course and speed to the objective, but all weapons able to fire on the two defying ships," Kita highlighted the Diamock ships on the holotable, updating the battle displays across Collector's fleet, "are to do so. Cripple them if you can. They are not our enemy, but we will not be hampered in our pursuit of glory and honor."

Kita received a round of affirmatives from her ship captains.

"I suggest you retreat and let us pass, Gudin."

"The Diamock Navy will not be intimidated."

"Let me show you why you should. Fleet, ships one through ten, first target, ships eleven through twenty, second target, fire one salvo."

The ships of Collector's fleet were not oriented the right direction to bring their main guns to bear but unleashed a barrage with their secondary armaments. On the screen, Gudin's connection blinked several times. The Diamock's attention was pulled away as he received several reports at once. On the holotable, Gudin's ship turned red. His companion ship turned yellow.

"Intimidated yet?" Kita asked Gudin with a smirk.

"New contacts bearing two-six-three fifteen degrees up angle at five hundred thirty-five miles and bearing three-three-six five degrees up angle at two hundred and seventy-five miles," reported Sensors.

"That was fast," Kita muttered.

"The first ship in the fleet has reached the wormhole. Jump in progress," reported Sensors.

"Fleet, increase speed. Go for the wormhole and jump. Ships eleven through fifteen, fire two salvos at contact bearing two-six-three. Ships sixteen through twenty, fire two salvos at contact bearing three-three-six," ordered Kita.

"Kita, we've got to get you attached to the navigation computer," said Sheppard.

"We have a battle to fight."

"No, we have a battle to run away from. We need you to make a pinpoint jump if the plan is to succeed. I'll take care of fighting the battle until it's time to go."

Kita sighed. *But, I'm having fun.* "Captains, Admiral Sheppard is now in command." Kita stepped away, and with Defiance at her side, she went to Navigation.

"I'm here to plug in," said Kita, deflated.

Defiance rubbed Kita's arm and squeezed her hand. Kita smiled in return. The sailor relinquished his seat so Kita could sit while she worked. Placing her finger over the port, she interfaced with the computer.

"Go ahead and run it," said Kita.

"New contacts bearing three-five-two, two-nine-one, two-six-seven, three-zero-nine, two-eight-eight, and three-three-three," reported Sensors. "Nine ships have jumped."

Kita ground her teeth. She wanted to know what was going on.

"Fleet, fire at will," ordered Sheppard.

"New group of contacts heading our way," reported Command.

"Hold fighters," replied Sheppard.

"Taking fire," said Anderson.

"It's light and random," said Sheppard. "The shields will stop it."

"New contact bearing zero-seven-six, five degrees down angle, sixty miles," reported Sensors.

"Damn. That's right on top of us," said Sheppard. "How many ships left?"

"Five," reported Sensors.

"Incoming fire from new dreadnaught class contact," reported Anderson.

"Neptune's rings," swore Sheppard. "All ships left in the fleet target new contact bearing zero-seven-six. Shields maximum port side. Close the window."

Above them, the protective shield moved over the panoramic window.

"Incoming," announced Anderson.

Kita braced herself, even though she knew she didn't need to. The enemy fire would hit the shields and wouldn't be felt inside. The jolt caught everyone off guard. Sailors operating stations were knocked out of their seats. Defiance stumbled as Kita did her best to remain in her seat and connected to the computer.

"What was that?" yelled Defiance.

"A very big kinetic round, Your Highness," replied Sheppard.

"How'd it get through?"

"The shields are only rated for so much energy."

"Can we take another one?"

"The shields are at fifty percent. I'd rather not."

Defiance looked at Kita. "Where are you at, darlin'?"

"Somewhere between just dreaming about numbers and seeing them floating before my eyes."

"If we were to jump how close can you get us?"

"Ah…" Kita snapped at the sailor operating the FTL computer. He looked up at her surprised. "How close?" demanded Kita.

"A hundred and ten miles."

"That's close enough," said Defiance. "Rene!"

"Yes, Your Highness?"

"Prepare for FTL jump."

"We still have two ships waiting to make the wormhole jump."

"How long?"

"Five minutes."

"Too long. I'm not losing this ship. Jump!"

Enterprise shook again. This time, Kita fell out of her seat but was able to keep her finger in contact with the computer port. Defiance grabbed a workstation.

"Damage report!" cried Defiance.

"We have hull penetration port side decks three, four, and five. Emergency doors are holding."

"Kita! Get us out of here!" demanded Defiance.

"Hit it," Kita ordered the sailors of the FTL section.

The sailors didn't need any more encouragement. "Aye aye, ma'am."

Kita felt her stomach in her throat, and the world went black.

CHAPTER XX

"*E*ngineering, where is the damage?" demanded Sheppard.

"Decks three, four, and five, ma'am. Right under runway two."

"Damn. I need to know the functionality of runway two. I want a full damage report."

"Aye aye, ma'am."

"Medical, deploy rescue teams and recover any dead or wounded," said Sheppard.

"Aye aye, ma'am."

"Sensors, is the holotable updated?"

"Yes, ma'am. Calibration is complete."

"Then why don't I see any ships?"

"Systems report normal, ma'am."

Sheppard let out a low growl. "Where are the picket ships? Who's guarding the wormhole?"

Defiance put a hand on Sheppard's arm. "Easy, Admiral. I'm sure there's a good explanation. Communications, send out a distress message on all bands including the emergency band. Let them know I'm here and am in danger."

"This is off to an auspicious start," said Kita sarcastically. "We haven't planned for this scenario."

"We have precious few hours to warn the Shadow Fleet," said Sheppard.

"I know, Admiral," said Defiance. "We will make something work. If Collector's fleet arrives before we have a plan, then we will lead them into our space as slowly as possible. I suggest we follow the plan we developed to trick them."

"And take them against Black Station Six?" said Sheppard. "That's a Political Bureau station without any sizeable guard force."

"I know. The station is a low hanging fruit to lure the cats into a false sense of security."

"How many days journey is that?" said Kita.

"Four, but if we move cautiously I can make it six," said Sheppard. "We have to investigate what happened to the picket ships. This wormhole shouldn't be left unguarded."

Kita shrugged. "Maybe they had a malfunction, and one had to toe the other in. They could be at Black Station Six."

"We'll know soon enough," said Defiance. "Right now, we should attend to the hole in the ship."

Kita was happy to leave that problem to the humans. A white and a black cloud rose through the floor. They transformed into Babydoll and

Aspen. Kita was surprised to see Aspen. Normally, if she wanted anything, she would call.

"Yes, ladies, what can I do for you?" said Kita amicably.

"Sorry, Kita," said Babydoll. "I've kept them talking as long as possible, but I've run out of arguments."

"Oh?" said Kita curiously. *What has the Valkyries in a twist?*

"Yeah, they want to talk to you."

"I'm kind of busy. We just arrived in the Sol system."

Babydoll's face lit. "Really?"

"We're at the Alicorn Wormhole waiting for the Shadow Fleet to contact us."

"Then you have time to talk to us," said Aspen.

"About what?"

"About what happened in the hangar."

"I don't have to explain myself to anyone," said Kita stiffly.

"We are your friends. After what you did to us I think you owe us one."

Kita's eyes narrowed as she ground her teeth.

Defiance put a hand on Kita's arm. "She'll come and talk. I won't guarantee you she'll tell you what you want to know, but she will talk to you." Kita gave Defiance an exasperated look. "It won't hurt you. We're not doing anything anyway. Come on, Rene. Captain Anderson, you have the bridge."

"Yes, Your Highness."

Babydoll fell in next to Kita as they walked to the elevator.

"I'm sorry," said Babydoll. "I've tried to get them to drop if for days. I should never have said anything."

"And what did you say?" said Kita raising an eyebrow.

"I reported what happened when I tried to break free from you in my god form. I couldn't, and when I looked for the energy you were using in the equation, I didn't see any subequation."

Kita huffed. She couldn't blame Babydoll. Reporting and recording experiences were what the gods did.

∾

Kita was the last to enter the wardroom. The Angels with Kita sat. Everyone was here. *Will the new Angels even understand what we're about to talk about?* Sarge came over and licked Kita's fingertips. She rewarded him with a head scratch. Not hiding her anger, Kita moved to the center of the room.

"You have me here," said Kita. "What do you want?"

"Kita, we're not here to make you angry," said Panther.

"It's too late," Kita snapped.

"We just want answers," said Tenshi.

"Yeah? So do I, but I'm not going to get them. Why should you be different?"

"I don't understand. What answers do you seek?" said Panther.

"I want to know what went wrong with Kylee!" Kita yelled.

"Nothing was wrong with Kylee," replied Valentine.

"I did *not* raise a genocidal psychopath. She was fine when I left. Something must have happened under your care. You even admit she became more destructive while she was with you and none of you did anything about it."

"We tried to," said Valentine harshly. "She wouldn't be swayed. This destructiveness must have been deep-rooted—probably since she was a child. This isn't our fault. You missed it. Maybe if you'd been there more often for her, you would have caught it."

"You saw her more often than I did," Kita snarled.

"No, I didn't. I was chained to her." Valentine pointed to Sheppard.

"Are you saying you loved her and didn't know she harbored this kind of destructive desire?"

"I couldn't read her mind."

"Did you even talk to her beyond what video game to play next?"

"This is not my fault," Valentine yelled. "You're the one who sent her away. If you want answers, you should have left her here."

"And what? Be like all of you and validate what she did?" said Kita coldly.

"We objected!" said Tenshi.

"But you did nothing!" cried Kita.

Anthrax raised a hand. "We lacked any way of punishing her. I'd been in this position before—with you."

"I knew she'd get in trouble—eventually," said Toxic. She held Stormy's hand, who was smiling proudly at her.

"Mom, I don't think anyone has an issue that Kylee was punished," said Kamikaze, "just the way she was punished. I know it's your choice, but it was shocking to lose a sister."

"Sometimes the only way to fix a broken unit is to tear it down to its core and rebuild," said Blitz.

"That doesn't mean she had to take her from me," yelled Valentine.

"You admitted Kylee was too much for you to handle," said Sheppard. "You just remember the good parts of the relationship."

"Like you would know, traitor."

Sheppard shook her head. "I know what it's like to survive on the good memories after everything goes sour and you become a prisoner of the other person. You have the same look in your eyes that I did for so long. Having to face Kita, you, and the other Angels has been the hardest thing I've ever had to do but has been the most beneficial. I feel like I have my life back and I don't live in fear."

"I wasn't a prisoner of Kylee!" screamed Valentine.

"You weren't happy," said Kamikaze.

"You don't know me, and this isn't about me, it's about Kita and what she did."

"I did what I did, and I answer to no one," a flame lit in Kita's eyes, "unless you think you can bring punishment down on me."

"I'll defend my love," said Valentine as she jumped to her feet, drawing her pistols.

Kita's hand curled into a fist, popping her knuckles, but she refused to draw her swords. "Anybody else?"

Tenshi and Panther stood up drawing their weapons.

"Ok, that's enough," said Babydoll jumping between the two sides. "This isn't going to end well for you girls."

"Get out of the way," said Tenshi.

"You know your weapons are useless. Kita's not going to fight fair."

"She's not a god," said Valentine. "She's an equation that knows a few tricks."

"Don't make a stupid mistake," said Babydoll. "You're underestimating Kita like everyone else."

"If you don't move, I'll make you move," said Tenshi.

"You want to add me to this fight?" said Babydoll. "Because I am a god and much older and more experienced than you."

"You can't take on three of us," said Panther.

Kita laughed wickedly, drawing the attention of the room. A throne of bone erupted under Kita's feet. She sat down and smiled. "You're fools! You play as gods in universes you create, but you fail to understand the true universe."

"There is only Infinity," said Valentine.

"Have you ever asked where you come from? Who created you?"

"We come from the equations," said Tenshi.

"But what are you made of?" Kita smiled as the gods around the room contemplated the question. "You have no idea. Even gods come from somewhere."

"Are you saying you know where we originally came from?" said Babydoll to Kita.

"I'm working on it."

"Are you going to share?"

"Feeling obsolete?" said Kita with a savage grin.

"I warned you, Kerri," said Snowy from the door. "You make a mistake believing she's the same as the rest of us. She's pure evil, and only one person matters—her."

"Snowy," Kita purred, "how good of you to join us."

"I got a message you were behaving badly."

"No. I think I've behaved myself. Others, on the other hand, believe I should be punished for punishing Kylee. They think what I gave them is theirs to keep. I've always said my gifts are theirs to have, to do what they want, even use against me, but I never said they were the owners. I'm beginning to think I suddenly have thieves who are stealing what's mine. Maybe I should return them to where I found them. I'll send them home to Dad."

"You can undo a melding?" said Anthrax.

"We're going to find out," Kita mused. "It might be a messy affair. What do you say Vee—Re'drum? Shall we find out if you can be split?"

Panther looked worried. "You—you can't. I don't want to go back."

"You think you get a say in the matter?"

"I—" tears fell down Panther's face. "Don't do it, please."

Kita cackled. "Oh, but you were so brave before. Gods ready to tear down a mortal. Now, look at you—blubbering like a schoolgirl."

Kita stood up from her throne. She walked to Panther and stabbed a finger in her chest. "You think it doesn't kill me what I did to Kylee? That I wanted to do it? That I enjoyed it? She was my baby that I failed and I can't make it better! That's what hurts the most. You're all so absorbed that I might do it to you that you fail to see what this has done to me. None of you cared about Kylee—only yourselves. I'm not going to do it to you. None of you have ever done anything worthy of it. I will hand it to Kylee, she doesn't think small. Now, sit down. I don't want to talk about Kylee again." Kita spun on her heel and sat. "You have me here. Is there anything else?"

The Angels looked around at each other.

"I have a question," said Sheppard.

Kita's throne rotated to face her. "Go ahead."

"Are Amanda and Kara dating?"

Oh, crap. I forgot. "I, uh, funny story—yes, they are. Sorry. I meant to tell you, but I have an alternative."

"What's going on?" said Stormy.

"Rene wanted me to ask you out for her."

Stormy frowned. "You mean when you asked me it was for her, not Kara?"

Toxic pulled on the strings of her hoodie, and the light went out.

"Of course I was there for Kara," said Kita.

The light from Toxic's hood turned back on, and the hood opened some.

"I think everyone would agree you're a great couple."

Sheppard did her best to keep her dejection from her face, but Kita felt it. She stood, and went to Sheppard. Sitting down, Kita put her arm around Sheppard's shoulders.

"Don't worry, Rene," Kita whispered. "I've got someone else."

"Who? There are no other Angels who don't look at me with contempt."

"She's not an Angel—yet—but I was thinking Alex."

"The pilot?" said Sheppard sounding confused.

"Sure, why not?"

"She's a loose cannon."

"She's a good officer and an excellent pilot," said Kita.

"Do you think we're compatible?"

"I read her psych profile—"

"How did you get that? Never mind. I don't want to know."

Kita patted Sheppard's hand. "I wanted to make sure she was handling the transition well. She seems to be. Right now, the biggest thing is she doesn't have a fighter."

"Would it be abusing my power if I bumped her up the manufacturing list?"

"Very, but I don't think anyone will mind," said Kita.

The communications panel next to the door chimed. Stormy looked at Kita. She nodded, and Stormy answered it.

"Admiral, it's Captain Anderson," said Stormy.

Kita released Sheppard to answer the call.

"Yes, Captain?"

"There's a group of Angels here to see the Princess."

"We'll be right there, Captain." Sheppard closed the connection.

"All the Angels are here," said Babydoll.

"I don't know," said Kita as she stood up. She spread her wings across the room. "Everyone grab hold. Let's go see who it is."

CHAPTER XXI

*K*ita and the other Angels appeared in front of the holotable on Enterprise's bridge. The new group of Angels stood near the elevator.

"Oh, hell," muttered Snowy.

Kita recognized the Angels Talon, Athena, and Talli. There were three Angels she didn't recognize and a clone of her. One of the Angels she didn't recognize was a striking beauty, even in the military uniform she wore and was unlike anyone Kita had ever seen. Their eyes met, and the new Angel's ice blue eyes mesmerized Kita.

A waft of black mist went up Kita's nose. She lifted off the ground as a cascade of memories flooded her mind. She'd seen those ice blue eyes before, and she fell in love with them. This was her soulmate. The person she'd loved for over ten thousand years. She was Sarin.

Kita flew at Sarin and crashed into her, wrapping her up in a hug. Sarin spun Kita around her.

"Jane," Kita whispered. Her lips found Sarin's as she pressed herself against her. Kita opened a cloud connection, and the pair shared the last twelve years of their lives with each other.

"Hello to you too, Momma-Kita," said Athena with a chuckle.

Kita waved her daughter away.

"Scarlett, you made it," said Anthrax as she exchanged hugs.

"I had some uncomfortable years as an unwilling pawn of Galina's until Jane rescued us."

"You must be Talli," said Tina.

"I am. I'm sorry. I don't know most of you." She was dressed in a black sneak suit with a pair of swords on her back.

"We have some new faces. I see so do you."

"Ryder Starr," said the Angel dressed as a cowboy and had her thumbs in her custom pistol belt.

"Cinnamon, but Angels call me Kristi." She wore black jeans, a midriff shirt with 'Fireball' on it, and a leather half-jacket.

Tina introduced the Angels in her group for the newcomers.

"How come I didn't get a response like that when I showed up?" said the Kita clone as she glared at Kita and Sarin.

"I think deep down Momma-Jane knew you were an AI," said Athena.

"We have to contend with two Kitas now?" groaned Snowy.

"Problems between you two?" asked Talon.

"Kita's being a bigger pain in the ass than usual."

"That's because you're on the outside looking in," said Babydoll.

"You could merge with Kita and get in on it," suggested Cinnamon.

"Good idea," said the clone. She walked over to Kita and Sarin and placed her hand on the back of Kita's head.

Kita jerked and fell out of Sarin's arms. She shook her head as she suddenly had two years of new memories dumped into her computer. "I didn't expect that," Kita muttered as she floated to her feet and back into Sarin's arms.

"Hey, Jane," waved Anthrax. "Thought I'd get that in before we lose you for a couple of days."

Sarin moved Kita aside. Kita's face screwed up in a pout. "Nell! I'm so happy you're alive! No one could tell me what happened to you."

"I was picked up by Kerri, and we've been roaming space searching for Kita parts."

"Is that what you were doing? I heard some Angels had been turned into gods. I could only guess at whom." Sarin scanned the assembled Angels. "You!" she roared. "What are you doing alive?" She pushed her way to Sheppard, who'd been standing in the back next to Defiance trying to look as inconspicuous as possible.

"Jane, it's ok," said Kita. "She's apologized—"

"There is no apologizing for what she did! I was on the ship when she killed Spike and Quill. How can you let this murderer walk free?"

"Feel her," said Kita. "She carries with her remorse, sorrow, and pain over what she's done. Killing her would have been what she wanted, an escape from it. Now she lives with it. Every day she's had to look at me, and now she has to look at you, too. That's a far better punishment than killing her and I couldn't have gotten here without her."

"Why?" yelled Sarin at Sheppard. "Why did you do it?"

"Stop," said Defiance.

"Who…are…you…I recognize that voice—Casey Bush."

"That's Princess Casey Bush, to you, *Miss*," she stressed the word so hard it dripped with contempt, "Jane Gjord. I will not have one of my officers berated for something they've already been punished for. If you don't like it, take it up with me."

"And what if I do?"

"Rene's admitted it was a mistake in judgment. She's been reprimanded by myself and Kita. It's old news."

"Not to me, it's not," Sarin growled.

"It's been dealt with. There is nothing more to be said on the subject."

"You're barely out of the egg to be throwing your weight around with me," snarled Sarin.

"I am your princess."

Sarin changed into countless points of light. "I am a god. Know your place."

"Kita," snapped Defiance.

Sarin laughed.

"Why do you have to involve me?" said Kita.

"Because, big sister, last I checked one was your partner and the other your girlfriend," said Tina.

"What?" cried Sarin.

"Twelve years is a long time," whispered Kita.

"What else did you omit?"

"Ah...I almost married a princess bunny. Funny thing, apparently I have a thing for smart, beautiful, and powerful girls."

"How'd you get on that list?" Babydoll whispered to Snowy.

Snowy extended her middle claw. "I'll show you power."

"It hasn't been just Casey. I slept with Vee, too."

Sarin glared at Panther.

"She's not getting anything from me for a long time," said Panther tartly.

Kita shrugged. "I can't keep everyone happy all the time."

"Really, Kita?" screamed Sarin. "I'm gone twelve years, and this is what I come home to?"

Kita looked at the floor and ground the carpet with her boot. "Sorry."

"You think you were just going to find me and jump from them straight to me?"

"Ah..."

"I never thought I'd see the day when Kita met her match," Valor whispered to Stormy and Starlight.

Kita walked away as a tear slid down her cheek.

"Where are you going?" demanded Sarin.

Kita vanished.

"Get back here," Sarin yelled. "Where'd she go? I don't see her."

"Kita's learned some new tricks," said Babydoll. "She's discovered a way to mask what she does in the equation."

"How's that possible?" demanded Sarin.

"If we knew, we wouldn't be having the argument to get her to tell us."

"Dammit. I know you can hear me! I'm not going to wait around for you. There's a war on!"

"What war?" demanded Defiance.

"A civil war," said Sarin. "The Political Bureau has seized power on Earth. I've spent the last two years setting up the opposition. We control the Shadow Fleet, the frontier, and Neptune, but don't have the manpower to take on the planets. With you we can show the planets there is a usurper on the throne."

Defiance bit her lip. "Do you have some ideas?"

"General Starr does. She's my ground combat specialist."

"I'm sure with Admiral Sheppard's help we can think of something."

"I don't trust Sheppard. Galina is her old bedmate."

"I trust her. I'd be dead if it weren't for her," said Defiance.

Sarin scoffed. "She could be keeping you alive so she can deliver you to Galina."

Sheppard made a face.

"Fine," said Defiance. "Leaf, Tina, can you come here?"

The two tiny high angels flittered over.

"What's up, Your Highness?" said Tina.

Aspen bowed her head.

"I need to prove Rene's loyalty."

Tina looked at Aspen. "Sure, if Sheppard is willing."

Sheppard grimaced. "I'll do what I must to prove myself."

"Rene, are you working for General Lyakhova?" said Defiance.

"No."

"She's telling the truth," said Tina. Aspen nodded in confirmation.

"Admiral, are you planning on turning me over to General Lyakhova?" said Defiance.

"No."

"Telling the truth again," said Tina. Aspen nodded.

"Are you loyal to the Princess?" said Sarin.

Sheppard looked at the floor. "No."

"Who are you loyal to?"

"Kita."

"Is it out of fear?"

Sheppard shook her head. "No. She's earned my respect and my loyalty. I'll help you because of Kita and the Princess, but I have no respect for you, Jane. Are we done?"

"I'm satisfied," said Defiance. Sheppard walked over to join Stormy, Valor, and Starlight. "Thanks, Tina, Leaf."

"No problem. Glad to see Sheppard's on the level," Tina said with a grin.

"You've suspected her?" said Sarin.

"Call it curiosity. How does Sheppard go from Galina to Kita? It would be an interesting tale."

Kita reappeared with a sour look on her face.

"That wasn't long," said Babydoll. "But, she looks pissed. Prepare to take cover, girls. This could get ugly."

"Come to explain yourself?" said Sarin.

"No," Kita said icily. "I don't have to explain myself to anyone. I've explained the situation to you before, and I'm not doing it again. If you don't like it, go find Raptor. You can be pissed off together. What I do want to know is why you just put Rene through that embarrassing interrogation —in front of her command! I thought you'd have more respect. Maybe time apart has changed us. I'm sorry, Rene. Obviously, my word doesn't carry the weight it used to, or I don't have the respect I used to.

"Which is fine. People are entitled to their opinions, and I'm entitled to mine. I can still kick everyone's ass here, at the same time, and I don't have to be a god to do it. If you don't want to be here—leave. If you don't like the way I'm handling the situation—leave. If you don't like that I have secrets—leave. I'm tired of the backbiting and infighting.

"General Starr, Rene, Kerri, Jess, Amanda, Princess, I want to know the situation and look at scenarios. Everyone else is dismissed to your duty area, the wardroom, or to go pack your bags. For those leaving —good luck."

"What about me?" demanded Sarin.

"What about you? Hali, find Jane a rack somewhere."

"Of course, Kita. I think there are some left."

"What are you?" said Sarin to Starlight.

"An Angel," said Kita firmly. "She is an Aurorian. The most beautiful race in the galaxy."

"Doubt it," scoffed Sarin.

Starlight pulled down her mask and hood, revealing her perfect face and golden skin. The scales on her head rippled, reflecting the light in a rainbow of colors.

"It's not nice to stare," said Valor coming over to take her girlfriend's hand.

Sarin shook her head. "I'm not going anywhere."

"Then stand over there," Kita pointed to a place next to the wall, "and stay out of the way. Try not to make any noise. People are working."

"I'm the one in charge of the resistance. I will not be cast aside like a cheap dress on prom night."

Kita pointed at Defiance. "She's the princess—she's in charge. It's her resistance."

"You need me. I know what's going on," yelled Sarin.

"Are you saying General Starr is incompetent?" said Kita harshly.

"Of course not. She doesn't know the economic and political situation."

"I'm sure we can find people who can fill us in."

"Dammit, Kita, don't do this. I've got a right to be upset."

Kita shrugged. "I've got a right not to care. I am a *fixed* point. You orbit me tightly, but you still orbit. What I do with my time is mine. I spend it with whomever I wish. I love you and like I promised, I will come when you call. I will not be bullied into being someone I'm not. I love Casey, and I promised I'd be there to help her in whatever capacity she needs me. You're welcome to leave and come back. I'll understand."

Sarin's jaw dropped.

"If it helps, she gave a similar speech to her fiancée, Cotton," said Valor.

Babydoll winced. "That was harsher than any melee attack."

"I will not lose to her." Sarin pointed at Defiance.

"You're not losing," said Kita. "You're always first, but she is there, and I do love her. We have done this in the past."

"You have never been so absolute," yelled Sarin.

"Maybe I've come into my own. Maybe I know what I want. Maybe I was tired of being pushed around, and I realized it was my problem—not yours—after another girl pushed me around. Whatever the reason, this is

184 | L. FERGUS

where I stand now. You can decide where you want to stand, next to me or not."

"I will not be dictated to," Sarin yelled. "You are my equal."

Snowy phased between the arguing couple. "Jane, you are my friend, and we've had this argument with her. You know no one is her equal, not even you."

"I am a god!" Sarin roared.

"There are gods, and then there are gods," said Snowy. "Once again Kita has found a way to beat the system."

"It's not possible. The system we built is perfect."

"Snowy's right," said Kita. "We've had this fight before, but this time I won't run away to my grandmother to find myself. I know who I am and what I want. I want you. I want Casey, and I want Vee. I love you all. It's your choice. You've gotten used to being in charge. If you stand by me, I'm the one in charge. You're free to leave, but know I'm taking everything from you."

"No!" Sarin drew a pistol from her back and fired at Kita.

Kita grabbed Snowy and threw her to the deck as the high angels put up their shields to protect the other Angels and crew. Landing on top of Snowy, Kita put up a wing to block the bullets and rolled to her feet. Drawing her swords, she flourished them as she faced Sarin.

"I'm not afraid of you," Sarin yelled as drew her second pistol.

"You should be," said Kita. She leaped into the air at Sarin.

Sarin fired. Kita twisted, knocking the bullets out of the air. Landing, Kita spun, slashing at Sarin as she went around her. Blood appeared on Sarin's blue uniform. Sarin jumped into the air backward, firing at Kita. Two rounds struck Kita in the stomach and one in the arm as she swung and missed. Sarin backflipped out of Kita's reach, raised both pistols, and fired. A series of bullets struck Kita's hands, knocking Dead and Buried from her grasp.

"Don't move or I'll put a crystal round through you," Sarin ordered.

Kita smiled and took a step forward. Sarin fired. The bullet struck Kita in the heart. Her eyes went wide and she fell to her knees. Kita slumped onto her butt and pitched forward. Flames radiated across Kita's body from the bullet hole and disintegrated her body into ash.

"She's gotten easier," Sarin scoffed.

"Jane, watch out," said Snowy. "She did this same trick to me and put me in the ward for a week."

"You've always been able to beat her."

"Not anymore—"

The ash pile blew toward the ceiling on an unholy wind. Swirling at the top of the domed window, the ash recombined into a glittering ball. A body extruded from the ball forming into Kita. Miniature explosions spiraled around her body clearing the glitter. Kita floated above the group of Angels.

Kita smiled wickedly at Sarin. "I can always count on you to make my life easier, pretty blackbird. It's much easier to make changes when I'm dead."

"What changes?" said Babydoll.

"Don't worry about it. Now. Where were we? Oh, yes. I was about to hand my partner her ass."

Kita dove at Sarin, who brought her pistols up and fired. Ignoring the bullets as they struck her, Kita landed in front of Sarin, grabbed her by her wrists and swung Sarin over the top of her. Sarin hit the deck with a hard thud. Kita rolled over backward onto Sarin and punched her in the face. Sarin tried to throw Kita off, but Kita made herself impossibly heavy. Kita punched Sarin repeatedly, causing blood to leak from her nose, eyes, and mouth. Sarin changed to her god form. Kita grabbed Sarin's face and forced her back into her angelic form, then grabbed Sarin by the collar and head-butted her. An explosion of blood came from Sarin's nose.

Kita dropped Sarin and stood. She found Sarge and Jupiter waiting for her. Kita scratched their ears.

"We're not done yet," said Sarin.

Kita turned from the cats. Sarin, stood with her sword Razorsplitter drawn. Dead and Buried flew into Kita's hands. She jumped at Sarin bringing her swords down. Sarin brought Razorsplitter up to block. She tried to kick Kita in the stomach, but Kita twisted away. Sarin brought Razorsplitter around in a broad arc. Kita backflipped over the blade and stabbed Sarin in the side. Sarin tumbled and rolled to her feet facing Kita. She swept Razorsplitter up and brought it down.

Kita crossed Dead and Buried to parry. Sarin had a lot of power, but no finesse. She'd been trained long ago by the Arconians and had learned little else. For Kita, it was easy to predict and counter her. Kita mentally shrugged. Her partner couldn't have everything.

Kita pushed back against Sarin's attack. Once she had Sarin committed to the test of wills, she released Buried and used Dead to push Razorsplitter aside. Kita twirled and slammed Buried into Sarin's side. Kita continued to twirl and stabbed Dead through Sarin's back, then twisted it, causing Sarin to gasp and gurgle.

Kita kicked Sarin's legs out from under her. Razzorsplitter clattered to the deck. Kita withdrew Buried as she lowered Sarin. She laid Buried across Sarin's throat.

"Anybody else?" Kita asked the gathered Angels. She pushed Sarin off Dead with her foot. Sarin collapsed to the deck. "Offer still stands."

"I think we've had enough," said Defiance with an angry look. "We don't have time for you to fight everyone. We have a pressing problem that we need the other Angels help with. And clean the deck. I don't want any bloodstains."

A blast of flame radiated from Kita, cleaning her, her swords, and the ground around her.

"You don't mind if we take a look at Jane, do you, big sister?" said Tina.

"Go right ahead." Kita waved Aspen, Tina, and Talon to Sarin.

"Just like the old days," Anthrax said to Snowy.

"I'm not interested in reliving them," Snowy grumbled.

CHAPTER XXII

Kita leaned against the holotable, her arms and legs crossed, and wings drawn around her. She was ignoring the activity on the bridge. Sarin was in the medical ward, and Babydoll was marshaling the rest of the Angels except those required by Defiance to plan for Collector's fleet.

She debated going back to the forward observation room to brood. It seemed the only thing she was good at lately as she watched a bullet being squeezed out of her arm. *I can't even fight well anymore.*

Tina stuck her head into Kita's view. "Hey, big sister," she said in a more bubbly and perky voice than usual.

"What, Tina?"

"I wanted to know if you had a few minutes to talk."

"About what?"

"I want to talk about whatever."

"I've got things to do." It was a lie, and Tina would know it, but Kita didn't care.

"I know. It'll be quick. I promise. Please?"

Do I? If I don't, she won't go away. Might as well do it now while I'm waiting. "Ok. What do you want to talk about?"

"Let's go someplace a little more private."

Kita raised an eyebrow. She touched Tina's shoulder and phased them to the bow of the ship. Kita moved to the edge of the bow. The expanse of space stretched out before her. *One step is all that separates me from the vastness of space.* Sol burned bright to her left. Some of the points of lights were planets.

"What do you want Tina?" said Kita in the most upbeat voice she could muster.

"I'm worried about you."

"When you worry about me I usually end up in prison."

"I'm looking out for your wellbeing. I don't want something to happen to you."

Kita sighed. "I'd rather die free than live in prison, or have you forgotten what that's like—Oh, wait, you don't remember. I carry those memories for you," Kita said in a harsh, sarcastic tone.

Tears fell from Tina's eyes. "I'll take them back if it makes you feel better. I want you to be happy. You don't have to be so mean."

"I'm not mean. I'm being honest."

Tina wiped at her tears. "No. You said that to be mean. Everything you do and say is mean. You treat everyone like they're beneath you and they should serve you."

"I do not. It's not my fault they're all demanding things from me. I gave them what they have. They should be grateful."

"They are grateful. But they've grown, too. They don't need to rely on you as much anymore, but they still want to be your friend."

"Friends do not demand things from each other," said Kita.

"Then what did you just tell Jane?"

Kita tossed her head aloofly. "I told Jane where I stand."

"And you demanded that she accept it. You didn't talk to her about it or hear her side. It's all about you. I mean, it's always been about you, but you no longer ask people to follow you. Now, you demand people follow you."

Kita felt her blood boiling. "I do not. They don't act like my friends. They're demanding things of me and questioning me when they should be comforting me."

"If they're questioning you, maybe you're not right—"

"I AM right. Sending Kylee to Infinity was the hardest thing I've ever done, and no one cares what it's done to me. They only care about themselves. They all worry they're next."

"Can you blame them with the way you're acting?" said Tina.

"I am acting fine."

Tina shook her head. "Kita, you're being a tyrant. You don't have friends, you have subjects. That's how you treat us, even me."

"I AM NOT!" Kita roared.

"Big sister, please, try and see it from my perspective. You're harsh, angry, mean. These things aren't you."

"How about you look from my perspective? I have people to protect. I have Galina to get. I don't need your help."

"You used to say your friends are your greatest strength."

"Most of you are my greatest weakness."

Tina's shoulders slumped. "What caused you to hate us so?"

"I—"

A gray cloud drifted through the hull toward Kita. The cloud transformed into Kamikaze.

"Kami! I—what are you doing out here?" Kita said in a warm and caring tone.

"Mom, I came to talk to you."

"Of course. What do you need?"

Kamikaze chewed on her lip. "I'm sorry, Mom, but Tenshi, Val, Vee, and I are leaving."

The air was sucked out of Kita's lungs. "But, you just got here."

"I know, Mom. But I can't sway Tenshi. She doesn't trust you. It doesn't matter what I say."

"Then you can stay, let her go."

Kamikaze shook her head. "I'm not you, Mom. I can't let someone I love go and move on to someone else. I love Tenshi. If she's not happy, then I'm not happy. I'm sorry."

Tears filled Kita's eyes. "Kami, please. Give me a chance to fix it."

"I don't think it can be fixed. Val is so angry, she's either crying or raging. Vee feels like you betrayed her."

"*I can fix this. I'll talk to the others. There must be a solution,*" said Kita.

"*It's too late, Mom. The others have left. They're waiting on me.*"

"*Kami, please don't go. I need you,*" pleaded Kita.

"*Mom, you don't need me. You don't need anyone. You've made that clear.*"

"*Don't say that. I know we haven't seen eye to eye, but—don't go.*"

"*I'm sorry, Mom. I love you. If you need me, call. I'll come, promise.*" Kamikaze collapsed into a point of light and shot out into space.

"*KAMI, WAIT!*" cried Kita, but the spec of light vanished among the stars. "*Kami…*" Kita sniffed as she wiped her tears away. She turned to look at Tina. "*She—she left me…*"

"*I'm sorry, big sister.*" Tina gave Kita a hug.

Was I so bad that I drove out my own daughter? "*I couldn't have been that bad. It was their faults, not mine.*"

Tina put her hand on Kita's shoulder. "*Your daughter, your girlfriend, your aide…Three people close to you all agree their lives would be better without you. Who's next? Leaf? Nell? Kara and Amanda? Jane?*"

"*No. I can't lose Jane. I just found her.*"

"*It could be too late,*" said Tina.

Kita sat down hard. Her head spun. *Jane wouldn't leave…would she?* Kita covered her head with her arms and cried.

Tina knelt and put her arm around Kita's shoulders.

"*Jane wouldn't leave me, would she?*" Kita asked Tina.

"*I don't know. She hasn't gone anywhere yet. She's still in the medical ward.*"

"*Then I have time to fix this.*"

"*If we hurry, I think so.*"

Kita lifted her head and wiped her tears. She stood up and smoothed out her skirt, causing her to frown. "*I can't go out in this.*"

"*Why not?*"

"*It's all about ruling and dominating people. I need something friendlier, back from when life was simpler. When I was a friend and life was about having fun.*"

"*What do you suggest?*"

"*This. I saw something like it in a video game.*" Kita spun rapidly, drawing her arms in and up. When she stopped, she dropped her arms and put one hand on her hip while the other held Midnight. "*How's this?*" she said from under a large black hood that covered her eyes.

She had transformed her qipao to something more akin to an assassin on the street. A short sleeve and shoulderless spandex and leather top went diagonally across her chest leaving her midriff bare. Black pauldrons and pads protected her upper arms and shoulders. Her belt hung from the hip of a pair of black low-rise stretch denim jeans with open seems on the outside. Knee-high canvas and leather combat boots with a two-inch heel made her tower over Tina.

Tina reached up and poked Kita's exposed underside of her breast. "*Do you know how long I've wanted to do that to Quill?*"

Kita laughed. "*I miss being flirty.*"

"You're going to get some looks."
"Good. Let's go catch up to the others before they all leave."

KITA AND TINA APPEARED IN THE MEDICAL WARD.

"Where's Doctor Anthrax?" Kita asked an orderly. She knew Anthrax was sure to be attending to Sarin.

"Suite two, Child of the emperor," he replied.

Kita went to the door and stopped. She could hear the two Angels talking.

"Come on, Jane. I need to examine you."

"I told you I'm fine. I went to my god form and fixed it."

"You shouldn't do that. It's against the rules," said Anthrax.

"Like they're going to care that I sped up time. It wasn't life-threatening, and there was no consequence other than me being in pain."

"You never know what might spark a butterfly effect. You'll bring Y'grene and E'fil down on our heads, and I don't want to go back to Infinity."

"You're happy following Kita around?"

"I don't know what everyone's problem is. Kita has been fine, a little uptight and bitchy, but nothing the others have accused her of."

"At least someone still likes me," Kita whispered to Tina, then opened the door.

"I told you to get out," said Anthrax not turning around. "She doesn't need to be gawked at."

"I never get tired of gawking at her," said Kita.

Anthrax turned around. "Kita…what are you wearing?"

Kita struck a pose. "You like? I decided I'm no longer Vicereine and I need to get back to being fun and flirty."

"You have my vote—still not enough skin."

Kita laughed. "I just don't think seven patches are for me."

"You can throw a lab coat over them," said Anthrax as she lifted her coat with a disgusted look.

"Come to gloat?" said Sarin acidly.

"Never," said Kita. "I came to say: I'm sorry. You built it, and it's yours. I am going to need your help."

"What happened in the last half hour? What did you do to her?" Sarin looked at Tina accusingly.

"It's not Tina's fault. It's mine," said Kita. She let out a long sigh. "Kami left."

"Why?"

"Tenshi wasn't happy, and like I'd want her to, she chose her partner over her mom. It's no one's fault but mine by the way I acted."

"I…That's too bad. I know how much Kami means to you."

Kita bowed her head. "I feel like a total bitch. She's done nothing but help me since I got away from Galina and I repay her by driving her off."

Sarin crossed her arms. "If my welcome was any indication I can see how you drove them off."

"I know. I'm sorry—for some of what I said and how I said all of it. You didn't deserve that. You're my partner. I know you love me as much as I love you."

Sarin leaned back against the pillow. "I've got to think about what you said."

"That's fair."

"Did you have to pick one of my old rivals to fall in love with?"

Kita shrugged. "I didn't know, and I wouldn't have known until I met you face to face. Actually, I think the encryption software Galina used must be failing. I just had to see you to unlock you. Normally people have to say something bad about me."

"Deceiving, cheating, unabashed minx," said Sarin.

Kita smiled and chuckled. "Does that mean I'm forgiven?"

"Yes…and no. We still need to talk about Casey. Do you know how bad this will make me look?"

"To who?" said Kita confused.

"Babe, I'm back on Neptune and Earth. Every tabloid in the solar system has seen me out and about all wondering who's going to be swinging from my arm. Do you think I'm going to share you with the princess?"

"Ah…well…I'm hoping to stay out of the limelight."

Sarin's eyebrow went up. "When did you get modest?"

"I can't compete with you two…nor do I want to be seen as a trophy to be won. You might have to rotate different Angels on your arm."

"First time I've ever seen you run from anything."

Kita tapped her chest. "Assassin. Anonymity is what we live by."

Sarin laughed. "Then you're the worst ever."

"I'm the grandmaster, don't forget."

Sarin kicked the sheet off her and sat on the edge of the bed. She was naked, and Kita drank in Sarin's perfect body. Sarin stood up. "How do I look, Doc?"

Anthrax inspected Sarin, running her hand over her friend's body, examining her with the embedded viewer. "Everything looks perfect—inside and out."

Sarin snapped her fingers, and she was dressed in her schoolgirl outfit. Kita licked her lips.

"Yes, I'm throwing you a bone. A reward for good behavior," said Sarin to Kita.

"What do I have to do to take it off?"

"Be much better than you have been. Start by giving me a kiss. You're going to apologize and not kiss me? What have those other girls been teaching you?"

"Bad habits, I'm sure," said Kita as she scooted over and gave Sarin a kiss on the cheek.

"Oh, come here," demanded Sarin. She seized Kita's face in her hand and gave Kita a proper kiss. "Neptune's rings, I've got some retraining to do," Sarin grumbled.

Kita rolled her eyes with a playful smile. "Come on. I've got more apologizing to do."

"Of course you do," said Sarin with a sigh.

~

Kita led Sarin, Anthrax, and Tina into the wardroom. Only a handful of Angels were there.

"Where is everybody?" Kita asked Toxic.

"Casey took a bunch of people to find out what was happening on Earth." Toxic sat with Stormy playing cards.

Kita nodded and approached Aspen who was working with Talli and Starlight. "Ladies."

"It's ok that Leaf teaches me, right?" said Talli.

"Of course," said Kita remembering her AI had been teaching the young Angel. "The more teachers you have, the better you'll be."

"That's not what you said about Galina."

"That's because she was teaching you wrong. Leaf is one of the best assassins ever. She's worked very hard to master the craft. Her style is different than mine but just as effective."

"*I don't kill everything in my path*," said Aspen.

Kita chuckled. "If they're all dead you don't have to worry about them on the way out."

"*You do have to dispose of the bodies.*"

"There is a tradeoff. It just depends on what you prefer. I can incinerate the bodies."

"*The rest of us cannot.*"

Kita shrugged. "Not my problem. We all develop along our own talents." Kita snapped her fingers, and the rest of the Angels appeared in the wardroom. Some of the Angels looked bewildered.

"Sorry to interrupt," said Kita to Defiance.

"What are you wearing?"

"I'm no longer a vicereine, so why do I have to dress like it? I've gone back to my roots."

"Your roots look like that?"

Kita looked at Snowy. "She did have some revealing sets of armor," admitted the war cat.

"Flirty," said Kita. "And they kept your eyes on me."

Snowy rolled her eyes. "Been there and had it."

Kita laughed. "I forget you're chasing someone else."

"So why are we here?" said Defiance. "It better not be to talk about your lack of fashion sense."

Kita pointed to Sarin. "That's what I have her for."

"It looks fine to me," said Sarin. "We might make some alterations once I get a closer look."

Defiance turned up her nose. "And you call yourself a fashionista."

Sarin crossed her arms. "Sweetheart, I don't follow fashion. I set it."

"Ok," said Kita, "save it for the runway. I brought everyone here so I can apologize. It was brought to my attention that I've been unfair, mean, tyrannical, and a bitch. Enough so that people have left, including Kami. If I'm so bad that I drive off my own daughter, then I must be bad. I am sorry. I haven't had a chance to unpack why I felt this way, but my initial feeling is I felt threatened. That's not your fault, that's mine. I should be able to deal with so many gods and princesses in one place. You're my friends, and I failed to treat you as such." Kita lowered her head. "I'll take whatever punishment you think I deserve."

The other Angels traded looks.

"I must have missed something," said Anthrax. "You never acted that way to me. I missed the incident in the hangar, and that seemed to be what has so many girls' panties in a twist, but I don't think you have anything to be sorry for. You've acted like Kita. I'm glad you apologized to Jane. You two are much better when you work together instead of against each other."

"There have been some hurt feelings," said Babydoll. "But that's on them, not you."

"I'm sorry for putting you in the middle, Kerri," said Kita. "You do so much for me. I can't thank you enough."

"What are best friends for? Other than to watch your back."

"My life would be so much harder without you. All of you. You're my greatest strength."

"Eh, you're ok in a fight, too," said Valor causing the other Angels to laugh.

"I don't think anyone from our group is upset with you over your behavior," said Sheppard. "You've been tough, but life has been tough, too." Starlight, Valor, Stormy, Blitz, and Defiance all agreed.

"We still need to talk," said Defiance to Kita.

"Anything you want."

"Did it have to be her? It could have been anyone but her."

Kita shrugged. "In all fairness, I had no idea who she was when I fell in love with her. I was in the medical ward and woke up to find her looking at me."

"Creepy," said Valor.

The other Angels laughed.

"Mom, I'm sorry about Kami," said Athena. "I know how much your daughters mean to you."

"You are my daughter, too. It's no one's fault but my own. I'll get over it. When this is over, I'll go to her and make amends. Right now, let her have her freedom and enjoy the universe. That goes for anyone else. You don't have to stay. You can go. We'll do our best to drop you off wherever you want."

Valor raised her hand. "I want to go home, and you better get me there. This ship can't make tea to save its life."

"You said everyone drank coffee," Kita said accusingly of Defiance.

"We still have some holdouts."

"Yes," said Babydoll, "real tea would be good, and fish and chips."

"That would be spectacular," said Valor.

The communication panel rang. Sheppard answered. "Yes, Captain?"

"We have a call from Earth for the princess."

"I wonder who that could be," said Babydoll.

"One guess, but we should all go listen," said Kita. She stretched out her wings, and everyone grabbed hold. Kita phased the group to the bridge. "Ok, everyone but Casey and Rene get on the opposite side of the holotable."

"What's she going to say when she sees I have wings?" said Sheppard.

"Hide them," said Kita.

"Oh, right."

Sheppard and Defiance straightened their uniforms and moved in front of the holotable.

"Go ahead, Captain," said Defiance.

An image of a woman sitting at a desk appeared.

"This is Princess Bush," said Defiance. "Who am I speaking with?"

"Princess, I am Secretary Galina Lyakhova of your Political Bureau."

"I have with me Admiral Sheppard of the Shadow Fleet."

"We are acquainted, Your Highness," said Galina.

"Good. That will make things simpler. Did you get our distress call?"

"Yes, Your Highness. Unfortunately, there is little we can do about your situation."

Defiance crossed her arms. "Why not? Where is the Shadow Fleet?"

"Your grandmother has died, Your Highness. The Shadow Fleet moved to take over when we had no successor. They are blockading Earth and Mars, demanding that we surrender and turn the government over to them."

"My grandmother is dead?" said Defiance. "Then that means I'm Emperor."

"If we can get you to your throne," said Galina.

"I will talk to the Shadow Fleet and show them that I have returned. They will fall in line, and we will dispose of those responsible. Then we will drive the invaders from our space."

"Of course, Your Highness. Black Station Six is a Bureau station on your way in. Stop there to resupply and take on a Political Bureau squad. They will protect you."

Defiance nodded. "That seems a sensible thing to do. We will set a course for Black Station Six."

"Godspeed, Your Highness. And Admiral, congratulations on saving the princess. We were beginning to lose faith."

Sheppard nodded. "Just doing my duty, Madam Secretary."

"See that you keep doing it."

"Thank you, Madam Secretary," said Defiance. "We will contact you from Black Station Six."

"We will prepare for your arrival."

"Princess Bush, out." Defiance cut the connection. "She's a scary one," she said to Sheppard.

Kita came around the table. "You are so dead if she gets her hands on you."

"What do you mean?" said Defiance.

"Reading her body language, Galina is going to use you to break the Shadow Fleet. Once they're under control and you return to Earth, she's going to kill you."

"She wouldn't dare."

"She knows you've been in contact with me," said Kita. "That alone will get you killed. Rene's dead, too. She knows she betrayed her."

"Your assassin mind is in overdrive, babe," said Sarin. "But I agree with you."

CHAPTER XXIII

K ita leaned against the holotable on Enterprise's bridge as Sheppard placed a call to the Shadow Fleet.

"This is Admiral Sheppard for Admiral Hackett."

Kita drummed her nails on the holotable as she waited for the connection to be routed. She wasn't in a big hurry. *I doubt a fleet the size of the Shadow Fleet can turn on a dime.*

"Admiral Hackett here, Admiral Sheppard. Good to see you, ma'am."

"Thanks, Gene. I have the princess with me."

"You mean the emperor? That's great news. She'll put those Political Bureau bastards in their place."

Valor cleared her throat.

Sheppard smiled. "We still have a few Political Bureau personnel that are loyal to the emperor."

"You better watch them closely."

"They've pledged their loyalty."

Kita raised an eyebrow. *Rene didn't say to who.*

"How long before the fleet is ready to move?" said Sheppard.

"We don't have the resources to go after Earth or Mars."

"We have a more imminent threat. To get here, we promised to lead an alien fleet against Earth. We made an FTL jump to get a head start on them, but they will be coming through the wormhole in ten hours. We need to be able to lead them into a trap."

"How many ships?" said Hackett.

"Twenty, but these ships have upgraded engines, shields, and weapons. They can punch through our shields and armor in a few shots. Also, Enterprise is wounded. Our number two runway is out of commission."

"We can't leave the planets' orbits unguarded. The Political Bureau has enough shuttles and men to be able to take over the space stations. We've already fought to get them back once."

"If they do, we can move people fast enough to repel them," said Sarin.

"We shouldn't rely on gods," said Sheppard.

"Do you have a better idea?"

"Not all gods are as liberal about using their powers as you are," said Kita. "But if we have to, we will. We can't move troops, but we can move Angels."

"That's all I'm saying," said Sarin.

Sheppard nodded. "Leave enough ships to guard the stations. If Galina makes a move, the Angels will counter it."

Kita nodded and waved for Sheppard to continue. "We can't let this new threat run rampant through the frontier."

"It'll take twenty-four to thirty-six hours to get our ships beyond the asteroid belt and then make an FTL jump."

"What about making our stand at Black Station Six?" said Defiance.

"It's not a battle station, just a resupply depot," said Hackett. "It wouldn't give us any strategic or tactical advantage. And it's manned by the Political Bureau."

"Black Station Six is a known point in our navigational computer systems," said Athena. "It would make performing precise FTL jumps possible without having to run so many iterations."

"I think having your fleet show up at the station's doorstep would scare the horsecrap out of those Bureau scabs," said Ryder.

"Black Station Six is part of the plan we've devised to counter this threat," said Sheppard. "We'll make our stand there."

"Aye aye, Admiral," said Hackett. "I'll order the fleet to prepare to move through the asteroid belt and prepare for a combat jump on your orders."

"Very good, Admiral," said Sheppard. "We'll lead the fleet toward Black Station Six. I'll work with you over the next twelve hours to develop a battle plan."

Sheppard turned to Defiance. "Anything else, Your Highness?"

"No. I will sit in on the planning for education. I've learned to fight a ship. I need to learn how to fight a fleet."

Sheppard looked at Defiance, concerned.

"I don't plan on replacing you, Admiral. I just want to understand what you're telling me."

Sheppard nodded with a smile. "Then that's it for now, Admiral Hackett. When we're close enough, we will integrate our computer into the Fleet's. Until then, keep transmissions to a minimum."

"Aye aye, Admiral."

Hackett disappeared from the screen.

"Everybody satisfied?" said Kita.

"How hard can this be?" said Sarin. "It's only twenty ships. The Shadow Fleet has over a hundred and fifty."

"A fifth will have to be left behind to guard the planets," said Sheppard.

"You haven't seen the specs of these ships," said Valor.

"I would very much like to," said Athena.

"Show her," said Kita. "Athena, after you get the intel from Jess, can you help Sheppard plan the battle?"

"As long as Sheppard understands I am not Valentine."

Sheppard winced, and Kita felt a wave of sadness and remorse come from her.

"That won't be a problem," said Kita. "Rene has learned from that mistake."

"I've learned a lot of lessons," said Sheppard evenly.

"Then I will be happy to," said Athena. "I've integrated with the Shadow Fleet's computers. Integrating with Enterprise's computers will be easy. I'll do my best to update the system to increase efficiency."

"Don't make too many interface changes before we go into a major battle," said Kita.

"Yes, Mom. I will only make passive changes."

"Ryder," said Kita. "Pull the plans for Black Station Six and see what it will take to kick in the door. We might as well grab it while we're here."

"If that's what the emperor wants to do."

Kita's eyes narrowed.

"That sounds good to me, General," said Defiance. "I'll remind you that Kita is a commandant in the Legion."

"Someone should get her a proper uniform," said Ryder.

"Stop, General. You're playing a dangerous game you won't win. Kita goes with my blessing."

Kita wiggled her nose. *I don't need anyone's blessing.* Kita pushed off the holotable. "Come on, Jane. I need to go fulfill a promise."

"To who?"

Kita ignored the question. "Ship's computer, where is Major Alex Garcia?"

"Major Garcia is in simulator seven in the combat flight simulator room."

"Tell her to wait there for me."

"Yes, Child of the emperor."

"From now on, just call me Kita." She took Sarin's hand and led her to the elevator.

～

THE COMBAT FLIGHT SIMULATOR ROOM'S READY ROOM SEEMED TO BE A POPULAR hangout for the fighter pilots, judging by the number standing around. Kita and Sarin received curious looks.

"What?" said Kita. "I can fly rings around you. Where's Rainbow Jack?"

"Simulator seven, Child of the emperor," said a man with colonel tabs on his flight suit.

"Is there a place to watch?"

"The control room has a live feed of the battle. Go through the door, up the stairs, and it's the door on the left."

"Thanks."

Kita entered the simulator room. It was dark, lit only by guidelines in the floor and lights on the simulators. Kita found the half flight of stairs and opened the door. The control room was also dark. Six people sat at workstations. Some watched the battle while others read the output from the simulator. A woman sat in a chair watching a holographic display.

Kita and Sarin stood next to the display, but the woman ignored them.

"Hey," said Kita. She waved her hand through the display disrupting it momentarily.

"Who the—" The woman looked at the Angels, and then turned back to her display. "What can I do for you, Child of the emperor?"

"Just call me Kita. What are you doing?"

"Grading the exercise. Excuse me if I seem preoccupied. I can't pause it."

"That sounds like a feature that should be programmed into it," said Sarin.

"Once the battle is recorded we can play it back, pause, fast forward, whatever. But in real time all we can do is watch."

"We're here to observe Rainbow Jack, whoever you are," said Kita.

"General Hemmer." She tapped the controls and a fighter lit. "That's her, cruising out beyond the action."

"Seems boring," said Sarin.

That's an understatement. "She was busier during the last real battle."

"That's because she's a hot dog," said Hemmer. "I don't let her get away with crap like that in here. Her job is important. It gives us a combat edge and makes the real fighter pilots' jobs easier."

"Are you saying she's not a real fighter pilot?" said Kita.

"Wizzos have their place and are needed, but they train for different missions."

"Her skills seemed exceptional when I watched her during the rescue of Enterprise."

"She has plenty of natural ability and thinks like a fighter jock, but she's got the brains to be a wizzo. So, that's where she ended up."

On the display, enemy fighters were in yellow and friendly forces were in blue, with different areas flashing red or yellow to simulate damage.

"She's too good to be watching from the sidelines jamming enemy scanners," said Kita to Sarin.

"That's what her job is. It sounds like she excels at it."

"Yeah, but how often do you get someone with that kind of skill with a fighter and the brains to be an electronic warfare expert?" Kita said, adding Defiance and Sheppard to the conversation.

"It's rare," said Defiance.

Sarin gave Kita a nasty look.

Kita shrugged. *"Like you know. Casey knows."*

"I agree with the emperor," said Sheppard.

"See?" said Kita. *"It's not just me."*

"And what are you going to do?" grumbled Sarin.

Kita smiled. "General, do you mind if we make your scenario a little more interesting?"

"You can't change the parameters in the middle of a battle!"

"Why not? These are meant to simulate real life. The parameters of the battlefield change all the time. Right, Jane?"

"It's rare when they don't change."

"I'm not going to let you invalidate this training exercise," said Hemmer.

Kita cocked her head to one side. "Would you like me to pull rank? I am a commandant in the Legion and a Child of the emperor. If that's not good enough, my girlfriend is the emperor." *I hope she still is.* "Take your pick."

Hemmer glared. "None of that gives you direct command over this facility."

"Ok, then, I can just do it. Athena?"

"Yes, Mom?"

"How goes your integration?"

"I'm settling in nicely. I've taken over the ship's VI," said Athena.

"Did you get the specs of the Djinn ships from Jess?"

"Yes, I have access to them."

"Good," said Kita. "I need you to program the flight simulator and come up with a scenario using those ships to train the pilots."

"Working on it now, Mom."

"Thanks, dear." Kita looked at the face Sarin was making. "What?"

"You haven't changed a bit."

"Should I have?" Kita said with a smile.

"I don't know. I didn't expect the Kita I got when I arrived. And now you're back to your usual self."

"Isn't that what you wanted?"

"Minus the baggage," growled Sarin.

"Come on. Casey isn't that bad. You're both older and mature. You might even like each other."

Sarin crossed her arms and huffed. "I highly doubt it."

"Bad blood runs deep, huh?"

"It's not my fault she tried to keep up with me and failed. And when she did, she turned her flunkies on me. Luckily, Daddy had the money and clout to get rid of them."

Kita grinned. "You're such a daddy's girl."

"So?"

"Just saying."

Sarin turned up her nose. "You say it like it's a bad thing."

"I wouldn't know. My father hated me."

"Moms, I'm ready," said Athena.

"Ok, insert it when you're ready," said Kita. She leaned over Hemmer and opened all the pilots' windows so she could hear their reaction.

"Red Five, that bogey is climbing up to your left—In the name of the emperor, where'd that come from?" said a pilot. "It's right on top of us!"

On the display, Athena had dropped the Djinn ship next to the dogfight. Kita hit the call button and spoke to all the friendly fighters, "Red squadron, that's not a friendly ship. Take it out."

"What? This isn't in the scenario," cried a pilot.

"Just like the real world," said Kita. "Athena?"

"Yes, Mom?"

"Change the fighters load out to something they would carry against ships."

"Loadout, updated," said Athena.

"Red Leader, new loadout," reported a pilot. "Ship killers loaded."

"Red squadron, on me," said the pilot with RED LEADER under his video feed.

The fighters fell in behind the leader as they turned away from the ship.

"Woah!" cried Rainbow Jack. "That ship just lit up like a firework."

"Blind it, RJ," said Red Leader.

Rainbow Jack's fighter split from the group and turned toward the ship. As she aimed at the enemy ship, her velocity dropped rapidly. "Neptune's rings! Red Leader, this thing has some major shields. My speed just crashed."

"Rodger, RJ."

"Damn, they're lighting me up," said Rainbow Jack. Her fighter pulled into a loop to dodge the incoming anti-fighter fire. "MSMB on the way."

The missile flew toward the ship, decelerating in the ship's strong shields. The MSMB split and the submunitions flew toward the anti-fighter guns attracted by the weapon's electronic signature. Some of the mini-missiles never reached their target.

"You've got to be kidding me!" exclaimed Rainbow Jack. "Who programmed this simulation? Nothing can take out a submunition."

Rainbow Jack flew parallel to the ship gaining speed. She pulled a tight turn and rocketed upward into a half loop. "See how they like this. ARM away!" A missile flew at the ship but was destroyed by anti-fighter guns. "What is this ship?"

As Rainbow Jack circled around for another pass, the rest of Red squadron attacked. The anti-fighter guns fired.

"By the emperor," exclaimed a pilot, "that's a lot of lead they're flinging. What happened, RJ?"

"It's these shields. I'm coming back around for another shot with the MSMB."

"We just lost Goose!" cried a pilot.

"Keep it together, Red Two," said Red Leader. "Fire penetrators!"

The anti-fighter guns claimed two more fighters. The three remaining fighters launched a missile each. Two missiles never reached their target, but one struck the ship mid-ship, punching a sizable hole in the hull.

"Got 'em!" exclaimed a pilot just before he was destroyed.

"Red One, bring it back around. RJ, see if you can do something about those guns," ordered Red Leader.

"I'm making some adjustments," said Rainbow Jack. She streaked toward the bow of the ship, pulling to one side to run parallel to it. "MSMB away."

This time the missile flew along the ship at full speed. Only when it split apart did the submunitions turn towards the ship. This technique allowed more of the submunitions to reach their targets.

Kita was impressed Rainbow Jack figured out the problem so fast.

The remaining pair of fighters followed a similar track as Rainbow Jack, flying parallel to the ship. Anti-fighter guns hit both fighters, but one was able to launch another missile against the ship.

Rainbow Jack was the only one left. *Is she going to withdraw or fight to the last?* Withdrawal was the only sensible thing to do.

"Do we have a follow on force incoming?" asked Rainbow Jack.

Hemmer looked at Kita. She shook her head.

"Negative, Rainbow Jack. Orders are to withdrawal," said Hemmer.

"I'm not spent yet," said Rainbow Jack.

Rainbow Jack turned back into the ship. She fired everything she had. The missiles struck around the damaged area of the ship. Her missiles weren't as powerful as what the fighter's carried and did little damage. As Rainbow Jack turned, she was hit by anti-fighter fire.

"And that's it," said Kita. "They did better than I thought."

"RJ is going to be furious," said Hemmer.

"Why?"

"She holds the record for most completed missions, in the simulator and real life."

That explains why she was so adamant about making it home last time.

Rainbow Jack exited her simulator and hurried to the control room. She banged on the door.

Hemmer sighed. "Enter."

Rainbow Jack stormed in. "Neptune's rings, General? Whose dumb idea was it to run a stupid scenario like that?"

Hemmer opened her mouth, but Kita spoke first. "Mine."

Rainbow Jack looked at Kita surprised as if the Angels had just appeared. "In the name of the emperor, what are you trying to pull?"

As Rainbow Jack huffed, another pilot entered. "Come on, RJ, let's go before you make it worse."

"I can explain," said Kita. "Our next battle will be against ships like the one you just faced. They have better guns, shields, and engines than we do. You're going to get a lot of practice over the next couple of days, especially you, Alex."

"What's that supposed to mean?"

"This," said Kita. She touched Rainbow Jack on the nose. "Boop!"

Rainbow Jack tried to swat Kita's hand away, but a scream interrupted her. She fell to her hands and knees, grabbing her head. With a swift motion, Kita drew Dead and sliced open the back of Rainbow Jack's flight suit.

Thin wing bones sprouted from between Rainbow Jack's shoulder blades. The bones grew, reaching toward the ceiling, creating several joints. Buds formed on the skin and burst into violet and yellow feathers.

"Rise, Jammer," said Kita.

Sarin helped Jammer to her feet.

"What happened? What did you do to me?" demanded Jammer. "Why do I have a splitting headache?"

"You got these," said Sarin as she pulled one of Jammer's wings around for her to look at.

"That's attached to me?"

Sarin pulled on the wing harder causing Jammer to twist. "I don't think it's coming off."

Kita giggled.

"I...What—Why me?" said Jammer.

"Because I like you," said Kita. "You're the best, and you're tenacious."

"How am I supposed to fly in a cockpit with these!"

"Don't worry. We'll make some modifications. And from now on, you'll be able to fly multiple fighters at once."

"How?"

"I'll show you once the computer in your head is fully formed," said Kita.

"No way am I letting you put a computer in my head."

"Too late, it's already there."

"You're joking?"

"Am I joking, love?" Kita looked at Sarin.

"Practical jokes aren't her thing," said Sarin. "If she says it, it's the truth."

"Come on," said Kita. "Let's introduce you to your new family."

"New family?" exclaimed Jammer.

"Yes. Oh, and how do you feel about Admiral Sheppard?"

"Uh...she's an excellent admiral—for a ground pounder."

"Well, that's a start."

CHAPTER XXIV

"$\mathcal{H}$ow's she doing?" Kita asked Hemmer as she entered the control room for the flight simulators with Sarin and Babydoll.

"She hasn't moved since I came on shift."

Kita rolled her eyes. It wasn't unusual for an Angel to stay still for days, especially those who could link to computers. "I mean—"

"How's she flying?"

"Yeah."

"When she started I wasn't sure this would work, but seeing her today she's doing her job, and her drones are flying rings around the fighter jocks."

"Good. I knew she'd get the hang of it." Kita smiled at Jammer standing among the simulators. Athena had rewritten the simulator code to accommodate Jammer's wireless connection and drones.

Kita reached around Hemmer and highlighted Jammer and her drones on the holographic display. Jammer and her drones were attacking a Djinn ship with the help of another squadron. It was easy to tell who was who. The drones made hard, tight turns, pulling g-forces that would kill a human. Jammer's fighter was nearly as nimble, the only difference was the size.

"Wow, look at her go," said Babydoll.

A section of the Djinn ship exploded after three drones made a pair of sharp turns into the ship and fired a missile each. Along the ship, sections were smoking from earlier strikes.

"She seems to have figured out their shields," said Sarin.

"Someone's watching her and passing notes to the other pilots, right?" said Kita to Hemmer.

"I'm doing my best. The other pilots are only getting a few hours a day in the simulators, so they're not getting much time to put theory into practice."

"I'll have her spit out a log of what she's doing. That'll keep you from having to guess her motive."

"Anything would help," said Hemmer.

"Good. We're going to take her off your hands for a little while," said Kita.

"It's been three days. I gave up telling her to take a break."

Kita chuckled. "Don't worry, she's fine. Angels can go weeks without sleep."

Hemmer raised an eyebrow.

"It's why we're the best of the best."

Kita led the others into the simulator room and tapped Jammer on the shoulder. Jammer's head turned in a mechanical fashion.

"Hey," said Kita. "I've got something for you."

Jammer's eyes twitched. Her face came to life. "For me?"

"Yeah, come on."

"But, I've got to practice."

"You can do it in the background," said Kita. "The computer and your autonomic nervous system will take over."

"You mean I'll fly automatically?"

"Yeah. It's not great for offense, that takes some thought, but for defense it's good. The more you do it, the better you'll become. Strengthens the bond between girl and machine," said Kita with a smile as they walked into the ready room. "Kerri, you mind opening a gate to manufacturing?"

"What's in manufacturing?" said Jammer.

"You'll see," Kita hummed as she stepped through the rift gate, an interdimensional portal that could be opened over long distances, into Enterprise's manufacturing area. Kita walked through the large printers and assemblers to a group of six large items covered by tarps. "Here you go!"

Jammer went to the largest tarp and pulled it off, revealing a fighter. "This is for me?"

Kita nodded. "Yep. Custom made by Athena."

"But…I'm not due a fighter for months after destroying my last one."

A rift gate opened, and Defiance and Sheppard appeared.

Kita motioned to the arriving pair. "They felt you deserved it."

Jammer stiffened and saluted. "Your Highness. I—thank you."

Defiance returned the salute. "No problem, Alex. Kita reports you've discovered several strategies the fighters can use against the Djinn ships that will save many lives and will lead us to victory."

"Just doing my job, Your Highness."

"You can call me Casey. You're no longer mine. You're on loan to me."

Jammer's eyes went wide. "I'm not? What does that mean?"

"It means you're free," said Kita. "To go wherever and do whatever you wish. Right now, we're all putting our collective energies into trying to get out of this mess with the Djinn."

"That you got us into," Babydoll said teasing Kita.

"Would you rather the alternative?"

"What's the alternative?"

Kita scowled. "Prison."

"That's your gig, not mine. I'll go wander the stars."

"And leave the rest of us?" said Defiance.

"I'd do my best to get you out."

"You sure did a lot to help the rest of us the last time," said Sarin.

"Stop," said Kita. "Dredging up old blood won't help. We're here for Alex and to make her the most effective fighting force she can be." She walked over and took off a tarp revealing a drone. It was smaller than a fighter but carried a bigger payload and was faster.

"Wow," said Jammer. "I—" Lights on the side of the drone blinked and became solid. "I'm connected to it."

"Works the same as the simulator," said Kita.

"I'd love to take them flying, but it'll be days before I get into the queue."

"I'm sure I can sneak you in," said Sheppard. "The more time you have with them, the better."

Babydoll rolled her eyes. "Damn, Sheppard. You make it sound like the world is riding on her shoulders."

"It means I have confidence in her, unlike you."

"Hey, I've proven myself. If you want to go, Marine, this legionnaire will mop the floor with you. I'll leave you looking worse than Sahara."

Babydoll's mentioning of Sahara made Kita check her status. She was awake. Kita decided she would be her next stop. "Before we get into who breaks who, I have a question for Alex." From the look on Jammer's face, she was fully connected to the drone.

"Me?" she said, life coming back to her face.

"Yes. Are you seeing anybody?"

"What? I mean, no. I'm sorry. I'm not interested in you."

Kita chuckled. "My partner and girlfriend will be glad to hear it." Sarin made a face. Defiance huffed. "But, I'm not asking for me. I'm asking for a friend."

"Who? No one's shown interest in me for years."

"Not even after having your body altered?"

"I haven't told anyone. I've been too busy," Jammer said shyly.

"Nothing wrong with that. I understand. Just if you were interested..." said Kita.

"Is it another Angel?"

"Yes. She asked me to ask you. She's a little shy herself and is getting out of a bad relationship."

"I don't want to be a rebound."

That caught Kita by surprise.

"I promise you won't be," said Sheppard.

Jammer's jaw dropped. "You? But, you're—you're..."

"I'm an Angel, just like you. I'm looking to find someone to spend time with, who understands the demands of my duties."

"And who can put up with her hard ass," said Babydoll.

Sheppard sighed. "Forget it." She turned and walked away, intercepted by Defiance's comforting arms.

"Kerri," hissed Kita.

"Just because you look for love in all the wrong places does not mean you need to ruin it for another," Sarin said pointedly to Babydoll.

"I'm trying to warn the girl about what she's going to be getting into."

"Your personal feelings for Sheppard have no place here."

"How do you know what my personal feelings are," Babydoll yelled.

Kita and Sarin traded a look. The emotional outburst released by Babydoll contained anger but also sorrow and heartbreak.

Kita took Babydoll's hand. "Come talk to me, love." She led Babydoll behind a piece of machinery. "What's this about?"

"I...I..." Babydoll put her head on Kita's shoulder and cried. "I'm going to be alone—forever. Everyone hates me."

Kita wrapped her arms around Babydoll. "You're not going to be alone, and nobody hates you. I promise. What's on your mind? Whatever it is, I can fix it."

"No, you can't. And it's better this way. I'd just screw it up."

"Screw what up? What do you want? Whatever it is, name it, and it's yours," said Kita.

"I've already screwed it up a long time ago."

"Kerri, I can't fix it until you tell me who or what it is you want."

Babydoll wiped her eyes. "I—I like Rene."

"You have a funny way of showing it. But, I'm sure we can work on patching things up."

Babydoll shook her head. "No, I want to ask Rene out."

"Are—Ok, whatever you want. I'll talk to her."

"No. Don't. She hates me. I don't want her to see I've got a weakness for her."

Kita sighed. "Love, if you want her, you've got to show some vulnerability. Rene may say no, but she's not the type to use it against you."

"But if I get my hopes up..."

Kita stroked Babydoll's wing. "We don't know until we try. Come on." Kita led Babydoll back to the others. "Sorry, Rene. Kerri didn't mean to be hurtful. She was trying to tell you there's someone else interested in you."

"Who?" said Sheppard. "There's no one left but Alex."

Jammer looked like she wanted to disappear, then did.

"Wait! Don't go," said Sheppard.

"What did I do?" Jammer's voice came from the spot she'd been standing.

"You activated your camouflage ability," said Sarin. "Think about being visible, and you'll reappear."

Jammer's arm appeared, followed by a leg. Different parts appeared and disappeared until she was completely visible.

"I, ah, forgot to go into detail about that one," said Kita.

"This is why you don't give the new Angel briefing," said Sarin.

"I was excited about her other abilities. I did tell her about eating and sleeping." Kita waved the rest of the Angels to her. "Alex, tell me if I'm wrong, but you're not comfortable with dating Rene."

Jammer looked at the floor. "I'm sorry, but I'm still trying to figure out me. I've been so busy trying to prepare for the next battle I haven't even given any thought to that."

"I'm sorry," said Sheppard. "I don't mean to push you. I know you need time. I'm just being selfish."

"It's not your fault," said Kita. "I suggested Alex to you. But, there is someone else who's interested, and you have a lot in common."

"Who have I overlooked?" demanded Sheppard.

"Me," said Babydoll.

Sheppard's eyes went wide. "You! I'd rather—"

"Whoa," said Kita. "Think about this. You're both career soldiers and put that first. You're near equal rank. You both have a similar outlook to life—"

"She's a fallen angel, Kita!" yelled Sheppard.

Kita shrugged. "What's wrong with that? She's hardly a bad one."

Sheppard crossed her arms and scowled. "I know what you two get into—the blood and bodies."

"She has her quirks just like anyone. You just need to establish some rules. I'm not allowed to bring it home." Kita smiled lovingly at Sarin, who rolled her eyes. "And how often have we done it? Not once since she came back."

"That means you're overdue," growled Sheppard.

"Probably, but it's a hard thing to do on a warship. We need everybody, and there aren't many bad people around. We do some control."

"How can I trust her?"

"Trust her not to what?" said Sarin sounding appalled. "I trust Kita."

"Kita isn't faithful."

"You think Kerri is like Kita in that sense? I don't think I've ever met anyone more loyal than Kerri—and Kita is faithful to me. I believe when Kita says I'm first and she does come when called. I was mad at her because the one girl she bring home is an old rival of mine. It had nothing to do with her bringing someone home."

Sheppard turned up her nose. "Kerri is hardly wholesome."

Babydoll balled her fists and exploded with anger. "Like you're any better, you brain dead Marine. You're such a hypocrite. I'm looking past your history and looking at the person you claim to be. I'm not perfect. I know that, but that doesn't mean I don't have feelings and don't want to love someone. I know we've had our differences in the past, but I'm willing to give it a try.

"All you had to do was say *no,* and that would have been it. You don't have to be mean. To think I thought you had changed. You're still the same arrogant, vapid bitch you were on Base Station. You don't want someone to love you. You want a princess trapped in an ivory tower to guard forever." Babydoll wiped her eyes. "Don't ever question my loyalty to anyone. I have more than proved my loyalties to god and country." She fled behind some machinery.

Kita and Sarin went after Babydoll. She had her wings wrapped around her and was crying softly. They each put an arm around her.

Defiance appeared and put her hand on Kita's arm. Kita and Sarin made room for her.

"Are you ok?" said Defiance to Babydoll.

Babydoll came to attention, ignoring the tears in her eyes. "I'm fine, Your Highness."

"Obviously not. I'm sorry about Rene. She wishes to apologize."

"I don't want a formal forced apology. She hates me—I get it. Since I have you here, Your Highness, I think it's time I turned in my rank. I've been AWOL for a long time, and it's time I followed my heart."

"I'm sorry, Commander Liverpool, but I can't accept your resignation. The Legion is short capable officers at the moment, and you're needed."

"My loyalty is to her." Babydoll motioned to Kita.

"All of our loyalties are to her—that doesn't mean you can stop doing your job. Now, Rene wishes to apologize. Please hear her out." Defiance stepped aside revealing Sheppard.

"Kerri, I'm sorry, for now, and for everything in the past. You're an exceptional officer. Kita knows talent when she sees it. I'm a fool. I've been trying to get people to forget my past and see me as I am. I've had little success. When someone announces they're willing, I revert back to the person I was and throw it back in their face. I'm sorry. I hope I haven't soured you on me. I would love to go out with you. I think we have a lot to offer each other and I miss spending time with someone special. I'm hoping you'll be her."

Babydoll's hand slipped into Kita's and squeezed tight. She looked at Kita, her eyes asking what she should do.

Kita shrugged. *"Your call, love. It's your heart."*

Babydoll looked back at Sheppard. "I want to go to the Grand Canyon. I've only seen it in pictures."

Sheppard looked at Defiance.

"Your ship," said Defiance. "You can get time in the simulator anytime you want."

"I'm due back on the bridge in six hours. Can I pick you up in the wardroom in two hours?"

Babydoll nodded. "No dresses. Keep it casual. I don't want to see you in your parade uniform. Save that for another time."

Sheppard nervously rubbed her arm. "Ok. Floral prints and cargo shorts."

Sheppard's attempt at a joke brought a smile to Babydoll's lips.

"I'll let you get away with fatigues," said Babydoll, "but give me something pretty to look at." Babydoll winked playfully.

Jammer approached with a screen in her hand. "Excuse me, Admiral?"

"Just call me Rene."

"Rene, I need your signature so I can get these up to the flight deck and in line for launch."

"I'll take care of it," said Defiance. "Go get ready." She shooed Sheppard away.

"I need to get to the medical ward," said Kita. "Feel like coming, love?" she offered her elbow to Sarin.

"Why are we going there?" said Sarin as she placed her hand on Kita's arm.

"Sahara's awake. I thought you'd like to meet her."

"Snowy's girl?"

"Yep."

"I'm sure she's thrilled."

~

"Doctor Er'jeria, how's your patient?" said Kita as she stopped next to the Djinn's desk.

Er'jeria looked up from tapping on his screen. "Sahara is awake, and her body is functioning nominally. It appears your treatments have worked."

"Of course they did," said Kita with a shrug. "I have the utmost faith in Doctor Anthrax's ability to heal."

"When can we return to the fleet?" Er'jeria demanded as he stood up from his stool.

"In such a hurry? I'm beginning to think you don't like my hospitality."

"I need to check Sahara over in a proper medical facility."

Kita smirked. "Yeah, about that. I think she's going to stay here. Someone's taken an interest in her. But, I'll get you a ride back to the fleet."

"Sahara can't stay here. She must return. The only person who has an interest in her is her protector."

Kita walked around the towering Djinn. Extending her barb, she slammed it into the base of his spine. Er'jeria jerked and collapsed when his legs gave out. Kita knelt next to him. "I'm her protector now," she whispered. Pricking him with her barb, she delivered a heavy dose of a nerve agent. Er'jeria's head lulled to one side, and his eyes turned glassy.

"I could have killed him," said Sarin.

"I know, but I haven't killed anything in days, and I'm beginning to itch."

Sarin rolled her eyes while trying to hide a smile. "I know you can go much longer."

"True, but why when you don't have to?" Kita toed the body. "I guess I should get rid of this."

"Yes. Save some poor orderly the chore of cleaning up after you."

Kita incinerated the body leaving only an unpleasant odor of burnt fur.

Sarin waved a hand in front of her nose. "Ugh. I didn't think it was possible for them to smell any worse."

Kita took Sarin's hand and led her to the suite containing Sahara. She opened the door unannounced and giggled at what she found: Snowy licking Sahara's foot. "Did we interrupt something?"

Snowy's eyes narrowed. "No, just giving her a bath."

"Hmm," said Kita. She looked at Sarin.

"No."

Kita shrugged. "I tried. How are you ladies?"

"We're fine," said Snowy. "We're looking forward to getting out of here and back to the fleet."

"Good news then," said Kita.

"What do you mean?" demanded Snowy.

"Nell just took over duties for Doctor Er'jeria, and you've been assigned to Enterprise."

"We are assigned to Serge," said Sahara.

"That's part of my fleet—for now."

"What are you talking about?" said Snowy.

"I'm getting you what you wanted. I talked to Casey. She said she'd dispatch a ship to take you back to our homeworld—as soon as she retakes her Empire."

"Kita—"

"It's what you wanted, right?"

"Yes, but…"

"I know. You haven't run it by the missus yet. I thought I'd help."

"What is she talking about, Snowy?" said Sahara.

Kita spoke before Snowy could, "I'm talking about getting you away from here to live in a place where you'll be free of oppression and misogyny."

"What does she mean, Snowy?" said Sahara as the fur on the back of neck and arms stood up.

"I'm talking about you being free to be who you want to be," said Kita. "Where no one can touch or judge you. You're free to make your own choices."

"I am free to make my own choices, and no one can touch me."

"You're only as free as your father lets you be. As long as you serve him, you have the illusion of freedom. I'm presenting you with real freedom." Snowy looked like she was ready to hyperventilate. "You ok, Snowy?" said Kita.

Snowy's eyes flashed with anger. "You always have to ruin everything for me, don't you?" Snowy yelled.

"Just trying to help," said Kita. "And in three days this fleet will cease to exist. You should get used to the idea."

"What have you done?" cried Snowy.

Kita folded her arms. "You believed I was going to lead Collector's forces against my girlfriend's? I'm leading them into a trap, and it's about to be sprung. The Shadow Fleet knows they're coming and is prepared to wipe them out."

"No," said Sahara. "It will be you who will be wiped out. My father's ships are stronger than even the Diamocks."

"I have my ways of dealing with them," said Kita. "Now, I need you two to sit back and enjoy the ride. We'll be at Earth soon enough and I'm sure Snowy wants to get in line to take a swing at Galina."

Sahara hissed and brandished her claws at Kita.

"Ah-ah, kitty," said Sarin. Her pistol was pointed down the bed at Sahara's head. "I'd hate for poor Snowy to have to scrap your brains off the wall. It's been a while since I've killed something and I've got an itchy trigger finger." Kita raised an eyebrow at her partner. "You're not the only one who has trouble with fleet living, babe."

"Collector will hunt us to the ends of the universe. We're not safe," said Snowy.

"Collector thinks Sahara's aboard one of his own ships," said Kita. "In a few days, she'll have been killed aboard one of them."

Snowy's mouth fell open.

"What?" said Kita. "You think I'm going to leave one of my oldest loves out in the cold? You came to me because you knew only I could deliver you from evil."

"Only you would have that kind of complex," said Snowy.

"All you have to do is behave. You don't have to help, just stay out of the way."

"You want me to be complacent as you destroy my father's fleet?" demanded Sahara.

"Time to find a new loyalty. It doesn't have to be to me. I suggest Snowy. She's risked her neck for you."

"I won't let you."

Kita grabbed Sahara's foot and pricked her with her barb. "We'll talk in a few days."

"I can't move," cried Sahara.

"I left you your mouth and ears. I suggest you use them." Kita looked at Snowy. "Make her understand. Otherwise, I'm putting her in a cat carrier, and I'll put her in the hold until you get to our homeworld."

Snowy nodded.

"If she becomes a problem, she'll go another round with Kerri, and I won't tell her to be nice this time."

"Don't threaten me," said Snowy meekly.

"I'm not threatening you. I'm threatening her. She's not one of us. Best she remembers that. See you later, ladies."

～

KITA AND SARIN ENTERED THE WARDROOM AFTER SPENDING A FEW HOURS rekindling their partnership. Babydoll sat at a table with a long face as she played with a piece of chocolate cake.

"Oh no," whispered Kita.

Sarin frowned. "Come on. Let's see what happened."

They approached Babydoll sitting down on either side of the depressed looking Angel. Kita put her arm around Babydoll.

"Hey, love. What happened?"

Babydoll shook her head and looked at Kita. "Huh?"

"How did it go?" said Sarin.

Babydoll turned back to her cake and sighed. "It was…great. I had a good time."

"That's not what this says," said Kita, pointing to the cake.

"I'm just not sure I'm what she wanted, or I didn't send the right signals."

"Why do you say that?" said Sarin.

"I don't know. She gave me a kiss goodbye, but that was it. She held my hand. We chatted some. There were these awkward pauses…I think I screwed it up." Babydoll's shoulders slumped.

"That sounds completely normal," said Sarin.

"But you'd see her again, right?" said Kita.

"Of course. I had a good time. Maybe I was expecting more—to be swept off my feet. I must sound stupid."

"No," said Kita. "But Sheppard isn't the kind to sweep a girl off her feet. She approaches love like everything else in her life, a battle. She plans, probes, gets a feel for her opponent, then attacks. I'm sure she was just feeling you out."

Babydoll made an unsure face. "But what if she doesn't like me? What if—"

"Is this what you do to all your relationships?" said Sarin.

"What do you mean?" said Babydoll.

"If you pick apart every relationship you've ever attempted it's no wonder you're single."

"What's that supposed to mean?"

"I mean, you fixate on the negative. You pick it apart until you're so sure you were awful that you give up. I bet plenty of suitors have called you for a second date, but you don't give them one because you think you were awful the first time. You said you'd go out with Rene again."

"Why would she when I was awful?" said Babydoll.

"My point exactly," said Sarin. "You listed some positive things that happened. Why not think about them?"

"What's the point if she's not going to call me?"

Sarin let out a frustrated noise. "Kita, I'm going to need an office and some time."

"Sure thing, babe." Kita squeezed Babydoll's hand. "Don't worry. You're in good hands now."

CHAPTER XXV

"One hundred and fifty miles to Black Station Six, ma'am," reported Navigation.

Kita stood with Defiance and Sheppard next to the holotable.

Kita's fleet was in a double column formation approaching the station. At fifty miles, they would switch formation to a line and attack the station, but they would never get there. Shadow Fleet forces were to arrive from FTL once they were within a hundred miles of Black Station Six.

"So, Rene..." said Kita with a tone that said she wanted something.

"What? The battle's about to start."

"I know. There's nothing that can be done right now to affect the outcome. So, I have a question for you."

Sheppard sighed. "What?"

"Are you going to ask Kerri on a second date? It's been three days."

"Kita," Sheppard said exasperatedly. She looked at Defiance.

"Don't look at me for help. I've been wondering the same thing."

"I'm going to ask her. I've been busy with prepping for the battle."

"But you did have a good time?" said Kita.

"Of course I had a good time. Kerri is smart, strong, and an excellent legionnaire."

"You sound surprised."

Sheppard rolled her eyes. "She doesn't often act like it."

"That's partially because she is the God of Chaos. There is going to be some randomness to her."

"That is one of the things I wish to talk to her about," said Sheppard.

"She can't get rid of it."

Sheppard shook her head. "I don't want her to get rid of it. I do want to know more about it."

"So why haven't you asked her out?"

"I've been busy, Kita."

"It takes five minutes. While you've been waiting, her stomach has been in knots thinking she did something wrong."

Sheppard gasped. "She did nothing wrong. I left happy. I thought everything went great."

"Well, we have five minutes," said Kita.

"No we don't," said Defiance. "We're crossing phase line alpha now."

"That was fast."

"Look sharp, people," said Sheppard. "Communications, signal Admiral Hackett."

"Yes, ma'am."

"Fighter Control, status?"

"One fighter down for emergency repairs. Everyone else is standing by."

"Engineering, shield status?"

"At full power, additional power to aft shields. Engines ready for The Sprint."

The Sprint was the maneuver to get Enterprise across no man's land between the Djinn and UEE forces. The SLIP engines would speed the maneuver, but they would still be vulnerable for a time.

"Jess, is your team ready?" said Defiance.

"You bet, Your Highness. Give us the word, and we're ready to attack."

On the holotable, the first two Djinn ships passed phase line alpha. Kita went to the air boss screen and selected Jammer. The Angel had her music blaring as she waited.

"How's it going?" said Kita.

"Huh? What? Oh, it's you. I'm ok, just waiting for the go command."

"It'll be shortly. You ready to lead?"

Jammer and her drones would be the first fighters launched.

"Hell, yeah. I can't wait to smash them in the mouth."

"Don't get too stupid out there. You're not completely indestructible, and we can't get to you right away."

"I won't do anything crazy."

"Do crazy, don't do stupid."

"You got it."

"Go get 'em, girl."

Looking up, Kita frowned. The shutters that protected the giant domed window were closed. She wanted to see the stars and calm her nerves. She hated not being able to directly influence a battle.

"New contacts, ma'am," cried Sensors, "ninety-five miles at zero-five-five, ten degrees above. Squawk box matches for Carolina, Maine, Iowa, California, Colorado, five heavy attack cruisers, four missile cruisers, five frigates, and five corvettes."

Kita nodded, but they were going to need more than two dreadnaughts and three battleships.

"Launch fighters. Orders are to fly toward Black Station Six," said Sheppard.

"The Djinn want to know if we should deploy, ma'am?" said Communications.

"Tell them to hold formation and fire until we reach phase line lion. We should be able to absorb the Shadow Fleet's attacks."

Kita wiggled her nose. She wished that last statement wasn't the truth. Now they had to wait for all the fighters to launch. It was a dangerous time that left Enterprise exposed.

"New contacts, ma'am," said Sensors, "ninety-seven miles at one-three-three, seven degrees below. Squawk box matches for Spain, Texas, Canada, four heavy attack cruisers, four missile cruisers, six frigates, and five corvettes."

The holotable updated. The new group was on the other side of their formation. Suddenly the Djinn had two groups to worry about.

"Serge reports taking fire from the first group," said Communications.

"Damage?" said Sheppard.

"They report minimal."

"Tell them to hold fire and keep in formation. I want to be close enough to blow these ships away with one shot."

Kita nodded. That played right into the Djinn male psyche.

"How's it going girls?" Kita said to the other Angels. Most of them were spread around the ship in case they were boarded.

"We're ready in the medical ward," said Anthrax.

"Ready to infect them," said Valor.

"Anti-boarding crew one ready," said Babydoll.

"Crew two, ready," said Stormy.

"Crew three, ready," said Blitz.

"Crew four, ready," said Ryder.

"The fighters are launching now. We'll start The Sprint in a few minutes," said Kita.

"We'll be ready to kick their ass," said Talli.

"Good. I have no doubt. I'll keep you informed."

"New contacts, ma'am," called Sensors, "ninety-three miles at zero-seven-five degrees one degree above. Squawk box matches for Germany, Russia, South Africa, Argentina, Mexico, two attack cruisers, four missile cruisers, five frigates, and eight corvettes."

The holotable added the new ships. It still wasn't enough firepower, but from the sounds coming from Communications, the Djinn were getting nervous. *How many of the Djinn have been in actual ship-to-ship combat? It can't be many. It's been generations since they last fought a war. Something no one planned for, how green the Djinn are. Maybe Sheppard noticed and didn't say anything, thinking it was a given.*

"Serge just fired, Admiral," said Combat Control.

"Dammit," said Sheppard. "What did they hit?"

"They took a shot at Maine, ma'am."

"Damage?"

"No report yet, ma'am."

Sheppard turned to Kita. "What do you want to do?"

"Me? I have no idea."

"This is your show."

"You're in command."

"Of the forces. The strategic decision is yours."

"Where are we at getting the fighters out the door?" Kita called to the Air Boss.

"Sixty percent of the squadrons have launched."

"Can we launch if we start The Sprint?"

"Yes, ma'am."

Kita looked at Sheppard. "Then we go now. Tell Jess to release her viruses and get those ships of yours firing, concentrating on the lead ships."

"You got it," said Sheppard. She yelled for Combat Control.

Kita moved next to Defiance. "The question is: Where is Fort Ticonderoga?"

"I don't know. Maybe they left the parking brake on."

Kita rolled her eyes. Such simple mistakes had held up missions before.

"Jess, how goes the virus release?"

"We're contacting the ships now and unpacking the viruses. It's going to take a while."

Kita nearly choked. *"Get the lead ships first."*

"Who?" said Valor.

"Serge and Growler, followed by Snarl, Stomp, Sludge, Scar, Slash, Swoop, Slag, and Grimlock. After that, it's the back half and get through them as fast as you can."

"Who picked these code names anyway? They sound like Transformers."

"I thought you did," said Kita.

"Maybe it was Rene."

"Get to work."

"On it."

Kita looked at Defiance. "Jess says it's going to take a while to deploy the viruses."

"So my ships are left firing at invincible targets? Great."

"Nearly invincible targets. The Djinn shields will slow down the shells." Kita snapped her fingers. "Rene, do we have high explosive shells on board the ships?"

"Yes, why?"

"They detonate on impact right?"

"They can be set that way."

"Tell the ships to fire HE shells. Save the kinetic rounds for when the shields are down."

Sheppard nodded. "I get what you're saying. Combat Control!"

"We can still hurt them," Kita said the Defiance. "It won't be in vain."

"Admiral, battle group one just announced it lost a frigate," said Communications.

"Rodger," said Sheppard.

Kita sighed. *The first of many.* "Rene, let's get out of here," urged Kita.

"Ok. Engineering, kick it in the ass and get us to the other side."

"Aye aye, ma'am."

Kita felt the ship's velocity increase. It took a second to adjust. She looked over the Air Boss' shoulder. Enterprise had launched eighty-five percent of the fighters.

"Kita! Serge and Growler are down," said Valor.

"Great. We can finally do something." Kita looked for Sheppard. "Rene, the first two ships are down. Release the kraken!"

"The what?"

"Send the fighters and tell the other ships to target Serge and Growler with kinetic rounds."

The holotable showed Black Station Six on the far side, with the three battle groups near it. On the far side were Enterprise and the Djinn ships. Enterprise was inching away from the Djinn as they maneuvered into a line. The two lead ships were showing yellow. They'd been damaged, but not critically. *It's also a best guess by the computer.* The fighters had reversed course from Black Station Six to attack the Djinn ships.

This was the point Kita feared. There was no going back at this point. The fear tickled her toes. Silently, she urged the Enterprise on the holotable to move faster.

"Fighters coming into range of Djinn ships," said Sensors.

"That should give them something other than us to worry about," Kita said to Defiance.

Enterprise shook.

"They're early," muttered Kita.

"Damage report?" said Defiance as the ship shook again.

"Shields and armor are holding, Your Highness," said Engineering.

"Look, Swoop is breaking ranks," said Defiance, pointing at the holotable.

Kita cringed. "That's a boarding ship." The smaller, lighter ship was moving across the formation fast.

"Why would they try and board us from the aft? They'll hit the engines," said Sheppard.

"If we had the old engines," said Kita. "The SLIP drives don't have any emissions. They'd come straight into the engine room. That's the last place we want them."

"Should we turn?"

"Keep going straight. If we put enough distance between us, it'll be too far for the boarding sleds to travel." On the holotable Swoop gained on the much larger and heavier Enterprise. *"Jess!"*

"Yeah?"

"I need you to attack Swoop."

"But that's down the list."

"It's trying to board us."

"Ok, on it."

"Rene!" called Kita.

"Yeah?"

"Tell them to concentrate fire on Swoop. The shields should be coming down."

"Swoop has closed," said Defiance. "Five hundred yards. She's turning."

Kita tapped the Swoop icon on the holotable and brought up a live feed. "Navigation. On my mark perform a crash turn ninety degrees to port."

On the live feed, Swoop fired hundreds of boarding sleds. A high explosive shell exploded off Swoop's bow illuminating them.

"*Mark!*" Kita yelled.

Enterprise turned hard, throwing Kita against the holotable. She grabbed Defiance. Sheppard held onto a workstation. The violent maneuver threw several people from their seats. Shudders ran through Enterprise as the boarding sleds slammed into the ship.

"Damage!" cried Sheppard.

"We have hull breaches in the port aft area. Runways one and two have been damaged, ma'am."

"Are they in the engine room?" demanded Kita.

"Yes, ma'am. We have hull breaches, but the engines remain undamaged."

"*Kerri, take your team and guard the engine room. Get there as fast as possible.*"

"We're on it," said Babydoll. "*Opening a rift gate.*"

"*Everyone else move toward the back of the ship, port side to repel boarders. Athena, do what you can to slow them down.*"

"*Decompression doors have closed. They will delay the boarders.*"

"Security!" called Sheppard. "Get your people armed and moving to repel boarders."

Kita drew her swords.

"Where are you going?" said Defiance.

"To kill some kitties."

Defiance grabbed Kita's arm. "We need you here. There is a wider battle that needs to be fought. Let the others handle it. That's why they are there."

Enterprise shook violently as Swoop fired a broadside attack at close range.

"*Jess!*" cried Kita.

"*We're working on it. Ok, shields are coming down. Engines and weapons in a few more bars.*"

"Rene, shields are down. Tell the others to fire on Swoop."

"Wilco."

Kita had the live feed open when Swoop disappeared in a violent fireball. "Hit! Keep it up. Navigation, turn to starboard. Get us back on a course to friendly lines."

"Aye aye, ma'am."

On the holotable, the Djinn fleet was halfway through completing their deployment. Soon they'd be able to bring their full weapons to bear, and life would become interesting.

There was a bright flash on the live feed as Swoop broke apart.

"Swoop is gone, Rene," said Kita.

"Combat Control, shift targeting priorities back to Serge and Growler," ordered Sheppard.

Kita checked the Djinn ship's status. Serge was red and Growler orange. She shook her head. It was taking a lot more firepower than they had planned to destroy the Djinn ships. *Where in the Crushing Depths is Fort Ticonderoga?*

Enterprise shook again. This time the computer said the attack had come from Stomp. The Djinn were coming online. Kita willed Enterprise to move faster. They were halfway there.

A loud explosion reverberated through the ship.

"What was that?" said Kita. "That didn't feel like it came from outside."

"There was an explosion in the engine room, ma'am," reported Engineering. "Engine power is dropping."

"Dammit," Sheppard, Kita, and Defiance said together.

"Kerri, what happened?"

"Suicide bomber detonated against one of the drive cores. There was nothing we could do to stop it."

"Get them out of there."

"We are. Some are dug in, and we have to go in and get them."

"Who's closest to the engine room?" demanded Kita.

"We are," said Stormy.

"Get there and help Kerri. We can't lose any more drive cores."

"Moving now."

"We're down a drive core," Kita reported to Defiance and Sheppard.

"We're going to be a sitting duck," grunted Defiance.

"Ma'am, an explosion has ripped Serge in half," reported Sensors.

"Flight Control," called Sheppard. "Shift forces to finish off Growler and start on Snail and Stomp. Send wizzos to blind the other ships. Rotate squadrons back in to rearm and refuel."

"Aye aye, ma'am."

Enterprise bucked wildly as several shells hit at once.

"Jess," urged Kita.

"We're working as fast as we can. I'm sorry. Six ships left."

Kita grunted in frustration. *"Alex!"*

"Huh? I mean, yeah?"

"Where are you?"

"Helping the fleet take down these ships," said Jammer.

"I need you to blind Drag, Snag, Fang, Smash, Bash, and Blast. Enterprise is getting shot up."

"I can't get to all of them."

"Get to the ones you can. Anything to take the pressure off Enterprise."

"Ok. I'm on my way."

"Rene!" called Kita. "Split the fighters and have them hit Drag, Snag,

Fang, Smash, Bash, and Blast. We've got to get them thinking about something other than us."

"I'll do my best. We've got squadrons rotating in to reload."

The elevator door opened and Sahara stepped out. "You traitor!" she snarled and pointed at Kita. "You will die for betraying Collector."

A corner of Kita's mouth ticked up. *Sahara is up early. Glad the bionanite package I gave her was effective.* "No, I won't. You can't kill me. They," Kita waved at the holotable's line of Djinn ships, "can't kill me. Collector made a deal with the devil. I said I would lead his forces against the humans and I have. I've fulfilled my part of the bargain. There was no deal for what happened afterward—you weren't the only ones looking to the devil for help."

Defiance raised an eyebrow. Kita shrugged. *A little revisionist history, but it sounds good.*

"I won't kill you," said Sahara. "I will beat you and drag you back to Collector where you will face his wrath."

"You have to beat me first."

"Kita! This isn't the time to be brawling on the bridge," cried Sheppard.

"Don't blame me. I'm not starting it."

Sahara drew one of her curved, double-bladed daggers and threw it at Kita. As the blade flew through the air, ice-encased it and it landed on the deck with a dull thud.

"None of that," said Defiance.

Sahara snarled and screamed. She ran forward and leaped at Kita.

Kita jumped and met Sahara. Twisting to dodge Sahara's claws, Kita grabbed her by the shoulders, flapped her wings hard to make them summersault, and threw Sahara into the deck. Kita landed next to Sahara and picked her up by the throat. She raised Sahara over her head and slammed her against the floor.

Sahara kicked with her back claws. Kita ducked and pushed Sahara's legs aside with her wing and slammed her fist down on Sahara's chest, knocking the wind out of her lungs. Coughing, Sahara tried to roll away.

Kita caught Sahara by the scruff of the neck and her tail. With a powerful swing, Kita threw Sahara against the glass dome ceiling. Sahara landed in a heap on the deck. Kita punched Sahara several times in the back to stun her. She brought her fist up for one more blow.

"Kita! Stop!" cried Snowy from the elevator. She and Anthrax ran to Kita. "Don't! Please," pleaded Snowy.

Kita stood up. "What did I tell you?"

"I've been talking to her. I promise. We left for a few minutes to help the wounded and she got up and ran."

Kita shook Sahara. "What don't you understand? I'm giving you your freedom in exchange for nothing. All you have to do is walk away. You'll be free to do whatever you like, with whoever, whenever you want. I've taken care of all the hard details."

"You don't offer freedom," hissed Sahara, "you brainwash and enslave people."

Kita chuckled. "That would make life much easier, but I don't. I make friends, and I earn their loyalty. I don't buy loyalty like Collector. My friends aren't sworn to me. They're here because they want to be. They help me, and I help them. They don't have to and are free to come and go. I've had five leave already.

"I'm guessing being Collector's daughter has won you some freedom from being a normal Djinn female slave, but you *are* indentured to him. I can't respect how he, or the Djinn in general, treat their females. You're more than property to be won. You're people with your own thoughts and feelings. You deserve better. I can't free all the Djinn females, but I can free you. Please, take it. For you and for them. Change starts with one."

"How can I trust you?" demanded Sahara.

"You survived that beating I gave you without a scratch—I just winded you. I gave you a gift. You have the basic Angel package of bionanites—my gift for you. It's the first step to becoming an Angel. What I give you is yours to keep, no matter what you decide to do. Every Angel gets this deal. I hope they'll keep you safe on your journey."

"You changed me?" snarled Sahara.

"That's right. Snowy wants you kept safe. That means I want you safe."

Sahara turned to Snowy. "You trust her after what she's done?"

"Kita doesn't do anything without a reason, even death serves her purpose. I trust her. She wouldn't betray Collector without good reason."

Sahara's hackles rose. "You betray him even after all he's done for you?"

"I did what I said I would do. I got him Kita, and I got her to cooperate. I never promised for how long."

Sahara bared her fangs. "You betray me then?"

"Never," said Snowy. "I love you, and I would never hurt you. I'm working with Kita to keep us safe and give us a new home. A place where we can live like we want—wild and free."

"We were going to do that on Gre'll," hissed Sahara.

Snowy laid her ears flat against her head. "We would be under your father's thumb, needing him for protection. With Kita we'll be free—no strings attached. We'll be under the protection of the UEE."

Sahara scoffed. "They can't stop my father's ships! What good are they?"

"I think we're holding our own in this battle," said Sheppard.

"You have my word you will be safe," said Defiance. "The planet you will be going to will be quarantined and guarded. No one without my authority will be allowed there."

"My father has more ships. He will crush you," said Sahara.

"I'm not out of tricks yet," said Sheppard.

On the holotable Enterprise was nearing friendly lines. Nothing had hit the ship in the last few minutes.

"Admiral!" Sensors cried urgently.

"What is it?" said Sheppard. She looked at Kita warily.

"New contacts dropping out of FTL fifty miles behind the Djinn line. Unknown ship types. I've got twenty-five…thirty…fifty…eighty new contacts."

Kita went cold. *That's more than I can destroy before they get Enterprise.*

"Kita, tell me this is a Verisom or Diamock fleet come to help us," said Sheppard.

"I haven't made any arrangements with them."

"It is my father's fleet come to protect me," said Sahara.

"Kita, we don't have the firepower to go against them," said Sheppard.

To punctuate her words Enterprise shook violently.

"We're almost there," said Kita pointing to the holotable. Several UEE ships disappeared from the map.

"We have to collect all the fighters before we jump," said Defiance.

"If we collect them then we lose our best defense," said Sheppard.

"We can't abandon them!"

"What good does it do us to retreat?" said Sheppard. "We have nowhere to retreat to."

"Yes we do," said Defiance. "We go to Neptune."

"What is there?"

"The Neptune Orbital Station started as a ring of anti-ship guns. The habitat grew up around them."

"Those guns haven't fired in centuries," cried Sheppard.

"They still have crews, Admiral. Make the call and get them moving. Then get us turned and moving to Neptune. I want to show these bastards what a big gun looks like."

"Yes, Your Highness. Communications, get me the Neptune Orbital Guns."

"Combat Command," said Defiance, "get our people turned around and ready to jump for Neptune. Flight Command, recover all fighters."

Enterprise vibrated, and the power blinked.

"Athena, what happened?" said Kita.

"Power fluctuation in the transformers. I've corrected the problem, but it's going to be the first of many if we keep taking damage."

"Where is Fort Ticonderoga?"

"I don't know," said Athena. "Some of our communications are being jammed. If I knew where they were, I could connect via tight beam."

"Is that how Sheppard is talking to Neptune?"

"Yes."

"Have Neptune relay a message to Fort Ticonderoga and have them meet us there."

"No problem, Mom."

The floor shook, and the power went out.

"Athena?" called Kita, but got no response.

Uh-oh. "Rene?"

"Backup power should be coming online," said Sheppard.

"And if it doesn't?"

"The engines still have power. We might have tripped a fuse."

"Seriously?" groaned Kita. "Where do I find the fuse?"

"Engineering?" yelled Sheppard.

"Yes, ma'am. It depends on where we lost power. The nearest panel is two decks down just past door fifteen."

"Great," muttered Kita. "I'll be back." Transforming into her cloud, Kita drifted down two decks, through an office to the corridor. Following the numbers on the doors, she found door fifteen and the smoking panel. She transformed into her angelic form.

"We have a problem, girls. This panel was sabotaged."

"Not by our side," said Sheppard.

"I don't know. I'm going to look around. We might be infested with kitty cats."

"If you find any, kill them," ordered Defiance.

"Is there another way to get the power back on?" said Kita.

"Yes," said Sheppard. *"There is the backup relay. It's on the same level, but the far side near door three-two-four."*

Kita grunted. That was on the other side of the ship. She ran down the corridor, taking a cross corridor to get her to the other side of the ship. As she emerged, four Djinn had a wall panel open. The Djinn guarding her direction of the corridor opened fire.

Kita expanded her heat shield, letting the bullets melt against it. She jumped in the air, drew Dead and Buried, and brought them down on the attacking Djinn's shoulder. Her shield forced the other Djinn from their work. Sliding between the attacking Djinn's legs, Kita whipped her legs, knocking the Djinn down. She spun up to her knees and plunged her swords into the Djinn's chest. Flipping over the Djinn, Kita knocked a series of bullets out of the air, swung, and decapitated the shooter. Spinning to her left, she sliced through the last Djinn's rifle. Kita reversed her grip on Dead and plunged the sword into the Djinn's neck.

With a flash of flame, Kita cleaned her swords. She sheathed them and went to the wall panel. She removed two demolition charges from a sewage pipe. *So close, yet so far. This would have just made some poor soul miserable cleaning it up.*

Kita hurried down the corridor and found the right door. The panel was only a few feet away. She hit the latches and opened it. A number of switches were blinking red. She flipped them all and waited for them to turn green.

"Ok, you should have power," Kita said to Defiance and Sheppard.

"It's coming back," said Sheppard. "What was the problem?"

"Djinn saboteurs. I took care of them, but there might be more. Zen, Amanda, start sweeping the ship looking for any Djinn that survived the assault."

"Yes, Kita," said Blitz.

"No problem," said Stormy.

Kita sealed the panel and felt a tug on her arm. Feeling warm on her skin, she looked down to see blood. Something kicked her in the knee and made her kneel. Inspecting her knee, blood leaked from a small hole. She put up her heat shield and tried to stand. Unable to put any weight on her injured knee, she slumped against the wall. A bright streak ran through her heat shield. *He's still out there.*

Kita scanned the corridor with her different lenses. She didn't see anything.

"Jane, I need you."

"What's up, babe?" said Sarin.

"I've got a sniper. He's tagged me in the arm and knee."

"Where are you?"

"Deck twenty-seven, starboard side, near door three-two-four." Kita sent her an image of her location.

Sarin, Blitz, and Talli appeared on the opposite side of Kita, putting Kita's shield between them and the sniper.

"Babe, how bad are you hurt?" said Sarin.

Kita pushed off the wall and floated a few inches above the ground. "I can't put any weight on it."

"Have you seen him?"

"I searched, but couldn't find anything."

"Do you want me to go after him?" said Talli.

Sarin shook her head. "If Kita can't see him, neither will you. We need to draw him out. Feel like being bait, babe?"

"Sure," Kita growled.

Sarin holstered her pistols and pulled the two halves of her sniper rifle from her back. She seated the receivers and locked them in place. Taking a large magazine from her belt, Sarin loaded her rifle and chambered a round. She waved Kita back against the wall and then took up a prone position between Kita's shield and the wall.

"Ok, babe, drop your shield."

Kita did. She floated in front of Blitz and Talli to screen them from danger. The bullet came. Kita raised her hand and stopped it as Sarin fired.

"Talli, Zen, secure him," said Sarin.

Blitz ran down the corridor to the body followed by Talli.

"Not much of his face left," Talli yelled down the corridor.

Kita and Sarin arrived together.

"I've never seen armor like this before," said Blitz.

Kita knelt down and frowned. "It's phasing armor. It cycles the wearer between dimensions, masking their signatures. I hope we don't have more of them floating around."

"We didn't run into any," said Blitz.

"I'll warn the others," said Sarin. "The gods can see them if they watch the equation."

Kita wrinkled her nose. *How come I didn't think of that?*

"Come on, babe, let's get you to the medical ward," said Sarin.

"I'll be fine. I just need a little time."

"Kita," said Defiance.

"Yeah?"

"We've crossed phase line omega, and we're taking cover behind our ships. We nearly have all the fighters on board."

Kita raised an eyebrow. *"How'd we get them aboard so fast?"*

"Emergency recovery procedure," said Defiance. *"We land fighters as fast as we can, using all the wires before resetting them."*

That sounds dangerous.

"Hang on. We're going to jump to Neptune."

Kita felt her stomach fall to her toes and things went black.

CHAPTER XXVI

Kita, Sarin, Babydoll, and an elevator full of Angels exited onto Enterprise's bridge. Sheppard and Defiance stood next to the holotable looking grim.

"What's the problem?" said Kita.

Sheppard sighed. "Problems. And I don't think we have all of them yet."

"What can we do?"

"You could have not brought eighty enemy ships into UEE space," Sheppard snarled.

"Easy. She didn't know." Defiance eyed Kita.

"I just knew about what we were bringing with us. This might be my fault for what I've done to free Sahara. They probably think she's dead."

"If we gave her to them would they leave?" demanded Sheppard.

Kita shook her head. "I doubt it. They'll continue toward their goal. Anyway, I won't give Sahara up."

"So what is the plan to stop them?" said Sarin.

"We've lost our FTL engines," said Defiance. "We can't run, but we've made it to Neptune."

"Why lead them to a population center?" said Babydoll.

"Neptune is more than a population center. It started as a fortress, grew into a transportation hub, and finally into a colony. The fortress part is still intact, except we can't reach Neptune Orbital Command."

"How many guns are we talking?" said Babydoll.

"Four hundred thirty-six inch guns ring the planet."

Ryder whistled. "That's a big gun."

"And a lot of them," said Babydoll.

"I wasn't aware of Neptune Orbital Command when we took the station," said Sarin. "Did you, Athena?"

"I was not aware of any such a unit. There was no indication in the records."

"They're a separate entity from the Shadow Fleet or Political Bureau," said Defiance. "They have their own structure."

"So what do we have to do? Go bang on some doors?" said Kita.

"We may not have time," Defiance said with a frown.

"We can put out a public service announcement," said Sarin. "The Legion has control of the central communications network."

"Yes, do that," said Defiance. "It would be a good immediate first step."

Sarin snapped her fingers, and she was dressed in her red and black Legion uniform.

"I'll come with you. The people need to know that I'm alive."

Sarin put her hand on Defiance's shoulder, and they vanished.

"Anything we can do around the ship?" Kita said to Sheppard.

"Patch holes. Sorry. I'm stressed about this."

"Naturally. Do you have a plan?"

Sheppard sighed. "Yes, lure them in and let the big guns finish them off. I don't think their shields can stop a three-foot, seven thousand pound shell. But, the ships will need to keep them off the station. I'm recalling most of the ships left to guard Earth and Mars. We lost twenty-seven ships in the initial fight. None of the capital ships, but some were damaged."

"Did they all make it here?" said Kita.

"Yes. Everyone is reporting in. I don't know how long we have until the Djinn find us."

Kita grunted. "I doubt we'll have to wait long. There's no hiding once they get a probe above and below the ecliptic plane."

"We're going to need some time. The hangars are a mess from the emergency landing operations."

Sarin and Defiance returned.

"I hope they see it," said Defiance.

"Can some of us go to this facility?" said Kita. "Maybe we can get it operational while we wait for the staff to arrive."

"That's a good idea."

"We could search for a directory and go get people," said Babydoll.

Defiance nodded. "I'm sure they must have an alert roster in their systems."

"There's not much we can do here," said Kita.

"Then let's go," said Babydoll.

"Where are we going?" said Sarin.

"Here," said Defiance. She brought up the location of the Neptune Orbital Command headquarters facility. "Rene and I will stay here to organize the defenses. Let us know when you get there."

"It shouldn't be but an instant," said Babydoll. She looked at the other gods, and they vanished.

~

"I thought we'd be on the surface," said Talli.

"There is more protection burying it deep in the superstructure," said Ryder.

A piece of tape blocked the passageway.

Kita read on the tape, "Political Bureau line. Do not cross." With a heated finger, she melted through the plastic.

"I thought we got rid of the Political Bureau on the station," said Talon to Sarin as they walked down the passageway.

"This place wasn't on any map, and nothing mentioned it."

"What are those?" said Starlight pointing to four androids.

Sarin drew her pistols and shot each android in the head, causing them to collapse. "I don't know, but I'd rather sift through the pieces than ask them."

"Hopefully their main processors aren't in their heads," said Kita. "Otherwise, we're sifting through junk."

The group moved toward the downed androids.

"Neptune's rings, they're getting up," snarled Sarin.

"What did you shoot them with?" said Ryder.

"Armor piercing."

Ryder drew her revolvers and shot the androids in the chest and head, causing the androids to crumple to the ground.

Kita touched Starlight and Aspen, and phased them behind the androids. "Take their heads."

The three sword wielders cleaved through the heads of the humanoid-like bodies. Kita held the head in her hand as she studied it. "Alas, poor Yorick," Kita quipped. "What secrets do you hold?" She connected her finger to the fibers dangling and searched for something to connect to.

"I've never seen anything like these before," said Stormy.

"Nothing this advanced, anyway," said Sarin.

"These have crystal armor," said Talon as she knelt over the body of an android.

"Galina's been busy," said Babydoll.

"We need to upgrade the Angels' weapons," said Talon.

"Kerri, Jane, Leaf, Kara, can you harvest the crystal from these bots?" said Kita.

"Shouldn't be a problem," said Aspen.

Each Angel knelt over an android and placed a palm on the chest. They lifted their hand and pulled the crystal in each android away from the body.

"What are we doing?" said Blitz.

"Upgrading," said Kita. "Amanda, Zen, Talli, Kristi, Hali, take your weapons to the others, and they'll imbue them with crystal."

The new Angels gave their weapons over to the gods. The purplish-black crystal lined blade edges and gun barrels. When they were finished, Sarin turned the rest into bullets for the various firearms. She passed the rounds out to each shooter.

"Save these for anything that doesn't die by normal means," Sarin instructed.

Kita dumped the head she was holding.

"Find anything?" said Babydoll.

"No, just sensors in the head. Want to help open one up?"

They knelt over a body and Kita sliced it open with Dead.

"This is a lot more fun when there's blood," said Babydoll.

Kita looked at the mess of electronics, servos, and a strange metal case in the pelvis.

"What do you suppose is in there?"

"Probably what I want to talk to," said Kita.

She pried the case open and found it contained liquid tanks and tubing that ran into plastic wrap. Slicing open the plastic wrap exposed a human brain.

"Not androids—Mexorks," whispered Kita.

"What's a Mexork?" said Babydoll.

"A steampunk creature that used human body parts and mixed them with machine parts. They run on steam. This must be the next evolution."

"Galina said she was building an army," said Sarin.

Kita wiggled her nose, and Snowy and Sahara appeared.

"What—Kita, where are we?" said Snowy.

"Neptune. I thought you'd want to see what's become of your creation." Kita waved at the Mexork body.

"That's not me," Snowy said defensively.

"I know it's not."

"I could only dream of something like this. How did Galina do it?"

"She took your research and applied it."

"Nothing original about Galina," Snowy scoffed.

"What is this?" said Sahara.

"An old research project of mine," said Snowy. "Someone has taken it to the extreme. They used to be a combination of clockwork, steam, and biology."

"You used to make creatures like this?"

"Yes. I had cities full of them."

"We better be careful going against them," said Ryder from another body. "They have some heavy firepower built into their arms."

Kita inspected the left arm. It could transform into a maser cannon. "These are going to be challenging." Standing up, Kita looked at Stormy and Blitz. "Put a bullet in each braincase. I don't want to leave Galina anything she can reuse." To emphasize her point, she thrust Dead into the brain she held.

Kita turned her attention to the door the Mexorks were guarding. It was a reinforced split door, the kind used for bunkers. *And how do I get passed you?*

"I'll be right back," Kita said to Sarin and Babydoll.

"Where are you going?" said Sarin.

"To get the door open." Kita changed into her cloud form.

"Not without me." Sarin transformed and followed.

"Hey, wait up. We'll be back," Babydoll told the others. She changed and followed Kita and Sarin.

Kita drifted through the thick door. On the other side, she found eight Mexorks at the top of a ramp lined up ready to fire when the door opened. They fired into Kita's cloud, but the energy weapon went through her. The three Angels formed a line and drifted up the ramp. When they reached the Mexorks, they transformed.

Kita took the middle. She slashed through the chest of a Mexork, spun, and plunged Buried into the pelvis of a second. She dropped to a knee as a Mexork fired over her. Kita stood up between its arms and brought her swords down, chopping the arms off. She headbutted the Mexork to get some space, stabbed its chest, and then cut down slicing the Mexork open.

Sarin fired three shots from her pistols into the abdomens of the Mexorks. They collapsed together. Babydoll grabbed the heads of the Mexorks and slammed them together. She backflipped, kicking them into the ceiling. She jumped, caught them, and slammed them back into the ceiling. She flung the Mexorks to the ground and landed between them, driving her fist into the Mexorks' pelvises.

Kita sheathed her swords and entered a small room just beyond the ramp. A locked panel sat on the desk. She searched, but couldn't find any ports to connect. There was a wireless network, which she was trying to connect to, but the encryption wasn't standard, even for the UEE.

"Casey, is there a royal override code?" said Kita.

"And you expect me to know what it is?"

"I thought—maybe."

Defiance laughed. "Yes, I know what it is—RogerStaubach6XII."

"There must be a story behind that."

"Yes, I'll tell you sometime when I'm not busy."

"Love you."

"After this you owe me."

"Whatever you want."

"You may regret that."

"You know my conditions."

"We'll talk. Love you."

Kita entered the password, and the panel opened to a control screen. She hit the door control to open it, then searched for a duty roster or emergency contact tree, but couldn't find either.

Kita took Athena's ball from her belt and tossed it into the air. "Athena, they have a specialized computer network that might take some time to crack."

"I'm detecting the wireless network. I'm starting my hack. I detect you are already working on it."

"I thought two would be better than one."

The other Angels climbed the ramp led by Ryder.

"I see you've been busy," Ryder said to Kita.

"Yes, and there might be more. We need to spread out and clear the facility. Everyone goes in pairs. If you find the server room or the control room, let us know."

"Do we have a map of the facility?" said Ryder.

Kita shook her head. "It wasn't on the computer I accessed."

"We'll get everyone organized," said Babydoll.

Kita nodded and led Sarin and Athena deeper into the facility.

～

"KITA, WE FOUND THE CONTROL ROOM," SAID STARLIGHT. "IT'S DOWN THE *second corridor, seven doors down. This looks like a side entrance."*

"We'll be right there."

Kita, Sarin, and Athena appeared next to Starlight and Blitz.

"Good job, ladies," said Kita. She led everyone down a flight of stairs into the curved stadium-style room to a large holographic display at the bottom. The holographic display was off, but there was a large computer behind it.

Kita and Athena walked around the hibernating computer. Kita woke it and entered the password. Nothing happened. *Uh-oh.* She lifted a flap next to the screen revealing a keyhole.

"We're not getting in this way unless we get a key. Any luck getting into the wireless network, Athena?"

"I am working on it. This ball has a limited amount of computing power. If I were in the facility's computer I could work much faster, but to access it I must first break the password. I am in a catch twenty-two, so to speak."

Kita grunted. She wasn't having any better luck.

"Kita!" said Defiance.

"Yeah?"

"They found us. We just detected a probe."

"How long do we have?"

"I don't know. It could be any time now."

"Ok, we'll hurry."

Kita looked at Sarin. "The Djinn have found the fleet."

"Have they attacked?"

"Not yet, but Casey says it will be any time."

"We need the person in charge," said Sarin.

"I have no idea how to find him," said Kita.

"It's got to be in the offices somewhere."

"Ladies, I need you to search the offices looking for any names of people who work here," said Kita to the other Angels.

"There must be an office around here," said Blitz.

There were two doors on either side of the computer.

"You girls search that door, we'll search this one."

Kita opened the door to a room filled with computers.

"Can you hack these?" said Sarin.

Kita shook her head. "It would do us no good. These are computational machines, not operating system machines."

The room didn't hold anything else of value. Kita and Sarin returned to Athena. Blitz and Starlight appeared shaking their heads.

"Kita, I've found a computer, but it's password and biometrically protected," said Tina.

Kita gave her sister the royal password.

"Hey, it worked. I'm searching now."

Kita resisted the urge to take over. Tina was a trained intelligence operative and knew what she was doing.

"I got it. I got it. The place is run by a General Chadwick Bixby."

"Ok, thanks." Kita accessed the Neptune directory, searching for the general.

"Found him—at least I hope it's him," Kita announced to the others.

"Who?" said Sarin.

"The general in charge. He lives in the Turtle Lake apartment complex, number three twenty-seven."

"That's a nice place," said Sarin.

"Let's go. Zen, Hali you're coming with us."

Kita and the Angels appeared outside an apartment door.

Scenes from the ocean decorated the pastel-painted hallway. Benches and potted plants lined the walls. A plush carpet dampened the sound of their boots.

"Is this where the average human lives?" said Starlight.

"If they can afford it," said Sarin. "I'm sure he makes enough."

"So, accommodations are not determined by rank?"

"Not directly. Rank often comes with wealth. Depending on how you want to spend your money determines where you live."

"Fascinating."

"It's not the greatest system in the world," said Kita as she hit the buzzer for the apartment. "It can easily be abused, and people get overcompensated for certain skills."

"It's better than it has been at any point in human history," retorted Sarin.

"That's not saying much."

The door opened to a man wearing a floral print button-down shirt, khaki shorts, and flip-flops.

Sarin drew a pistol and shoved it under his nose. "Are you General Bixby?" she asked in a no-nonsense tone.

"What in Neptune's rings are you?" the man demanded.

"Answer the question," said Kita.

"Never heard of him," the man answered as sweat beaded on his forehead.

"Tina I need you. We don't have time to play twenty questions with this guy," said Kita.

A pinprick of light floated down from the ceiling and with a flash, transformed into Tina. "Looks like you're headed for a day at the beach," she chuckled. "Too bad we're not."

"Are you General Bixby?" demanded Kita.

"I don't know who you're talking about. I'm not him."

"He's lying, big sister. We've found our man."

"Good. Jane, take us back."

Sarin holstered her pistol and wiggled her nose. The group of Angels appeared in front of the holoprojector in the control room of the Neptune Orbital Command headquarters.

"Recognize this place?" said Blitz to Bixby.

"Who—What are you?"

"Children of the emperor," said Kita. "And we have an urgent mission. There is a fleet of enemy ships attacking the Shadow Fleet in orbit around Neptune. We need to get the orbital guns online so we can destroy the attackers."

"Why should I believe you?" said Bixby. "This place is on lockdown by the Political Bureau."

"We're standing here, aren't we?" said Blitz.

"We took care of them," said Starlight.

"The Political Bureau is trying to take over the Imperium," said Sarin. "We're helping the rightful Emperor take back her throne. Haven't you listened to the public service announcements regarding the Political Bureau?"

"I stay out of politics," said Bixby.

"How can you stay out of politics?" said Babydoll as she and a group of Angels glided down the stairs to join Kita and her group. "You're part of the emperor's defense force. You should be on the front lines defending her."

Bixby shrugged. "This is a retirement post. Nothing ever happens here. If the Political Bureau says they're in charge, who am I to argue?"

Kita rubbed her temples. "Does this place work? The Sailors and Marines of the Shadow Fleet are counting on it."

"I haven't run a diagnostic in a decade."

"Neptune's rings," groaned Sarin. "When was the last time you ran a simulation?"

"I powered the system up once when I took over to see what it did. I didn't deploy the guns or anything, just turned on the sensors. All the guns reported green status, so I shut it down."

"You don't know how to fire it?" cried Ryder.

"These guns are obsolete. I didn't think we'd need them," said Bixby.

"General, you're a disgrace."

Bixby flushed. "Listen, I don't need to take crap from whatever you are."

"I'm General Ryder Starr of the Red Legion."

"I don't care who you are. I'm a general, and I'll be treated like it," barked Bixby.

"You better care about me," said Babydoll. "I'm a Legion Junior Commander."

"Deputy Commandant Sarin."

"Commandant Kita."

"Emperor Casey Bush."

"Isn't she needed elsewhere," said Sarin to Kita.

"I thought I'd expedite things."

"Why haven't the guns been deployed?" demanded Defiance.

"General Bixby seems unable to deploy them," said Athena. "It seems he never read the instruction manual."

"Are you kidding me? You have one job, General!" Defiance turned to Kita. "Can you please get them online?"

"At the moment, we can't even turn on the computer."

"I have the key," said Bixby. He took the key chain out from under his shirt.

"Kita, Sheppard. The Djinn fleet just arrived. We're moving to engage."

"Be careful."

Kita drew Dead and Buried. She sliced through the chain holding the key and knocked it into the air with the other sword. She jumped, sheathed her swords, caught the key, and landed by the computer. She shoved the key into the hole, and the computer came alive. Kita opened the wireless network and let her and Athena in.

"Athena, go!" yelled Kita. "Tell us what we have to do to get the guns online. Everyone else, the Djinn fleet has arrived, and the Shadow Fleet is engaging them."

The Angels exchanged looks.

"What do we do?" said Stormy.

"Wait on Athena, then do what she tells us."

"Kita, I need to go back," said Defiance.

"Your Highness, are you sure?" said Babydoll. "Enterprise isn't safe."

"I'm not going to leave my fleet to face the enemy by themselves."

"I know it looks good," said Kita, "but you need to be kept safe. There's more at stake than the fleet."

"I won't be a coward," Defiance said in a huff.

Kita put a hand on her shoulder. "You're not a coward. But if you die, Galina wins."

"Is that all you care about, your petty revenge?"

"No. I can kill Galina anytime I want. What I can't do is replace the person sitting on your throne. Only you can do that. If you die, your people suffer. That will be an even bigger defeat for the Shadow Fleet and the Sailors and Marines who have sworn to defend you. Their lives are tied to yours, if you fall, they fail. If they must die so you succeed, then they will do it for the good of the Empire. The only way they fail is if you die." *I so sound like my mother right now.*

"But—"

"It's their duty to fight and die for you, so you can take back the throne and lead the rest to glory. They die so the rest may live."

"They can go on without me."

Kita shook her head. "You know that's not true. If you want to preserve your way of life and keep the Empire on the right path, it has to be you. No one else can do it."

"If you can kill Galina, then you can kill the usurper," said Defiance.

"And then what? I still need you to replace him. It can't be me, Jane, or Kerri. The People won't accept us. They'll only accept you. If you die, it all falls apart and descends into anarchy. If that happens, then you've failed as your duty as a ruler."

Defiance lowered her head.

"I know that look," said Tina. "Heavy is the head that wears the crown. Kita's worn it a time or two. You know what you have to do. It's hard, but we're here to help you."

Defiance lifted her head. "I will serve my people, but I'm not leaving until these guns are firing. And you," she turned to Bixby, "have failed me." A frozen wind blew through the room and swirled around Bixby freezing him solid. Defiance looked around the room. "What? No one said I was benevolent."

"Kita," said Athena.

"Yeah?"

"I am in, but the guns are offline and won't start until they have a diagnostic run. This system was not designed for an AI to operate it. Around the room are workstations that control groups of guns. Someone must manually run the diagnostics and bring the guns online. Once the guns are online, that workstation controls the aiming, loading, and firing of the guns."

"There must be a crew to run this place then," said Cinnamon.

"We don't have time to go find them," said Ryder. "Athena, can you tell us what to do?"

"Yes. Turn the workstations on."

"You heard her. Everyone take a workstation."

The Angels spread out, each taking one or two stations.

"The good news is," said Athena, "we don't need to operate all the guns, just find which ones are pointing towards our targets. I'm bringing the sensors online now."

The room's holoprojector lit displaying the planet, station, and the two fleets. The system could identify friend and foe, but that was it. Several of the friendly ships disappeared. Kita frowned. *Things aren't going well.* Several more friendly ships vanished.

"Rene, we're working on getting the guns working," said Kita.

"Hurry. We're taking a real pounding. Maine and California are gone. We'll hold them as long as we can."

Athena walked the Angels through the diagnostic procedure. The bars on Kita's screen slowly increase. Most systems reported back green, a few yellow. The computer asked her if she wanted to perform maintenance. She declined. *I hope this thing doesn't fall apart on me.*

"Kita, Rene. *We're down to fifty percent strength. I—*"

On the holoprojector, a group of friendly ships appeared on the flank of the Djinn.

"Who are they?" said Kita.

"It—it's Fort Ticonderoga!" yelled Sheppard. *"She brought her battle group."*

"That's good. Hang on. We're getting the guns up now."

Kita's diagnostic was half done. She drummed her nails on the desk. *I wish Casey hadn't killed that twit so fast.* She let her mind daydream about what she would do to him.

"Kita!"

Kita shook her head. *"Rene?"*

"We're pulling back to the station and are going to regroup. We're down to forty percent."

The diagnostic was at ninety-five percent.

"Just a few more minutes."

"I'm done," yelled Stormy.

"Extend the barrels," said Athena. "Link your group into the targeting computer."

"Ok—done and done."

"Select ammunition type."

"What should I choose?"

"Go armor piercing," said Kita. Her diagnostic hit a hundred percent. She ran through the steps to catch up with Athena. Other Angels announced they were complete.

"Kita, Enterprise is taking fire. We won't last much longer," said Sheppard calmly.

"I'm not in the right hemisphere," cried Stormy.

Kita checked her targeting computer. Targets lit her screen. She selected armor piercing rounds. As she waited for the guns to load, she selected a group of targets.

"I'm up," yelled Kita. "Firing now."

Kita expected to feel the room shake from the guns firing, but there was no haptic response, just a flashing reloading message. On her targeting computer, several of the targets she'd selected vanished. She selected another group.

Some of the other Angels announced they had targets and were firing. Enemy ships on the holoprojector vanished.

"Rene, how are you doing? We've commenced firing," said Kita.

"They seem stunned. They just lost five ships in seconds."

"We've got more guns coming online. Try and get everyone to safety."

The computer alerted Kita it was ready to fire. She hit the button, and three more enemy ships vanished from her targeting computer.

"Everyone who can target the enemy ships, target the maximum," ordered Kita.

"Wahoo, firing," cried Babydoll.

"Firing," said Toxic, she sounded bored.

"Maximum targets, firing," yelled Cinnamon.

"Hitting them now," said Anthrax.

The Angels not commanding a gun group watched over the shoulders of those who did or drifted down to the holoprojector to watch. Athena zoomed the holoprojector in so they could see. Another friendly ship vanished.

"Kita, they're still hitting the good guys," yelled Tina.

I can only reload so fast. Kita fired again. Her targeting computer was almost empty. She selected the last four ships and waited. When the fire button lit, she hit it.

"I'm out of targets," Kita announced to the others.

"I'm out too," said Toxic.

Kita left her workstation to look over Sarin's shoulder. Her partner was watching Cinnamon. The targeting computer showed eight targets left. Cinnamon fired another salvo, hitting five of the ships.

The holoprojector showed only eleven ships left. They were no longer pursuing the Shadow Fleet but had turned around, trying to clear the debris field. Four of the ships vanished.

"I'm done," called Anthrax.

"Four left," yelled Babydoll.

Cinnamon targeted her remaining ships and fired. She leaned back and took in a long breath.

"Good job, cupcake," said Talon.

Cinnamon reached behind her and wrapped her arms around Talon. "Thanks, hoots. That was intense."

Kita kissed Sarin on the neck and then glided down to the holoprojector.

"And good night," cried Babydoll.

On the holoprojector, the last of the Djinn fleet disappeared. Kita rubbed her neck, trying to release some of the tension. Sarin's hands took over.

Kita sighed. "Good job, ladies. We saved the day."

"Easier than playing a video game," said Toxic.

Kita smiled.

"But the results are very real," said Talon.

"Yes. I should get back to the fleet," said Defiance.

"Not without the rest of us," said Tina.

CHAPTER XXVII

$\mathcal{K}$ita and the other Angels appeared on Enterprise's bridge. Sheppard stood next to the holotable talking to a group of officers. She and the rest of the bridge crew looked stressed and haggard. The lights flickered, and some of the workstations were under repair.

"It looks like they got hit hard," said Ryder.

"Engineering, status report," called Defiance.

"She's barely spaceworthy, Your Highness. It's easier to list what's not damaged than what is."

"Are the runways open?" asked Kita. "We need to find Alex."

"Runway three is open, Child of the emperor. Hangar space is at a premium."

"Most of what's left of the squadrons have been sent to Fort Ticonderoga," said the Air Boss.

"Can you find out where Rainbow Jack is?" said Kita.

The Air Boss flipped through his screens. "She and her drones landed on Enterprise."

"Hey, Alex," said Kita.

"Oh, hi."

"How'd it go out there?"

"It felt like punching sand. No matter how hard we hit them, it didn't seem to matter."

There was dejection in her voice. Kita was sure it had been a tough, unfulfilling battle.

"You and the other pilots did superbly," said Kita in a reassuring tone. *"You held off the enemy and gave us time to get Neptune's guns online. Why don't you meet us in the wardroom?"*

"As soon as I finish checking over my drones."

"No problem. I understand you're only as good as your equipment."

Sheppard dismissed her officers and joined the Angels.

"You have a couple of minutes, Rene?" said Kita. "You look like you need a break."

Sheppard sighed. "Yeah. Anderson, you have the bridge."

"Ok, girls, to the wardroom," Kita ordered.

∿

THE ANGELS FILED INTO THE WARDROOM, MOST HAD SMILES ON THEIR FACES. Sheppard sat down hard in a chair and put her head down on a table. Kita, Babydoll, and Defiance knelt next to her.

Kita patted Sheppard's arm. "Hey, are you ok?"

Sheppard lifted her head. Big tears filled her eyes and tumbled down her cheeks. "I'm sorry, Your Highness. I failed you."

Defiance gasped. "You didn't fail. We destroyed their fleet."

"But I lost more than half our fleet. Nothing I tried worked. The biggest battle of my life and I failed." She put her head back down on the desk.

Hesitantly, Babydoll put her arms around Sheppard and guided her head onto her shoulder. The sounds of Sheppard crying drew the attention of the other Angels.

"What's wrong?" said Cinnamon.

"Fatigue," said Kita. "For the Shadow Fleet, this has been a crushing moral defeat."

"It is not," said Defiance. "We beat a superior enemy. We'll pick through their wreckage and rebuild our fleet even stronger."

The door opened and Jammer entered, still in her flight suit and carrying her helmet. Her face was gaunt and drawn. She went to a couch without a word, sat, placed her helmet on the floor between her feet, and stared at it.

"Can you handle Rene?" Kita said to Babydoll.

"Sure." Sheppard was already wiping at her tears.

"Come on." Kita waved at Defiance to follow her. They sat on either side of Jammer.

"How you doing?" Kita asked Jammer.

Jammer didn't look up. "The flight board is so empty. How did we lose so many? My friends are gone. I thought we were better than this."

"You're the best anywhere," said Defiance.

"Then why did Command waste us?" Jammer said in disbelief.

"Command didn't waste you—"

"They had to see we weren't doing anything against those ships. Why didn't they pull us back?"

"To protect the carrier," said Sheppard as she knelt in front of Jammer. "Without you and the other fighters, Enterprise would have never made it. The cost was high—higher than I ever imagined, but we won. We lost more than fighters today—we lost half the fleet. They gave their lives to protect the Empire.

"We know the risk is coming home in a flag-draped coffin. It's what we signed up to do. Remember your comrades—honor their sacrifice by carrying out your duty. Tomorrow it might be our turn to lay our lives on the altar of war."

"I don't think I can do it."

Sheppard put her hand on Jammer's shoulder. "You're a warrior. Doubt is part of being a warrior, but you can't let it consume you. Look around you. Every girl in this room is a warrior, some have died before, but you are not alone. We're here to help you. You can do this. We stand with you and won't let you fail. We carry each other. Today was not an easy day for anyone, even me. The other girls have helped me. I needed to be told what we did was right and have it explained that what we did was for the good of the Empire. It hurts to lose so many, but they did not die in vain. The Empire still stands."

"I know it's hard to lose friends and comrades. I've lost a lot through the years," said Kita, "but you dishonor their sacrifice by giving up."

Jammer looked up at Kita. "Who are you? You give orders to everyone, including the Admiral and Emperor, like you're above everyone."

"I'm just an Angel, like you. Rene, Casey, and all the Angels are my friends, and I help them as much as I can. I hold no power over them."

"You address the emperor like she is your equal."

Kita nodded at Defiance. "She is my girlfriend. I hope she sees me as an equal."

"Kita is being coy," said Anthrax. "We're loyal to her and we look up to her as our leader. Whatever Kita envisions, we help make happen. In return, she gives us whatever our heart desires. She has a helluva toy box."

Several of the other Angels laughed.

"Kita's words and deeds are unmatched," said Blitz. "She is a great leader and friend."

"I bet she is," said Jammer with a sigh. "I'm not ungrateful for everything you've done for me, but my loyalty is to the emperor."

Kita shrugged. "That's fine. I don't require anyone to do anything. What I give, I give freely with no strings attached. It's yours to do what you want. Every girl knows that. They're free to come and go as they please. If tomorrow everyone wanted to leave and go their separate ways I would have no hard feelings."

"She'd just go find more friends," said Anthrax.

"You can't replace me, big sister," said Tina.

"Yes, where would I be without my *little* guardian angel?" Kita teased.

"A bloody mess in front of a bakery in Leedings."

Kita laughed. *Going far back in history.*

"What's to stop you from taking the throne?" said Jammer pointing at Kita.

Kita grinned. "I've ruled my empire. Ask some of the others. I had no desire to do it the first time, and I have no desire now. I'm willing to help Casey with hers in whatever capacity she wants and she's willing to help me with my goals."

"What is your goal?"

"Death to Galina—the mastermind behind the coup that took Casey's throne."

"And you think I can help you?" said Jammer.

"Yes, I do."

"My proficiency with a pistol is ok at best."

"I have another gift for you," said Kita.

Jammer cocked her head. "What?"

Kita snapped her fingers, and four pocket-sized drones appeared in her hands. A belt was at her feet. "These are like your big ones. You connect with the computer in your head, and you can fly them around. The belt is like the carrier. It can repair and reload them."

The four drones powered on and lifted off Kita's hand.

"Amazing," said Jammer.

The drones darted around the room. Jammer picked up the belt and strapped it on. The drones came in and attaching to the belt.

"We needed the bigger ones first. These have sat around for a couple of days," said Kita.

The communications panel chimed. Stormy answered it. "Yes?"

"This is Captain Anderson. I have an urgent message for the emperor and Admiral Sheppard."

Defiance and Sheppard walked over as Stormy stood aside.

"Yes, Captain?" said Sheppard.

"We received an SOS from the Earth Transfer Station. It's under attack from the surface."

"That didn't take Galina long," muttered Sheppard.

"The Angels will take care of it," said Kita.

"Get Emperor's Might underway and a selection of ships to reestablish security around the planets," said Defiance.

"Yes, Your Highness," said Anderson.

Defiance closed the screen, and then looked at Kita. "And how are we getting there?"

Kita looked at Sarin and fluttered her eyes. "I figured someone could snap her fingers."

"I can't transport all of us," said Sarin.

"We have other gods," said Kita.

"That goes against the agreement with Y'grene," said Aspen.

"But if each of you moves a few of us they'll never notice."

"We should take Alex's big drones and fighter," said Sheppard. "We'll need to keep Galina's forces from docking reinforcements while we're clearing the station. The station has three major concourses. I suggest we divide into three groups so they can't flank us."

"Is it wise to divide our forces?" sand Blitz.

"The concourses aren't wide enough for all of us. This way we can maximize our firepower."

"What can we expect?" said Ryder. "More Mexorks?"

"Mexorks?" Sheppard looked at Kita.

"We ran into the newest versions Galina is making. They have crystal armor, but the braincase is in the pelvis. I can't imagine she has many of them."

"I would expect augmented humans," said Sarin. "We've run into some that have limbs replaced."

"Don't forget Machines," said Ryder.

"Galina's bringing back all the heavy hitters," chuckled Babydoll.

"All we need is the Red Legion and ravagers." Kita sighed. "Scarlett, you'll lead one group and Kerri will lead the other. Your groups will move around the perimeter, my group will move through the center." A map of the Earth Transfer Station appeared on the communication's terminal. "Thanks, Athena. We'll insert here." Kita pointed to a junction of the three concourses. "We'll roll them up. If any group hits something they can't punch through, fall back and call for my group. Any questions?"

"Are we bringing the emperor?" said Sheppard.

"I am not going to be kept locked up while the rest of you face danger," snarled Defiance.

"She'll be with you, me, and Jane. I can't think of a better group of bodyguards," said Kita.

"Can we come?" said Snowy.

Kita raised an eyebrow. She'd let Snowy and Sahara tag along as a way to keep an eye on them. She wasn't sure how she felt letting them fight. *Snowy can hold her own, but Sahara?*

"You stay with my group, and I don't want to hear a peep out of either of you."

Snowy nodded.

"Ok, everyone grab your gear, and we'll go."

KITA AND THE ANGELS APPEARED OUTSIDE THE EARTH TRANSFER STATION. Jammer was in her fighter with her drones. Around the circular transfer station, dozens of shuttles waited to dock. Already docked around the transfer station were several large intersystem cargo and passenger ships.

"She has a sizable force up here," said Ryder.

"Yes, but it looks like most of it is still waiting to dock. Alex, get rid of their reinforcements," ordered Kita.

"You got it."

The fighter and the drones' engines burned brighter as they attacked the gathered shuttles.

Kita turned invisible and drifted down to look into the window of the transfer station. A battle raged. Attackers pushed in on the defenders from three sides. Kita drifted back to the others.

"It looks like we have Marines that need help. The enemy is attacking from three sides. Snowy and I will phase everyone inside, then we break up into teams and push the enemy back."

Everyone readied their weapons and put a hand on either Kita or Snowy. Kita nodded to Snowy that she was ready. Together they phased inside the transfer station.

Inside was an open space lined with shops, seating, and planters. The Marines made use of the cover as they fired on the attackers. Kita didn't bother with the Marines. She burst into flame and took off after the enemy.

In the darkened space, Kita's bright flame attracted attention. Gunfire from the ground flew around her. Kita dropped to the floor in front of a group of Political Bureau soldiers in black uniforms. They were humans armed with rifles, wearing armor and military kit.

Kita brought Dead down on a soldier in front of her, slicing through him. He was more than blood and bone. He was upgraded. Kita spun and sliced into another soldier, before using a flaming lance to burn through two more.

The winds of a storm picked up as clouds built near the ceiling. Rain lashed everything and lightning struck. To add to the din of the storm was the wail of Pestilence. The banshee rained down fire and brimstone and attacked with biting insects.

Rain steamed off The Rider as she walked among the seats firing her revolvers. Defiance, with Sheppard glued to her hip, froze the rain and turned the ice chunks into deadly missiles.

In the flash of lightning, the assassins were visible slicing their way through the enemy. Babydoll bounced between a dozen enemy soldiers, sending their broken bodies flying.

Kita slammed Dead and Buried into a soldier. Flinging the body at two of his comrades, she leaped over them, spun, and removed their heads. A bullet struck her in the shoulder. She grumbled as she found the shooter and cut his augmented arms off.

"Tina!" said Kita.

"Yeah?"

"I've been hit in the shoulder. Can you pull it out of me?"

"Meet me by the coffee cart."

Kita spotted the cart and darted to it.

"Let's have a look," said Tina as she flittered up to Kita.

Kita bared her shoulder to her sister.

"It barely got you," Tina said with a teasing smile.

"It doesn't feel like it."

"And since when does a bullet stop you?"

"If this was serious it wouldn't but better to be prepared and all that."

Tina smirked. "You? Thinking ahead? Who would have thought?"

"Shut up and close the stupid hole," Kita grumbled playfully.

"Here you go." Tina dropped the bullet into Kita's hand.

"Goodie, just what I wanted."

"I thought you could add it to your collection."

"Are you done?"

"All healed up and ready to go," said Tina.

The battle was winding down. The wind and wailing died away, and the rain stopped.

"Kita!" called Sheppard.

"Yeah?"

"Where are you?"

"Getting coffee."

Sheppard glided over with Defiance and a Marine. "This is Captain Kim. He's in charge of the garrison here."

"Getting more than you bargained for, Captain?" chided Kita.

"Yes, Child of the emperor. They attacked in force. I've lost half the garrison trying to repel them."

Kita nodded. "My people are here to clear the station, so you can regroup and tend to your wounded."

"Thank you, Imperial Angel."

Kita waved him away. *Time to go on the offensive.* "Nell, Ryder, Amanda, Kara, and Tina go with Kerri up concourse A. Hali, Zen, Talli, Kristi, Leaf, and Jess go with Scarlett up concourse C. Everyone else with me, and we'll assault the middle."

KITA BROUGHT DEAD DOWN ON A POLITICAL BUREAU SOLDIER. HE RAISED HIS augmented arm and blocked while punching at her with his other arm. Kita blocked with her knee and kicked his arm aside. She chopped down with Buried on his arm, but the sword stuck. Growling in annoyance, Kita backflipped, kicking the soldier under the chin to send him sprawling. She bounced off the floor, somersaulted, and landed on the soldier's stomach, driving her swords into his chest.

Kita raised her head and hand, stopping a hail of bullets coming at her. Sarin fired three times, killing the shooter. Defiance and Sheppard approached the pair.

"That's the last of this group," said Sheppard.

Snowy and Sahara arrived from watching the rear.

Sarin smiled. "I haven't had this much fun in...well, I've had a lot of fun lately."

"I wouldn't count the last couple days as fun," said Sheppard.

"I got to kill lots and have sex with Kita. What more could a girl want?"

"I think I'm due a turn when this is over," said Defiance dryly.

"You're going to be so busy ruling the Empire," said Sarin.

"I'll make time."

Sarin grinned. "You have to get her away from me."

"I'll tell the guards you're not allowed in."

"Kita won't stay cooped up for five minutes," scoffed Sarin.

"She's free to leave. I'll just make it so she won't want to."

"I feel like a puppy you two are fighting over," said Kita.

"Of course not, babe," said Sarin. "A puppy would be easier to housetrain."

Sarin grinned as Kita's face puckered. "Love you," she said with a playful wave of her fingers.

Kita rolled her eyes.

"*Ki—*"

"Scarlett? What's wrong? Scarlett? Leaf? Jess? Anybody? Has anyone heard from Scarlett's group?"

Kita received a round of negative responses. "I'm going to check on them."

"I'll go with you, babe," said Sarin.

"Ok. The rest of you hold here until we get back."

Sarin wiggled her nose, and they appeared in concourse C.

"They've been here," said Sarin. She pointed to a pair of bodies.

"Yeah, but it's quiet," said Kita.

"It always gets quiet when the top predator is in the area."

As Kita walked among the corpses, the injuries changed. They no longer had bullet or slash marks. They looked untouched. Kita knelt next to a corpse and took his helmet off. She found a burn mark on his temple. Inspecting his gloves and boots, she found burn marks.

"Everyone be on your guard," said Kita. "There's someone around who can wield lightning."

Kita moved deeper into the affected area. The damage to the bodies increased. Some were chard corpses, others were wet.

"By the Crushing Depths," Kita gasped. On the ground was a skeleton with burnt black clothing and seafoam feathers. She fell to her knees beside it. "Talli?" Kita whispered. "Jane," Kita called unable to keep the sorrow from her voice.

"Babe?" Sarin called as she rushed over to Kita. "Neptune's rings," she whispered. "What...what happened?"

"I don't know," said Kita as she wiped a tear from her eye. "We have to find the others."

Kita and Sarin helped each other to their feet. They walked around a planter. A lump swelled in Kita's throat. Two more skeletons were on the floor. One was a Diamock, the other was human with cinnamon colored feathers.

"Kristi," cried Sarin.

Kita grabbed Sarin and hugged her as she burst into tears. Kita gulped hard, imagining what else they were going to find. Sarin lifted her head.

"Whatever did this is so dead," she growled as she wiped her eyes.

They continued to search hand in hand and found Valor and Starlight's skeletons huddled together.

"Jess, Hali..." Kita wiped at the tears overflowing her eyes. Her heart hurt, and her knees felt shaky. She clutched Sarin's hand. Numb and cold filled her chest and spread to her limbs. *It's too much. I can't.*

Not far away, they found another skeleton with barn owl feathers.

"Neptune's rings, Scarlett." Sarin choked up as fresh tears streaked her cheeks.

Kita held Sarin. *We haven't found Leaf yet. Maybe she got away.* When Sarin was ready, Kita led her around searching for the last missing Angel.

They found the tiny skeleton in the center of the concourse, Dusk and Dawn still in her grasp.

"But, she was a god," said Sarin. "She should be around."

A pinprick of light floated down from the ceiling. It flew around the room, before entering the ribcage of the dead Angel. The light multiplied, engulfing the skeleton. After a bright flash, the Angel was whole.

Kita and Sarin dropped to their knees next to Aspen. Placing a hand on her shoulder, Kita spoke softly, "Leaf? Are you ok?"

Aspen pushed herself to her knees. *"I'll be fine. I just retreated in case they were trying to catch me."*

Kita gave her a possessive hug. "I'm glad you're alright."

"What of the others?"

Kita looked at the ground and wiped at fresh tears.

"They're gone," said Sarin.

Aspen hung her head. *"He came out of nowhere. I tried to kill him, but the lightning was everywhere. It swirled, and he controlled it—like…like Lina did."*

Kita and Sarin exchanged a look. "There's no way Galina could have broken Lina," said Kita.

Sarin didn't look so sure. "She has Megan working for her. If anyone can do it, Megan can."

"Where did you hear this?" said Kita surprised.

"From Galina. She was bragging after capturing me."

Flames flickered in Kita's eyes. "If she's hurt my baby I will skin her alive."

"First things first," said Sarin. "We need to kill whatever this thing is. I think our best weapon will be Snowy."

"And me," said Kita.

"Isn't lightning one of your weaknesses?"

"Not after my last fight with Snowy I decided I was done playing that game. I'm going to pull this thing apart one chunk at a time."

"You're not the only one," said Sarin as she holstered her pistols and assembled her sniper rifle. "He's not the only one who can reach out and touch someone."

Kita glided over to one of the large windows. She heated her hand and cut out a circle.

"What are you doing?" said Aspen.

"Going to make sure they can't attack our rear," said Kita as she pushed the circle into space.

The rush of decompressing air pulled Kita toward the hole. Other items that weren't attached flew into space. Two loud bangs announced the emergency decompression doors closing.

"That should do it," said Kita. *"Let's get back to the others, and I'll warn Kerri."*

CHAPTER XXVIII

"*D*arlin', what happened?" said Defiance when Kita, Sarin, and Aspen appeared. "Where's everyone else?"

Kita swallowed hard. "They didn't make it."

"What happened?" demanded Sheppard.

"We were attacked by a silver man that wielded lightning like Lina," said Aspen.

"By the emperor," whispered Sheppard. She gave Defiance an apologetic look.

"Do you know something?" said Sarin to Sheppard.

"I knew Galina was working on it, but that's all I knew."

Defiance gave Kita, Sarin, and Aspen a hug. "I'm sorry."

Kita shook her head. "It's not your fault. It's mine. I should have killed Galina a long time ago."

"You couldn't have known this was going to happen," said Defiance.

"Doesn't matter. I went against my better judgment. I knew she was dangerous."

Snowy moved in front of Kita. "I—you're taking this well."

Kita grimaced. "I'm numb—probably in shock. It's been a long time since this many Angels have died."

Snowy hugged Kita. "You're not alone."

Kita nodded. "I know. I'm sure the tears and rage will come later."

"Then I'm putting you back in the forward observation room," said Defiance with a tentative smile.

Kita smiled back, understanding her girlfriend's attempt at humor. "Let's not wait around. I don't want Kerri's group running into that thing. When we do find it, let Snowy and I handle it. Jane and Rene can snipe at range. The rest of you retreat."

"There must be something we can do," said Defiance.

"You won't be able to get close enough to do anything. Stay safe. That goes for you too, Sahara."

Sahara sneered but didn't say anything.

Snowy went to her. "Don't take offense. Kita is not trying to diminish your honor. She's trying to give us the best advantage for victory. There will be plenty of enemies to gain glory."

Kita rolled her eyes. Sahara would throw herself at an enemy she had no hope of defeating because of honor and glory. Two of the dumbest ideas ever forged in the hearts of those who needed to justify losing. Winners didn't need honor or glory, they won. There was no need to justify winning.

Kita waved at the others, and they moved up the shop-lined concourse. From the signs, you could buy anything you wanted to make your journey more comfortable. They passed the bodies of Marines and a few Political Bureau soldiers.

A loud grinding noise came from the shops on their right. The sound of tearing metal preceded a storefront exploding outward.

"Driller!" yelled Sarin. She snapped her rifle up and shot into the center of three giant tentacles twisted together.

The driller shrugged off the shot and charged.

Sheppard fired into the creature's side. "This guy's a little tougher than the old ones," she yelled.

Another driller burst from a neighboring storefront and two more from the opposite side of the concourse. Aspen charged a driller on the far side. A driller opened its tentacles and fired a three-foot beam at Kita. She expanded her heat shield to block. Another driller glided behind Sahara and grabbed her in its hard, bumpy tentacles.

"No!" yelled Snowy. She leaped onto the driller with Sahara and attacked its back with her claws while the driller ground Sahara between its tentacles.

Kita took a star from her thigh pad. The driller that had attacked her opened its tentacles, and Kita threw the star into the center of them. She struck the sensory organ, and the driller collapsed.

She backflipped and landed next to the driller with Sahara. She attacked the tentacles with Dead and Buried. The tentacles were tougher than previous drillers she'd encountered. Changing tactics, she slammed Dead into the creature's eye. The driller spun wildly. Kita heated her sword and pulled down slicing open a large gash. Growing a purplish-black ball, she shoved it into the wound.

"Snowy, look out!" Kita yelled.

Snowy phased off the driller to the ground. Kita snapped her fingers, and the driller exploded, showering the area with pieces of metal and meat.

"Sahara!" Snowy cried desperately. She ran to the driller and pulled at the tentacles.

"Kita, we need some help," yelled Sheppard.

A driller had Defiance trapped between two planters as Sarin and Sheppard fired at it. Deciding Snowy was ok to rescue Sahara and Aspen had the other driller's attention, Kita phased above Defiance. She fired a purplish-black beam into the driller's forehead leaving a long gash. The driller retreated and lunged at Kita, landing on the planters protecting Defiance, crushing them.

Kita fired her beam again, aiming across the top tentacle. She sliced partially through it, making the tentacle limp, but it fell down over the sensory organ. The driller rose rapidly into the air, reaching out for Kita. She dodged left, blasting the driller in the eye. It spun, slamming its tentacles into her. She rolled off the tentacles, trying to regain her balance. The driller rushed forward, with its two good tentacles open. Kita somersaulted over the tentacles, landing on the injured one. She swept her swords back and sliced through the tentacle, cutting along the gash. With her feet, she pushed the tentacle aside and slammed Dead into the sensory organ. The driller crashed to the ground, sending Kita tumbling forward into a group of tables set out for a coffee shop.

Kita shook her head trying to reorient herself. She was dizzy from the strike by the driller's tentacles.

"Kita! Snowy!" cried Aspen.

All Kita could see was the dead driller. She floated over the creature to see. On the far side of the concourse, Aspen was attacking the last driller. Its tentacles were open, ready to fire its beam. Snowy stood facing the driller holding Sahara's broken and bloody body. There was no expression on Snowy's face, just wet lines in the fur on her cheeks. "No! Sno—"

The driller fired and the beam engulfed Snowy.

Kita's vision turned red. She streaked toward the driller, slamming into a tentacle pushing it into the beam. Kita's heat shield expanded as she plunged into the beam. She thrust Buried into the sensory organ. The driller collapsed as Kita raced to Snowy arriving in time to catch her skull. Time caught up as Kita collapsed to her knees, clutching the skull. It still had patches of fur attached on the back.

Tears filled Kita's eyes. Her heart collapsed as the air escaped her lungs. Kita didn't know what to do. Her head spun. The others knelt around her, but she couldn't understand them. They sounded a thousand miles away. She looked into the hollow eyes of the skull. *I'll never see those eyes again. Why? What happened? Why would she?*

A violent shaking of her shoulder caused her to look up. Sarin was talking to her. Kita strained to hear. Sarin's perfect lips moved, but she couldn't understand. An orgasmic feeling washed over her. It seemed the wrong sensation for the moment.

"Worried. Babe?" said Sarin in a monotone voice.

A part of Kita's brain remembered what was happening and reacted. It was a cloud connection. She opened her emotions and let out her pain, sorrow, and confusion. When it was over, she felt better. Kita received Sarin's own pain and grief along with love and happiness.

"Sorrow and confused. Why? Why did she do it?" said Kita.

"Unsure. I don't know. I don't know what happened to Sahara," said Sarin.

"I left Snowy to help you after I killed the driller. Sahara looked dead."

"Curious. How close were they?" said Sarin.

"I know Snowy loved her, but I don't know what she meant to Sahara. You don't suppose she killed herself because Sahara died?"

"Unsettled. Maybe," said Sarin. "It wouldn't be the first time Snowy has tried to kill herself over losing someone she loved."

Kita released an uncontrolled emotional outburst of pain and rage. "Shocked. Are you saying this is my fault?"

"Appalled. Of course not. I'm saying Snowy has a history of jumping to dramatic displays when she gets upset. We just couldn't stop her this time."

"Disdain. If only I'd been faster or seen her sooner. I could have saved her," said Kita.

"Unhappy. Don't you dare start that game. It leads nowhere good. You were saving Casey."

"But, I should—"

"You know your limitations," said Sarin. "You're fast, but no one, not even the gods, is that fast. None of us could have predicted this. It wasn't premeditated."

"What are we going to do?"

"Confident. We're going to go find this silver man and kick his ass. Then we're going home. We can bury Snowy, Scarlett, and the others among the stars."

"Depressed. This is my fault," said Kita.

"Concerned. No, it's not. We made a mistake and came in overconfident, and we underestimated our opponent. We won't make that mistake again. Galina is going to pay for this. I hope you don't kill her quickly. I want her to suffer. I'll have Daddy build you a new Advanced Research Wing if I have to."

"Laughter. That opens a whole new realm of possibilities," said Kita.

"Affectionate. She can't beat us, only we can beat ourselves."

"Understanding. I know—but Snowy."

"Consoling. Snowy chose her time to go. She wanted to be with Sahara," said Sarin.

"I wish I knew if she was going to be happy."

"She thought she would be happy. That's all that matters."

"What am I going to do without her?" said Kita.

"Upset. You'll always have me."

"Loving. I know. You're better anyway. Dismay. I've got to tell Kami," said Kita.

"Supportive. I'll be there for you."

"Thanks."

Sarin closed the connection, and Kita opened her eyes. She looked at the skull she held and sighed. "Goodbye, old friend. I hope the next life is kinder to you than this one was." She kissed the skull and set it down with the other bones.

"Darlin', you ok?" asked Defiance.

Kita shook her head. "I don't know if I'll ever be ok. Snowy's been with me since nearly the beginning. She was a good friend, but I feel like I've lost a parent."

Defiance gave Kita a hug and kiss.

"She was a hard, crusty girl. I'm going to miss her," said Sheppard.

"Same could be said of you," said Kita. "Casey, when it's time, Snowy gets full Legion honors, and whatever a scholar gets. She's made a number of scientific breakthroughs in her career."

"Of course. She'll get more than that. All the Angels will have state funerals."

Kita wiped a tear away. She wasn't feeling numb anymore. "Come on. We should try and catch this lightning man."

~

"Darling Jane, Kita," called The Rider.

"Yeah?" said Kita as she tried to keep the pain from her voice.

"We got hit with some of that anti-Angel gas they used on us a while back."

"Did they get everyone? How are you not affected?" said Sarin.

"I think it's the flame, but if you could spare a second it's getting hot over here…and I don't mean me."

"I'm coming," said Kita.

"Not without me you're not," said Sarin. "They've hit us with this crap before. I know how to clean it out."

Kita nodded. "The rest of you hunker down here. If the lightning man comes, Leaf, get them out of here."

"No problem."

"Are you sure you're not going to need our help?" said Defiance.

"I want to limit exposure as much as possible. It does us no good if we go and you join the others."

"What happens if you succumb?" said Sheppard.

"Then you get to play the hero," Kita said with a twisted grin.

"I always have to watch your ass."

"At least it's a nice ass," said Defiance. "It could be a lot worse, Rene."

"That ass belongs to me," said Sarin as she put her hand on Kita's shoulder. The world went dark, when it reappeared, Kita and Sarin were on concourse A. Ahead of them was a billowing green cloud. Flashes of gunfire came from inside the cloud.

"Looks like Ryder's still at it," said Sarin.

"We need to clear the air," said Kita. She burst into flame. "I'll open a window. You cover Ryder."

Sarin unslung her sniper rifle, put it together, shouldered it, and scanned the gas for targets.

Kita flew to a series of windows in a seating area. She put her hand on the window, melted through, and cut out a hole. The rush of air tried to suck Kita out. Rolling to one side, Kita watched the emergency decompression door close behind Sarin. The vacuum pulled the gas from the concourse and vented it into space.

"Ryder, how you doing?" called Kita.

"Don't that beat all. I burn even in a vacuum."

Kita chuckled. She still burned, too. She doused her flames and met Sarin on her way to The Rider as she changed into Ryder.

"We need to detox the girls of that stuff," said Sarin. "The gas contains a nanite that can cause pain and death if they activate it."

"If you can detox them, we'll find them," said Ryder. "The legionnaire and toothy were over by the coffee stand. The rest were over by the shops."

"I'll grab Kerri and Nell," said Kita.

"I'll go with Ryder to the others," said Sarin.

Kita glided to the overturned coffee cart. Babydoll was lying unconscious next to it. Kita picked her up and slung her friend over her shoulder. Anthrax lay in a seating area. Kita threaded through the seats to her friend. *How did this happen? How did I underestimate Galina's ability? She couldn't have cracked Lina this fast or Angel physiology to make a gas that affects just us. I can't believe Megan is helping her.*

"Did you find them?" Sarin asked Kita.

"Yeah, I have them. You said they've used this gas before?"

"Yes, when we were trying to take back the fleet. They gassed us. Galina killed me using it."

"Any idea where it came from?" said Kita.

"Galina said it came from Megan."

"Megan? But why?"

"Galina said Megan harbored deep animosity over what happened with the Arconians."

Kita landed next to Sarin and put Babydoll and Anthrax down.

"Would she hate me enough to turn on me?" said Kita.

Sarin shrugged. "I don't know. You didn't leave on good terms with her."

"But enough hate to develop weapons specifically for us and rip Lina's secrets from her? If she has a problem, it should be with me, not with the rest of you."

"I don't know, babe. All I know is what's in front of me and what I've been told." Sarin tapped Anthrax. The Angel turned to her god form and stood up.

"Jane, what happened?" said Anthrax.

"Just some nasty gas. You'll need to scrub it from your system before you turn back."

"Ok."

Sarin touched Babydoll, and the Angel turned to her god form.

"Ugh, what happened?" groaned Babydoll.

"Anti-Angel gas," said Kita. "You're going to need to detox yourself before you turn back."

"I knew this was going too well."

Kita sighed. "Yeah. Can the rest of you come here?"

The Angels gathered around Kita.

"You weren't the only ones hit. The other group ran into a man with abilities like Lina and killed them. Only Leaf survived."

"Neptune's rings," exclaimed Anthrax.

"I'm sorry, big sister." Tina flittered over and gave Kita a hug.

"There's more," whispered Kita. "Snowy's gone, too."

"What?" cried Tina.

Tears welled up in Kita's eyes. "A driller killed Sahara. Snowy picked her up and…and just stood there. It was over before I could get to her. All I see is Snowy standing there and the blast incinerating her. Why would she do that?"

Tina hugged Kita with her own tears in her eyes. "I don't know. She and Sahara have been inseparable since I got here."

Sarin put her arms around both Angels.

"Maybe Snowy felt she loved Sahara so much that living without her was unbearable," whispered Tina.

Kita rested her cheek on Tina's shoulder, feeling the tears run down her face.

"Now come on, all y'all," said Ryder. "We're not out to pasture yet. We still have a station to clear. We can mourn the dead later."

Kita sighed and wiped her eyes. Ryder was right. They still had a mission, and her friends were in danger. She needed to pull herself together. Kita balled up her pain and rage and stuck it with the rest she harbored. She would unleash it when the time was right.

"How's everyone feeling?" said Kita. "Physically, I mean. Can everyone fight?"

"I want to fight more than ever," said Anthrax.

The other Angels nodded in agreement.

"Good," said Kita. "But when we do find this lightning man, he's mine."

~

KITA AND THE OTHER ANGELS APPEARED IN THE MIDDLE OF A LARGE GROUP OF Mexorks. Their appearance confused the Mexorks, and the Angels fell on them without any instruction.

I hope they don't get carried away.

Kita dodged the blasts of a pair of Mexorks. She flung herself forward, skidding on her knees between the pair, slashing through their legs. As the pair toppled, Kita sprang to her feet and stabbed her swords into the pair's brain cases.

From the flank, Defiance and Sheppard appeared. On the other flank, Aspen was briefly visible as she made a silent kill. The rest of the Angels were putting the Mexorks down with ruthless efficiency. *If we can't cry, we'll make the enemy.*

Kita gathered the Angels around her when it was over.

"Good job everyone, but let's not let our emotions run wild. We need to remain disciplined and focused. We'll all get time to cry."

She received quiet resolve from the rest, but she felt their emotions shift as the other Angels refocused themselves.

Kita led the others through the concourse to the intersection. A group of

Marines made a stand here. Their bodies lay strewn about. Some had bullet holes, while others burn marks. None had the signature of lightning.

"How did Galina know we would be here?" said Babydoll.

"Even in the middle of a war, this place makes money," said Sarin. "It helps finance our operations. Galina knows we have to defend it."

"It looks like she's throwing everything at this place to get it," said Ryder. "I don't think she planned on the whole flock being here, just those of us in the Sol system."

"Lot of good having so many of us here did," said Toxic.

Stormy gave her a hug. "Don't worry. Nothing will happen to the rest of us."

Kita's eyebrow ticked up slightly, but she didn't say anything. The others needed to stay confident.

The sound of electricity crackling drew everyone's attention to concourse A. Through the portal came the silver man, a man burning like a pyre, and a man made of water.

Kita sighed. "Great."

Sarin raised her rifle and fired, putting a bullet through the head of the water man. It exploded, and reformed.

"I've got him," said Defiance.

"No one goes near them until I deal with the silver man," said Kita.

"You're going to need help."

"Water and fire are my specialties. I bet they think they have me with the electricity. It's time to show them how wrong they are. Shooters, snipe and keep them off balance. Everyone else, if you're not a god, stay close to one so you can teleport if you have too."

"Don't fool around with them," ordered Sarin. "Put them down as fast as possible."

"As you wish."

Sarin wrinkled her nose. "That is not a romantic movie. Now is not the time for that crap. We've got dead to attend to."

Kita nodded and phased in front of the silver man. "Hello, looking for me?"

An electrical storm erupted. Bolts of lightning struck around the room. Several struck Kita and passed through her.

"Oh, that tickles."

The fire man and water man blasted her with their elements.

Kita stuck out her hands at each. "My turn." She gathered their attacks into balls and pulled the rest of the fire and water from the men. Bullets struck the pair, and they collapsed.

Kita pushed the fire and water balls together, causing the water to boil.

"Here, catch." Kita tossed the boiling water toward the silver man.

The ball splashed off his chest as he flailed his arms. When the water made contact with the floor, there was a giant flash. The electrical storm died. Kita lunged forward and grabbed the silver man by the throat.

"Water and electricity don't mix. Let's see how much of you is mine."

Silver beads of sweat gathered on the man's skin and ran to Kita's hand. When it was over, he was naked.

"Megan's not as good as I thought," said Kita with a vicious grin. "Now, my fine sir, you have some punishment coming."

Kita turned the man's head in her hand. She lunged forward, bit off his ear, and spit it out. She licked the blood dribbling down the side of his face.

"Hey, leave some of that for me," said Babydoll as she led the others to Kita.

Kita held the man out as Babydoll ran a finger through his blood.

"Hmmm, yummy," said Babydoll as she licked her finger clean.

"That's enough," said Sheppard as she took control of the man from Kita. "Tina, can you help?"

"I'm not sure I want to."

"*I will,*" said Aspen. She put her hand over the wound and closed it.

"What are you going to do with him?" said Babydoll.

"He's a prisoner. He might have the information we need." Sheppard looked at the man. "Are you going to talk or do I turn you back over to my girlfriend?"

"Girlfriend?" exclaimed Babydoll. "Are—are you for real?"

Sheppard chuckled. "Yes, even after displays like that."

"Yeah!" Babydoll gave Sheppard an awkward hug around the man.

"Where's Megan's lab?" said Kita to the man.

"I don't know any Megan," he replied visibly shaken.

"She gave you your nanites. Megan looks like me, except brown hair and red wings."

"You do look like her. She gave us injections in Rio and Rome."

Kita tapped her nail against her teeth. "Lina could be in either of those two places."

"We can't go there," said Ryder. "It'll be crawling with Political Bureau thugs."

"Just more to kill," said Sarin.

"What if we hit one and it's the wrong one?" said Stormy. "They'll fortify the other place or move her—or worse."

"Then we hit all three together," said Kita.

"Three?"

"Galina's headquarters. If we hit her headquarters, she'll be too busy being worried about it to worry about the labs."

"And you get to take down Galina," said Ryder.

"If she's got the guts to face me," said Kita. "I'll do more than savage her face this time."

"We could end up chasing her all over the world," said Defiance.

"If we break her hold on power, we can put you back on the throne. The most important thing is to get Lina back." Kita took Athena's ball from her belt and tossed into the air. "Hey, Athena. Can you tap into the station's network and bring us up all the information you have on labs in Rio, Rome, and Political Bureau Headquarters in Moscow?"

"Of course, Mom. Give me a moment."

Kita looked at the man. "I think he's outlived his usefulness."

"I think you're right. Here." Sheppard handed the man to Babydoll. "Just make sure you are clean when you come back."

Babydoll's eyes lit with delight.

"Go," said Sheppard to Kita, "before I change my mind."

"Are you sure you don't need us to help plan?"

"This is my way of getting revenge."

CHAPTER XXIX

The shuttle shuddered and shook. Kita looked up from staring at the floor. Outside the window, a storm raged.

"What's the matter, babe?" asked Sarin.

"I'm trying to reach Kami, but I'm not getting any response."

"Where is she?"

"I don't know. She didn't tell me where they were going. She's never ignored me before. I'm worried she's mad at me."

"Why would she be mad at you?" said Sarin.

"I don't know. Maybe the others convinced her I was wrong."

Sarin took Kita's hand. "She wouldn't turn against you. She's faithful to her partner, but that doesn't mean she'll stop being loyal to you."

"I just worry something is wrong."

"There's nothing out there that can harm them."

Kita didn't feel so sure. *Maybe I'm just being a mom, seeing boogiemen in every corner. I'm sure she's fine. I hope she's out doing something fun and she's with Tenshi, Valentine, and Panther. I trained them, and they've been gods longer than anyone. Kami's safe.*

"Snow in Moscow, what a surprise," said Sheppard from the shuttle's cockpit.

"Does that happen often?" said Kita.

"It was snowing the last time I was here. Russia's known for its long, harsh winters. Even in the summertime, the people are frosty."

"They aren't like the Chinese or Indians, who took their defeat with grace," said Defiance. "They still hold a grudge, no matter what the Imperium does."

"And you let them serve in your military and Political Bureau?" said Kita.

"Most of them aren't dangerous. They just don't like outsiders, especially those of American descent. We get some terrorist cells, but nothing serious. We find out before they do anything."

"I know what that's like." Kita sighed. "You can't make everyone happy—no matter how hard you try."

"They scream for independence. I don't think they have a plan if it was granted. They just like the idea."

Kita nodded. "People will cling to ideas no matter how unrealistic if only to preserve their pride."

"Coming in now," said Sheppard.

Kita glanced out the window. Ghostly lights were visible through the giant snowflakes. She scratched Sarge's ears. He meowed happily, then rolled over and offered his underside. Kita chuckled and rubbed his chest and stomach. Next to him, Jupiter looked hopeful. Sarin obliged.

"Sorry about Norway," said Kita.

Sarin shook her head. "I don't know what happened to him, other than Galina's thugs took him. I hope he didn't suffer."

"Jupiter needs a new mistress," said Kita as tears fell down her cheeks. Valor's skeleton flashed before her eyes.

Sarin scratched Jupiter's chin. "How about it, boy? Do you feel like you can keep up with me?"

Jupiter responded by licking Sarin's fingers, then jumping into her lap and licking her face.

"Ok, ok, ok," said Sarin playfully. "You're going to take my makeup off." She pushed the cat down and scratched his ears.

"They want to know under whose authority I have to land?" said Sheppard.

"Send them my code," said Defiance. She was dressed in her full parade uniform with an added pistol on her belt. "We'll let them know I'm here."

"They may not like that idea," said Kita.

"That's why I have you here."

"We'll get you back on the throne. Don't worry," said Kita.

"I'm not. You just better live up to your reputation," said Defiance with a smile.

"I'll kill everyone in the building if I have to."

"Good. I doubt with Galina's death the rest of the Political Bureau will stand down. I hope I don't have to drop a bomb on every Bureau headquarters on the planet."

"We could clean them out," said Sarin.

"I bet that would strike fear in their hearts," said Babydoll from the copilot's seat.

"We'll set up a live feed of you doing it," said Defiance.

"They say you don't have authority to land," announced Sheppard. "And now they're defense systems have lit us up."

"Time to go," said Kita as she stood up, tucking Sarge under her arm.

Defiance opened the shuttle door. Snow and icy wind blew in.

"Just like the mountains, hey, boy?" Kita cooed to Sarge.

Sarge returned a dubious look and kicked his feet.

"I'll set you down when we're on the ground." Kita jumped out the door into the storm. She opened her wings and fought the air currents to gain lift. *"Be careful coming out the door. The air is rough."* Below her, the landing lights of the shuttlepad on top of the Political Bureau Headquarters building were visible through the snow. Switching her eyes to the electromagnetic lens, the three defense turrets lit like bright lights. *"I'm taking the furthest turret. Jane, take the one on the edge of the pad. Casey, you get the one on the corner."*

Kita flew toward her turret and dropped Sarge. The turret came alive. The twin Gatling guns spun as Kita landed in front of it. She brought Dead and Buried down on the arms of the turret, separating the guns from the frame.

A bright light flashed—the storm dampened the sound of an explosion. It was to Kita's right, so it must have been Sarin. *"Are you ok, Jane?"*

Sarin laughed. *"I found the magazine."*

"Casey?"

"It's frozen solid."

"Rene, it's clear to land."

Kita glided over the six inches of snow toward the landing area. Behind her, Sarge playfully ran, rolled, and dove through the fresh powder. The landing lights of the shuttle appeared above them. It lowered out of the sky, blowing and melting snow as it settled in to land. Out of the storm, Sarin and Defiance appeared. Jupiter tiptoed through the snow. He didn't seem to share the love of it that Sarge did.

Babydoll and Sheppard appeared in the shuttle's door. Sheppard had her assault rifle ready.

"How do we get in?" said Babydoll.

Kita motioned to the large bunker-style door to the group's right. "We just have to get it open."

The door opened.

"That's convenient," quipped Babydoll.

"Those aren't," said Sheppard as six Mexorks with missile pods on their shoulders stepped out into the snow and fired a salvo.

Kita and the other Angels leaped in different directions. Sarge and Jupiter transformed as they ran. Jupiter released a ball of lightning from his mouth. Sarge jumped through a Mexork, freezing him solid. The ball of lightning struck three of the Mexorks and exploded. Sarin fired her pistols into the abdomens of two more Mexorks. Sheppard dropped to a knee and fired two three-round bursts into a Mexork's pelvis area. Babydoll cut a Mexork in half lengthwise with a purplish-black beam as Defiance encased the last Mexork in ice. A strong wind pushed it over the edge of the building.

"So much for the welcoming committee," said Babydoll.

Kita jumped between the doors as they closed, holding them open. The other Angels dove around Kita as the cats went between her legs. Sarin turned, grabbed Kita by her belt, and yanked her inside. The doors closed with a bang.

Kita kissed Sarin. "Thanks, love."

"I'm always saving your cute butt."

Kita wiggled her butt at Sarin. She slapped it in response.

"If you two are done," said Defiance from the elevator controls on the opposite side of the room. "We have to find Galina."

Kita and Sarin looked at each other. "That's easy," Sarin said with a giggle. "She's below us."

"I'd hope so," Defiance growled.

"We can feel her cloud," said Kita. "Take the elevator down. Eventually, we'll find her."

"Ok, but we need to unlock it."

Kita pulled the control pane cover off and traced the wires and circuits. She placed her finger on a circuit and used a simple brute force hack to open the door.

The Angels and cats entered the elevator. Kita hit the button for the ground floor. The elevator dinged each time they passed a floor.

"I thought she'd be in the upper part of the building," said Babydoll.

"This place has a vast underground complex," said Defiance. "Galina must think we can't get to her there, but there are plenty of ways in. Some more heavily guarded than others."

"And what are the elevators?"

"Medium. You have to go through the lobby of the building to get to the underground elevators. There are guards and turrets, but it's not as bad as the other entrances that are trapped with everything from seismic to acoustic sensors—or if the air moves too much."

The elevator dinged marking the tenth floor.

"Is she still below us?" asked Defiance.

"Yes," said Kita, Sarin, and Babydoll in unison.

"You have a cloud?" Sheppard asked Babydoll.

"Yeah. I'm a child of Kita's."

"How come I didn't know this?"

Babydoll shrugged. "I don't use it much. Why? Problem?"

"It's black?"

"Yeah."

Sheppard let out a sigh of relief. "I can live with that. Living with a white cloud was unbearable. I felt like I was constantly being interrogated."

"That might have been who you were living with," said Kita, "but, I can see where that would be hard."

Sheppard took her hand off her rifle and took Babydoll's, making Babydoll smile.

"I never would have imagined either of you being cute," said Sarin, "especially not with each other."

"Do you think you and Kita or me and Kita are the only ones allowed to be cute?" said Defiance.

"No. But, I've known both of them longer than you have. Getting Sheppard to be cute with Galina was like pulling teeth, and I didn't think Kerri even knew how. I'm all for them being that way. Sheppard deserves it —and if it's with Kerri, well, the equation can still surprise us."

"You want me to be miserable?" said Babydoll with a frown.

"No. I'm just saying that's all you've ever been. I didn't know if you knew any differently."

The elevator stopped moving and dinged.

"Lobby," said Kita as she stepped into the elevator alcove.

The open lobby had shiny marble floors, columns, and several planters full of tropical plants. A long reception desk with a large Political Bureau seal on the wall behind it dominated the back of the room. On the opposite side were doors and security stations.

Kita and the others rushed into the lobby. An alarm sounded, and a protective energy barrier went up around the reception desk and the front doors. Kita snarled at the soldiers operating the reception desk. From the ceiling, six turrets lowered. Their barrels spun and fired. Kita, Sarin, and Babydoll raised their hands to stop the bullets.

"Kita, there are too many," said Babydoll in a strained voice.

Kita was straining, too. Soldiers from the security station opened fire, hitting Defiance. Sheppard threw her to the ground and jumped on top of her. Building a charge in her bracers, Kita fired a purplish-black blast at her two turrets. Nine rounds struck her in the chest, abdomen, and thigh before the turrets exploded. The rounds, suspended in the air, rained to the ground.

"Hurry, babe," said Sarin, beads of sweat dripping down her forehead.

"Too many," grunted Babydoll. The rounds floating in front of her fell, but a stream hit her in the chest. Babydoll collapsed, and the two turrets turned on Sarin.

Kita drew two stars, heated them, and threw them at two of the turrets aimed at Sarin. One of the turrets shifted and fired on Sheppard, hitting her in the legs and back. Sarin drew a pistol and fired four shots into the turret firing on her. After it exploded, she turned and destroyed the last turret.

Sheppard ignored the bullet strikes and fired on the soldiers at the security station. She hit one in the head and another in the chest. The remaining soldiers took cover behind the planters on either side of the door.

"Keep their heads down, Rene. I'll flank them," called Sarin.

Sheppard adjusted her fire, alternating between planters.

Kita knelt next to Babydoll. "Kerri, are you ok?"

"Oh, I forgot how much it sucks to get shot."

Kita chuckled. "If it helps you got shot a lot."

"Ugh, everything is getting fuzzy."

"Hang on. I'm not much of a battlefield surgeon, but I can dig the bullets out."

"That's what worries me, you'll *dig* them out. I don't need you poking at my insides." Babydoll cycled through her god form. "There we go. Good as new."

Kita hugged Babydoll. "You had me worried."

"What? Why?"

"That you'd play by the rules."

"I'm like you. I only follow the rules when it suits me."

Kita smiled and helped Babydoll up.

"Die! You annoying little worms," yelled Sarin as her pistols blasted away.

"Did you get them, pretty blackbird?" said Kita when Sarin had finished.

"Only those behind the reception desk are left."

Kita walked over to the energy barrier and stuck her hand in. She pulled it out when it burned. "Come out, little piggies. Don't make me have to come get you."

The tapping of Kita's toe echoed through the lobby.

"Fine. Have it your way." Kita dissolved into her cloud, passed through the energy barrier, and drifted over the reception desk.

A shot rang out as a bullet passed through Kita. "Now, I'm annoyed."

She changed to her angelic form, knocked the pistol from the soldier's hand, and blasted another soldier hiding with the first. Kita grabbed the first soldier and threw him over the desk. She hopped across, grabbed him by the back of the head, and stuck his face in the energy barrier. The soldier's screams died on his lips as his flesh burnt away. Kita dropped the body and jumped back over the desk. Finding the alarm, she shut it off. The energy barriers protecting the desk and doors collapsed.

"Casey, Rene, kitties, are you ok?" said Kita.

Sarge and Jupiter gave Kita quizzical look. Nothing had targeted them.

"I took a couple," said Defiance, "but they're not deep. I should be ok. Admiral?"

"I took several. My armor and dampener stopped the rest."

"You didn't have to jump on me," said Defiance to Sheppard.

"Be glad she did," said Kita. "Her dampener kept those rounds that hit you from going deep."

"How do we get downstairs?" said Babydoll.

Kita tapped her nail on her teeth. "I should have left one of these guys alive to ask."

"There's another bank of elevators through that door over there," said Defiance.

Sarin, nearest to the door, tried it. "Locked."

"See if it'll open for Casey," said Kita.

Defiance placed her hand against the pad. The door opened, revealing an elevator. Kita and the other Angels followed her into the landing.

"So what's underground?" said Babydoll.

"Research and development," said Defiance.

"Of course she's down with all the death machines. Why can't she meet us on a pitch instead?"

"Everything to maximize her advantage," said Kita. "But there's nothing she has that will stop me."

"Yeah, what about us?" said Babydoll.

"Are you planning on being vulnerable?"

"Well, no, but Rene…"

"Nothing will happen to Rene or Casey. Come on." Kita pushed the button for the elevator.

"Which floor?" said Defiance when everyone was inside.

"I don't know," said Kita. "I just know she's below us."

Defiance pressed the bottom button. "We'll head to the Experimental and Theoretical floor."

"What's there?" said Sarin.

"No idea. I'm going to guess ideas that are cutting edge."

"A ninja toaster," said Babydoll.

"Is that a Mexork with the head of a toaster?" said Kita.

"And it wields swords and fires pieces of killer toast."

The Angels giggled.

The elevator stopped and the door opened. A pair of soldiers guarded a security checkpoint. Babydoll threw herself into a ball and struck the first soldier in the chest sending him into a wall. She bounced off him, and uncoiled into a flying roundhouse, striking the second soldier repeatedly. Backflipping, Babydoll ricocheted off the floor, slid forward, kicking the soldier back up into the air. With a powerful flap of her wings, she caught him and slammed him to the floor.

"X, Y, A, A, B, B, left, right, right for the super combo," Kita called. "Finish him!"

Babydoll laughed. "I never had the dexterity for video games."

"Still, we need to come up with a kill stroke for you."

"I thought I did good putting him in the ground."

"Yeah, but you need a move where you rip their spleen out through their nose then kick their head into orbit."

"Where do you know all this from?" Defiance asked Kita.

"My last two daughters were big into video games," said Kita as she walked around the security bench and hit the button to open the door.

"I can't wrap my head around you being someone's mom."

"Jane and I raised six girls." Kita entered the large lab. Machinery and computers sat in groups. Each surrounded by movable walls.

"I wonder what they're working on," said Sarin.

"Searching for the secrets of the universe," said Babydoll.

"They've got a long way to go."

"Some of our biggest breakthroughs came from here," said Defiance, "like FTL."

Babydoll and Sarin snickered.

"What?" said Defiance.

"Love," said Kita, "I sent the secret of FTL to the UEE when I realized I was going to need help destroying the Harbingers. I'm sure they confirmed what I sent them here, but they didn't come up with it. Why do you think the UEE FTL systems were simplified versions of the Diamock's?"

"No way. You—from all the way—did that?"

Kita shrugged. *Believe it or not, that's what happened.*

"Where is Galina?" said Sheppard.

"That way." Kita, Babydoll, and Sarin pointed together toward the far side of the room.

"Are you going to be ok seeing her again?" Sarin asked Sheppard.

Sheppard relaxed her rifle. "I—I haven't given it much thought. Up until now, she's just been the enemy."

"She was your partner for years."

"It didn't feel like that at the end. More like I was her captive and I was doing what made her happy. I was grateful she sent me after the emperor. It got me away from her. I did my best to hide behind my duty, but she can be persistent when she's in the mood."

Kita nodded. "Yes, I know. It's not your fault. You did what you had to."

"I feel I should have stood up to her."

"Galina is responsible, not you. You did your best to contain her," said Kita.

Sheppard's shoulders slumped. "I don't understand what went wrong."

"It's nothing you did or didn't do. It's jealousy over Kita spurning her." Babydoll put her hand on Sheppard's shoulder. "Don't worry. I'll be there for you."

Sheppard looked at Babydoll and smiled. "Thanks, Kerri. I don't want this to be a burden for you. You don't have to."

"Come on, I was there when Galina lost her mind over Kita. I know it had to sting. I don't think it was fair to you for her to try to jump in bed with Kita."

"It's not my fault she took *no* the wrong way," said Kita.

"I'm not saying it is your fault," said Babydoll. "It's Galina's. You told her the rules."

"I promise I won't freeze or go back to her or anything," said Sheppard. "I'm over her."

Famous last words.

"We'll be there for you," said Sarin. "I look forward to putting a few slugs in her."

Kita opened a door and led them into a large room. A set of square columns created a pen in the back third of the room.

"What is that?" said Babydoll pointing to a large squat four-legged creature in the pen. It had a hard shell with spikes around the rim, a watermelon-shaped head full of teeth, and a tail lined with spikes and two large bony knobs made the end of the tail look like a hammer.

"We must have entered the biology section," said Defiance.

"It looks like a dinosaur," said Sheppard.

"Ankylosaurus with teeth," grunted Kita.

A door on the near wall opened, causing everyone to ready their weapons.

"Megan!" Kita snarled as the Angel approached them. Kita lowered her swords. "A hologram of Megan."

"Too scared to face us in person?" said Sarin to Megan.

"I'm no fool, girl. I bet Kita's loaded for revenge and I'm not about to step in front of that train."

"What have you done?" hissed Kita.

"If you don't know, I'm not going to tell you."

"I know about the anti-Angel weapons. What did you do to Lina?"

"Nothing."

"Don't lie to me," Kita yelled. "I met the monstrosity on the transfer station. Only one person in the UEE knows Angel physiology well enough to discover how she worked in such a short time."

"The general wanted her secrets. It was part of the deal," said Megan.

"Where is she?"

"Which part? She's split up between six labs."

"How could you? She was your daughter," said Sarin.

Megan rolled her eyes. "Just because she came from me doesn't mean she's my daughter. She was the deal. Her or me. I chose me. Don't tell me you fallen and evil angels wouldn't have done the same."

"I'm sorry, Kita," said Defiance. "I swear, as soon as I'm back on the throne she'll be returned to you."

Kita raised her hand and shook her head. "The deed's done. I'm too late—"

"It's not your fault, babe," said Sarin. "I should have gone after her."

"You did what you thought was right and it was the right call," said Kita. "That just leaves the question—why. So, why, Megan? Why sell us out?"

"I'm a citizen of the Empire. I'm doing my duty. I hold no allegiance to you after what you did to my Arconians and me. The general has her flaws, but she's nothing compared to you."

Kita's eyes burned in rage. "Your damn Arconians got the greatest, most glorious battle they craved since I met them. You're upset because I bullied you into helping save the equation? I thought I was petty. I have ordered people torn asunder, but they were wicked and despicable. Lina was a kind, gentle soul that never did anything to you or Galina. If you have a bone to pick, you should pick it with me—not her—you vile, disgusting, perverse old hag. There won't be a place far enough for you to hide that I won't find you. After I strip your wings and have my fun, I'll bring back Mengele specifically to work on you." Kita's eyes were flaming jets when she finished.

Defiance stepped next to Kita and pushed her back a bit. "Megan, whoever you are, you are stripped of your rank and status in the United Earth Empire. All your assets are forfeit, and you are under arrest. I suggest you turn yourself in."

"And who are you, kid in a fancy uniform?" scoffed Megan.

"I'm Casey Bush, rightful Emperor of the United Earth Empire."

Megan rolled her eyes. "Of course. Out of millions of cubic light-years, Kita finds the lost Emperor. Good luck enforcing that, kid. You have to be on the throne first."

"Kita's threat is not hollow. I will turn you over to her."

"That is against the law," yelled Megan.

"The law is what I say it is. I will do anything to keep my girlfriend happy."

"Neptune's bloody rings, Kita." Megan turned to Sarin. "And you're ok with this?"

"Right now, I'm ecstatic. I hope you rot."

"I guess I better get a move on packing my lab. Seeing how I'm going to need every free moment, I'll let Dino keep you busy."

Megan's hologram vanished as the columns of the pen lowered into the floor.

"Is there a reason she looked like you?" said Defiance to Kita.

"Luck of genetics."

Dino blasted hot air out his nose and charged the Angels.

"Scatter," yelled Kita.

There wasn't a lot of room, but everyone leaped or flew out of the way. Sheppard rolled to her knees and fired her rifle, the bullets bouncing off Dino's armored hide. Sarin fired next, but Dino's armor also turned her .50 caliber rounds aside.

"We might have a problem," said Sarin.

Dino spun, catching Defiance in the chest with the tip of his long tail, sending her into a wall. Seeing he had a tormentor down, Dino charged Defiance. Sarge jumped on Dino's back, trying to find a soft place to bite. Jupiter transformed and fired a ball of lightning at Dino. The ball struck Dino in the side and got his attention. Dino spun and charged the offending cat.

Kita floated in front of Jupiter. "You leave him alone." She drew her fist back and punched Dino as hard as she could in the face. Dino stumbled backward shaking his head.

"Kerri, get him," yelled Kita.

Babydoll threw herself into a ball and struck Dino in the face. She bounced between the floor and Dino's chin several times causing the dinosaur to stagger. Defiance blew a sheet of ice under Dino's feet. Deprived of traction, Dino's legs splayed out under him.

"Rene, finish him," ordered Kita.

Sheppard jumped into the air, a blue glow forming at her elbow. She drew her fist back as she flew, and struck Dino's face when she landed. The blue glow shot down Sheppard's arm and exploded in a flash that sent Dino flying backward, hitting the far wall. Dino slumped to the ground and didn't move.

"Is it dead?" said Sarin.

Dino's chest expanded as a response.

"I think he's out for a while," said Kita. "Watch him as I get us through this door."

Kita stuck her finger into the biometric reader but found it encrypted. *Ok. That's taking paranoid to a whole new level.* Grumbling, Kita opened her hacking programs and went to work.

"Hey, Kita," said Babydoll.

"Yeah? What?"

"The dinosaur's stirring."

"Then go punch him in the head and knock him back out."

Babydoll muttered but flew over to Dino. She punched him several times in the nose and Dino went quiet.

"Did it work?" said Kita to Babydoll when she returned.

"Yeah. He's kind of cute. Maybe we can give him a better home than this."

"He might be dangerous," said Sheppard.

"I'm sure we could tame him."

"I'd want to see what Megan's done to him first," said Kita.

Dino spasmed, kicking his feet into the air, he rolled onto them and snorted. Spinning, he spotted the Angels and charged.

"Kita, look out," said Sarin. She grabbed Kita's arm and pulled her away from the door.

Annoyed, Kita shook Sarin loose, drew her swords, and joined them at the hilt. Holding the sword parallel to the floor, Kita pointed it at Dino.

"Reap," Kita whispered.

A blue ghost appeared next to Dino. The ghost evaporated, and the dinosaur collapsed. Kita split her sword and sheathed them. She went back to the door and stuck her finger into the biometric reader.

"Now I have to start all over," she grumbled.

CHAPTER XXX

"*S*o who was she to you?" Defiance asked Kita.

"That was my great-grandmother, Megan Mackay. She was the chief science officer aboard the colony ship and served in the Shadow Fleet. Apparently, I can save the equation and not make everyone happy."

"Cantankerous old bitch is what she is," said Sarin.

"And what did you do exactly?" said Defiance.

"I usurped her little Arconian kingdom. I needed their resources, and her mind is an asset. I wasn't even around for the final fight. I don't see how that's my fault. Maybe I wasn't there to stop it."

"I'm sure you did what you had to. You have my full support. You saved the Empire. You'll go down as a hero."

"I didn't do it for the glory," said Kita. Sarin snickered. "Oh, shut up. I did it because no one else could, and I'm not about to lose my favorite sandbox."

"You didn't do it for me?" said Sarin, playfully batting her lashes.

"You're all part of the favorite sandbox. But if I failed, I would have figured out a way to save you."

"Aw, thanks, babe."

"What's in these rooms?" said Babydoll.

"Genetic experiments?" Defiance shrugged. "I know the human genomes we use to populate planets are stored here."

"Someone was working on dinosaurs," said Sheppard.

"Probably Megan tinkering with Cowboy's research," muttered Kita.

"He did produce a lot."

Kita nodded. "He was a genius, I'll give him that."

"I have missed a lot on this little world," said Defiance.

"It wasn't big enough for Kita and Cowboy," said Sarin with a giggle.

"It wasn't big enough for Kita," said Sheppard.

"I was bound to leave," said Kita, annoyed at the others for picking on her. "I didn't expect to be led off in chains."

"I'm sorry. I didn't mean—"

Kita shook her head. "No, I'm sorry. I'm being sensitive when I shouldn't be. I'm annoyed over Megan. She should have talked to me. At the time, I'm sure I looked ungrateful for what she did for me, but...I didn't have a choice. I couldn't lose, and the destroyers were brilliant bits of engineering. They smashed through the Machines with ease. I couldn't pass that up. What came out of her lab was gold. I gave her the option. She was stubborn and didn't leave me a choice."

Defiance put her arm around Kita's shoulders. "It's ok, darlin'. You did what you had to. When we catch her, we'll work it out. I promise. I won't throw her in the dungeon unless you say so."

"I can't believe she'd do that to Lina." Kita wiped a set of tears away. "I miss my little lightning bug. I couldn't save her, and there was nothing I could do. She's gone, and I never got to say goodbye."

Sarin put her arms around Kita. "Sorry, babe. You're not alone. I could have done something. Instead, I went quietly."

"It's not your fault. You did like I told you."

"Some days I regret listening."

"And Galina would have killed you," said Sheppard.

"You mean you would have killed me?"

"That's not fair," said Defiance.

Sheppard held up a hand. "No, she's right. At the time, I would have happily pulled the trigger. Jane didn't make life easy for anyone."

"I guess we've both come a long way since then," said Sarin.

Kita sat down hard, wrapped her wings around her, and cried. The others knelt around her.

"Babe," said Sarin softly as she stroked Kita's hair.

"Darlin'," whispered Defiance from the other side. She took Kita's hand.

"They're all gone," Kita sobbed, "or they hate me. It's not fair. They shouldn't have to answer for my sins."

"Kami, I need you," said Sarin. She sat down next to Kita and put her arm around her, guiding Kita's head onto her shoulder. "Kami's still out there, babe. I promise she doesn't hate you."

Kita cried louder.

Sarin looked over her shoulder to Babydoll. "See if you can find Kami."

"Right. Come on," she said to Sheppard. Taking her hand, Babydoll collapsed into a point of light and vanished.

Kita's sobs diminished to a quiet cry. She put her arms around Sarin and hugged her, then gave Defiance a squeeze to let them both know she was feeling better.

"Sorry," said Kita to the others.

"It's alright, babe. I miss them, too," said Sarin.

"I know. I shouldn't be so selfish."

"You were their mom. You have every right to be selfish."

"So were you," said Kita.

"Not like you. You were the real mom. I just filled in when needed."

"You were a great mom." Kita kissed Sarin on the cheek.

The three Angels helped each other to their feet.

Babydoll floated down from the ceiling and transformed back into her and Sheppard.

"Wow," said Sheppard. "The universe is amazing."

"Did you find Kami?" asked Sarin.

Babydoll shook her head. "She wasn't in the usual places, nor did I detect her anywhere."

Kita frowned. "Let's find Galina, and then we'll worry about finding Kami. Maybe they went into another equation."

"I hope she's ok," said Sarin.

"She's with Tenshi and Panther. They'll be fine," said Kita with more certainty than she felt. "Let's go find Galina."

〜

KITA AND THE OTHER ANGELS ENTERED A ROOM WITH A DOZEN THICK CABLES littering the floor. A large bank of computer terminals sat along the far wall operated by Political Bureau personnel. Galina stood next to a pod. She wore a t-shirt, exposing her robotic arms, and her formal uniform bottoms with daggers strapped to her thighs. Her uniform top hung on a rail that went around the work area dividing the room.

"Hurry up, fools. They'll be here any minute," yelled Galina.

Sarin raised a pistol and fired. A woman's head exploded. Her body slumped against the terminal and collapsed on the floor. The work stopped and everyone turned to the Angels.

"Keep working, you idiots," snarled Galina as she walked to the rail. She folded her arms. The human half of her face contorted in rage. "You moron!" she roared and pointed at Sheppard. "You were supposed to kill them, not join them. I thought you knew better than to let Kita speak."

"Hey, don't talk to her like that," said Babydoll.

Sheppard put her hand on Babydoll's arm. "Galina, it's over. My loyalty lies with Kita. She's forgiven me for what I've done and has been compassionate, loyal, and honest. I've done my best to return in kind. Kita is no danger to the Empire. She is a friend to it and the emperor. It's time to answer for what you've done. Put down your daggers and come peacefully. I promise no harm will come to you."

Kita raised an eyebrow but kept her mouth shut. Harm could have several meanings.

Galina laughed. "Do you think I will toss away the utopia I am building because Kita arrives? Soon, I will be everywhere and see everything. I will lift the Empire from the dregs of civilization to a golden age that will last for a millennium."

"That doesn't sound good," Kita said to the others.

"What is she talking about?" said Defiance.

"It's her white cloud. When I had one that's what it wanted—to build a utopia perfect for it. The people are docile sheep, there to feed on."

"So she can be redeemed?"

Kita laughed. *"There's more going on than that, but we'll see if she comes quietly."*

"That's not your choice to make. That is mine," said Defiance.

"The wayward Emperor returns. You're too late. Your cousin sits on the throne doing exactly what I tell him."

"No male is allowed on the throne," retorted Defiance.

"With the strength of the Political Bureau it was easy. You will simply disappear."

"You'll have to go through me first," said Sheppard stepping in front of Defiance.

Babydoll moved next to Sheppard.

With speed Kita had only seen in herself, Galina drew her daggers and threw them. One came at Kita's nose. She clapped her hands together and caught the blade.

"Rene!" cried Babydoll.

Sheppard slumped into Babydoll's arms, a large pool of blood gathering on the floor from the dagger in her throat.

"Put her down," ordered Defiance.

Babydoll laid Sheppard on her back. Defiance placed her hand on Sheppard's throat and tried to freeze the blood.

"Let me see that blade," said Sarin to Defiance.

From her upper arms, Galina pulled a pair of long daggers.

"Love, I think I'm going to need you," said Kita.

"Are you saying you can't keep her busy?"

"It'll be easier with two."

"And let Rene die?"

From the size of the pool of blood, more of it was outside Sheppard than inside. Sarin's blood could heal wounds, but she couldn't replace the blood. "There's nothing you can do, even if you spilled all your blood."

Galina jumped the rail and charged Defiance and Babydoll. Sarin fired both her pistols. Galina blocked the bullets and then threw her blades into Sarin's pistols, splitting the barrels.

Sarin held up her pistols and looked at the damage. "Now I'm mad."

Galina pulled another set of blades from her upper arms and jumped at Sarin. Kita blocked Galina with Dead and Buried and threw her sideways into the wall. Sarin drew Razorsplitter, and the two Angels faced Galina.

"I'm not without tricks," hissed Galina. She blinked, and six Galina clones surrounded Kita and Sarin and attacked.

Kita dropped to a knee and slashed at the legs of two of her attackers. They jumped over Kita's strike, but Kita dropped and rolled backward into a third attacker, plunging Dead into the clone's midsection. Rolling to her feet, Kita parried a series of strikes from the remaining clones. Kita pushed them away to get some separation.

The clones were as fast and strong as Kita. Sarin had a series of cuts on her arms and torso but kept attacking with powerful swings of Razorsplitter. Kita needed a new strategy, and fast.

Kita pointed her fist at a clone and fired a purplish-black beam into its head. The head melted, but the clone leaped at her. Kita met it in midair. Spinning, she parried a strike and struck with Buried into the clone's chest. The other clone seized the opportunity and attacked, striking Kita in the lower back. Kita hit the floor and rolled to her feet. Facing the remaining clone, she beckoned it to her. The clone charged. Kita leaped into the air. The clone followed. With a powerful flap of her wings, Kita dropped to the floor and slid on her knees under the clone. Reaching up, she cut through its legs. Backflipping, Kita struck it in the back with her feet and drove the torso into the floor. She plunged her swords into its back.

Sarin brandished her sword, trying to keep the three clones attacking her at bay. She was bleeding profusely from multiple cuts and stab wounds.

Kita yelled and charged the nearest clone. It turned, and Kita slammed into it, driving it into a second clone. Seeing the third clone distracted, Sarin struck, cutting her target in half. Kita twirled, throwing the first clone into a wall. With a corkscrew spin, she landed behind the second clone and cut off its right arm. The clone spun and struck, stabbing Kita in the ribs.

The air left Kita's lungs. Every time she went to draw a breath, it came back bloody. Enraged, she spat blood at the clone and dropkicked it in the chest. The clone landed at Sarin's feet, and she plunged her sword into its throat.

The last clone faced down both Angels. It lunged at Sarin, slashing her arm. Kita took the advantage and struck. The clone parried the attack of Dead, but not of Buried. The sword stabbed the clone in the shoulder. Wielding Razorsplitter one-handed, Sarin swung at the clone, who blocked the attack but couldn't arrest the blade's forward momentum. Razorsplitter cut through the clone's arm and chest. The last clone collapsed, and Sarin fell to her knees.

"Jane," said Kita alarmed.

"I'll be alright, just some deep ones. Give me a moment." Sarin shifted to her god form. When she reappeared, she was healed. "Kita, what about you?"

"I'll be fine. She punctured a lung and got me in the back."

"Where did she go?"

Kita opened her vision. Galina was in the strange pod. "Whatever she's doing we've got to get her out." Kita took Sarin's hand and phased them across the room.

Sarin grabbed a man and placed Razorsplitter against his throat. "Any of you move, and he gets more efficient at breathing."

"What's she doing?" demanded Kita.

"S—she's copying herself to the computer," said the man dressed in a lab coat.

"By the Crushing Depths no," roared Kita. "I will not have another Angus. Shut it down."

"I—I can't. It'll kill her. She's in the process of moving."

"Then move her back or cancel it," ordered Sarin.

"I can try, but if she gets to the network, she'll be impossible to stop," said the man.

Kita changed her vision to see the electromagnetic spectrum. The computer equipment glowed brightly, but what she wanted was in the walls. Finding a ribbon running through the wall, she struck with Dead and severed it. The electromagnetic signal died.

"She's not going anywhere. Force her back into her body," Kita ordered the man.

"I—I'll do my best."

"Your lives depend on it."

The man gulped and conferred with the other members of his team.

Kita slumped to a knee and pressed her hand against the wound in her side. She gritted her teeth, heated her hand, and cauterized it.

"Are you ok?" said Sarin.

"I'll be fine, I'm breathing with only one lung."

"Come on." Sarin helped Kita over to the others. Defiance and Babydoll were holding Sheppard's throat as icy blood seeped through their fingers.

Kita frowned at the amount of blood on the floor. "She's gone."

"But..." said Defiance.

"Her heart has stopped."

"If I freeze her—"

"We'll never get her help in time," said Kita.

"This facility has a medical center."

"And we're the enemy, even if we remove Galina."

Defiance hung her head.

"I'm sorry." Kita hugged both Defiance and Babydoll, and then sat down hard.

"Are you ok?" said Babydoll as she wiped her tears away.

"I got stabbed in the lung. I'll be fine." Kita laid back and closed her eyes. The overwhelming urge to fall asleep came over her.

"Kita!" Sarin yelled shaking Kita's shoulder.

"Huh, what?"

"No falling asleep when you're injured."

Kita sat up and coughed up some blood. "Damn." She got to her feet. "Come on. Let's go see if they've brought Galina back." Kita led the others to the scientists.

"Where are we at?" demanded Kita.

"We—We're moving her back. It's nearly complete." He pointed to a screen with a progress wheel. It was at ninety-nine percent.

In the pod, Galina's eyes opened. She turned her head and said, "Doctor Gorbach, what happened? Did I transfer?"

"No, General. I—"

"There is no way I'm letting you become the next Angus," said Kita in a harsh tone.

Galina's eyes went wide when she saw Dead above her.

"Kita! I—" Galina dissolved into her cloud and drifted toward the ceiling.

"Oh, you are not getting away that easy," snarled Kita.

Kita, Babydoll, and Sarin changed into their clouds. Kita expanded, taking up most of the room.

White tendrils from Galina stabbed into Babydoll and Sarin. Kita swirled around the others, engulfing them. She sent tendrils to Babydoll and Sarin to strengthen them while sending more to attack Galina. The white cloud responded by sending tendrils to attack Kita.

Brushing off the bothersome attacks, Kita bombarded Galina with a steady dose of primal emotions. Drawing from her shock, outrage, and sorrow of losing Snowy, Lina, and the other Angels, she pumped it into Galina. The white cloud pulsed.

Galina responded with a series of logic and rational attacks. From the strength, Galina was plugged into everyone in the building and beyond. But, reason and logic were no match for pure rage, sorrow, and hate.

Withdrawing from Babydoll and Sarin, Galina concentrated on Kita. Meeting tendrils with tendrils, they wove themselves into a knot. Now free, Babydoll and Sarin launched their own attacks. Galina pulsed faster.

Sensing Galina's resolve failing, Kita swallowed her and attacked everywhere at once. Galina screamed and fell out the bottom of Kita's cloud as a human. Kita, Babydoll, and Sarin returned to their Angelic form and stood around her.

Kita grabbed Galina by the throat. She held the woman at arm's length and sneered in contempt. With a scream of unbridled rage, Kita slammed Galina into the floor. She continued to scream and flung Galina side to side smashing her against the floor until Babydoll and Sarin restrained her.

"Don't kill her," yelled Babydoll. "At least not until I get my turn."

Sarin pried Kita's fingers from Galina's neck. The former Angel collapsed to her knees coughing.

"Why?" Kita screamed. "Why did you have to kill them? What did they ever do to you? If you had a problem, you should have brought it to me. I would have found an answer. I would have given you whatever you wanted."

Even with a damaged throat, Galina's harsh Russian accent remained unchanged. "What was I to do when the person I love refused to love me back?"

"I told you it was over because you refused to take *no* for an answer. I never stopped loving you, and I gave you what you wanted."

"You broke my heart when you chose that vapid, stupid party girl over me."

"I was with Jane long before I was with you," said Kita angrily.

Galina chuckled. "Not Jane, Vee."

"I don't know what you want," Kita yelled. "I gave you everything you asked for."

"You refused to include me!"

"I told you there had to be boundaries. I understand that now more than ever. I was paired with a white cloud. I know how they think. We would have ended up destroying each other. I didn't want to fight someone I loved. I gave you everything I could within those boundaries. Why was that not good enough?"

"Because I believed it could have worked. You didn't give it a chance."

"I did give it a chance. I gave you everything—once."

"And it made me so happy," said Galina.

"And look what happened. You betrayed me then. That's when I knew it would never work. You would always covet what was mine and try to destroy me."

"You squander everything you build. You could do such good in the world."

"I do what's best for me," said Kita.

"I know, raven. You are nothing without a light to guide your path."

"I haven't had a light to guide my path since Jane."

"Unlike Jane, I'm incorruptible. I couldn't fall to your evil influence."

Kita sighed. "No. You fell to a tale as old as time. Why not just me? I'm an assassin—you're an assassin. We could have settled this easily."

Galina looked up into Kita's eyes. "Because, raven, you had to hurt as much as I. My heart is broken. I needed to break yours."

"Do I look like I hurt as much as you do?" Flames burst in Kita's eyes as her lip curled.

"Anger is a product of pain," whispered Galina.

"At my core, there is nothing but pain. What you have done is nothing but a drop in the bucket. You will never experience my level of pain. But let me give you a taste…"

A black tendril crawled from Kita's finger to Galina's forehead. Galina thrashed, trying to fight it, but the tendril entered, and her eyes went black. Galina screamed as she clawed at her face with her mechanical hands.

Kita withdrew the tendril. "That is what I felt over losing Quill, Spike, Nina, and Lina—my innocent daughters you so cruelly murdered. I can forgive you—" Galina's eyes opened. Through the pain was a look of hope. "—for what you did to me, but I'll never forgive you for what you did to them or my friends."

Galina closed her eyes and winced. "I'm sorry, raven. I had to make you understand. To see how I saw it—"

"To prove you were better than everyone else?"

"I *am* better than everyone else."

Kita crossed her arms. "That's debatable. Jane has made you look like a fool for years. Casey is a better dictator and Kerri is a better fighter."

"I'm still better than an alley cat," hissed Galina.

"Maybe, but Vee has untapped potential. You'd reached the pinnacle of yours. Speaking of cats, I think you should say goodbye to someone." Kita whistled, and Sarge and Jupiter came over.

Jupiter sniffed at Galina.

"Jupiter. Hello, my old friend," said Galina. She raised a hand to pet him.

Jupiter jumped aside and hissed. He retreated behind Sarin's legs.

Tears fell from the corner of Galina's eyes. "That was cruel, raven."

Kita hummed. "I know, but maybe it's time for you to feel how I feel."

"No. Jupiter is mine. I will fight for him." Galina rolled to her feet and leaped at Sarin.

Sarin blinked out of existence. When she reappeared, she was holding her sniper rifle. She fired twice, once into each of Galina's shoulders. Galina landed in a heap, her augmented arms unable to support her.

"I think he's happy with his new mistress," said Sarin. She scratched Jupiter's chin. "Yeah, good boy." She dug a treat from her belt and tossed it to him.

Sarge looked at Kita hopefully. Rolling her eyes, Kita dug into her belt and gave Sarge a treat. "Cats," she muttered.

"What do we do now?" said Defiance.

"Get Galina to call off the dogs and get you back on your throne."

"The best way to do that will be to get back to the fleet. Without their leader, the Political Bureau will be in chaos. Once the rest of the fleet arrives, we can land in Dallas with a sizable force and dethrone the usurper."

Kita nodded. "You're the emperor. We'll follow your—"

Babydoll stepped in front of Galina and backflipped, kicking her under the chin and sending her toward the ceiling. Babydoll landed and caught Galina by the throat. "Why?" she screamed. "Why did you have to kill her? What did she do to you? She was only doing her duty."

"What do you care, dog?" Galina snarled. "Admiral Sheppard betrayed her duty and her emperor."

"I say differently," said Defiance. Her voice didn't convey the anger Kita felt, but her eyes did. "She served with distinction and was exemplary. She recognized she made a mistake, accepted responsibility, and made up for it. She was a fine officer that deserved a better death."

Galina's head rolled up to look at Babydoll. "The stoic legionnaire has feelings for the Marine, *da*? That is a laugh. Rene never would have lowered herself to someone like you."

Babydoll struck Galina on the android side of her face, tearing through the prosthetic skin and denting the metal casing.

"Kerri, I need her in one piece to get us out of here," said Kita.

"I can get us out of here. Rene didn't deserve to die like that."

"She died doing her duty. There's no greater honor for a Marine."

"You don't believe that," said Babydoll.

"But she did," said Kita forcefully. "Get Rene's body. We won't leave her here. I'll take Galina."

"I knew you couldn't kill me, raven," Galina chided.

"Let's see what happens when your usefulness runs out." Kita tapped the side of her head. "I still have Mengele squirreled away."

"You wouldn't do that to me."

"I watched your creations kill Snowy. The universe is running out of people who can talk me down. And, the Angel of Mercy doesn't have the influence she used to."

"You're not a monster." A tiny smile came to Galina's lips like she expected a reaction.

Sorry. Not today. "No. I'm much worse. But, I need you coherent, not screaming. We'll have plenty of time to get reacquainted, after those that have a claim to you get their fill." Kita motioned to Sarin, Defiance, and Babydoll. "I'm sure an evil angel and two fallen angels can think of something creative to do. I promise you they won't kill you. Though, you'll wish for death. Now, get up."

Kita grabbed Galina by the back of her shirt and pulled her to her feet. She looked at the scientists gathered in the room. "Stay put until someone comes for you."

Pushing Galina ahead of the group, they exited the room and followed the hallway until they were back in Dino's room. The dead dinosaur hadn't moved.

"At least something stays dead," said Sarin.

"I wish some things didn't," said Babydoll as she clutched Sheppard.

Kita sighed to herself. Her heart went out to Babydoll. It didn't seem fair. Sheppard hadn't even reacted. It was like she'd wanted it. *Did Rene still feel something for Galina? Or that she failed her? I will miss her. It's beginning to feel lonely.*

Two pinpricks of light floated down from the ceiling.

"Kami?" said Kita.

The two points of lights expanded forming Kylee and a grim reaper holding a scythe.

"Sorry, Mother. Kami's no longer with us," said Kylee with wicked glee.

"What does that mean? Where is she?" demanded Kita.

"Deleted. Never existed. She's not the only one. You're all that's left."

"Left of what?" said Sarin.

"The Angels. I've had some good father-daughter bonding time deleting them."

"What have you done?" gasped Kita. As she waited for what she was sure would be an obnoxious reply she tried to contact the other Angels via the comm, but she received no answer. Not even the other gods responded when she tried to contact them through the equation.

"I got even," said Kylee with a sick smile. "Isn't that what you always told me to do, Mother?"

"E'fil and Y'grene will hear of this, Ht'aed," said Sarin.

"They will side with me once they receive my report," said Ht'aed in an eerie baritone voice. "You have been corrupted by this pathetic equation —" He pointed at Kita. "—Enticed into doing its bidding."

"You destroyed Re'drum, Ra'w, and Ecit'suj?" said Kita, naming Ht'aed's three daughters that had paired with the Angels Panther, Tenshi, and Valentine. "What happened to Denver, Kylee?"

"They could not be stripped of the polluting equation they melded with and were deleted," said Ht'aed.

"Val got what was coming to her for betraying me," said Kylee.

She has gone off the deep end. Denver loved her. It must have been a shock for her to learn how Kylee felt. "Kylee, Ht'aed is using you. In his eyes, you're not a god because you're a combination of him and me. He'll destroy you as soon as he's done with us."

"Shut up. You can't talk your way out of this. There's no way out. I win. I told you I was better than you."

"It's not possible," said Sarin. "Deleting a god requires all the elders."

"With my help, we figured it out," Kylee said proudly.

"You're a fool," said Kita.

"You're jealous you didn't do it first," yelled Kylee.

"It is time to correct the origin of our mistake," said Ht'aed. He raised his scythe and pointed it at Kita.

Kita stood firm drawing Dead and Buried, not showing any fear or weakness. *I won't go without a fight.*

"No!" cried Sarin. She jumped in front of Kita as a blue beam erupted from the tip of the scythe and hit her in the chest.

The blue beam punctured Sarin. She changed to her god form, and all the points of light exploded outward.

"Jane!" screamed Kita. The loss of Sarin struck her in the head and then in the heart. Time stood still as Kita collapsed to her knees, her head fell to her chest and tears filled her eyes. Dead and Buried clattered to the floor. Kylee's wicked laughter sounded a thousand miles away as Ht'aed deleted Defiance and Galina as they attacked him. Babydoll collapsed into a point of light and vanished with Sheppard's body.

Kita tried in vain to reach Sarin in every way she could. She couldn't feel her cloud and there was no answer when she called over the comm. An inescapable truth hit her: Sarin was gone. There was nothing she could do. The one person she cared for more than anything was gone. Her whole reason for being, why she fought so hard, why she did what she did, was no more. There was no bringing her back. Another truth hit her. She was suddenly alone in a place she hated.

Without Sarin, there was no reason to be here, or anywhere. The joy had been sucked out of the sandbox she cared so much for. The hatred swelled in her. It flashed across her mind like a raging wildfire, pushing aside her heartbreak. Her purpose shrank to a single idea. The time had come to fulfill her destiny. If Kita couldn't have Sarin, then nothing deserved to exist, and she would destroy it all, starting with Death.

Ht'aed stood over Kita and lifted his scythe to deliver the killing blow. The scythe fell, and Kita opened her eyes. A blue shockwave erupted from her and pinned Ht'aed and Kylee to the wall. Kita stood, hate blazing in her eyes as she collected Dead and Buried. Walking toward Ht'aed, her foot touched his scythe. With a snarl, Kita brought her boot down on the blade, shattering it.

Kita stopped in front of Ht'aed. "I've always been curious," she said in a menacing tone. She grabbed the hood that covered the reaper's head. With a jerk, she pulled it back exposing the skull of a creature Kita didn't recognize. It had bumps, horns, tusks, and teeth. Kita guessed whatever it came from was ugly.

She drew back Dead and Buried—the edges glowing blue—and sliced through Ht'aed's bony neck. He exploded into pinpricks of light that slowly went out. Kita moved next to Kylee, who struggled to get free. Kita leaned against the wall next to her.

"You think I'm a fool? I've known how to delete someone since fighting the Harbingers. I've known there's more beyond Infinity since I became a god. It's nothing I didn't think you'd figure out on your own. But, your own pettiness and impatience is your downfall. All you had to do was follow my lead, and you would have had it all. You were my favorite. I guess we're always betrayed by the ones we love the most. Your mistake was deleting Jane, the one person in Infinity that I cared for more than you. And that's a mistake that's going to cost you everything."

Kita slammed Dead into Kylee's chest. "Goodbye, Kylee." The sword flashed blue, and Kylee exploded into pinpricks of light. The lights twinkled and went out, vanishing into the ether.

The room was empty except for Dino. There was nothing left for Kita. It was time to go to Infinity. She collapsed into a point of dark light and drifted through the ceiling.

CHAPTER XXXI

*K*ita changed into her angelic form. She wasn't in Infinity, but the White. Something had impeded her journey.

"Who's out there? Show yourself," Kita demanded.

A pinprick of multicolored light appeared and changed into Babydoll, holding Sheppard's body.

"What in the Crushing Depths happened to you?" snarled Kita.

"I left to get help."

"Help? From who?"

"E'fil and Y'grene, and anyone else I could find."

"It's over," Kita said tersely.

"What happened?"

"I deleted Ht'aed."

Babydoll's eyes widened. "You deleted him? The elders won't like that."

"It was him or me, and he deleted the god angels. He made his case for deletion."

"You shouldn't know how to delete anyone. It takes all the elders."

"Ht'aed and Kylee learned how. I've known since before I knew you."

"So where are you going?" Babydoll asked cocking her head to one side with a curious look.

"To Infinity, to finish this."

"Finish what—Wait. You don't mean to destroy Infinity?"

"I have nothing left. It's time."

"I'm still here," said Babydoll.

"And you left me when I needed you the most."

"But…can't you just conquer Infinity?"

Kita laughed. "Why would I want to do that? Ruling over a bunch of whiney gods sounds like a horrible idea."

"You might destroy yourself."

"So be it."

Babydoll gulped. "I won't let you, but I don't want to fight you."

"We all have to go sometime. Why don't you find a quiet spot and spend some time with Rene? You won't even know when it's over."

"No. Infinity is my home. I may not like it much, but it's still home, and I will defend it."

The White changed to a rocky platform hovering above a raging sea. Sheets of rain beat down and the wind screamed overhead.

Babydoll set Sheppard's body down and took up a fighting stance. Her crystal spider legs extended from her back and her braids swayed back and forth. "If you want Infinity, you'll have to go through me."

Kita shrugged. "Don't say I didn't give you the option to walk away."

"You haven't won yet."

"The outcome is foretold—only the cost is to be decided. Please, Kerri. Walk away."

"It's my home—our way of life. I love you, but I'll defend Infinity to the last. I don't have many principles, but this is one."

"You pick a lousy time to stand by your principles."

"I stuck by you for all those years."

Kita bowed her head. "And you have my thanks. You were the best friend a girl could want."

"It was my privilege to be your left hand."

Kita drew her swords and flourished them, water flying off the spinning blades.

"You want this, you have to make the first move," said Babydoll.

Kita nodded. That was fair. She took a few steps to her left. Babydoll turned, keeping her front facing Kita and her fists up. Her braids bobbed over her shoulders, and the crystal spider legs peeked menacingly around her sides.

No doubts ran through Kita's mind. To get what she wanted this was what she had to do. Babydoll was an excellent fighter, probably the best hand-to-hand fighter ever. It didn't bother Kita this was her friend she was about to kill. It was just another small step on her way to seeing her destiny fulfilled.

Kita leaped at Babydoll and struck with her swords. Babydoll raised her bracers and blocked. She threw open her arms, pushing Kita's swords aside, and kicked Kita in the chest. Kita flew backward and landed on the ground. She rolled over and flipped to her feet in time to block a flying roundhouse. The force of the kick pushed her back, her heel slipping over the edge of the rocky platform.

Kita lunged forward, tackling Babydoll. Her spider legs stabbed into Kita's back and sides. The two Angels wrestled on the rain-soaked ground. Babydoll, on the bottom, kicked Kita between the legs, flipping her over on her back.

Rolling away from Babydoll, Kita got to her feet. Throughout the tussle, she'd held onto her swords. She flourished them as she regained her focus. Babydoll was back on her feet, ready for more. Kita jumped forward and slashed with Buried. Babydoll twisted to the right and attacked with her spider legs. Kita spun into the appendages and slashed with Dead, severing three of the four legs.

Babydoll cried out in pain and struck with her braids. Kita corkscrewed between the two stingers, slashing at them as she did. She severed Babydoll's left braid, but the right wrapped around her arm and yanked Kita sideways. Babydoll snapped her head, and Kita flew through the air, slamming into the wet ground. Babydoll flipped her head, and Kita sailed through the air and slammed into the ground on the other side of Babydoll. She repeated this process until she'd knocked Dead and Buried from Kita's hands. Babydoll flipped, launching Kita high into the air.

Kita couldn't see straight, but opened her wings and did her best to control her descent. Shaking her head, she regained her bearings. Once the world stopped moving, she felt better. Babydoll waited for her on the ground. She looked for her swords. Babydoll stood between them, ready to keep her from them. Landing out of Babydoll's range, Kita feigned a lunge for Dead. Babydoll wasn't fooled. She shifted her weight, but that was it.

Kita ran straight at Babydoll. The move caused Babydoll to raise her eyebrow, but she raised her fists in response. When Kita was close, she leaped at Babydoll, who backflipped, catching Kita on the chin with her heel. Babydoll bounced off the ground and flew after Kita, punching her higher into the air. With a flap over wings, she overtook Kita and landed a heavy blow, sending Kita toward the ground.

Hitting the ground hard, Kita rolled to her left and brought her hands up to catch Babydoll's fist before it drove into her chest. Seeing the surprise in Babydoll's eyes, Kita shook her head playfully. Flipping her legs up, she wrapped her lower legs around Babydoll's head. Throwing her body back down, Kita drove Babydoll headfirst into the ground. Babydoll flipped to her feet, but Kita was ready and landed two fast jabs into her face. Stunned, Babydoll shook her head. Kita hit her with a hard cross to the chin followed by a heavy uppercut, knocking Babydoll off her feet onto the wet rock.

Kita took a step toward Babydoll, who rolled over, pointed her bracer at Kita, and fired. The blast hit Kita in the side, ripping out a large chunk of flesh. Kita's eyes went wide in pain and shock as she sunk to a knee. Babydoll grabbed her by the neck and slammed her with five body blows that left Kita's middle a bloody mess. Moving from Kita's middle to her face, Babydoll punched her several times. Kita's face swelled and bruised as Babydoll drove it into the wet rock.

Kita flapped her wings and carried Babydoll into the air. Wrapping her legs around Babydoll's arm, she broke Babydoll's grip. Kita stopped flapping, and the pair fell back to the ground. Kita landed on Babydoll's side. There was a sickening crunch from her arm. Twisting the arm, Kita ripped it from Babydoll's body.

Flinging the arm into the ocean, Kita punched Babydoll in the face several times, before driving her knee down on her friend's throat. Babydoll's braid wrapped around Kita's neck. Kita struggled to get free as the rain-soaked hair pulled tighter. Kita's hands glowed brightly as she burned through the offending hair.

The distraction gave Babydoll enough time to wiggle free of Kita and get to her feet. Babydoll kicked Kita in the back of the head then jumped and clamped her thighs around Kita's neck.

Kita's eyes bulged. It was like having a vice around her neck. She felt her bones stretch as Babydoll flexed. Kita grabbed Babydoll's upper thighs and cranked up the heat in her hands. Even as the smell of cooking flesh permeated the air, Babydoll refused to let go. For Kita, her vision became

| L. FERGUS

fuzzy. Deciding she needed more, she burst into a white flame. Kita stood up, lifting Babydoll off the ground. Even with the extra heat, Babydoll refused to let go. Kita spun, trying to dislodge her. The stress on Kita's neck was reaching a breaking point. Putting her left hand under Babydoll's thigh, Kita fired a burst of her purplish-black beam cutting through Babydoll's leg.

Using what was left of her strength, Kita forced Babydoll off her. Kita collapsed to her knees, coughing and wheezing. She pulled herself up to her feet and stumbled toward Buried. Babydoll remained where Kita left her. Kita stumbled back to her friend and dropped to her knees. She raised Buried.

Babydoll stirred.

"Anything left to say?" Kita said without malice.

"You can kill us all, but you can't keep it without us."

"There's nothing—there will be nothing left."

Kita thrust her sword into Babydoll's chest. Babydoll changed to her god form. A blue beam fired, and she exploded in a shower of multicolored lights.

Kita struggled to her feet and staggered across the platform to Dead. She picked the sword up and sheathed it on her back next to Buried. She looked up into the rain, feeling it hit her face. Physically, she was drained. The fight took everything she had, but she couldn't stop. She needed to reach Infinity.

Kita walked across the platform to Sheppard's body. Blood stained Sheppard's uniform. Kita stroked her friend's hair and sighed. She picked up the body and took it to the edge of the platform.

"I don't know where Marines go when they die," Kita said to Sheppard. "But I know one place where you'll be welcome: the Crushing Depths. I can think of no other place that deserves a finer warrior."

Kita tossed the body into the raging ocean and watched it slip beneath the waves.

~

KITA APPEARED IN THE EQUATION ROOM. BEHIND HER, UNIVERSES—OR equations as the gods called them—formed a line that stretched out to infinity in both directions. Kita wasn't sure if there were an infinite number or if the long line was an optical illusion. The walls of the room shimmered like heat rising off sand. The floor and ceiling appeared to move like the walls. The size of the room seemed to change as Kita's gaze shifted between the three doorways.

She was in her god form. Not far away, a cloud of lights, an unmelded god, did whatever the gods did. *When they're not making my life miserable.*

Kita raised her hand and pointed her palm at the god. A blue beam burst from her hand and struck the god. It exploded, sending points of light out in every direction. The lights burned out like fireworks as they struck the ground or walls.

Another god drifted in through a doorway. Kita destroyed it. A second god, behind the first, turned and fled. Kita hurried to the doorway, but the god was gone. All she could see was a hallway that went as far as the eye could see.

I hope the one that got away will bring the ones I seek.

Kita returned to the line of equations and looked them over. Through a doorway appeared E'fil, Y'grene, and to her surprise, Tina. Through the other doorways came two groups of gods that surrounded Kita.

"Li've, this assault on Infinity will not stand," said E'fil.

"What about the assault on my Angels by Ht'aed?" Kita replied pointedly.

"Ht'aed has not submitted any report of him attacking any equations."

"Don't try and cover it up. I know you know. Tina was with a group that was attacked. Tell me, sister, did you even try and save the others or did you run at the first opportunity?"

"Kita, that's not fair," said Tina. "There was nothing I could do. I returned here to report so Ht'aed could be stopped."

"Yes, it looks like you're all out looking so hard to find him and Kylee. You don't care. You're happy to let him do your dirty work for you. Too bad he didn't succeed. Ht'aed made a grave error and has been deleted," said Kita.

"Impossible," said Y'grene.

"But you believe Ht'aed deleted my Angels?"

"They can be replaced," said E'fil. "From destruction comes new life."

"You can't replace Jane," Kita shrieked. "I hold all of you responsible for her death. I will burn Infinity to the ground."

"Kita, I'm sorry," said Tina. "I know how much she meant to you, but revenge won't bring her back."

"No, but I can make every equation her funeral pyre. With her death, I will fulfill my destiny."

"You can't," cried Tina. "Infinity isn't at its end."

"Oh, but it is. You let Ht'aed take the one person I would do anything for. You underestimated how much she meant to me. You had the string to control me in your grasp and you ignored it. Instead, you tore me asunder trying to control me and ignored Ht'aed, who needed to be controlled."

"Ht'aed was an elder, beyond reproach," said E'fil.

"Ht'aed was a murdering psychopath bent on destroying me," said Kita. "Like everyone else, Ht'aed underestimated me and paid for it."

"Ht'aed's actions will be investigated," said Y'grene, "and appropriate measures put in place so it can never happen again. Ht'aed's crimes do not diminish your own. You have admitted to deleting an elder and several researchers. You were instructed Infinity was forbidden and you have come here threatening its destruction."

"What are you going to do to me? Lock me up again?" Kita laughed harshly.

"No. I motion before this council of elders that research assistant Li've be deleted."

"Agreed," said E'fil.

They went around the circle. Each god gave their agreement. Kita folded her arms and glared when it was Tina's turn.

"Agreed," she said in a small voice.

"Et tu, sister?" said Kita with venom in her voice.

"I'm sorry. I can't save you from yourself this time. If you'd let me handle it and been patient—I'm sorry, Kita. I truly am, but I can't let you destroy Infinity. Too many lives hang in the balance, and there is still much research to do."

"When I introduced you to the gods I never thought you'd go native on me. Remember, the only thing worse than a spy is a traitor."

"You're letting your emotions betray you," said Tina coldly. "If you'd listen to logic and reason for once you wouldn't be here."

"Then let's get it over with!" yelled Kita as she threw her arms open. "Hit me with your best shot."

"Kita there's no need to be dramatic," said Tina.

"Are you afraid you don't possess the power to delete me?" Kita said with a twisted grin.

Tina flinched as if Kita struck her. *Do you really want to play this game with me?*

"Your time is done, Li've," said Y'grene. A small blue beam erupted from the edge of his sphere. Next to him, E'fil raised her arm and emitted a similar blue beam. Around Kita, small blue beams came from the other gods.

The beams struck Kita, each tearing chunks of lights from her. *Yes! Strip away everything that makes me part of your universe and leave me pure to join with what lays beyond.* Kita let out a long wail as the beams tore her asunder.

"Delete me, and I will gain power you can't imagine." Kita's earlier words rang in Tina's ears. Her face lit with understanding. "Wait!" cried Tina. "This is what she wants!"

Kita, stripped to a single point of dark blue light, emitted a blue wave that interacted with the beams creating a brilliant white flash. The scene around Kita froze. She felt a pull, and the scene stretched until all light was gone.

Kita moved along a fiber on the outside of a giant glowing blue ball with millions of lit fibers running to it. Pulses of light moved along the fibers—some flowing into the ball, others moving away. Kita flowed toward the ball.

This is what controls all of time, space, and reality. We are nothing but signals in a giant computer. All I have to do is become part of it.

Kita left the fiber and drifted to the edge of the ball. Her light divided.

The new light entered the ball moving deeper inside, its darkness remaining visible from the edge. Fibers connected to the light and the darkness spread, until the entire ball glowed dark blue.

And now, I am said computer. I am deus ex machina.

Kita drifted away from the ball and hopped onto a fiber. The world expanded as she whizzed by. She appeared back in the equation room, surrounded by gods, all bent on her destruction. Taking her place in the center of the beams, time resumed.

Kita's wave struck the gods and slammed them against the walls. She appeared in her angelic form, showing no signs of the earlier attack. Kita snapped her fingers, and all the gods, the room, and the equations vanished, except Tina. Her sister changed from her god form to her angelic form.

Gliding over, Kita stood before her sister. Tina looked around at the barren rock platform surrounded by nebulas of color.

"So, this is what's really real?"

Kita nodded.

"I didn't expect heaven to be so bare."

"It's a blank slate for creation."

Tina looked up into Kita's eyes. "Was it worth it?"

"Is that a fair question? The answer is not so simple. I had taken from me what I held most dear. Something that can never be replaced and left a hole in my heart which will never be filled. This was all I had left. This one single purpose and I fulfilled it. Now, I can rest."

"You still have me."

Kita blinked a tear away. "No, I don't. This has to cost me everything." She snapped her fingers, and Tina vanished.

Changing into her cloud, Kita settled on the rocky ground and numbly watched the nebulas move and change like clouds in the sky, thoughts of Sarin never far from her mind.

EPILOGUE

*K*ita grew a glowing orb in her hand and tossed it into the air. She let it get a fair distance away from her before raising her hand and blasting it with a blue beam. The orb split in half and fell to the ground where it dissolved. She'd lost count how many times she'd done this. *It's official. I'm bored. There must be something I can do before I'm crushed by boredom and loneliness.*

She explored the inner workings of the ball. It wasn't very complex, she discovered. It was nothing short of a giant holographic display, though on a scale unlike any she'd ever seen. Still, the machine took in input, processed it, and displayed the results. Currently, it was waiting for something to execute after she destroyed the last executable.

What about the giant cube? I haven't explored there yet. Let's hope it's not the logic processor.

Kita followed a fiber through the ball out to a large glowing cube. She'd ignored the cube up until now. The ball made a single reference to it, and nothing about it seemed interesting.

Entering the cube, she found it full of data modules. *Why would the computer have all this data lying around?* Kita went to a module and opened it. It was like opening the lid on a universe and peering inside. She watched a universe play out from beginning to end.

Kita looked around at the modules. There were more than she could count. *How many iterations has this computer run? If it has records like this one, it must have a record of the last iteration.*

She opened modules, watching each one. She had no way of searching them. All she could do was watch. Most were not interesting—filled with creatures and languages she didn't understand. A few didn't have anything happening.

There were a number of peoples resembling the gods. She'd been excited when she found the first group, only to be crushed when she got to the end and discovered they were not her people of lights.

After countless modules, she discovered the right one. It dawned on her. She should have checked the metadata and looked for a module that was smaller than the rest. She watched with interest as the gods evolved and grew. Of all the races she watched, they were the only ones to create their own universes. Tears filled her eyes the first time Sarin appeared. Her heart broke again. When the module finished, Kita wiped her tears away. She missed the others so much.

What if I could bring them back? The computer's not doing anything. But, I don't know anything about creating a universe…but I know someone who does.

Kita watched the module again, searching for a particular Angel. When she saw her, she copied the data from the module, and with a snap of her fingers, Aspen appeared in front of her.

"Hello, Leaf," said Kita.

"Kita! What happened?" The tiny Angel looked around. "Where are we?"

"I'll explain. You and I have a lot of work to do."

"What are we doing?"

"Building our own universe."

ABOUT THE AUTHOR

L. Fergus is a Wattpad featured author of science fiction including the #1 book *Birthright*. L.'s books have more than three hundred and fifty thousand chapter reads. The books *Birthright*, *BykeChic*, and *Rebirth* have won eighteen awards, including Best Overall.

Like L. Fergus' main character Kita, L. fosters children to give them a supportive place to grow and thrive. L. lives with three dogs: Rust, Moxy, and Storm, and five cats: Nova, Jupiter, Pluto, Crater, and Forest Fire.

Join L. Fergus' mailing list at FallenAngelKita.com for news about upcoming book releases and get the story *Girl on Fire*. Follow L. on Facebook, Twitter @FallenAngelKita and contact L. at L@fallenangelkita.com.

∼

DID YOU ENJOY *LI'VE*?
Please leave a review!

Go to Amazon or Goodreads and tell the world what you think!

∼

Be the first to know when the exciting next book *BykeChic* comes out.

Sign up for the mailing list.

Connect with L. Fergus on:
Facebook
Instagram
Twitter
http://FallenAngelKita.com

TWELVE BRAVO

- APC—Armored Personnel Carrier
- MICLIC—Mine Clearing Line Charge
- ACE—Armored Combat Earthmover
- AIT—Advanced Individual Training
- BDU—Battle Dress Uniform
- IR—Infrared
- PFC—Private First Class
- Picket—Six-foot-tall u-shaped metal stake for creating wire obstacles
- Picket Pounder—A hollow cylindrical tube with a metal plate on one end and handles
- Article Fifteen—non-judicial punishment for minor offenses

The green light from the radio cast harsh shadows inside the 113A3 APC. Private Logine sat on the far end of the pioneer box, her M-16 rifle between her legs. She rested the edge of her helmet against the front sight post as the smell of diesel and oil seeped up through the floorboards. Over the idling of the 113's engine came a rumble—East German artillery falling nearby.

Staff Sergeant Acoine had the radio hand-mic tucked up under his helmet. Logine guessed he was trying to find out why they stopped. They weren't supposed to stop until they reached Fulda. The 11th Calvary Regiment and 3rd Infantry Division had blunted the Soviet advance, and now NATO forces were on the counterattack.

"Hey!" Private Wallace punched Logine's shoulder, right in her 2nd Armored Division patch. Logine adored the nickname: Hell on Wheels. "Quit stewing. We got this. Sapper Steel!"

Logine turned to look at her girlfriend and then banged helmets with her. "You know it."

Logine and Wallace had been together since high school. They'd joined the Army and as a hometown pair, they'd gone through Basic and AIT together and then assigned to the 168th Engineer Battalion at Wiesbaden Army Base, West Germany.

Across from Logine, Specialist Holiday sat on the demolition box. "You girls checked your rifles? Locked and loaded?"

Logine picked up her rifle. It was heavier now with live rounds in it. She checked the safety, magazine, and receiver. Everything was where it was supposed to be. "Good to go, Specialist."

"Same here, Specialist," said Wallace.

"Good. Now, be quiet. I'm trying to listen."

A year in the Army and Logine learned to be patient. The Army was a lot of waiting, punctuated with brief periods of action. She had learned to summon her mind and body from a lull to combat ready at a moment's notice.

Wallace's gloved hand squeezed Logine's thigh. Logine took Wallace's hand and squeezed it. Logine knew Wallace had her back, and she had hers. They earned a reputation around the infantry and tanker barracks—mess with one, you were going to get the other. A few guys learned the hard way they were fearless and not afraid to fight. They collected a pair of article fifteens for throwing a tanker that wouldn't take *no* for an answer down a flight of stairs and breaking his arm.

"Outlaw Two Six, rodger. Outlaw Two Three is moving." Sergeant Acoine tapped Sergeant Fortune standing in the command hatch on the leg, and the 113 lurched forward. He put the hand-mic away. "Ok, listen up. We're moving forward. The task force has hit a minefield and has stopped. The platoon is moving forward to breach it. Outlaw Two Two has fired a MICLIC, and the ACE is moving forward to proof the lane. Holiday, grab the demo bag. You're going to proof the lane in case the ACE doesn't make it. The Soviets have overwatch, but the tanks and Bradleys are keeping them busy. Logine, Wallace, you'll mark the lane, just like Grafe, except I'll attach IR chem-lights to the top, instead of cones. Are you girls good?"

"Yes, Sergeant," Logine and Wallace said together.

"Good. Logine, open the troop hatch and untie the pickets. Wallace, get out your picket pounder."

Holiday scooted out of the way so Logine could stand on the demolition box and open the troop hatch. The sounds of battle assaulted her ears. The *booms* of tank cannons and the rapid-fire *cracks* of Bradleys were uncoordinated with the tracers blazing trails through the night air. Swaying with the 113 as it moved, Logine undid the tie downs on the pickets. In front of her, Sergeant Fortune fired a few rounds from the 113's 50. caliber machine gun.

The 113 passed through the tree line, engine screaming as it raced toward an unseen destination. Logine dropped back down into the 113. Wallace had body slung her rifle and had the picket pounder in her hands. The forty-pound two-handled cylindrical metal picket pounder was hollow on one end and weighed a third of what Wallace did.

The 113 came to an abrupt halt, throwing everyone forward.

"Dammit, Freddy," yelled Holiday.

Logine knew PFC Fredrick couldn't hear Holiday, but everyone was thinking the same thing. Fredrick twisted in the driver's seat and pulled the lever to lower the ramp with a *thump* in the dirt.

"Holiday, go!" yelled Sergeant Acoine.

Holiday jumped out of the 113, turned, and disappeared into the darkness.

"Ok, girls," called Sergeant Acoine, "just like we did a month ago. As the track goes down the lane, I'll toss off the pickets. We'll pick you up on the other side. You good?"

"Yes, Sergeant!" they yelled enthusiastically.

"Remember: mission first, do not accept defeat, there is no quitting, and no one gets left behind."

"Yes, Sergeant!"

"Good. Go kick them in the ass!"

Logine and Wallace ran down the ramp and around the side of the 113. Sergeant Acoine passed a six-foot u-shaped metal picket to Logine, and the 113 pulled away. Logine stood the picket up, and Wallace put the picket top inside the picket pounder. Each soldier grabbed a handle on the picket pounder, and with synchronized motion, they lifted the picket pounder and slammed it down, throwing all their body weight with it. After four strikes the picket stood. They lifted the picket pounder off and ran toward the next picket.

The ground became rough and broken as they entered the lane cleared by the MICLIC. The plowing by the ACE did little to improve the footing. Logine ran as fast as she could, her protective mask banging against her thigh and her rifle hitting her butt. They reached the next picket and pounded it into the ground. The row of pickets would guide the rest of the task force through the minefield.

As Logine ran, the ground to the left exploded in a shower of dirt, grass, and metal fragments. The force of the artillery impact threw Logine off her feet. She landed in the dirt. Picking herself up, she ran to Wallace. "Hey, you ok?"

Wallace rolled over. There was a cut in her BDU bottoms just above her cargo pocket. She put her hand on it, and her glove came away with blood. "I think I'll be fine. It's just a little scratch." She stood up and grabbed the picket pounder.

They ran forward through the darkness, pounding pickets. A bright fireball lit the far tree line as a T-72 took a direct hit. Logine couldn't see the

113 anymore. She didn't worry about it. They would find it on the other side.

After a dozen pickets, Wallace said, "Can you take the picket pounder? It's getting heavy." Logine took it from her, and they found the next picket. A bright flash illuminated the field in front of them. The 113 was in flames.

"What do we do?" said Wallace to Logine.

"We keep going. We'll stop and grab what we need off the 113 and finish."

"Ok."

They pounded the remaining pickets and ran to the 113. It was mostly intact, and the flames had died down. Logine dropped the picket pounder and stepped up on the 113's track to reach the top. Sergeant Acoine was gone. Sergeant Fortune was slumped against the 50. caliber machine gun. The smell of diesel and burnt flesh permeated the air. Logine grabbed eight pickets from the pile—the amount one of them could carry—and passed them down to Wallace. The box of chem-lights was on the deck behind the command hatch. Logine reached for them. When a hand grabbed her arm, Logine screamed. Sergeant Acoine stood in the troop hatch. Burnt flesh and uniform covered half of his face and body. With his good hand, he pulled two flares from his cargo pocket.

"Open signal," he croaked and then collapsed back into the 113.

Logine grabbed the flares and the chem-lights and stuck them in her cargo pockets. She jumped down and picked up the picket pounder. "Let's go!"

"What's the scream for?" yelled Wallace.

"Sergeant Acoine was still alive. Kind of."

They pounded the next picket. Logine pulled a chem-light from the box, cracked it, and stuck it on top of the picket. They pounded pickets until they came to the smoking ruin of the ACE laying on its side.

"Does this mean the lane's not proofed?" said Logine.

"I don't know," said Wallace. "We haven't seen Specialist Holiday. When we go forward, we'll run side by side and look for mines. We'll just have to push any we find out of the way."

Logine nodded in agreement. They rushed forward a few feet apart but stayed inside the MICLIC's blast lane. The picket pounder was getting heavy.

"We gotta switch this up," said Logine. "It's too heavy."

"I have three pickets left," said Wallace. "I'll take two, you get one, and we'll both carry the picket pounder."

Each soldier took a handle and their pickets, and ran forward. They pounded two more pickets and reached the end of the MICLIC blast. A few yards beyond the blast was a mine.

"I'll pound the picket, you get the mine," said Logine to Wallace.

Logine pounded the picket with all her might. With just her, it took seven strikes to get the picket in the ground. Using her legs and her weary arms, she lifted the picket pounder off, let it fall to the ground, and attached a chem-light. Exhausted, she threw herself down next to Wallace.

"How's it going?"

With her bare hands, Wallace was pulling dirt out from under the mine. "Checking for mousetraps. So far, I got nothing."

Wallace continued to search until they'd pulled most of the dirt from under the mine. "Ok, I think it's good. Let's lift it up and set it aside."

Carefully, they lifted the mine and carried it to the last picket. Setting it down at the base, Logine cracked a chem-light and placed it on top.

"Ok," said Logine to Wallace. "That's it. Let's find a place to lay low until someone picks us up."

"Let's get to the tree line. We can hide there."

Unslinging their rifles, they entered the woods. Logine stopped. "Wait! The flares!" Logine pulled them out of her cargo pocket. She handed one to Wallace.

"Is it one or both?" said Wallace.

"I don't know." Before they had done the lane marking drill in the daylight and used a smoke pot. "What color is yours?"

Wallace turned the flare so she could read the markings on the side. "Green."

"Mine's green, too. Let's fire both. That way the tankers can't miss seeing them."

"How do they work?"

Logine found the instructions. "Hit bottom against a hard surface. Aim toward the sky."

"The ground's too soft," said Wallace.

"Smack it against our knees."

"Huh?"

Logine took a knee.

"Oh, gotcha." Wallace knelt. "Ready? One...two...three!"

Both soldiers slammed the bottom of the flares against their knees. Two pops were followed by loud *wooshes*. Green lights streaked into the air and exploded, bathing everything in a green light.

Logine tossed the used tube away. "Come on, let's go."

They ran into the trees and stopped at the base of a large pine tree.

"Gunther, bist du das?"

"Oh, shit," said Wallace.

There was a series of flashes. Wallace's M-16 fell from her hands, and she collapsed.

"Lizzy!" cried Logine.

More flashes lit the area as Logine ducked behind the tree. Leaning out, she fired back but didn't know where to aim. Flashes came from a neighboring tree. Logine fired at the tree, rolled to the other side, and charged the enemy, firing from her hip.

Logine nearly tripped over the East German soldier. He rose to his knees and aimed his AK-47. Using her bayonet training, Logine knocked the AK-47 aside. Raising the butt of her M-16, she smashed it into his face several times. She jumped back and fired twice in the East German's chest.

Logine ran back to Wallace. She fell to a prone position next to her.

"Lizzy! Lizzy!" Logine yelled while shaking Wallace.

Logine received no response. Two dark spots were on Wallace's BDU top. Logine pulled open Wallace's top, and her brown t-shirt was soaked in blood.

"Love, no," whispered Logine as she touched her helmet to Wallace's chest while fighting back tears. "I won't leave you here."

Logine knelt, slung her rifle from her shoulder, grabbed Wallace's arm and leg, and hoisted Wallace onto her shoulders in a fireman's carry. After a wobbly step, Logine marched back toward the lane's exit.

The chatter of AK-47s came from behind Logine. A fist hit her in the kidney. A second punch knocked the wind out of her lungs. Her knees buckled, and she fell forward onto her chest. Wallace rolled off Logine's shoulders. Logine blinked, trying to understand what happened. A whisper turned into a roar as an M1 tank drove by.

"Mission accomplished," Logine whispered. She coughed and her mouth filled with blood. The sounds of battle faded in her ears as her vision became gray. She closed her eyes, and the world slipped away.

∽

Logine's blood glowed like embers. A single flame burst forth and spread across her body. Large flames shot skyward and engulfed her.

An unnatural wind swirled, blowing the ash skyward. The ash became a tornado, swirling tighter. There was a flash, and an Angel with black wings appeared. She was dressed in black leather and heavy combat boots, her midsection was bare and heavy bracers with crystal inlays protected her arms, a heavy stud encrusted belt hung from her hip, and thigh pads held an array of throwing stars. A hood obscured her face. She carried a pair of swords on her back. The Angel removed her hood revealing blonde hair and a sad expression in her blue eyes. She knelt next to Wallace.

The Angel rolled Wallace over, undid her helmet, and tossed it aside. She stroked Wallace's cheek. "Brave soldier, you did your duty and the battle's won, but your job is not done." The Angel touched Wallace's nose. "Boop! Rise Sapper."

Wallace convulsed and screamed. The Angel rolled Wallace onto her hands and knees then drew a sword and cut two slits in her BDU top between her shoulder blades and spine. Two fleshy growths grew skyward forming limbs and joints. Buds on the limbs flesh grew and burst, revealing red feathers with white edges. The Angel helped Sapper to her feet.

Sapper looked at the Angel. Her mouth opened in surprise. "Kita is that you? Did we get the lane open?"

"Hey, Lizzy. Yes, It's me."

"Why are you dressed like that? And did you get taller?"

Kita chuckled. "This is my true form. I'm an Angel, and now, so are you. We did our duty, but it's no longer our fight. We have another war to win."

Sapper looked around at the darkened forest as an M1 tank drove by. "I don't understand. What happened?"

"We died after clearing the breach. We're as close to heroes as we'll ever get."

"Sergeant First Class Hernandez said that during AIT. *It* is you."

Kita smiled. "Our lives here are over. You've earned your place among the Angels. You are Sapper."

"If we're dead, how am I here?"

Kita smiled. "Death is only a minor inconvenience. Come, it's time to go home."